COVE OF CROSSING

Nezkwah Trilogy Book One

Jo Hannah Afton

Mind & Mythos
—Media—

MIND AND MYTHOS MEDIA

Dedicated to my eldest, Morgan

First Edition, June 2025

Softcover ISBN 978-1-967802-01-2

Cover photograph by Jo Hannah Afton.

Book cover illustrated and designed by Morgan Afton.

Visit mindandmythosmedia.com

CONTENTS

Chapter One

SOMETHING WAITED

Inside a shadowed cave, something waited.

Hidden along a forgotten trail in the Smoky Mountains, something crouched in the shadows, its chest rising and falling with ragged anticipation. Each breath it drew was labored, rattling in the thin, stagnant air. Tucked beneath the moss-covered granite ledge, the creature retreated deeper into the cave as heavy, lumbering footsteps echoed along the trail outside. A mortal was approaching. The thought sent a ripple of anticipation through the watcher. It glanced at the cave walls, glimmering with mica, catching the last fading threads of daylight.

The creature dug its fingers into the earth, lifting a fistful to its face and inhaling deeply. The soil was dense, pungent with age, its scent telling a story of decay. *How can anything survive here?* And yet, it had. A sudden gust of wind slipped through the cave's entrance, carrying a momentary breath of fresh air, and the creature tilted its head back, inhaling the brief gift. The leaves outside swayed and danced, grateful for the same fleeting mercy.

Beneath the ground, an ancient oak's sprawling roots, tangled beneath the cave floor, sent a message, vibrating through the earth, traveling up the creature's bare feet. *Take nothing.*

"Os kandinade ka tisaha wi os nazokwa, ka ouri kan si," it murmured, its voice low and respectful. *I take only what I need, but not from you.*

The footsteps grew closer, accompanied by the light tinkling of a bell, its soft clink hanging tinny and flat in the thick, quiet forest. The creature strained to listen, hoping to sense the mortal's intent through the intricate network of roots and fungi beneath them both. But the earth told little. Only the steady crunch of leaves beneath indifferent feet.

This mortal did not commune with the soil. His scent arrived before he did—a dense, bitter aroma that only mortals bore.

The creature's muscles trembled from holding still for so long, crouched on a soft mound of clay and decomposing leaves. Finally, the lone hiker appeared near the cave's mouth. An overstuffed pack hung tightly against his back, trinkets dangling from every possible loop. He wore a floppy tan hat, and his feet were shod, not in strips of bark or animal skins, but in something dead, blunt, and flexible. The creature watched closely, analyzing him. *If this mortal can speak with the earth, he chooses to block it with those strange boots.*

The mortal looked young. His pale face was kissed lightly by the sun, speckled like the eggs of the Yula Bird of the southern bogs. His hair, golden and soft, fell just below his ears, damp at the neck. His forearms were covered in fine down, neither smooth nor thick with fur, but something curiously in-between. He was the right age—healthy, virile. Much better than the last two. His demeanor was relaxed, as if the ancient forest had washed his worries away, leaving him to wander free.

He ignored the cave entirely, oblivious to the eyes watching him from the dark, and shuffled over to the edge of the path to a clearing. He stopped briefly to enjoy the view from his vantage point, the mountains rolling like waves in the distance. He shuffled around, surveying the small campsite, eyes landing on a battered, neglected table beneath the overhang. With a grunt, he shrugged off his pack, letting it drop onto the table, then stretched his arms wide to the sky, soaking in the cool late afternoon breeze. His sweat-soaked shirt came off in one fluid motion, and from his pack, he pulled out a morsel wrapped in bright packaging. He tore into it, chewing greedily, reminding the foreigner of the Kudlah at harvest time.

The being lifted its nose, trying to catch the scent of the food, but there was nothing—no freshness, no life. Whatever it was, it had not been harvested recently. Intrigued, the visitor blinked as the mortal set up a small metal device, filled it with water from a canteen, striking fire from a tiny object in his hand. *Perhaps not completely unintelligent,* it mused. *He creates fire without song.*

Water boiled in a small pot, and after some rummaging, the mortal dropped a tiny satchel into a metal cup. The aroma of chamomile soon filled the air, confirming that the brew was plant-based, edible, and, more importantly, an effective carrier for its intentions. The creature's two hearts quickened in anticipation. This one would be easy. After several suns of waiting for a suitable subject, the moment had arrived.

As the water steeped, the mortal soaked his shirt in the steaming pot, wringing it out with satisfaction before hanging it on a low-hanging pine branch. The creature watched with mild amusement. The smell was gone from the cloth, but not from him. *What was the point?* No matter. This was a place of dull-witted creatures, and as fascinating as the mortal was, the mission demanded focus. *This will not be pleasant. For either of us.*

When the mortal turned his back, the creature moved. It slipped silently from the cave, stepping into the last dappled rays of daylight, just long enough to drop a fine yellow powder into the man's mug before retreating to the darkness. The dried fungus, carefully prepared, dissolved instantly into the brew. It was a delicate balance—just enough monkwort for paralysis, not death. Too much risked disaster; too little would result in a fight. But this powder was expertly crafted, designed to leave only the faintest bitterness behind.

The creature slipped deeper into the shadows, its pulse racing. It watched as the man cupped the mug in his hands and brought it to his lips. *Excellent. Drink.*

As the mortal drew the tin cup closer, he took pause, inhaling the new aroma. He glanced inside the cup, as if something was off. He took a small sip to test and swallowed. He glanced over his shoulder, his instincts prickling.

Hearing only the rustling of leaves in the trees overhead, he savored his tea, while pulling out a small, flat device from his pocket, peering into it with interest. A flicker of sound and light flashed from its surface. *A looking pond? In a box?* The creature's eyes widened in fascination. It edged closer to the cave entrance, intrigued by this strange tool. "Supreme Court preserves immigration restrictions amid legal challenges," a voice droned from the box. "The Court voted five-four in favor of the measure."

It must be their prophet in the box, the creature concluded, imagining the amazement such an object would cause when it returned. The Keeper would marvel. *How clever, to carry a looking pond in a pocket!*

Another sip of the tea. The leaves in the cave rustled under the creature's feet, drawing the man's attention. He froze, head snapping toward the sound, body alert. Slowly, cautiously, he took a step forward, gripping a stick in one hand, and a small folding knife in the other. "Hello?" His voice trailed off, uncertainty hanging in the air. He moved like the Long-necked Neena bird in the mating season, awkward and obvious in his attempts at stealth.

The creature almost pitied him. *Too late for sneaking now.*

A quiet tap—stone on stone—echoed from deep within the cave as the creature beckoned him inward.

Tink. Tink. Yes, come closer, curious mortal.

"I'm not messing around," the man announced, though the knife trembled in his hand. His voice faltered, the poison taking hold. He stumbled, his body swaying, a hand braced against the cave wall to steady himself. The creature could see it now—his energy field glowing red with fear, his pulse quickening, his eyes glassy. He was slipping, the elixir doing its work.

He fell to his knees, blinking rapidly, trying to focus. His limbs twitched, confusion written across his face. The creature knew the sensation well: dizziness, warmth, and the creeping fog of paralysis. The drinking of Monkwort was one part exultation and two parts nightmare. With luck, the man would remember little and awaken before dawn, unharmed.

But for now, he was trapped, limbs frozen, breath shallow. The creature emerged from the shadows, revealing itself fully at last. The man rolled onto his back, eyes wide, paralysis overtaking him, the shock of what he saw written in his glassy horror-struck eyes.

The creature knelt beside him, resting a small, thin hand on his heaving chest. "Ouri nilane ri," it whispered.

Do not fear.

CHAPTER TWO

THE ḤIDING PLACE

Some moons later, Máhí clutched the fur-wrapped bundle tightly against her chest as she spread her black wings and flew over the rolling foothills of the ancient mountain range. The night air was soft and heavy with moisture, much like the valley she had left behind. New spring leaves, green as malachite, dangled from the trees and waved gently as she swooped low to peer into the windows of the tidy, square log nests below.

This place reminded her of home, yet something about it unsettled her deeply. The forest here was sick, burdened with an invisible weight that stunted its growth. Something noxious clung to the leaves and soaked deep into the earth, burning the saplings at their roots.

Under the dark sky, Máhí was nearly invisible on her clandestine mission. Her black, downy feathers, soft as hair, and deep coffee-brown skin marked with olive green stripes, gave her perfect camouflage among the trees. Her eyes—a striking cavernous gold rimmed with black—were protected by a third, diagonal membrane that flickered when she blinked. She moved imperceptibly through the oxygen-starved air. Yet the wicked atmosphere clung to her feathers, weighing her down, slowing her progress. And this, she knew, was the cleanest of the mortal places. Other locations were choked with murky air, bizarre illuminations, and towering structures made of steel and glass. In those places, she couldn't hear anything of value—just an incessant, mind-numbing cacophony that left her head spinning with panic.

Above her, the sky was cloudy and sparkled with lights in small patches. The skysigns were mostly absent, making navigation more tiresome. She was forced to rely on the outlines of mountains and valleys, landmarks barely visible in the darkness. But Máhí's vision, a gift from her father's bloodline, allowed her to see the finest details even in the low light of night. She could spot the smallest movements in the underbrush, distinguish the subtlest hues, and catch distant shapes with effortless clarity. Her hearing, too, was superior—capable of picking up conversations from behind walls or the sound of approaching footsteps long before they arrived. Yet here, where sound bounced erratically off the rocky trails and square structures, it was more a distraction than an advantage, further slowing her down.

As she flew, an unnatural vine, pulsing with energy, hanging from poles along the trail's edge, caught her attention. Her feathers bristled instinctively at the strange energy it emitted, and she veered upward, covering the bundle in her arms. *The mortals have found a way to protect their nests,* she thought warily. The intensity of the vibrations made it impossible to approach. *How do they drape these vines from pole to pole without harming themselves?*

The farther she ventured, the more disoriented she became. This land seemed designed to confuse—her migration impulses disrupted by a subtle yet persistent current running through the air, scrambling her instincts. *How do these mortals find their way through such a place?* she wondered.

Below her, a growling creature with glowing eyes roared down the trail, moving faster than any creature had a right. *These must be the rulers here,* Máhí thought. *They are so unafraid.* She hovered, watching in horrified fascination as the beast hurtled toward a four-legged creature with antlers. At the last moment, she looked away, unable to witness the moment of impact as the animal was thrown violently into the air. Its body landed with a sickening thud on the side of the trail, legs jerking helplessly as it struggled to stand.

The monster stopped. Máhí, her hearts racing, snatched a laughing potion from her belt, hoping to distract the creature and spare the wounded animal. With expert aim, she hurled it through the air. It shattered, releasing a small pink cloud which billowed up between predator and prey. But the monster merely stared at it for a moment, then sped off as quickly as it had arrived, leaving the animal in its misery.

Impervious to potions? Máhí shivered at the thought. These were terrifying creatures, indeed. She hoped she wouldn't have to face one on this mission. Though time was short, she couldn't bear to leave the injured animal in such pain. Once the trail was quiet again, she landed in a shadowy hollow nearby and pulled a vial of green liquid from her belt. Approaching the creature cautiously, she knelt beside it, letting three drops fall onto its tongue. In moments, it sprang to its feet and dashed off into the woods.

She knew tonight was critical to the future of the valley—finding the right hiding place, the right mortals. Her mother languished, captive, in the dungeon of Peregrine's

Keep, and she had suffered far too long already. Tonight, she would set their plan in motion, and if all went well, an end to her mother's captivity would be in sight. Peering into the bundle she carried, she gently parted the fur blanket to reveal her sister's face.

Sekowah's luminous emerald eyes blinked up at her, innocent and unaware. Her skin was a translucent olive, with her mother's distinct markings on her belly. Her pointed ears, still floppy at the tips as newborn ears often were, twitched slightly in the night breeze. Máhí's hearts ached with guilt. Soon, she would have to leave her sister here, alone in this strange and dangerous world. It was for the Good of All, she reminded herself—her duty to her people, to her mother. This child, conceived on the border of two worlds, a changeling—half mortal and half Nezkwah—would someday, she hoped, forgive.

Sekowah was the sole survivor of the Dasheah invasion that had decimated the most recent generation of newborns. This alone was proof that *the Verses* were right, that the Prophecy was unfolding. *This child is bound by destiny,* Máhí thought, her voice a whisper. "Si wi kanuta mayen," she told her infant sister. *You are a powerful combination.*

Clutching her bundle closer, Máhí sprang into the air again, nerves jangled.

Unlike most of her people, Máhí had been granted special privileges. As both Lirian and Nezkwah, and the King's daughter, she was allowed to travel between kingdoms. But unbeknownst to her father, her mother had given her permission to travel between realms. It was a secret privilege bestowed upon her by her mother and the Keeper—one she dared not mention to her father. He would be outraged if he knew anything of her mission or whereabouts.

Her mother's instructions had been clear: *Do not upset the balance.* The crossing between worlds was delicate, and a single misstep could disrupt the equilibrium of Futures and Pasts. For every item taken, something must be returned in its place. Everything had a purpose; nothing could be stolen or destroyed without consequence.

Though young, Máhí had shown promise from an early age, excelling in both healing and battle arts. This was her fourth journey to the mortal world—the first three had been purely preparatory—gathering items to put in her portal stash. But this mission was different. Historic. The fate of her people rested on its success, and Máhí was determined to see it through.

Below her, the log nests lay nestled snugly among the pines, maples, and oaks, arranged in orderly rows. They were neither stone fortresses nor nests woven from branches. In front of each nest, a sleeping monster—sometimes two—stood guard. *Are they protecting the mortals or holding them captive?*

She flew in near silence, her movements so delicate they barely disturbed the air. Her wings carried her with the grace of an owl, lifting her effortlessly from window to window. Her head was a short garden of black curls and feathers—signs of her maturing powers—and it buzzed with questions.

Harsh voices from one of the nests snapped her back to the present. Two mortals argued inside, their energy fields blazing red with anger. The room itself seemed to pulse with their heated exchange, glowing a deep, ugly scarlet. Máhí winced at the sight and quickly covered Sekowah's face with the blanket to shield her from the waves of discontent. Swiftly, she moved on to another nest. *These mortals are a wretched lot,* she thought. *Aggressive, mean-spirited, and rash.*

In the next log nest, she spied two mortals entering a room. With a flick of a lever, they caused the room to fill with light. But it was an unnatural light, harsh and buzzing, stinging Máhí's sensitive eyes and ears. *What is this strange magic?* She marveled at their ability to conjure light without gems, though it made her uneasy. If she had time, she would return to investigate this strange power—another mystery of the mortal world.

Her attention shifted to a small nestling, swaddled in flannel cloth in its mother's arms. *Why don't they wrap their newborns in fur?* Máhí's hearts quickened. After a long journey, she had found the right place.

Hovering silently outside the window, hidden in shadow, she lit down on the bough of a kind needlewood overlooking the nest. The night wind, heavy with the stench of the rancid air, tugged at her feathers, but she resisted the urge to cough. Instead, she pulled a small twig of Sleeproot from her satchel and sucked on it, hoping to calm her nerves.

The sight of the small infant inside filled her with equal parts excitement and terror. This was the moment. If she was to succeed, she would have to act now.

CHAPTER THREE

THE MIDNIGHT SWAP

T he nursery walls were painted with a soft cherry hue, with borders of white and red flowers brightening the edges. Everything in the room was square and angular, except for a small round table in the corner, holding a peculiar light. The sharp lines gave the space a rigid, orderly feel, in stark contrast to the circular warmth of the nests in Máhí's beloved valley.

A soothing sapphire glow radiated from the mortal mother as she gazed lovingly into her infant's eyes. The father's energy field, too, glimmered with an energetic jade, though it shifted now and then, flickering with shades of ginger and rose. Máhí watched with curiosity, enjoying the way their light intertwined as they exchanging glances—perhaps sharing thoughts, as nestmates do during mating season.

Máhí was still too young for such concerns. Nesting, accepting seeds—these things were far from her mind. There was too much to explore, too much to learn, to be tethered to one place, even for a season. As a warrior-in-training under her father's tutelage, she couldn't imagine taking on the responsibility of a nestling, even under the best of circumstances. Still, she couldn't help but admire the bond between these mortals, the deep connection they shared with their child. It was enviable, in a way, to be so closely linked to another, to feel such profound love for an offspring.

The mother carried her child over to a small cage in the corner, a sight that baffled Máhí. *Why would they place their nestling in a cage?* It was a strange contraption, with no top and wooden spindles along the sides. Stranger still, an enchantment hovered above it—menacing dragonflies suspended on strings, as if waiting to pounce on the little thing. *What a horrible thing to place over a nestling's sleep. Cruel.*

"Goodnight, little princess," the mother whispered as she laid her child down in the cage, brushing a tender kiss on her forehead. Her energy brightened to a vibrant violet with the touch. *A Princess,* Máhí thought. *What luck! It must be a sign.*

The father leaned in, letting the child's tiny fingers curl around his own. "Sleep now, Jade. No funny business tonight," he said, his voice gentle. His energy blended with the infant's, turning her essence a deep emerald. Another sign. There was love here—strong, true. Máhí hoped these mortals would love Sekowah as they loved their own.

The fate of Máhí's people rested on the ability of these mortals to protect her precious sister, to raise her with care, and to teach her the ways of their world. Yet Máhí and her mother had found no way to ensure that Sekowah would learn the ways of the Ancients. That part of her education would have to wait for her return to the valley. Nothing could be done about it. It was simply too dangerous to leave Máhí here permanently to watch over her, or to send her sister back too soon. The arrangement wasn't ideal, but it was the best solution they had.

The parents left the room, pulling the small lever by the door. Only the soft glow of an unnatural light on the wall, shaped like a dolphin, kept the nursery from complete darkness.

Máhí wrinkled her nose at the sight of the light. Though it was an advantage now, allowing her to move more easily, she disliked it all the same. In the Jasper Valley, nestlings, particularly flightless ones, were never left unattended. They slept in the nest with their charm, protected and cared for until they were strong enough to fly. Máhí plucked nervously at her fore feathers, the weight of time pressing down on her. *This will have to do,* she thought. *It's the best nest I've found, and I cannot wait any longer.* She could feel the dullness of this place sapping her strength. If she stayed too long, she might not have the energy to carry the mortal infant back with her.

"You'll be safe here," Máhí whispered to her bundle. "I'll return for you. I promise."

With that, she leapt to the window, wings spread for balance. But just as she moved forward, a fine mesh net appeared, bouncing her back mid-air, throwing her off balance. *What strange magic is this?* She inspected the mesh closely, realizing the mortals had placed it over the window to keep intruders out—perhaps to guard against the Dasheahs of this world.

Máhí drew her obsidian-and-steel dagger from her boot. Careful not to disturb the bundle in her arms, she pried the edges of the net away from the window, letting it drop into a bush below. She held her breath, listening for any sign that the mortals had heard, but the house remained still. Satisfied, she gripped the window ledge with her delicate fingers, folding her wings tightly to fit through, and silently moved inside.

She approached the cage, where the tiny mortal—blue-eyed, with strange strawberry curls—looked up at her, utterly unalarmed. Máhí pitied the little creature, knowing her world would change forever this night. With a soft breath, she unfurled her arms and placed Sekowah gently beside the mortal infant. Sekowah blinked with discomfort as the unnatural light temporarily blinded her.

Side by side, the two could not have been more different. Though Sekowah was part mortal, her olive skin was delicate and dainty. *Much cuter,* Máhí mused. The mortal child was round and pale, like a milk slug from the southern bogs.

What must be done, must be done, she reminded herself. Soon, this mortal would grow up in the valley, learning the ways of forests and flora, while Sekowah would hide here, safe, until it was time to bring her home.

From her satchel of dried leaves, birch bark, and amber-hued sap, Máhí drew out a small yellow vial, twisting the cap free with a careful, practiced motion. Attached beneath the cap was a slender golden wand, which she brushed softly against the sole of the infant's foot, gently scraping the skin. Once satisfied with her skin sample, she returned the wand to the vial and shook it vigorously, watching as the contents swirled and mingled. This time, when she uncapped it, she tipped the vial over her sister's lips, allowing a single, honey-thick drop to fall onto her tongue. She held her head gently as the golden liquid trickled down, coaxing her to swallow.

Next, Máhí reached into her satchel and withdrew a pouch of gold dust and two hollow spheres, each suspended from a chain. She took a deep breath, letting the mountain air fill her lungs, then lifted the spheres, allowing them to swing and collide with a soft, resonant chime. The birth notes, clear and pure, rang through the quiet space. Máhí matched the tone with her own voice—a low, vibrating hum that seemed to ripple through the air, ancient and powerful. Holding a pinch of dust between her thumb and forefinger, she sprinkled it over the infants, watching as the shimmering particles settled on their skin like glimmering stardust. Finally, she pressed her thumbs to their tiny foreheads, her fingers gentle but firm, and focused her thoughts into the sound, sending her song into the very core of their beings.

"Inal am gu wi, moma wi nai. Silami mikale, waynitu kanuta," she spoke. *Where once was one, now shall be two. The spirit doubles, a body new.*

The dust dissolved and the glowing particles receded into their skin, transforming their skin into a mosaic of shimmering light. The hexagons pulsed and sparkled, and with Máhí's concentrated energy, the energetic fields of the two babies began to shift and mesh. A bright green flash of light twined into an emerald vine of energy, spiraling from Máhí's thumbs into their bodies. In an instant, the transformation was complete. Sekowah was now a perfect imitation of Jade.

Máhí admired her handiwork. *Two little milk slugs. Perfect.*

She set to work swapping their clothes. The mortal child let out a giggle, and Máhí froze. She ducked behind an oversized chair, trembling with fear, clutching Sekowah to her chest.

The door creaked open. Máhí held her breath, eyes squeezed shut. The father leaned into the room, smiling as he whispered, "No funny business now. Close your eyes." Jade cooed adoringly at him, and with a nod of satisfaction, he closed the door.

Máhí exhaled slowly, calming her nerves. She finished the swap, carefully placing Sekowah back in the cage before wrapping Jade in the soft fur blanket. The child would need the warmth—the crossing was long and cold, and the transition back to the valley would be difficult. *If she survives it at all,* Máhí thought grimly. The Keeper's mandates were clear: for everything taken, something must be returned. The Balance had to be maintained. If she left her sister here, she had to bring another nestling back.

Securing the bundle to her chest with thin vine rope, Máhí glanced one last time at Sekowah, who now stared up at her with wide, alarmed eyes. Máhí knew that look well. It would soon be followed by a piercing wail.

She slipped back through the window and out onto the branch, wincing as Sekowah's cries echoed from the nursery. No sooner had Máhí reached the cover of the leaves than the nursery light flickered on.

The cries intensified. Máhí hovered outside, hidden among the branches, as the mother scooped Sekowah into her arms.

"Shhh, shhh," the mother whispered, rocking her gently. She glanced toward the open window, her body lights flashing red. She furrowed her brow, stepping closer to inspect the netting that now lay tangled in the bushes below. Her eyes scanned the yard.

Máhí clung to the branch, blending in effortlessly with the shadows. The mortal child stirred in the fur, squirming against Máhí's chest. Afraid the infant might cry out, Máhí blew softly on her face, causing her to inhale sharply—but the cry came all the same.

The mother's head snapped upward, eyes searching the tree. Máhí pressed her hand over the child's mouth, her hearts pounding in her ears.

A long, tense moment passed. Finally, the mother shut the window and returned to the chair, settling in with Sekowah, humming a soft lullaby. Máhí listened to the gentle song, her mind drifting back to Peregrine's Keep, where Jájá's mournful melodies would lull her to sleep on long, restless nights when she was a nestling herself.

It pained her to leave Sekowah in such a strange, wretched place, but there was no other choice. *For the Good of All,* she reminded herself. The song, however, did little to soothe Sekowah, whose cries continued to pull at Máhí's heart. It took every ounce of courage for her to tear herself away from the sound. With a mighty sweep of her wings, she turned her gaze toward the moon and launched herself swiftly into the night, leaving her sister behind. As she soared over the pines, Sekowah's cries faded into the distance.

CHAPTER FOUR

THE IN-BETWEEN TIME

Sekowah, now known as Jade Mills, twelve years old on this very day, was sprawled out across her bed, a colorful explosion of art supplies surrounding her like confetti—sketchbook, colored pencils, pastels, charcoals, and bright markers scattered across the rainbow comforter. Her sketchbook, filled with thick stock paper and ragged edges, bore lovingly crafted doodles of unicorns, dragons, faeries, tigers, flowers, and plants. She didn't know why, but the pictures she imagined and brought to life on the page always came to her during what she called "the in-between time," those fleeting moments between sleep and waking, when the world was soft and her mind drifted freely.

Some days, it felt like those moments were all that really mattered—the in-between time. The rest was just noise, static, a distraction from the vivid worlds she glimpsed when she lingered on the edge of dreams. In that space, her body sometimes tingled or went numb, as if caught in a strange, magical paralysis. Some mornings, she'd lie still for as long as possible, holding onto that dreamy state, wishing it could last forever.

Above her headboard, the only remnant from her old nursery remained in place: wooden block letters spelling her name—**JADE**. She lay there now in an outfit as colorful and mismatched as her imagination. An olive-green T shirt and orange shorts, with lavender-and-black striped socks.

Lost in her world of sketching and erasing, Jade wore her favorite Elton John-inspired sunglasses: hot pink, with silver feathers glued to the top edges, the mirrored lenses shielded her from the glaring light of the lamp beside her bed. She scribbled across the page, utterly absorbed in her art. Around her, an army of stuffed animals stood guard—unicorns, dragons, mermaids, and her constant companion, Olo, an owl with sewn-on sunglasses. Olo used to accompany her everywhere, but once she started kindergarten, she had to leave him behind, though he still kept her company at home, perched next to her on a ruffled white pillow.

"What do you say, Olo?" she asked, tilting her head toward the owl. "Tiger stripes or zebra stripes?" She paused for a moment. *Tiger stripes it is,* she thought, reaching for a carrot-orange pastel stick. Her room was a kaleidoscope of color—rainbow curtains to match her comforter, and shelves brimming with books: fantasy novels, geology textbooks, and biographies of queens from centuries past.

Amidst the books, an impressive collection of faery figurines danced across every available surface. Monarch faeries, moth faeries, angel faeries—winged sprites made of glass and porcelain perched on shelves, clung to bedposts, and even hung from the ceiling on threads of fishing line. Each one had a name. Each one had a story.

There was Marigold, a faery with black skin, bright ginger curls, and a knack for finding gold in creek beds. Jade took her to the creek behind the house often—just in case Marigold decided to lead her to a hidden treasure.

Her desk, however, was the one place in her room that wasn't swarmed by faeries. Neatly organized on its wooden surface was her rock-tumbling system. The cylindrical machine hummed softly, grinding stones she'd found, mostly from the creek, until they were smooth and polished. It ran almost constantly, drowning out the awful buzzing from the lights above. Next to the tumbler was a stack of polishing cloths, and above the desk, a display case proudly held her most precious rocks—smooth and shiny trophies of her expeditions.

Inside a metal trunk by the desk lay her collection of uncut geodes, nestled in pine straw like dinosaur eggs waiting to be hatched. She liked the mystery of them, not knowing what was hidden inside each one. Whenever she felt down, she'd select one, take it to the garden, wrap it in a sock, and smash it open with a hammer on the patio. Sometimes it revealed quartz or calcite. But on the best of days, she'd discover amethyst or agate, and the thrill of it would lift her spirits.

Holding rocks, crystals, and gemstones calmed Jade. They had a sacred energy, like they were alive in some way, though her father often reminded her they were nothing more than minerals shaped by heat, pressure, and time. *He doesn't understand,* she thought. *He can't feel it.* To Jade, each rock had a unique life energy, a purpose, a vibration she could sense with her fingertips. They were alive. She knew it.

She saved her allowance—five dollars a week—until she had enough to add a new stone to her collection. Last year, after saving for 52 weeks, her parents took her north to

Franklin, North Carolina, where she visited Gem World and bought a polished septarian "dragon's egg." That prized piece sat on a wooden pedestal beside her bed, where she could gaze into its swirling patterns before drifting off to sleep. The dragon's egg helped her focus during the in-between time, bringing her visions into sharper detail.

One vision in particular, from a few months ago, still lingered in her mind. It had come to her after a trip to Lake Jocassee. In her dream, she was underwater, surrounded by crystal-clear water and sunlight dancing through the ripples. And then, she saw it—a face, calm and peculiar, with copper skin and gentle gold eyes rimmed in black. The creature floated beside her, communicating without words, and though Jade couldn't recall what it had said, she remembered the sense of reassurance it brought. That vision had made its way into her sketchbook, and now the drawing hung on her corkboard, alongside dozens of other magical creatures. She glanced at it again, feeling a tingle on her skin, as if the cool, pristine water of the dream were washing over her once more.

Back in the present, sprawled across her bed, Jade wrenched herself out of the trance and focused on the sketch before her—another creature from last night's dream. This one, a mythical being, half tiger and half bird, was taking shape under her pencil. She worked meticulously, perfecting the stripes on its tail, when the door creaked open just a sliver, and her mother peeked in.

Worst timing, Jade thought with a sigh. "I still have to finish the wings," she said, not looking up from her work.

The soothing sound of water filling the washing machine in the basement floated into the room, mingling with the hum of the rock tumbler. Jade found the sound comforting, almost as good as the babble of the creek out back, where she often wandered to pass the time.

Her mother, Mindy, stepped into the room, wearing her favorite black yoga pants and a flowy, pale-yellow tunic. "Dress for comfort," she always told Jade, though Jade preferred to dress for color, for vibrancy. The more colors, the better. A waft of lavender drifted in with her—a signature scent that clung to her skin from lotion, candles, or the pillows she spritzed downstairs. Mindy's deep blue eyes, full of warmth and a touch of amusement, reflected a mix of admiration and puzzlement as she looked at her daughter. Her hair, tied back in a low ponytail, was streaked with dirty blonde and silvery gray at the temples, neat and deliberate, just like the rest of her.

"Jade, sweetie, you can't hide up here all day. Why don't you come downstairs and help me?" There was a hint of excitement in her voice, the kind that grated on Jade's nerves. *Why does she care so much about a birthday party that no one will even come to?*

"Nobody's coming," Jade replied flatly, her eyes still on the sketch.

"Of course they are," her mother countered cheerfully. "I talked to Sophia's mom this morning."

Sophia will never come, Jade thought. She wouldn't even eat lunch with her at school, let alone show up at a birthday party. Jade didn't dare tell her parents how the girls at school treated her, how they didn't understand her. Her parents meant well, but they had a habit of making things worse by calling the other parents whenever something unpleasant happened.

Mindy stepped closer, peering over her shoulder. "Oh Lord," she said with mock horror, "that's terrifying. Good job!"

Jade rolled her eyes. "It's not terrifying, it's a biger. Half tiger, half bird. The faeries ride them."

"Is that so? And how do you know that?"

"I saw it in a dream," Jade hesitated, quickly retreating from the truth. "I mean, I made it up. It's imaginary."

Her mother smiled tenderly. "Well, maybe you should call it something else. Like a gryphon, maybe?"

"I don't name them. I just draw them." Jade picked up a light chartreuse pencil and started filling in the creature's eyes.

Mindy sighed and put her hands on her hips. "Well, I've got cupcakes downstairs with no icing. It's a tragic situation. I'm going to the store, and we can stop by the farmer's market if you want."

Jade let out a deep sigh. *Another birthday spent at the park, or the playground, with no friends. Why do they keep trying?* She'd told her mother plenty of times that she liked being alone, but Mindy never listened. She didn't understand how hard it was to make friends, how none of the girls at school liked her or understood her. It was easier this way—to keep to herself, sketch, polish rocks, and talk to Olo.

She picked up a stuffed dolphin and swam it through the air. "Do you ever have dreams where you're underwater, but you can still breathe?" she asked, her mind drifting back to her dream of swimming with dolphins, using her tail to leap into the air before crashing back into the waves.

"Noooo, can't say I do," her mother replied, interrupting her reverie. "Come on. We can't have naked cupcakes."

Jade reluctantly hopped off the bed and grabbed her ballet slippers.

"Outside shoes, please," Mindy reminded her.

"Fine," Jade muttered, swapping her slippers for high tops.

"I can talk to whales and dolphins, you know," Jade announced, making a series of clicking, moaning, and screeching noises to demonstrate her newfound ability, which had come to her during the in-between time. But her mother just looked at her, amused.

"I said, 'Let's race to the island and find some lunch!'" Jade explained. But her mother gave her the same clueless look—raised eyebrow, crooked smile, and shifting body lights, the tangerine shade that meant she was getting annoyed.

"I have a vivid imagination, don't I, Mom?"

Mindy's energy shifted to a deep cobalt. "Okay, Flipper. March. Or swim, as the case may be."

Jade sighed, grabbed Olo for a final hug, and "swam" down the hallway, making mournful whale noises as she followed her mom downstairs.

At the farmer's market, they made their usual stop at the "Adopt a Forever Friend" booth, where Jade petted the puppies, begged for one, lost the argument, and left in a huff—same routine as always. But she still held on to the hope that one day, her mother would give in. Today, though, wasn't that day.

As they strolled through the market, Mindy picking up fresh produce and kettle corn, Jade's attention was caught by a sound—delicate and enchanting, unlike anything she'd heard before. She followed the sound to a booth selling garden plants and herbs. Off to the side, potted Lily of the Valley plants bloomed, their tiny bell-shaped flowers trembling ever so slightly. As a customer lifted one of the pots, the blossoms chimed softly, a high-pitched, sweet sound that made Jade's nose tingle.

"Ooooh, I love that sound," she said, her eyes wide with wonder. But the customer only glanced at her, confused.

"She has quite an imagination," her mother said with a sheepish smile, stepping up behind her. "Come on, Jade. Time to go home."

"Didn't you hear it? Shake them again so she can hear!" Jade insisted, but her mother just looked at her with exasperation.

"Mother Nature speaks to us in mysterious ways," the attendant with the bright blue scarf said kindly, giving Jade a wink.

But it was the older man to her left who caught Jade's attention. He was dressed in a light-yellow linen shirt, his long silver braid gleaming in the sunlight, and his sparkly blue eyes twinkled as he crouched down to her level.

Taking her hand in his, he smiled warmly. "Lily of the Valley is a magic plant," he said in a low voice. "Did you know the faeries ring those bells to hypnotize people?"

"Really?" Jade asked, transfixed by his gaze. She felt a strange kinship with him, a deep stirring in her belly that she couldn't quite explain.

"Oh yes," he said, giving her hand a gentle squeeze. "But be careful. Faery magic is nothing to trifle with."

Jade watched as he let go of her hand, stood up, and wandered off, his basket filling with herbs and flowers.

CHAPTER FIVE

DECAPITATED

B ack home, in the kitchen, Jade used a butter knife to spread lemon cream cheese icing—her favorite—across the top of a warm vanilla cupcake, sneaking in a lick here and there as she went. The scent of lemon was clean, intense. Other than her room, the kitchen was her favorite place. A window box over the sink grew a variety of herbs in clay pots: basil, sage, oregano, thyme. Simply walking in enveloped her in delicious smells—herbs, lavender dish soap, fresh bread—and the small plants dancing in the window sun seemed to like her. Their body lights were always a warm orangey-yellow, accepting and kind. It was why she volunteered for dish duty as her main chore... she could stand right there, breathing it all in, letting the plants whisper to her. *Good morning*, they seemed to say. Or, *would you be kind and sprinkle some water on me?* Which, of course, she would do, though she had long stopped talking back to them, out loud at least, as this habit bothered her mother, who would say idiotic things like 'You know that plants can't talk, right?'

She admired her mother's optimism today. Party plates had been carefully placed out on the dining room table, with party hats and kazoos. Balloons drifted about the downstairs, hugging the ceiling, their colorful strips dangling down making a ribbon forest of the living and dining rooms. She ran a circle through the living room, into the dining room, her arms outstretched, letting the ribbons follow in her wake, the balloons bouncing against the ceiling.

Jade stopped at the dining room table, and stared at the festive plates, knowing they would stay empty and be thrown in the trash later that evening. *But lemon icing! It was almost worth the disappointment just to have unfettered access to lemon icing.* She buzzed through the dining room, snatching a balloon on her way back into the kitchen, where she snagged a spoon and dipped it into the creamy bowl.

Her mom only glanced over as Jade dipped the spoon into the bowl. She smiled at Jade, the kind of smile only a mother can give—equal parts forgiving and amused.

"Caterpillar guts." Jade stuck her tongue out at her mother, icing smushed across it. "Ewww."

"Mmmmmm. I love caterpillar guts." She enjoyed teasing her Mom almost as much as she loved lemon icing.

"And I love you!" Her mother gave her a quick kiss on the top of the head before handing her another cupcake.

Just then, the front door opened. Jade's ears perked up; her dad had been gone most of the afternoon, and she'd noticed the secret glances and murmured conversations he'd shared with her mom before he left. Whatever it was, it was something *big*.

"Dad!"

She almost put the cupcake down to greet him, but he hollered back at her from the front foyer. "Whoa, whoa, whoa! Stay where you are! No peeking!" She heard a commotion in the hallway, with doors opening and closing. Jade held tightly to the icing bowl; her eyes wide open in surprise.

She smiled at her mother and whispered, "What is it?"

"Oh, nothing," she replied playfully. But Jade could tell from her look that she and her dad were up to something all right, as her mom was as excited as she was.

Finally, her dad appeared in the kitchen doorway, throwing a wink at her mom. Brandon Mills was a tall, plain looking 'Minnesota Man,' as he liked to say, with a soft belly, thick, wavy, chocolate brown hair and goatee, a gentle nature, and a big heart. Especially for his girl. She was his only child, his 'pride and joy' and when he wasn't watching the Braves on TV, or outside mowing their clover-filled lawn (a horrible habit), he enjoyed planning outings for the family. He loved boating, fishing and drinking beer, all of which he could do while camping, which they did twice a year, when he was on vacation from Clemson where he taught Economics. Affable, practical, and conservative, he had a strong handshake and even stronger opinions, mostly about things that Jade didn't understand nor cared to understand. His face was kind but stern, and he was never too busy to sit with Jade and help her with homework.

"As you were. Ooooooh. Cupcakes." He reached for one on the kitchen island.

"Those are for the guests," her mom scolded, as she swatted his hand away.

He glanced at the clock over the kitchen sink. It was half past three. Nearly thirty minutes after the party was due to start. He moved to the sink to wash his hands. Jade could tell from his body lights that he was trying very hard not to say anything, as his throat glowed red where the words got stuck.

"I'm sure they're just running a little late," her Mom lied.

Her Dad crouched down next to her and put a reassuring hand on her back. "Uh oh. Do I need to go beat up some sixth graders?"

Jade iced a cupcake, putting an extra blop on the top of it. "You can't *make* them like me." She made a swirl, like an elf hat, on the top of the cupcake and handed it to him, forcing a smile through her hot tears. "It's okay. Here, I made this one just for you." She reached into a bowl on the kitchen island and finished it off with a green M&M before handing it over. She looked into his eyes. *I don't want to talk about it.*

He understood her look instantly.

He took a man-sized bite out of the cupcake, which left yellow icing along the bottom of his mustache. Jade giggled.

"What? What's so funny?" He grinned at her.

"Your mustache ..."

"My mustache? What? What's wrong with my mustache?" He planted a kiss on Jade's cheek, leaving a smudge of icing behind, and followed it with a hug and a pat.

"Oh, honey. I'm so sorry. We'll have our own party," her mom said, an exaggerated frown across her face.

Jade snatched a wooden spoon off the counter and grabbed the icing bowl. "No thanks," she said as she stomped up the stairs to her room.

U p in her room, Jade, still sniffling, held Olo in her arms as she wandered over to her desk. She opened her rock tumbler to check on the progress of her latest batch of river stones. The rocks tumbled out into her hand, still dull and unfinished, their surfaces rough under her fingertips. She sighed, placing them back inside, and reached for a polishing cloth from her stack, choosing her favorite egg-shaped crystal to work on.

"Stupid Sophia," she grumbled under her breath. She never liked her to begin with, so why her mother had insisted that they get together for movies and theme park trips, she didn't know. *Just because Sophia's Mom worked with her Mom at the hospital? Stupid. Stupid. Stupid.*

As she rubbed the crystal in slow, deliberate circles, her mood began to soften. She lost herself in the slow, soothing rhythm, feeling the stone warm against her skin, the buzz of energy within it. Sometimes, when she polished her crystals, her mind would drift somewhere else entirely, to a place where strange, fleeting images would flicker like scenes from a half-remembered dream. Once, while polishing her pink crystal, she'd seen a little boy chasing a ball into the street, just as a car barreled toward him. The very next day, she overheard her mother on the phone, talking about a boy from town who'd been hit by a car while chasing a ball.

Now, Jade held the crystal close, willing herself to see something good this time. Her fingers moved in gentle circles, eyes half-closed, her mind slipping into that quiet, shadowy place. Slowly, an image began to form—a frightening figure, a man with a bald head and dark piercing eyes.

A strange noise outside her door jolted her eyes open. A whiny, swishy, shuffly noise.

The door opened. Her dad, half laughing and half struggling with something on the other side of the door, peeked in. "Hey, birthday girl. We got a surprise for you."

Jade stopped polishing and wiped the remnants of her tears away.

"What's white and white and white all over?" he asked.

She knew exactly what he meant. *It couldn't be!*

She squealed as she raced to open the door. As it flung wide, what greeted her was the fluffiest, cutest, most deliciously soft puppy she had ever seen. A snowball of joy: a mix of Husky and Alaskan Malamute with spectacular blueberry eyes.

She looked at her mom, who gave her a gentle nod, eyes brimming with happy tears. "The one you wanted, from the farmer's market."

"Thank you, thank you, thank you," was all she could say before the puppy bounded into her room, springing onto the bed, covering her with wet, eager kisses and clumsy, playful paws. She buried her face in the puppy's fur, inhaling that warm, new-puppy smell, feeling her heart swell with the purest kind of joy. Finally, a real friend—one who wouldn't judge her, who wouldn't leave her out or ignore her.

"I love her," she cried, laughing and crying all at once. But just as the words left her mouth, the puppy spotted Olo. In one swift motion, she snatched the owl by the neck, shaking her head wildly, her tiny jaws clamping down with playful ferocity.

"No! Leave Olo alone!" Jade shrieked.

But it was too late. With one last enthusiastic shake, the puppy ripped off Olo's head, sending a cascade of white stuffing spilling across the floor.

Jade stared at the mess, her heart dropping as the puppy looked up at her, tail wagging, completely oblivious.

CHAPTER SIX

PLACE OF THE LOST ONE

J ade's heart sank as they pulled into the parking lot at Devil's Fork Park at Lake Jocassee an hour later in the SUV. She was hoping for a deserted park, where she could walk the edges of the lake and listen to the lullaby that the water hummed for her as the smallest of waves lapped against the rocks. She held her puppy in her lap, and they gazed out the window together at the boat ramp as the SUV shifted into park. Her mother opened the passenger side door but stopped short when she caught sight of the activity near the beach.

"Oh. Look who it is," she grumbled.

Sitting at a picnic table next to the boat ramp, engrossed in a cosmetics lesson, were three girls: Sophia, Kaitlyn and Marie. Behind them were Sophia's parents, with, she assumed, the parents of one of the other girls. Kaitlyn wore a light pink sweat suit, and white leather sneakers with pom poms on the laces which matched her insufferably bouncy personality. Marie wore a black tank top and jeans with patches. Sophia, in jeans with holes fashionably cut across her thighs and a grey hoodie, flipped her hood up upon catching sight of the Mills' SUV.

Jade held tight to the leash as her puppy whined and strained to jump into the front seat to make an exit.

Her father blocked the eager dog with his forearm and turned to face her, a look of worry in his eyes. "We can go somewhere else," he said as he paused his fingers on the ignition keys.

Jade swallowed. "No. It's fine." It wasn't fine, but if they didn't go to this park, she'd end up at the playground in the city park and that was just plain senseless. That park was for little kids.

"Okay. But hold on to that leash. We don't want to lose—what are we calling her?"

"Ningo."

"Ningo. I like it. Like Bingo. B. I. N.—"

Jade rolled her eyes. "No. Stop singing. That's not it." She placed her hand on the door handle and paused. As she opened the heavy door and dropped her feet to the pavement, her heart fluttered, and she felt lightheaded. She cleared her throat and stiffened her abdomen to raise her blood pressure and avoid a fainting spell—which happened rarely, but enough to make her cautious nonetheless.

As she stepped out, the yank on the leash snapped her to attention and she immediately felt better. The fresh air enlivened her, and out in the naked sunlight, she removed her sunglasses to see the glorious glow of the forest all around her. With Ningo in the lead, she hurried across the asphalt, eager to chuck her shoes and feel the wet grass between her t oes.

Lake Jocassee was a strange but beautiful place, still wild, undeveloped, with hidden waterfalls along the banks that were only accessible by boat. The shores of the lake were lined with boulders and small rocks that glinted in the sun from the mica embedded in the granite. The spring-fed emerald water was pristine, and on sunny days, clear almost to the bottom in places. Low lying mountains surrounded the lake in gentle waves, having eroded over the millennia, leaving the ancient blue ridge mountains populated by old growth furs, mushroom covered oaks, and the Oconee Bell, an endangered white and yellow wildflower found almost exclusively inside these woods. The name Jocassee, in Cherokee, meant "Place of the Lost One," which Jade liked.

Her father had brought her to the lake on the summer solstice many times. The ritual had become habit, and now every year, rain or shine, they packed up a cooler with snacks and drinks, and journeyed to their special place—a large rock just off the hiking trail where you could see the greatest expanse of water possible—and sit quietly waiting. Most visits ended at sunset, but on the rare occasion the full moon was out, they would stay longer.

Jade tumbled into the grass, removed her tennis shoes, and let Ningo sniff and tug as she pleased, listening to the puppy's thoughts as she explored the world with her little pink nose.

Bunny. Bunny. Worm. Leaf. Where bunny? Bunny...

"Did you find a rabbit trail?" Jade was delighted to hear Ningo so clearly here. Her thoughts, and the ruminations of the birds all around her, were amplified here. Clear. She hardly had to try at all.

But then came a ripple of laughter, harsh and sudden, shattering the moment. She looked up to see the three girls by the picnic table watching her. Marie, holding a pair of tweezers, leaned in close to Sophia, whispering something that made the other two girls snicker. Kaitlyn's gaze rolled over Jade's outfit—hot pink leggings and lime-green T-shirt—and she stifled a smirk, leaning in to say something that Jade couldn't hear.

Marie's voice drifted across the grass, low but unmistakable. "Oh, gross. It's that weird girl from the gifted class." She plucked at her eyebrows with practiced precision. "Here, you try," she said, handing the tweezers to Sophia, who put them down on the table.

"Hi, Jade." Sophia slid off the table to meet her halfway. "You got a puppy?!"

"Her name's Ningo," Jade replied, uneasy as Marie looked her over. She could feel the awful knot in her stomach return. *Here we go*, she thought. *Let's get this over with already so I can play with Ningo in peace.*

Marie, her black hair in a ponytail curled just so, into one giant ringlet, and ruby lipstick to match her nail polish, stood up and crossed her arms over her chest. "Ningo? That's a stupid name for a dog."

"It means 'snow' in Latin." She regretted the words as soon as they left her lips. *Latin was for nerds. Should have told them I picked it because it rhymes with Bingo.*

Sophia, crouching to pet the puppy, offered a small smile. "I like it. She's so cute!"

"I got her for my birthday," Jade said, feeling a flicker of relief. For once, Sophia seemed to be on her side.

Kaitlyn stared at Jade's outfit, a smirk rising on her face. "You get those leggings for your birthday, too?"

The girls laughed. Except Sophia, who gave Jade an apologetic half-smile.

Jade's shoulders slumped. She wanted to say something back, to stand up for herself, to put Kaitlyn in her place, but all she could do was stare at the ground, then up at Sophia, the hot sting of rejection welling up in her eyes. "Come on, Ningo." She tugged on the leash and led Ningo away as the girls resumed their make-up lesson at the table. As she walked away, she could feel them staring, the low grumble of hushed gossip on their breath.

· · · · ● ⊙ ● · · · · ·

B randon and Mindy eavesdropped from their bench by the water, where they settled in with a cooler full of sandwiches and cupcakes.

Mindy's face darkened as she watched the girls, her eyes narrowing. "Those little—"

Brandon put a calming hand on her knee. "Back off, Momma. She has to learn to fight her own battles." The helicopter Mom thing was getting out of hand lately, and he knew it. Jade needed to learn how to socialize, to stand up for herself, to make her way in the world without Momma Bear holding her hand or taking over. She babied her too much, and this was the result.

Mindy's gaze drifted over to a group loading a cooler and life vests into a small motorboat at the dock. Sophia's mother was among them, making a deliberate effort not to look their way. "I can't believe her," Mindy muttered, her voice low. "This is what was more important? A boat ride? They could do that any weekend."

Brandon gave her knee a pat. She was exhausted, as was he. They both forced a smile as Jade picked Ningo up in her arms and carried her. "*She* likes me," she said as her new puppy licked her face and nuzzled her neck.

"Awww. She's tuckered out." Mindy stood, giving Ningo a pet.

Jade nuzzled Ningo back. "She's sad. She told me."

"Why would Ningo be sad? This is the day she found her forever home," Brandon said.

"She misses her brothers and sisters. And her Mom." She lowered the puppy down and retreated with her to a small grass clearing next to the woods, away from everyone.

Brandon and Mindy watched their daughter as she plopped down in the grass and sulked.

"Hello, puberty," Brandon mused.

Lately, he'd felt a strange, unnamable worry when he looked at his daughter—a glimpse of something wild and unknowable behind her eyes, as if she were slipping further into a world that neither he nor Mindy could follow. She was growing up, pulling away from them in ways that felt as inevitable as they were painful. He'd heard horror stories from the guys at work about their teenage daughters, and if he was totally honest, the prospect of it intimidated him. Economics and geometry, he could handle. But mood swings were not in his repertoire.

Mindy sighed. "Intelligence, imagination, plus a sensitive heart. Those kids'll be working for her someday. You'll see." She glanced back at Jade, who sat cross-legged in the grass, weaving a dandelion chain while Ningo chased a dragonfly that hovered just out of reach, teasing the puppy with its bright, iridescent wings. The puppy chomped at the air as the playful dragonfly flitted and darted about and then buzzed away into the woods.

When Ningo took to chase and bounded away and off into the woods in pursuit, Jade sprang up, close on Ningo's heels. The two of them disappeared into the adjoining woods.

"Oh, good grief," Mindy muttered, scooping up the remnants of their lunch and dropping them into the cooler.

Brandon took her hand, helping her up. "Looks like we're going on a hike." He pushed aside the underbrush, holding the brambles back to create a path as they followed their daughter into the shadows.

CHAPTER SEVEN

SPELLBOUND

Jade ran after Ningo, the puppy's fluffy white form bounding through the shadows, darting around tree trunks, disappearing into the thickening underbrush, with leash trailing behind. Branches whipped against her face, leaves crackling underfoot as she sprinted, heart pounding, keeping her eyes fixed on the spot of white fur bobbing through the ferns ahead. The dragonfly led them deeper into the woods, its wings flickering in and out of sight like a shimmer on the edge of a dream.

The tall pines loomed around her, pillars of rough bark stretching high overhead, and the hardwoods—maples and oaks—twisted up toward the canopy, their branches intertwined in a dense lattice that filtered the sunlight into soft, dappled patches on the forest floor. Jade gasped for breath, the forest air rich and strangely alive with scents she couldn't quite place, a wild perfume that made her feel both dazed and exhilarated. It was nothing like the forests she remembered from her hikes. Here, everything felt sharper, more vibrant, as if a veil had lifted from the world and she was seeing it for the first time.

Ahead, Ningo stopped at the base of an enormous oak, her leash caught on a low branch. She barked up at the dragonfly, which had alighted on a high branch just out of reach, wings still pulsing with iridescent light. Jade slowed, taking in her surroundings. The clearing was like a hidden world—quiet, enclosed, as though they'd slipped into a place untouched by time. The oak was ancient, its trunk thick and gnarled, with rows of soft blue-gray mushrooms growing in horizontal lines, like little awnings. The branches fanned out overhead, casting a vast circle of shade across the ground below, where the moss grew thick and plush.

This forest was different. Jade felt it immediately. The air was thick with the smell of damp earth and green life, tinged with the freshness of rain, though the sky was clear. It reminded her of her mother's garden after a summer storm, a smell that made her feel safe, cocooned. Around the oak, a circle of mushrooms—brown with red speckles—formed a natural boundary, and beyond it, ferns as tall as her waist swayed gently, their fronds brushing against one another in a whisper of sound. A small creek wound its way through the clearing, its water so clear that she could see each stone on the bottom—a bright mosaic of emerald, scarlet, and neon green pebbles, some flecked with crystals, others shot through with bands of color. She'd never seen stones like these, anywhere. In all the time that she had explored the park, she'd never come across this creek, which she would have remembered, as the stones were bright, irresistible. Surely, she would have wandered through it, picking up as many rocks as she could carry.

"There you are! Silly Ningo," Jade huffed, still catching her breath. She bent down, hands on her knees, and gazed at the creek. "Look what I found. A creek."

But Ningo was still fixated on the dragonfly, barking and bouncing, her paws scrabbling at the tree trunk. Jade laughed, charmed by the puppy's single-minded determination, then crouched beside the creek, drawn by the strange stones glinting in the shallow water. She reached in, scooping up a handful, feeling the coolness of the water and the smooth weight of the stones against her skin. There were fossils embedded in some, tiny spiral shells that seemed to curl endlessly inward. Others were glossy, their surfaces polished by the current, and a few were flecked with veins of crystal, catching the light in tiny prisms. She slipped several into her jacket pocket, imagining how beautiful they'd look once she polished them.

She looked up to find Ningo still circling the tree, nipping at the air, eyes fixed on the dragonfly with a look of determined focus. Jade chased after her, stepping into the ring of mushrooms, her shoes sinking slightly into the damp moss, which felt soft and springy beneath her feet.

At the base of the old oak, which was hollow in the center and big enough to hide, was a small patch of delicate white flowers, like little bells, hanging from the stems, near perfection. She halted upon seeing them. She knew this plant.

Lily of the Valley.

Jade secured Ningo's leash around her wrist and squatted to examine the mysterious, delicate bells. She carefully picked a small bouquet and showed them to Ningo. "They're magic. The faeries ring the bells to hypnotize people. Did you know that?"

Ningo's ears perked up as she shook the bouquet.

"See?! It's so sweet. The bells ... " She flopped down under the tree and yawned.

"They sound like peppermint candy," she murmured, leaning back against the rough bark of the oak. She yawned, stretching her arms, and the tension seemed to drain from her body all at once. Ningo settled into her lap, curling up into a warm, soft ball. Her eyes grew heavy, her whole body sinking into a pleasant, dizzy warmth. The air felt thick, almost syrupy, and her mind floated in a hazy, half-awake state, where colors seemed sharper, sounds richer. The dew-laden delicate moss was soft under her legs, and the lingering sweet perfume of the bells delicious. She leaned her head against the enormous oak, savoring the feeling.

The dragonfly hovered in front of her face, close enough that she could see the lavender sheen of its wings, the tiny flecks of gold dust that clung to its body, shimmering like stardust. It had an olive-green body, segmented and delicate, with two large, black eyes that seemed to watch her with a strange intensity.

Jade blinked, trying to focus, her lungs paralyzed.

In a swirl of emerald and gold dust, it spun in the air, growing larger, its wings elongating, its body shifting, reshaping itself with each turn. Arms and legs emerged, and a face took shape, fierce and strange, with eyes that gleamed in the dim light like twin embers. Jade watched, frozen, her mouth half-open in wonder as the creature settled before her, hovering just above the ground.

It was like a faery, but unlike any she'd ever imagined or sketched—a creature of sinew and shadow, with skin a deep olive brown, painted in dark stripes that ran across her face and down her arms. Her hair was a crest of feathers, black and iridescent, sweeping back like the plumage of some wild bird. Rings glittered on her fingers, and bracelets clinked softly around her wrists, made of stones and metals Jade couldn't identify. She was beautiful and terrifying, her yellow eyes bright with a serious kind of mischief, studying Jade as if deciding whether she was worthy of something important.

Jade tried to speak, but her voice was trapped somewhere inside her chest. She wanted to ask *Are you real?* but the words wouldn't come. The creature leaned closer, her intense gaze never wavering, as though she could read every thought flickering through Jade's mind. Jade's heart raced, caught between fear and exhilaration, certain that she'd fallen asleep, that this was one of her strange, vivid dreams. *I'm in the in-between,* she told herself. *It's not real.*

But it felt real—the dampness of the moss beneath her, the solid weight of Ningo curled against her leg. The faery's presence, her breathing, her scent—everything was as tangible as the forest itself.

"Is this real?" Jade whispered, her voice barely a breath.

The creature stepped closer, her movements precise and fluid, her fingers reaching out to gently brush Jade's hair away from her face to examine her ears. Jade shivered at the touch, feeling the light scratch of her nails, the warmth of her skin. The creature tilted Jade's head, inspecting her as though searching for something hidden in her eyes, her expression fierce and curious.

Jade's hands flew up instinctively, and the creature's wings flared, feathers bristling with a soft hiss. The hiss shifted, melting into a voice that spoke directly into Jade's mind: *Don't be upset, sister. You're not dreaming.*

· · · · • ◯◯ • · · · ·

B randon and Mindy pushed their way through the thicket, their voices rising in the silent expanse of pines and holly trees. Branches crackled underfoot, and brambles clung to their clothes, but there was no sign of Jade, only the echo of their own calls bouncing back through the forest.

"Jade! Jade, honey, this isn't funny!" Mindy's voice was sharp with worry as she scanned the shadowed woods, her eyes darting between the trees.

Brandon cupped his hands around his mouth. "Olly olly in come free!" But the only response was the distant rustle of leaves, the quiet murmur of distant water.

Mindy's fingers tightened around her cell phone, ready to dial, and she glanced at Brandon, her voice trembling. "Should we call someone?"

Brandon placed a steadying hand on her back. "No. She's here. She's hiding. We'll find her. She wants to play, we'll play." He pressed a finger to his lips, signaling for silence. They stood still, ears straining, until a faint rustle caught their attention from behind a low hill.

Moments later, Ningo appeared, bounding over the crest, her tongue lolling, eyes bright. Behind her came Jade, her face flushed, her eyes wide and shining with a strange intensity. She looked... different. Transformed. Mindy's heart leapt as she ran to meet her, ready to scold, but Jade's breathless words tumbled out before she could say a thing.

"Come see! Come see! I told you they were real! She was a dragonfly, but then she turned into... I don't know, she had wings and feathers and she called me sister!" Jade's hands clutched at her parents', tugging them toward the woods, her face alight with urgency.

Brandon and Mindy exchanged a bewildered glance but allowed themselves to be pulled along, stumbling over rocks and roots as they followed Jade's frantic steps. But as they climbed the hill, cresting it with their hearts pounding, they found nothing on the other side. Just trees. Pines and oaks, tall and silent, stretching endlessly into shadow.

Jade's expression shifted, her excitement giving way to confusion. She scanned the forest floor, her eyes searching desperately. "She was right here! And the creek—it was full of gems." She dug her hands into her pockets, her face crumpling as she found them empty. "No! I had the rocks. I put them in my pocket." Her gaze darted around, her voice rising in a frantic call.

"Sister! Siiissterrrrr!" she called. A sudden downpour of tears spilled forth.

The silence that followed was heavy, final, as if the forest itself were holding its breath.

Mindy and Brandon watched, helpless, as Jade's face twisted with anger and heartbreak. And then, with a shuddering gasp, she let out a scream—a high, screeching sound that tore through the air, raw and piercing, vibrating with a resonance that was anything but human. The sound was unnatural, and it sent a chill down her parents' spines, the kind of chill that settles deep and lingers, refusing to be shaken. How their daughter summoned the sound, they didn't know, but it was bone-chilling, otherworldly, and it shook them to the core.

J ade sat curled on the leather sofa in the psychiatrist's waiting room, her legs tucked under her, clutching Olo to her chest. Her fingers traced the line of stitches around her neck, where her head had been carefully sewn back on. She drew comfort from the softness of her fake fur, though her mother's expression offered no such comfort. There was a new, unsettling edge to the way her mother looked at her, a wariness that made Jade feel like a stranger.

"You don't need to be afraid," her mother was saying, her voice tight and overly calm. "Dr. Sullivan is a professional, and she knows all about how the mind works. She can help you."

Jade hugged Olo tighter, anger flaring in her chest.

"She doesn't know what I know," she replied, her voice flat, defiant. They didn't believe her. No one did. But she knew what she'd seen, what she'd felt. She would tell the doctor everything—someone had to understand, eventually.

The door to the psychiatrist's office opened, and a woman stepped out, dressed in a bright floral blouse and black slacks, her smile warm, inviting. "Jade? It's very nice to meet you. Do you feel comfortable coming in by yourself, or would you like your mom to come in too?"

Jade had a lot to say, and the last person she wanted in that room was her mother. She glanced back at her mother, feeling a surge of defiance. "By myself." She shrugged off her mother's attempted hug and walked through the door, holding her head high.

· · · · ● ◯◯ ● · · · ·

Mindy stood nervously, phone in hand, dialing Brandon's number as she paced the waiting room. She was too unsettled to sit, avoiding eye contact with a teenage boy across the room who was chewing his nails and bouncing his knee in agitation.

Brandon's voice came through the phone, steady, calm. "How's it going?"

"She went in by herself," Mindy replied. "She seemed... I don't know. Confident. Like she wanted to be alone with the doctor. It was strange. I thought she'd want me with her."

"That's a good thing," Brandon reassured her. "She needs someone she can talk to openly. I'm sure it will be fine."

Mindy's hand tightened around the phone as she looked out the window to the street below, cars idling at the stoplight, pedestrians wandering past with easy smiles. "No, Brandon. She's not fine. Something's wrong. She's not like other children." Her voice trembled, and the words spilled out. "Remember that day she stood by the chimes in that trance, humming? That was years ago. I knew then—"

"—that she's unique. She's special, Mindy. We just have to help her navigate that."

"Special?" Mindy's voice cracked. "No. It's more than that. I think she may never be okay. Are you getting this at all?" Her voice broke, and she drew a shuddering breath. "I'll call you when she's done." She ended the call without waiting for his response, dropping her phone back into her purse.

Mindy sank onto a sofa, watching the teenage boy across the room, who, despite his nervousness, appeared quite normal. Tears filled her eyes, blurring her vision as she sat there, alone, waiting.

CHAPTER EIGHT

TWO WORLDS

The University of Georgia was turning out to be an almost perfect fit for Jade as she settled into her second semester of freshman year. It was close enough to visit home on a whim, yet far enough away—a solid hour and a half—so that her mother couldn't hover. Mostly, anyway. The daily texts had finally trickled off, but her mother still insisted on evening phone calls, three or four times a week. Jade had quickly learned to put her phone on speaker and study during these conversations, offering the occasional "Uh-huh" or "That's nice, Mom," to keep her mother satisfied. Leaving home had been harder on her mom than she'd expected, though she'd tried to mask it with forced cheer. "It's just… I can't help worrying," Mindy would say, with a sigh that somehow sounded both theatrical and completely genuine.

But for Jade, the departure had been a liberation. She'd learned a long time ago—*that day,* when she was twelve—that some things were better left unsaid. She hadn't had another full "encounter," as she called it, since that day, but there were flashes sometimes: a glimpse of something dark and watchful hiding high in the trees, or the echo of a whisper threading through the forest. She saw her sister in dreams now and then, feathers shimmering in twilight, eyes full of that knowing, half-mischievous light. But she *never* spoke of her. To anyone. Not even to Ningo, her faithful white-furred confidante.

After that first psychiatric appointment, she had learned to live in two worlds. The ordinary world—where she obeyed, smiled, laughed when she was supposed to—and the other world, hidden inside her mind, a world full of half-glimpsed visions and echoes of that strange, magnificent creature with peacock feathers and a voice like falling leaves. She'd stopped drawing, stopped talking about what she saw and heard, learning to be a model student, a perfect daughter. And she became remarkably adept at faking her way through conversations, blending into the regular world without stirring suspicion.

But some habits persisted. She still watched the shimmering body lights around living things—she'd since learned to call them "auras"—and held silent conversations with Ningo when they were alone. During breaks from the Discovery School, she often returned to Lake Jocassee, haunted by a quiet, persistent hope that she might glimpse her sister again.

In truth, her years at the Discovery School had been a gift, far more comfortable than the isolating halls of her old public school. She was one oddball among many there, a place where differences were the rule rather than the exception. Connor was deaf, Sharlene was blind, the twins were on the spectrum, and Robbie—her irrepressible, upbeat friend—had ADHD, dyslexia, and a paralyzed right arm from a childhood fall. Robbie had been the first to approach her on that nerve-wracking first day, barreling over with his typical exuberance.

"Hi. I'm Robbie. I have a gimp arm, but you can shake my *other* hand. Unless you'd rather have a hug—we're big on hugs around here. But no hugging without permission, so, would you like a hug? I'm the best hugger." Jade hadn't known what to make of him at first, but his openness was like a balm, and she'd grown to adore him. She didn't know what had become of him after graduation, though Sharlene mentioned he was working for his dad selling air conditioners in Seneca. Jade had texted him a few times, even left voicemails, but she'd never heard back.

Starting college had been strangely easy for Jade. Here, she was just another face in the crowd, her history known to no one unless she chose to share it—which she didn't. She'd become so practiced at navigating social situations that she could almost fool herself into believing she belonged. She stayed quiet in class, an attentive student who flew through assignments with a quiet efficiency that impressed her professors. No one had to know about her past, her visions, her peculiarities. She was simply Jade: bright, reserved, a little unusual but nothing more.

She liked the campus itself: old-fashioned brick buildings draped in ivy, stately but a little dull, softened by the canopy of enormous oak trees that dotted the grounds, casting dappled patterns across the green lawns. There were enough students to lose herself among them, to become just another body in the flow of foot traffic between classes. She often brought her backpack outside, spreading a blanket beneath one of the ancient oaks to read or work on assignments. The trees soothed her, their grounding energy seeping up through the earth, filling her with a calm that nothing else seemed to offer.

It was on such an afternoon, late in April, with finals just around the corner, that she sat beneath the largest oak in the commons, enjoying the rare warmth of the season. The tree was in full bud, tiny green leaves unfurling like a thousand delicate flags, the promise of summer thick in the air. The soil beneath her still held the dampness from the previous night's rain, and she could feel the life force pulsing through the roots beneath her, drawn up through the trunk in slow, deliberate waves, feeding the budding leaves above. She stretched out on a blue-and-white gingham blanket, letting the sun fall on her bare feet as she spread her books around her, a little fortress of paper and ink.

Her snack box, a sleek stainless-steel container her mother had given her, sat open beside her. Inside, a mix of dried fruit, nuts, and seeds—a vegan assortment that Jade had carefully curated. Coconut flakes, raisins, apricots, almonds, sunflower seeds. She only ate what the plant world released willingly: fruits, seeds, the bounty that fell freely to the ground. Whole plants, ripped from the soil, felt wrong to her, like a violation. It was an odd rule, she knew, but it made sense to her, and her mother had long since learned not to question it. Being vegan at college was easier with access to her own kitchen, a perk of her "special needs" status, which also came with the luxury of a single dorm room.

As she leaned back against the oak, feeling the cool, textured bark pressing into her spine, a shadow fell over her. She glanced up, startled, to see a tall, lanky boy hovering nearby, hands buried in his pockets. His hair was a tangle of black curls that nearly obscured his eyes, and his face was dotted with acne. He wore a campus sweatshirt, loose corduroys, and an awkward, hesitant smile.

"Oh, hey. Plant Bio, right?" he asked, his voice warm but a little unsteady. His energy field pulsed around him in an anxious red, flickering with spots of orange that wavered as he shifted his weight from one foot to the other.

Jade gave him a polite nod. She didn't recognize him, but that was hardly surprising. She always sat near the door in class, strategically positioned to slip out the moment lectures ended. "Tuesday, Thursday, one o'clock?" she replied, offering him a small, noncommittal smile.

His shoulders relaxed, and his aura softened to a dusky rose, a sign that he was beginning to feel more at ease. He flopped down beside her on the blanket, far closer than she would have preferred, stretching out his hand in an awkward attempt at a high-five.

"I'm Josh," he said, his grin widening.

"Jade," she replied, ignoring his hand.

"J's are the best," he said, lowering his hand with a sheepish chuckle. He leaned back, clearly intending to linger.

He was in her privacy bubble, as Robbie used to call it. Jade steeled herself for the inevitable: an invitation to some loud fraternity party or obnoxious end-of-the-year bash. She would decline politely, go back to reading, and that would be that.

Instead, he surprised her. "You have plans for summer break?" he asked, picking at his cuticles as he spoke.

Jade reached into her backpack, pulling out a bookmark, nearly ready to pack up and retreat to her room. "Going home," she said, snapping her book shut with a quiet finality.

"Oh. Cool. Me and some friends rented a condo in Panama City Beach for a week. My roommate's bringing his jet ski. You like to jet ski?"

"I like going home." She clipped the lid onto her snack box, signaling that the conversation was over. But when she glanced up, she caught the disappointment in his eyes, a brief flicker of hurt that softened his aura to a faded gray.

Feeling a pang of guilt, she forced herself to soften her tone. "But that sounds like a nice vacation," she added, trying to sound sincere. "I'm sure you'll have a great time."

"Yeah," he said, standing up, shoving his hands back into his pockets. "Sorry for bugging you." He gave her a little nod and headed off, calling to another student as he crossed the lawn. "Yo, Pigeon, wait up!"

Jade watched him go, feeling an odd sense of relief as she reopened her snack box and leaned back against the tree. Socializing had always exhausted her; she preferred the calm, steady presence of trees, the silent company of roots and leaves.

The drive home was its own kind of meditation. She felt safe in her mother's old SUV, cocooned in her familiar space, gliding down country roads lined with Loblolly pines that whispered secrets to each other as she passed. The landscape was quiet, dotted with run-down gas stations and the occasional boiled peanut stand, long stretches of farmland sprawled beneath the open sky. To most, it would have been a dull journey, but Jade savored it, the simple emptiness, the absence of people. She listened to an audiobook, *The Celestine Prophecy*, letting the soothing voice of the narrator fill the car, her mind drifting in and out of the story.

When she pulled into the driveway, a sense of calm washed over her, an unexpected lightness. She hadn't realized how much tension she'd been carrying until she saw the house—familiar, unchanging, solid as an anchor. Her mom must have been watching from the window because she flew out the door the moment Jade shifted the SUV into park, her arms already outstretched.

"Jade!" Mindy called, her face bright with joy. She wrapped her daughter in a fierce hug, squeezing so tight Jade could barely breathe, as if Jade had been gone for years instead of a single semester.

"I just finished a batch of lemon cookies. They're still warm," her mom said, grinning as she finally let go.

Jade smiled back. "Great. I love your cookies." She'd missed her mother's baking, the comfort of home-cooked food.

"Oh, and your father thought we might get out on the boat this weekend. He's at Ace Hardware picking up new paddles. The old ones, well—"

"I know, Mom. The old ones got lost." Jade slipped past her, grabbing her heavy tote from the backseat. "I left them on the dock last year." She hoisted her gym bag—stuffed with laundry—into her other hand, shooting her mom an apologetic glance. "Sorry."

"It's no trouble," Mindy said, rolling her eyes fondly. "Those things happen." She bent to lift the gym bag, struggling under its weight as she waddled up the path. "Goodness, whatcha got in here? A dead body?"

Jade laughed, following her into the house, letting the warmth and familiarity wrap around her like a blanket. Here, she thought, in this strange little in-between place—between childhood and adulthood, between ordinary and extraordinary—she could almost forget the other world. Almost.

Chapter Nine

WHISPERING FALLS

Save me. SOS. Jade typed the words into her cellphone, her thumbs moving with practiced precision, and sent the text off with a tiny flick of hope. Curled up on the family sofa, she glanced across the living room at her dad, who was engrossed in the Kentucky Derby on their oversized HDTV. He sat comfortably plumped into the cushions, a bag of nachos balanced on his lap, a beer resting in one hand. His silver-threaded goatee had grown fuller over the years, and his belly now settled firmly against his belt, a subtle shift from his leaner days.

"Texting friends from college?" he asked, not taking his eyes off the screen as the horses thundered around the track.

"No." It wasn't a lie.

"Oh. Speaking of which, I assume you made some friends this semester?" He tossed a chip into his mouth, crunching loudly, oblivious. "That first semester's always brutal, but by the second half, things start to relax. That's when people really connect."

Really? Jade resisted the urge to roll her eyes. *I've been home for one day and he's already launching into a lecture about socializing?* "Sure," she replied, in her best casual tone. "Lots of friends. Parties. All that." She kept her gaze fixed on her phone screen, unwilling to meet his hopeful look. The truth was, she hadn't made a single friend at college all year, and she preferred it that way.

Her phone buzzed, and her heart skipped. Robbie's text came in: *i dont do damsels in distress.*

Jade smirked, curling the phone closer to her chest, careful to angle the screen so her dad couldn't sneak a look. She texted back: *Kayak? Lake Jocassee?*

"Don't make any plans for tomorrow," her dad reminded her, his tone brightening as he leaned forward, eyes glued to the TV. "We're going to the lake. First outing of the season!" His face lit up, eyes crinkling at the corners. The races had reached the final stretch, and he practically shouted at the screen, "Go! Go! Go! Watch him, he's coming around the outside!"

Working tomorrow, Robbie replied. She narrowed her eyes, suspicious.

On a Sunday? she texted back.

Robbie's reply made her grin: *its friday snaggletooth.*

She loved it when he called her that. Even after the braces had smoothed out her crooked front tooth, the nickname still felt oddly comforting.

Rawr. No. It's saturday, mouthbreather, she shot back, smiling as she remembered how he'd once run headfirst into a door jamb, breaking his nose. He'd had to breathe through his mouth for weeks.

But this time, his response didn't come immediately. Jade tossed the sofa pillow she'd been clutching aside, stood, and slipped out onto the front porch, phone in hand. She dialed his number, pacing along the edge of the porch, watching a robin flit down to a branch on the crepe myrtle. She chewed on her thumbnail as she waited for him to pick up.

When he finally answered, his voice was flat, a bit rough around the edges. "Don't be a stalker."

Jade winced at the sharpness in his tone. She'd hoped his old anger might have softened over the year, but it seemed to be lingering like an old yellow bruise. "So, we're not even friends anymore?" she asked, trying to keep her voice light.

"No. You abandoned me," he replied, the words tinged with bitterness. "I'll hate you until the day I die."

She felt a pang, a mix of regret and frustration. "Doesn't seem fair. Couldn't you just hate me a little less each year? Maybe even, I don't know... until you like me again?"

There was a pause, a soft cough, and Jade caught a hint of sadness threading through his voice. "You got a boyfriend now, or what?"

"Good Lord, no," she said, letting a small smile play on her lips. "Or what."

"Well, I have a girlfriend," he retorted, but the words sounded thin, as if he was testing her reaction, waiting for her to protest.

"Good for you," she said, her voice deliberately nonchalant, though a tiny stab of jealousy prickled in her chest. "I don't care." She did care, of course, but she'd rather swallow glass than admit that to Robbie.

The silence stretched between them, weighted with unspoken things. When he finally spoke, his voice was softer, almost a murmur. "I can't."

Jade hesitated, then spoke quickly, hoping to catch him off-guard. "You can bring her. I just want to kayak over to Whispering Falls. She can use my mom's kayak. What's her name?"

There was a long, heavy sigh on the other end of the line. Finally, he muttered, "Okay. I don't have a girlfriend. And I don't want one. I'm too busy. Everybody wants their A/C fixed yesterday."

Jade couldn't help the laugh that bubbled up. Same old Robbie. She lowered her voice to a conspiratorial whisper. "I have a secret I need to tell you."

There was a pause, and she could practically hear his curiosity sparking through the phone. "Really?" he said, playing along, though she knew he could see right through her. "So, tell me now."

She let the silence hang, then whispered, "Meet me at the boat ramp. Eight tomorrow morning." Before he could protest, she hung up, tucking the phone into her back pocket as it began to ring. She ignored it, wandering along the garden path, her fingers brushing the edges of blooming tulips and daffodils. Their colors were vivid in the spring light—golds, reds, pinks—bright as fireworks. She could see their auras flickering with life, a soft, pulsing glow that made her feel like she was standing in the heart of some hidden, ancient magic.

Danger. Danger.

Jade glanced up to find the robin watching her intently, its round black eyes like a tiny window into a different world.

"Don't worry," she murmured, meeting its gaze. "I won't disturb your nest." She adjusted her path, drifting back toward the house, but caught a glimpse of her mother's face through the dining room window, her expression tight with concern. *She saw me talking to the bird,* Jade realized, feeling a flash of annoyance mixed with something softer—a pang of guilt, maybe, for worrying her mother.

When she returned to the living room, her father was still glued to the screen, watching post-race commentary with the sound on low. She waited until the commercial break, then spoke casually. "I'm going to the lake tomorrow with a friend. Is that okay?"

Her dad muted the TV, glancing up as her mom joined them, hands resting on her hips. "Thought we'd all go. You can bring your friend," her mother offered, eyes bright with that hopeful, expectant look that Jade found almost painful. "Who's this now? Someone from school?"

Jade forced a smile. "Yes. Someone from school." Also technically not a lie, she thought, suppressing the urge to smirk.

"Oh?" Her mother lingered, waiting for more.

"We're just going to kayak out to the cove," she added breezily, giving them her best "responsible daughter" smile. "Maybe hike a little. Without parents. Nothing personal."

Her dad leaned back on the sofa, studying her for a moment, a slight crease forming between his brows. Finally, he shrugged, letting out a soft sigh. "Guess it's about that time, then. I need to work in the yard anyway." He looked disappointed, but she knew he'd let her go without argument. Her mom, however, looked a little crestfallen, like she'd just been politely refused an invitation to her own party. "Too bad," her dad continued, half-heartedly. "I bought those meatless burgers just for you."

Jade almost felt bad for him, but the longing inside her was stronger. It had been simmering all year, an ache that had settled into her bones, tugging her back to the lake, to the one place where she felt closest to the truth she couldn't share. She needed to see her sister again, to look into those fierce, otherworldly eyes, to feel that electric, wild energy crackling through the air around her. Every trip she'd taken with her parents to Lake Jocassee had ended in disappointment. She couldn't explain it, but she knew, in the deepest part of her being, that her sister would return. She could feel it, like the tension in the air before a storm, a storm that no one else could see.

Except this time, she would go with Robbie. He would understand. She was certain of it.

· · · · ● ◯◯ ● · · · ·

The kayaks slid silently across the lake, their paddles breaking the smooth surface with each rhythmic stroke. Jade took the lead, instinct guiding her more than memory. She could feel a subtle pull in her gut, a tugging that grew stronger with each bend they rounded, like an invisible thread drawing her deeper into the lake's hidden heart. She gripped the paddle with steady hands, dipping it into the water and pulling herself forward, muscles warm from the effort, the water cool and dark beneath her.

It had turned out to be a perfect day. The lake was a sheet of glass, reflecting the sun in glittering points that danced across the surface like tiny stars. The air was warm but crisp, edged with the bite of early spring, and the sky was a flawless, cloudless blue. But beneath her, she felt an unexpected chill rising from the water, a subtle, ghostly coolness that hinted at the depths below. She could see all the way down through the clear water, where flashes of movement betrayed the colorful trout darting away from the kayak's shadow. The lake knew many secrets, she thought—secrets buried beneath layers of silt and time, lost to everyone but the few who were curious or brave enough to search for them

.

Deeper beneath the trout, the water darkened, stained by tannins that gave the lake its earthy, tea-colored hue. There was a smell here, subtle, of wet stone and decaying leaves—a rich, silty musk that carried with it the sense of something ancient, something alive and sleeping beneath the surface, as Nature quietly recycled life back into itself.

Robbie was a welcome presence at her side, his paddle dipping unevenly into the water, splashing as he tried to keep up with her. He had changed since she'd last seen him. His face had filled out, his jaw shadowed with a scruff that was thicker in some patches than others, giving him a slightly rugged, disheveled look. He seemed broader across the shoulders, his frame heavier with the beginnings of muscle, though he still carried that same air of irrepressible energy, bouncing from one thought to the next, his stories tumbling over each other in a mix of sarcasm, optimism, and his usual scatterbrained cha rm.

"So, are we racing, or what?" he called, flashing her a grin as he struggled to keep his kayak from veering off course. He'd brought his paddle mount with him, along with the rear stabilizer, which allowed him to paddle without much problem, but his speed was still no match for hers.

Jade set her paddle across her lap, letting the kayak glide forward as she uncapped her water bottle. Only now, pausing for a moment, did she realize how quickly she'd been moving, as if something in the lake itself had been urging her on. She took a long drink and offered the bottle to Robbie, who coasted up beside her, his eyes squinting in the sun.

"Sorry about that. You thirsty?" she asked, as he took the bottle from her.

He took a deep gulp, then tossed it back to her with a casual grin, stretching his chest and overworked shoulder. "You're not taking me to some remote location to have your way with me, are you?" he teased, leaning back in his kayak with a mock-serious look. "Because, just so you know, I'm not that kind of guy. And also—you promised me a secret.

Unless that was just a ruse to get me alone and defenseless in the wilderness." He winked, his lips curving into the sly, half-smiling expression that had always been his signature.

Jade's cheeks flushed, memories from long ago creeping up on her, vivid as ever. She was back in eleventh grade, sneaking out of the Discovery School with Robbie, a flashlight in her hand, his fingers laced through hers. They'd made their way through the dark, knee-high grasses to a small hill under a sky blazing with stars. She could still feel the warmth of his hand, the way he'd squeezed her fingers each time a meteor streaked across the night, his aura pulsing in shades of soft orange and pink.

She remembered the way his lips had touched hers that night, tentative and gentle, as if he'd been afraid of breaking the moment. When he kissed her, their auras mingled, a swirl of pinks and blues that seemed to glow in the dark, expanding outward until they surrounded them both, blending, pulsing, alive. Her skin had tingled where he touched her, a warm, electric thrill that had made her pulse race. Her lips buzzed and her fingers tingled, stirring all her senses and awakening her body. For all his clumsiness and brash, he'd been unexpectedly tender—gentle, tentative as he coaxed her, unbuttoning her blouse.

Their eyes met now across the lake, and she saw the memory flicker in his gaze too. He looked at her for a beat too long, and a small smile tugged at the corners of his mouth. Jade's lips began to tingle at the thought of it, her heart skipping as she imagined the two of them hidden away from the world once more, alone in the quiet places where only the trees and the stars bore witness.

But the moment was shattered by a strange, echoing call that came from somewhere high up in the woods. "Whaaaaaahhhh. Ca. Ca. Caaaaa." It was a hollow, haunting sound, bouncing off the trees, sending a ripple of unease across the air. The lake seemed to hold its breath, and the smell of moss and something ancient—something almost floral—drifted past her.

She stiffened, her heart suddenly racing for a different reason. She knew that call. Her hand shot to her paddle, her body already moving, instincts kicking in as she spun her kayak toward the shore.

A blue heron lifted clumsily from the shore, its wings beating against the air in slow, awkward strokes, as though it had forgotten how to fly. Jade barely noticed; she was already paddling as fast as she could, a sense of urgency building inside her, pulling her forward.

"Hey!" Robbie called after her, confused but following. She could hear him paddling hard to keep up, his breath coming in short gasps as he struggled to match her pace. "Where are we going? What's going on?"

The water grew darker as they approached the shore, thick with shadows. She felt a chill run down her spine, and a shimmer flickered in the corner of her eye—a flash of green, or maybe gold, in the trees ahead. The air around them felt heavier, as though it was charged with a current, a pulse that skimmed the surface of the lake.

The shore loomed closer, the trees casting long, twisted shadows. Jade felt her pulse quicken, her senses alive with the certainty that she was close—somewhere, hidden in these shadows, her sister was waiting.

And this time, she wasn't going to let her slip away.

CHAPTER TEN

THE PORTAL

J ade half jumped and half fell out of the kayak as the water shallowed, her feet splashing into the chill water. She tossed the paddle onto the rocky shore and clutched at the rope on the front of the boat, hauling it up onto the pebble-strewn beach. Her hands shook with anticipation as she looked around, trying to absorb the strange energy that pulsed through the air.

To her right, Whispering Falls cascaded down from above, a curtain of white water and mist fluting down into a deep pool at its base. The constant pounding of the falls had worn the rocks smooth over the years, carving a circular cavern into the cliff face, its stone walls polished and glistening as if by some ancient hand. The frothing rainwater swirled in eddies around bits of leaves and twigs, sucking them into the mysterious dark beneath the surface. Normally, she would stand here, captivated, letting the cool mist spray her face.

But not today.

She scanned the treetops, her eyes darting over the branches, alert to every shadow and glint. The woods felt alive, humming with a watchful silence.

Behind her, Robbie called from his kayak, his voice a mixture of confusion and impatience. "What is it?"

Jade put a finger to her lips, her eyes wide, signaling him to be quiet. She waded back into the lake, waiting until he was close enough to hear her whispered reply. "You know that secret I was going to tell you?"

"Yeah," he replied, still half out of breath, his eyes scanning the shoreline.

She pointed up, to a boulder three-quarters up the waterfall, where a perched figure crouched, covered in black feathers. The figure watched them with a stillness that felt ancient, her gaze sharp and unnerving. It was as if she had been waiting for them, watching from a distance all this time.

"Holy crap." Robbie's paddle slipped from his grip into the water. "Are you seeing—"

"Yes. Shhhh," Jade whispered, barely breathing. "Don't scare her away. I told you faeries were real, didn't I?"

The creature remained motionless, her gold, glistening eyes locked on Jade.

Jade felt herself drawn forward, her steps slow, reverent. She raised a hand to Robbie, signaling him to stay put, though he looked as though he had no intention of moving an inch closer. Her breath was shallow, her heartbeat a rapid rhythm in her chest. She didn't know how she knew, but something in her bones urged her on. She put her hands to her mouth and called out, a cry that had haunted her dreams for years, a sound that welled up from the back of her throat as naturally as breathing: "Whaaaaa-caaa!"

At the call, the creature shifted, her iridescent wings unfurling in a slow, deliberate spread. In one smooth motion, she leapt from the boulder, her wings catching the warm air as she glided down to the base of the waterfall, landing with a grace and silence that made Jade's breath hitch. She was even more magnificent than Jade had remembered, her wings gleaming in shades of deep purple and iridescent black, shimmering like glass in the sunlight.

Her feet were wrapped in what looked like leather-like strips, and her body was covered in a tight wrap of dark, earthy brown fabric bound with vines. Around her neck hung a primitive gold necklace, an intricate lattice that caged her throat, with crimson gems hanging from it like drops of blood. She was both fierce and delicate, her face carved in sharp lines, her eyes large and gold, except for a thin ring of translucent black at the edges. When she blinked, her eyelids slid sideways, a movement so alien that Jade felt a chill race down her spine.

The creature drew in long, heaving breaths, her chest rising and falling, the sound raw and powerful, before finally beginning to sing. A single note, low and resonant, poured from her throat, a sound so pure it seemed to vibrate the very air around them. Jade felt the note deep in her chest, a vibration that seemed to harmonize with her heartbeat.

In her hands, two gold spheres appeared, one large and one smaller, each hanging from a delicate gold chain. She swung the smaller sphere gently, letting it collide with the larger one, producing a deep, calming tone that merged with her voice. The sound filled Jade with a sense of weightlessness, an eerie clarity that made her feel as though she were floating.

Behind her, Jade heard splashing as Robbie retrieved his paddle and clambered back into his kayak, muttering something she couldn't hear, but his presence faded from her awareness. She was captivated, her entire being pulled forward, as if tethered to the creature by an invisible thread. She took a step, then another, her bare feet feeling the smooth pebbles pressing into her soles, grounding her, but even that sensation began to melt away. The closer she got, the more she felt as though she were dissolving, her edges blurring, her body filling with a strange, liquid light that seemed to flow through her veins.

Every step brought a tingling, a slight resistance, like walking through cobwebs that clung to her skin and then snapped away. Each thread that broke seemed to release something within her, an old ache, a forgotten fear. Her heart pounded, her hands trembling as she drew closer to the creature, her vision narrowing to the dark, hypnotic eyes that never left hers.

When she was only a few feet away, the creature moved with sudden, blinding speed, a blur of feathers and iridescent light. In an instant, Jade felt herself swept up, the creature's arms wrapping around her in a firm grip. She gasped as they plunged into the waterfall, the cold water crashing over them as they dove deep into the darkness below.

She wanted to scream, but she dared not, her mouth clamped shut as she was dragged through the water, her vision reduced to shadows and flickers of light reflecting off submerged stones. The journey seemed to last an eternity, an endless rush of cold and dark, before they burst from the water into an open cavern, gasping for air.

The creature hauled Jade up onto a smooth rock ledge. The cavern walls were slick, curving in strange, organic shapes, their surfaces shimmering with flecks of gold that caught the light filtering in from above. The air was damp, the sound of dripping water echoing off the stone in a disorienting, hollow rhythm. Jade shivered, the chill sinking into her skin as she tried to catch her breath, her mind disoriented, foggy.

She watched as her captor scrambled over rocks to the back of the cavern, retrieving a small satchel. She pulled out a handful of golden sand and returned, tossing it over Jade in a sweeping motion, and as the grains caught the air, her voice rose again, filling the cavern with the same haunting note. The sand transformed mid-air, turning into butterflies—hundreds of them, vibrant orange and black, their wings beating in a blur around her.

The butterflies swarmed her, landing on her arms, her legs, her face. She held her breath, frozen in place as they pulsed and buzzed around her, the gentle tickling of their tiny legs and wings against her skin sending waves of electricity through her. The tingly sensation intensified, and she could feel an overpowering, strange yet euphoric wave come over her entire body, causing her lips and tongue to vibrate. The vibrations grew stronger. Her skin flushed. Her breath halted. So intense was her euphoria, she thought she might be dying. She blinked her eyes to see, but her vision was only a kaleidoscope of colors and the blur of shapes as the butterflies swarmed her face.

Then, in an instant, the butterflies dissolved back into gold dust, coating her body in a fine shimmer.

She looked down and saw her own body glowing, a soft white light emanating from beneath her skin, speckled with flecks of gold. Around her arms, golden threads spiraled, winding around her limbs like vines. Her clothes were gone.

The creature stepped back, examining her, a strange satisfaction in her dark eyes. "Nai arma. Nai leiga. Nai tuysuh. Am noune. Am nasir. May am sakau," she stated. Then off Sekowah's perplexed look, she added, "Sorry. Two arms. Two legs. Two eyes. One nose. One head. And a mouth. Perfect," she murmured, her voice resonant and strange, each word echoing through the cavern.

Jade touched her ears, her fingers brushing against their new shape—pointed, like the creature's. She scanned her body more closely. She turned her hands over. Touched her hair. Her face. Everything felt different. Somehow cleaner, clearer, sharper, more real than she had ever felt before. Then, quite suddenly and without warning, the creature grabbed her by the waist once more, dove into the dark blue water with her, and the journey was reversed, through the underground caverns, through the crystal-clear pool of the waterfall once more.

The water crashed around them as they crossed the threshold again, the thunderous roar drowning out her thoughts. But as they emerged from the curtain of water, Jade gasped, staggering as her feet hit solid ground. The lake was gone. In its place stretched a wild, untamed river, its currents raging and churning with a dark, relentless power. The banks were jagged, lined with thick, twisted roots that clawed into the earth like grasping fingers. Ancient trees, their trunks draped with moss and vines, leaned over the water, casting long shadows that danced in the amber glow of the sky. She took a shuddering breath, the strange, humid air filling her lungs with a sharp sweetness that felt alien yet invigorating. She clutched her sister's arm, her voice trembling. "Where... where are we?"

Her sister looked down at her, something fierce and solemn in her gaze. "Welcome home, Sekowah," she said, her voice barely audible over the river's roar. "This is the Jasper

Valley." And as Jade looked out over the wild, untamed landscape, she felt the enormity of it settle over her, heavy as stone—the life she had known was truly gone, washed away in the river's furious current.

The familiar edges of Lake Jocassee had disappeared, and the thick air made her feel dizzy. She collapsed to the ground, her legs unable to hold her.

Graceful rainbow-colored birds flushed from a nearby tree, startling her. She covered her head with her arms, pulling her knees into her chest, and squeezed her eyes shut. Jade clamped her hands over her mouth, panic surging through her veins. This isn't happening. *This is a dream*, she tried to tell herself. *Just a dream.*

But this dream had become a nightmare.

The scream that left her lips did not feel her own as it echoed throughout the dense woods. It was primal, echoing out into the forest, scattering more of the strange, rainbow-colored birds from the trees. They took to the sky, their long, iridescent tails streaming behind them like comets, their calls filling the air.

The creature was beside her, watching her closely, her brow furrowed in concern.

Jade leapt to her feet, her legs moving with a grace and speed that startled her. She stumbled forward, her gaze darting around wildly, seeking any sign of her old world. "Robbie! Where are you?"

The creature caught her by the wrist, her grip firm but gentle. "Shhhh! Don't shout." She pulled a rough, brown tunic from her satchel and handed it to Jade. "Put this on."

Jade stared at her, dazed, taking in the peacock feathers that bobbed from her head, her strange, feathered body, her powerful wings folded neatly behind her. "What's happening? Who are you?"

The creature slipped another tunic over her own shoulders, adjusting the opening to fit her wings comfortably. Curiously, Jade noted, she had neither breasts nor a bellybutton. "I'm Máhí, your elder nestling. I've summoned you back from the mortal realm."

"Mortal realm?" Jade's voice shook as she eyed the creature's wings again, her mind spinning. "You have... wings."

Máhí stretched them out, a display of iridescent feathers, the tips gleaming purple in the amber light. "All Nezkwah have wings."

"Nezkwah?" Jade whispered, half to herself, a wave of dread settling over her. "Are you a fairy?"

Máhí looked at her with a strange tenderness, her gaze steady. "Fairies? I don't know about this. I am Nezkwah. So are you. We've been waiting for you, Sekowah," she said softly.

Jade felt the world tilt, the name sinking into her like a forgotten melody. She backed away, her eyes wide. "Sekowah? No. I'm Jade."

Máhí sighed, her expression both patient and sad. "No, sister. Your name is Sekowah. You were born here, in this valley. I hid you away among the hut-dwellers at our mother's request... your real mother."

Jade shook her head, squeezing her eyes shut, trying to dispel the rising panic. She was in a nightmare, she had to be. She opened her eyes, only to find Máhí watching her with that same steady gaze, as real as the stinging air in her lungs.

Máhí blew into a thin, bamboo whistle that hung around her neck. "All will be explained. Later. Here." She pulled a small root from her satchel and offered it to Jade. "Have a sleeproot. It will help the nerves."

Jade backed away, refusing the root, her mind reeling. "Where's Robbie? What did you do to him?"

Ignoring her question, Máhí chewed thoughtfully on the root. "You'll get used to all of this soon enough." Her tone was casual, as though they were discussing the weather.

Above them, a great fluttering sounded, and Jade's gaze snapped upward. A horse with wings swept down and landed in front of them, her feathers a mirror of Máhí's colors: black and deep brown. The saddle was adorned with fine felt and small red gems that caught the light, casting prisms across the ground. Jade's heart raced, torn between awe and terror.

Máhí patted the horse's neck, a smile breaking through her stoic expression. "Sekowah, this is Tahgeet."

As the winged horse moved closer, her dark, liquid eyes locked with Sekowah's. A subtle, unfamiliar pressure swelled in her mind, not painful but insistent, as though the air was vibrating at a frequency only she could feel. And then it came—a voice, clear yet formless, as if it emerged not from the horse, but from somewhere within herself: *Welcome back.*

The world spun, and Jade felt herself slipping, her legs folding beneath her as darkness closed in. The last thing she saw was Máhí's face, watching her with an odd mixture of pride and amusement as she faded from consciousness.

CHAPTER ELEVEN

NATIONS DIVIDED

Sekowah clung to Máhí's waist as they soared over the alien landscape atop Tahgeet. Her massive wings beat rhythmically beneath them, yet they cut through the air with an eerie silence, gliding like a shadow across the world below. Sekowah's stomach twisted with each dip and rise, and a low nausea simmered inside her—but beneath the unease, a strange excitement simmered. This place was nothing like home.

The trees below them were giants, towering and dense, cloaked in emerald shadows and shrouded by mist that settled thickly in the dips and creases of the mountains. The forest sprawled endlessly in every direction, untouched by any sign of civilization—no cities, no streets, no scattered farmhouses. Just wild, pristine rainforest stretching toward the horizon, the canopy teeming with movement and life. She could hear it: a constant murmur of unfamiliar sounds rising from below—chitters, clacking, and high-pitched calls. It was both thrilling and unnerving, a reminder that this place was as alive as any creature, breathing and humming under its heavy blanket of fog.

Where *was* she? And *what* was this faery-creature who called herself her sister? The dreamlike trance from earlier had faded, leaving Sekowah wide-eyed and tingling with a raw, uncertain awe. Bound to the saddle with Máhí, she couldn't shake the feeling that she might be both a passenger and a captive. Each steady beat of Tahgeet's wings only took her farther from the life she had known, and yet... she felt herself drawn onward. She could close her eyes, could whisper to herself that this was just a dream, but she knew it wouldn't work. This was real. The air tasted different; her skin was slick from the cool mist. There was no waking up from this.

Gradually, the dense rainforest gave way, and an immense valley opened before them, bathed in an otherworldly light. The sky was a translucent blue laced with amber, deepening to crimson at the horizon, where the sun, an enormous orange orb, cast a hazy, prismatic glow. Sekowah had never seen light behave this way—rays pouring down, making her feel warm and exhilarated, as if she were drinking in sunlight itself. Her skin tingled with it, and a strange calm settled over her, quieting her anxious heart.

Beneath them, a breathtaking mosaic of meadows sprawled out, arranged in intricate patterns that seemed too deliberate to be natural. Wildflowers bloomed in riotous colors, splashing the fields with pinks, yellows, and purples. Orchards—circles of apple, pear, and stranger fruits she couldn't name—intertwined with vegetable gardens and endless stretches of vineyards. At the center of each orchard stood a stone monument, shaped like a cone and carved with symbols. Trails wove between the circles in a complex web, connecting the patches of color to a center.

Flute music drifted up from below, haunting and pure, joined by deep, rhythmic drumbeats that pulsed through the air, pulsating in her bones. There were no buildings, no villages, yet the valley was filled with voices—a chorus of layered harmonies that seemed to swirl around her, lifting and falling in intricate patterns. She had never heard anything so beautiful, so heartbreakingly strange. The music wrapped around her like a warm breeze, and for a moment, she felt the same serenity she sometimes found alone in the woods back home. Here, the music was alive, the valley itself seemed to sing.

The wind played with her hair as she loosened her grip on Máhí's waist and soaked in the valley's beauty. Each breath felt purer than the last, clean and crisp. The burning in her lungs had disappeared, and with it, the constant hazy fog that clouded her mind. It was as if some hidden weight had lifted, and for the first time, she could see the world—and herself—clearly. She felt alive in a way she never had before, her senses heightened, her thoughts sharp and untroubled. The familiar, suffocating buzz that haunted her daily life at home had vanished.

But clarity brought new questions. Why did this place feel so familiar? Why did it feel like she was... coming home? Had she truly lived here before? And if Máhí was her sister, then who were the parents who raised her? The questions piled on top of one another, a frantic jumble that knotted her throat, making it hard to breathe. She took a deep breath, then another, counting slowly to calm herself, using the breathing exercises Robbie had taught her back at Discovery School.

Robbie. Her chest ached at the thought of him. She'd left him behind, on the lake, without any explanation. What must he think? Did he run off in panic, searching for help? Or was he still there, staring into the water, wondering where she had gone? The guilt gnawed at her. She should have prepared him, explained everything before dragging him into her world. But she hadn't known... how could she have known that this was where she would end up?

They drifted lower, skimming the treetops as the valley widened beneath them. Far in the distance, enormous, prehistoric-looking birds flew in formation, their silhouettes sharp against the amber sky, like something out of a forgotten epoch. The creatures below them resembled those of home, yet each was a variation on a theme—trees that grew taller and denser, birds that flew faster, plants in hues she'd never seen. It was like a glimpse into a world that had evolved on a different path, untouched by human hands.

They approached the valley center, and Sekowah spotted movement below. At first, she thought they were people, but as Tahgeet descended, she saw their details more clearly: tiny, blue-skinned creatures with elongated, translucent wings. They flitted about like dragonflies, their wings veined and delicate, catching the light in flashes of purple and green. They wore tattered rags of linen, their faces curious and bright-eyed, but she noticed something strange—they had no noses.

The tiny, winged people darted around them, creating a chaotic swarm in the air, some staring up in wonder, others hiding behind one another in fear. It was impossible to tell if they were frightened or overjoyed by her presence. Their quick, darting movements and wide-eyed stares reminded her of sparrows flitting through the trees, alert but wary.

She shouted to Máhí over the wind, "Who are they?"

Máhí's voice rang out confidently, her words carrying easily in the thin, bright air. "Zahnene," she said. "This is where you were born. This is the Jasper Valley."

Sekowah's heart skipped a beat. Jasper Valley. *Where I was born.* The words seemed both strange and familiar, an echo from a dream long buried and forgotten.

They circled the valley's edge, and she noticed tall, lean soldiers patrolling below—creatures like Máhí, but taller, with spotted feather wings, dressed in shining metal armor. They had bows slung across their shoulders and sharp, angular faces with long noses and pointed ears.

"And these?" Sekowah asked.

Máhí narrowed her eyes. "Lirian. Mountain warriors. They claim the valley as their own. But not for long."

Sekowah watched as an elderly Zahnene buzzed around one of the soldiers, gesticulating wildly. Two soldiers seized him by the arms and led him away. Sekowah watched intently as she wondered what crime he might have committed.

Máhí guided Tahgeet farther, toward a limestone wall that marked the valley's far boundary. Guard towers dotted the wall, each occupied by more soldiers. At intervals, fierce, wingless creatures—short, squat, with thick fur and large hands like spades—stood guard at the gates. Máhí called them the Utdaga. Their eyes gleamed with a brutal intelligence as they watched Tahgeet fly overhead, but they did not raise their weapons.

Beyond the wall, the lush green faded, giving way to barren stretches and a river that ran deep and red, as if tainted by blood. A creeping sense of dread wound its way into Sekowah's heart. She clung to Máhí, her earlier excitement dissolving into unease. This was not the paradise she'd glimpsed from afar. Something dark and twisted had settled here. Her thighs hurt from clenching them in the saddle to stay in place, and she wished they would return to the valley to rest. But each second took her farther away and into another new world. As she continued to look down from that height, her nausea came in waves, worsening with each tilt or lift in Tahgeet's movements.

Máhí patted her hand, perhaps sensing her discomfort. "Hold tight, Sekowah. Our journey isn't over yet."

As they crossed the river, Sekowah spotted more Utdaga laboring in mines along the hillsides. They loaded wheelbarrows with rough stones—*were those geodes?*—and hauled them to large wagons, where furry elephant-like beasts waited to pull them away. The Utdaga paid no attention to Tahgeet, moving mechanically, their faces grim, their movements weary.

The mountain range loomed closer, jagged peaks clawing at the sky. Steam rose from the craters of distant volcanoes, their flanks veined with rivers of red-hot lava. The land here was harsh, hostile, marked by towering cliffs and arid valleys. Between two peaks, a lake shimmered in the distance, reflecting the triple rainbow cast by a twin waterfall. The sight was beautiful, but unsettling. It felt like a world on the edge of chaos.

Sekowah's gaze was drawn to a fortress—a sprawling stone castle nestled against the cliffs, surrounded by clover fields and firing ranges where soldiers practiced with bows. Máhí pointed. "Peregrine's Keep," she said.

Máhí turned Tahgeet toward the waterfalls, swooping lower so Sekowah could see the skirmish unfolding on either side of the riverbanks. Armored warriors clashed in brutal hand-to-hand combat, steel ringing against steel. Arrows flew in every direction, glinting like deadly needles in the sunlight. She could see the whites of their eyes, the desperate grunts and gasps as swords found their mark, blood staining the ground.

Sekowah's hands flew to her mouth, her stomach lurching as she took in the sight. She had never seen death like this—real, up close, raw and violent. The horror of it clawed at her, a scream caught in her throat as each warrior fell, each life snuffed out in a flash of crimson.

A warrior on horseback, his black wings sleek and shiny, glanced up and gave Máhí a nod as they passed overhead. Behind him rode another, an older man wearing a silver crown and a blue cloak. He shouted commands, his voice carrying over the din of battle. "Hold the line! Stand fast!"

Máhí raised her fist in salute, but Sekowah could hardly bear to look. Bodies littered the banks, vultures already circling. Her vision blurred, her heart racing as Máhí turned Tahgeet south, away from the carnage. Overwhelmed, Sekowah leaned over the side of the saddle and retched, the horror of what she'd seen twisting her insides.

CHAPTER TWELVE

CELEBRATION SOUP

T ahgeet descended gracefully, her mighty wings slowing in long, soundless beats as they approached a clearing in the forest. Sekowah's entire body ached from clinging to Máhí, her arms trembling with the strain, her fingers numb where they'd pressed into the leather saddle. She felt a surge of relief as they touched down, a slight tremor in her legs as the earth came up to meet her. She leaned her forehead against Máhí's shoulder, heaving a quiet sigh. Her stomach, still churning, let out a low growl. She wasn't sure if it was hunger or the relentless queasiness that had plagued her since the journey began.

The forest around them was dense, shadowed, and dripping with moisture. They'd landed on the edge of a bog, its humid breath filling the air with the smell of decaying wood, and the lingering musk of swamp. The trees—old conifers with trunks the width of small boulders—were draped in bone-colored lichen that clung to the bark like ghostly fingers. Dew-drenched ferns crowded around their roots, and vast curtains of hanging moss swayed gently from the branches, stirring as Tahgeet folded her wings. In the mud and tangled undergrowth, creatures stirred—grasshoppers, scorpions, and centipedes, some as long as her arm, weaving trails through the shadows, their iridescent bodies catching flecks of light as they moved.

Through the trees, Sekowah spotted a small stone cottage, hidden under a thatched roof thick with tamarisk moss. The structure seemed to blend seamlessly into the forest, camouflaged by creeping vines and patches of lichen that climbed its walls. Máhí gestured toward it as she helped Sekowah dismount. "That's the medicine cottage," she said. "Its location is known only to the Nezkwah and to the healers who seek rare ingredients."

The cottage was nestled amid wild herb gardens, mushroom beds, and clusters of berry bushes, all connected by winding pebble paths. Small waterfalls trickled into jewel-colored ponds that ringed the clearing, each one a different shade of blue. Frogs and salamanders skittered around the pools, their jeweled eyes reflecting the dappled sunlight that pierced the canopy. The air was alive with the hum of life and the subtle scent of crushed herbs, heady and calming, joining with the earthy richness of wet leaves and moss.

Sekowah's exhaustion returned in full force as she took in the scene. The cottage felt like a sanctuary, a hidden place far from the violence and confusion of the mountains. She wanted to go inside, to sit alone and gather her thoughts, but the weight in her chest—a thick, dull heaviness that made each breath feel like labor—consumed her. She'd felt this kind of sadness before, the kind that seeped into her like dampness in winter, leaving her feeling empty and gray.

Máhí finished unbuckling the straps that held Sekowah in place and gently pulled a hood over her head. "You mustn't be seen," Máhí said in a low voice. "Not yet."

From within the cottage, Sekowah noticed a figure watching them through a gap in the flax curtains. It was a young woman, with eyes as bright and curious as her own. The woman's gaze was steady, and as they locked eyes, Sekowah felt an eerie twinge of recognition, like staring into a reflection with details subtly out of place.

"That's Jade," Máhí murmured, her tone both cautious and reverent. "Don't scream. She's your... spirit-double."

Spirit-double. The term hung in the air, heavy and strange. Sekowah's head swam, her vision blurring at the edges as her knees threatened to buckle. She bent over, focusing on her breath, the way her mother had taught her to avoid fainting spells. Spirit-double? What could that possibly mean?

As Máhí and Sekowah approached the cottage door, a flash of movement caught their eye—a bird, perched in a nearby tree, with salt-and-lime feathers and a long tail tipped in crimson. The bird watched them with a tilted head, its sharp gaze unblinking. Máhí tightened her grip on Sekowah's elbow, steering her firmly down the pebble path. "I'll explain later," she whispered. "Inside, quickly."

With a flick of her wrist, Máhí sent Tahgeet off into the sky. "Away to Peregrine's Keep. Tell Mother she's with me," she called after her.

As they reached the front door, it swung open, and the young woman—Jade—stood framed in the doorway, her face etched with a mixture of curiosity and something else, something fragile and uncertain.

Sekowah stepped inside, her gaze sweeping the room. The cottage was a marvel of organized chaos. Each wall was lined with shelves that held colorful glass bottles, silver flasks, bundles of dried herbs hung upside down, and small earthen jars crammed with various ointments and salves. Lamps glowed in the corners, each casting a different hue of soft light, hidden behind shades made from layers of birch bark. The illumination was gentle, soothing, and easy on the eyes, unlike the harsh lights of home.

In the corner, a stone fireplace crackled with a low fire, a cast iron kettle suspended over it, bubbling and hissing with something that smelled earthy. The room was filled with an overwhelming blend of scents—like a garden in full bloom interspersed with the pungent aroma of roasted garlic and damp soil. The floor was a slab of polished river stone, its edges woven with tangled roots that climbed up the walls, forming a lattice of flowering branches overhead. Clumps of crimson blossoms hung in clusters, their fragrance subtle but warm.

Sekowah's eyes roamed over the shelves, stopping when she noticed a collection of books. Her breath halted as she recognized their covers—*Where the Wild Things Are*, *My Side of the Mountain*, *The Fellowship of the Ring*, *The Mists of Avalon*—books from her own childhood. Books she thought she'd lost. She stepped closer, her fingers trailing over the spines until she reached *Where the Wild Things Are*. She pulled it from the shelf and opened it to the title page. There, in faded ink, was an inscription from her Aunt Judy: *To my dearest Jade, I hope you enjoy this as much as I did growing up. There are wild things everywhere, if you only look. Love, Auntie J.*

Sekowah's heart fluttered, confusion twisting through her. *How did my books end up here?*

As if reading her thoughts, Jade spoke. "Those are mine," she said simply. "They were always mine."

Sekowah turned to face her, the two of them standing in silence, staring. Jade's hair was long, braided down her back, and her eyes were the color of a clear summer sky. She wore a crown of twigs woven with wildflowers, a delicate arrangement that somehow suited her solemn expression. Her tunic was flax linen, a sash of muted rose-pink silk around her waist, its tassels a deep burgundy. She looked almost regal, yet something about her posture, the way her gaze kept flickering uncertainly, suggested fragility.

Sekowah glanced over at a mirror by the door, catching sight of their reflections side by side. Her own green eyes stared back, wide and haunted, while Jade's blue gaze mirrored her bewilderment. They were identical in every way except for the color of their eyes—and the subtle points at the tops of Sekowah's ears, a detail that filled her with an inexplicable dread. She raised her hand to touch her face, feeling the new angles, the slight elongation of her cheekbones, the fullness of her lips.

Jade, shaking off her uncertainty, peeked over Sekowah's shoulder to study their reflections. "My spirit-double." She wrapped her arms around Sekowah in an impulsive hug from behind.

Sekowah stiffened, recoiling, and turned to face Jade, trying to make sense of the warmth in her eyes. "We're the same," she murmured. "Except... your eyes are blue. And mine are green... and my ears are..."

"Pointy," Jade finished for her, her tone oddly matter-of-fact. She reached out and touched one of Sekowah's ears, as if to confirm it.

"You're half Nezkwah. A changeling," Máhí announced. "The crossings aren't perfect. Looks like you've got some remainders."

changeling. The word hung in Sekowah's mind, filling her with a strange sense of wonder and dread. "And Jade?"

Jade glanced at Máhí for confirmation, a smile on her lips. "I'm just... me. A hut-dweller." She shared a look with Máhí, and seeing her expression, grabbed Sekowah by the hand, leading her over to the kettle. "I made soup for us. Celebration soup. For our birthdays."

Sekowah released the handhold, now feeling doubly awkward at Jade's easy and confusing, and obviously false, affection for her.

"Can you let her sit down first?" Máhí waved at a table in the corner with three chairs made from tree stumps and gave Jade another stern look that spoke volumes.

Jade nodded. "I'm so rude." She pulled Sekowah to the table. "Pick a seat. Then we'll tell you everything."

The three of them sat together at the rough-hewn table, a worn wooden surface scarred by countless years of use. In front of each of them sat a crude, redwood bowl, its surface polished from wear but flecked with imperfections, as though carved in haste. The soup inside was a brilliant shade of blue, the exact color of Jade's eyes, and thin wisps of steam rose from it, carrying a delicate fragrance that seemed to perfume the air itself. Sekowah leaned forward, catching the scent—a strange, floral note that bore no resemblance to any soup she'd ever tasted. It smelled like summer gardens, damp grasses after rain, and something sweet, almost like... lilacs.

Jade sat across from her, her gaze fixed, watching Sekowah with a mixture of fascination and something else, an intensity that made Sekowah feel both exposed and unsettled. An itching under her skin rose up from deep within her body, a deep prickling that flared at random spots along her arms and legs. She scratched vigorously at her arm, then at her calf, trying to dispel the sensation, but it was relentless, like her skin was trying to shed itself. She looked down at the soup, unsure. Her stomach was still uneasy, her head spinning slightly from everything that had happened, and the thought of eating—even something as fragrant as this—made her hesitate.

"I'm not hungry, but thank you," she murmured, her voice more strained than she'd intended.

Jade didn't seem to hear her reluctance. She slid a gold spoon across the table with a brisk nod. Sekowah picked it up, marveling at the craftsmanship—a solid jade stone had been set into the handle, the gold curving around it in intricate, delicate filigree. She traced the stone with her thumb, feeling the cool, smooth weight of it in her hand.

"Go on, try it. It's lilac and ginkgo berry," Jade said, a hint of a smile playing on her lips.

"Ginkgo berry?" Sekowah echoed.

"It's a... constitutional," Máhí interjected, taking a spoonful herself and nodding in approval. She was watching Sekowah closely, as though gauging her reaction.

Jade took a hearty gulp and sighed with satisfaction. "Transformational, actually. Soothes the nerves after the change. Takes away the itchy-scratchy. Or so I heard. I've never—"

"Lilac is the favored remedy after making the transition," Máhí explained gently, her eyes softening. "You'll need it to keep your thoughts clear and... your hearts calm."

Hearts? Sekowah's mind reeled. She looked from Máhí to Jade, who gave no sign that anything was amiss. She ignored the soup, even as the itching beneath her skin worsened, spreading over her entire body, a maddening, prickly sensation that made her want to claw at herself.

But worse than the itch was the storm of questions circling in her mind, each more insistent than the last. *Where am I? Am I still on Earth? Why did they take me and leave Jade?* And then, another thought, sharp and unsettling: *Why would they have my books?* She glanced at Máhí, who seemed to sense her frustration. Her expression was calm, though there was a hint of guardedness behind her eyes, as if she were bracing for questions she didn't want to answer.

Sekowah couldn't hold back any longer. "Why do you have my books?"

"Not yours. *Mine*," Jade replied instantly, her voice firm, her eyes narrowing with a flash of something close to resentment. "Says so right in the book. Jade. That's me. Not you."

Sekowah felt a flicker of anger at Jade's tone, an edge to her voice that made the bitterness between them feel visceral. She set the spoon down, her knee bouncing under the table. "So, let me see if I have this right. You stole Jade from my mom and dad, and—"

"My *mom and dad*," Jade interjected, her voice rising, her face flushed with sudden heat, as though she might explode at any moment.

"Hold on. Not stole," Máhí corrected, an apologetic half-smile crossing her lips. "Borrowed."

Sekowah narrowed her eyes, incredulous. *How does one borrow a baby?* She turned to Máhí, searching her face for answers. "Then what happened after we were switched? If my mom and dad are really her parents, then where are my parents?"

"Stuck!" Jade's voice cracked as she practically shouted, rising from her seat and pacing furiously. "That's what happened. I've been *stuck* here for twenty harvests!" Her hands trembled, and her eyes glistened with unshed tears. "And you're upset over a couple of books? Books that were supposed to be for me. From my Aunt. Who I never met! Not to mention the fact that I've had to watch you grow up with *my* family, while I've been alone—" Her voice broke entirely, and she gulped for air, the words catching in her throat. "Alone in this place without anyone to love me." She sank to her knees, pressing her hands to her face as she wept openly, her body shuddering with each sob.

Máhí knelt at Jade's side, rubbing her back in small, comforting circles. "I love you," she whispered, a quiet, steady reassurance.

"Oh, *shut up!*" Jade shoved Máhí's hand away, her voice raw with anger and pain.

Sekowah felt a wave of guilt crest over her, a heaviness in her chest that made it hard to breathe. She didn't even know what she felt guilty for—it wasn't as if she'd chosen any of this—but watching Jade's anguish stirred something deep and uncomfortable in her. "I'm sorry. I'm not upset. Just... curious," she managed, her voice hesitant.

"Seems a small thing, doesn't it? When you had my mother. My father. All this time. Books. Who cares about *books?*" Jade's voice was bitter, almost mocking, as she returned to her seat, wiping her nose with the sleeve of her tunic. "They're yours now anyway. I've read them all. Over and over. Take them."

Máhí leaned closer to Sekowah, her voice low and pointed. "The stuck part," she said, shooting a glance at Jade, "not my fault." She jabbed her spoon in Jade's direction for emphasis.

Jade let out a shaky breath, composing herself with visible effort. "It's his fault. *Zincubus.* He cast the 'Perimeter of Death' on the cottage grounds. Can you believe that? Can't go anywhere. It's like a prison." She waved a hand at Sekowah's bowl. "Go on. Drink already. I'm losing my patience."

Sekowah's patience, however, was wearing just as thin. "Well, *I'm* losing my patience. I don't know a thing about any of this! Where am I?!"

Máhí shifted in her seat, her gaze softening, but her tone remaining steady. "You're in the Jasper Valley. And I brought you here because this is the safest place for you to be. At the moment."

Sekowah wrung her hands under the table. "But where exactly is the Jasper Valley? It doesn't look like any place on Earth I've ever seen or read about. Even the sky here is strange. Hardly blue at all. Are we on... another planet?"

Máhí blinked, a crease forming between her brows as if she found the question perplexing. "Planet? I don't know what that is, but you were in the mortal realm. The place of the hut-dwellers. And we are here. As we've always been."

It appeared fruitless to ask again, so Sekowah leaned back, letting the silence hang in the air for a moment. She took in a full breath, releasing the tension in her hands, But the confusion didn't ease. She lifted a spoonful of the soup, inhaling its lilac scent again. Strangely comforting. It reminded her of the lilac bush in her backyard, the one that bloomed every spring. She took a cautious sip, then licked her lips as a subtle warmth spread through her body, gentle and immediate. "Ohhh," she murmured, cupping the bowl in both hands and taking a fuller gulp.

Máhí reached over and gently pulled her arm down. "Easy, easy."

Sekowah put the bowl down and resumed at a slower pace. Everything around her felt like quicksand, shifting and uncertain. Her irritation simmered, the nagging feeling of unfairness twisting in her gut. Jade seemed to have known all along, while she was left to wonder and suffer in silence. *changeling.* The word echoed in her mind, unfamiliar and foreboding. She finally spoke, her voice sharp. "What's a changeling?"

Máhí shrugged, her tone casual. "You know. A changeling. Part hut-dweller, part Nezkwah. Nothing to be ashamed of. You can't fly, but we can get around that."

The room fell into an uneasy silence as Sekowah finished her soup. Jade gathered the bowls and moved to wash them, while Máhí, preoccupied, paced by the window, glancing out now and then as if expecting something—or someone.

"So, who's Zincubus?" Sekowah asked, her voice barely more than a whisper, unsure if she even wanted the answer.

Máhí and Jade exchanged a glance. Jade put a finger to her lips, cautioning her to silence. "Shhhh! Not too loud. The spies... they'll hear you."

Máhí leaned closer, her voice a murmur. "He's why you were hidden away. If he knows you're here, he'll..."

"He ruined my life," Jade interrupted, her voice breaking as she held back tears. "Completely ruined it."

Máhí threw her a warning look. "Don't be dramatic. It was for the Good of All. You'll return soon, no worse for wear. You know what's at stake."

Jade sniffled, wiping her face bravely, and looked at Sekowah, her voice filled with bitterness. "You're welcome."

Sekowah glared at both of them, her heart pounding with frustration. *You're welcome?* she thought bitterly. *For what?*

CHAPTER THIRTEEN

THE LOOKING POND

Sekowah waited by the back door of the cottage, clutching her arms around herself as Máhí and Jade bustled about, gathering supplies, filling small satchels with dried herbs, jars, and other mysterious items. They moved with purpose, muttering to each other, barely glancing in her direction. Sekowah's heart hammered in her chest; whatever they were preparing for, it seemed urgent, and yet she remained in the dark, watching them with a mixture of anxiety and bewilderment.

The door she leaned against was crafted from polished cypress wood, its grain glinting in the low light. Intricate carvings covered its surface—twisting vines, blooming flowers, and symbols etched so finely that they seemed to pulse with life. The door arched gracefully at the top, held in place by hammered brass hinges that looked worn but sturdy, fastened with crude iron nails. The handle was carved from bone, smooth under her fingertips, with tiny glyphs etched along its length. It felt strange and wonderful, yet a dark knot twisted in her stomach as she took it all in. This place was beautiful, yes—almost intoxicating in its wildness—but something about it felt treacherous, too.

The strange, itchy sensation in her skin had faded, and her belly was full from the lilac-ginkgo soup, but the hollow ache of uncertainty remained. She pulled her hood up, as Máhí had reminded her, casting a shadow over her eyes.

Máhí knelt to adjust her boots and handed Sekowah a pair of moccasins made from soft gray wool felt, adorned with dangly green fringe. "Put these on," she instructed.

Sekowah slipped them on, noting how snug and warm they felt against her feet. She twirled her toes, marveling at their softness. "Where are we going now?" Her voice was quieter than she'd intended, thick with dread. The thought of another journey unsettled her. The images of the bodies in the river—the fallen soldiers, the vultures—still haunted her, a vivid smear across her mind's eye.

Jade's face split into a mischievous smile, her earlier grief now turned to bubbling excitement. "You're not going anywhere. I, on the other hand, am going—"

"Not far at all," Máhí interrupted, her tone as firm as steel. "Just out to the looking pond."

Jade's shoulders slumped in exaggerated disappointment, but she fell in line, following Máhí out the door. Sekowah trailed behind, her curiosity tempered by caution. They stepped into the gardens, a sprawling, enchanted oasis bordered by towering hedges and regal ginkgo trees. Flat river stones formed steps that led down winding pebble paths, threading through an astonishing collection of plants that seemed almost too vivid, too lush, as if each leaf and petal pulsed with its own quiet magic.

The garden was a maze of exotic flora—enormous ferns and palmettos that cast deep shadows, lilies as large as wheelbarrows, and trumpet flowers that cascaded from trellises like waterfalls. Succulents grew in sprawling clusters, some shimmering with silver edges, and in scattered pots, carnivorous pitcher plants leaned forward hungrily, their open mouths wide and waiting. As they walked, Sekowah noticed each plant seemed to vibrate with color, their auras larger and more intense than any she'd seen back home. She could almost hear them, each one emitting a musical hum, like glass chimes catching the breeze.

The sound was strange, atonal, but oddly beautiful. It stirred a distant memory of lying in bed at night, hearing the distant buzz of insects outside her window, a soothing lullaby from nature itself. She had heard this sound before, in glimpses, in dreams—but here, it was louder, brighter, alive.

They wound their way through the garden, finally arriving at a large, flowering tree. Its delicate pink blossoms reminded Sekowah of the mimosa trees back home, but these flowers had fuzzy blue centers, and as she inhaled, she caught a scent that was both sharp and comforting, like rosemary mixed with fresh rain. Iridescent hummingbirds buzzed around the tree, dipping their needle-like beaks into the blossoms, their tiny wings a blur of green and violet. A cool breeze wafted through the clearing, brushing across Sekowah's face and cooling the nape of her neck.

Nestled beneath the tree was a small, round pond lined with cattails and dotted with lotus flowers, their white petals glistening with dew. Lily pads floated lazily on the water's surface, alongside patches of water moss. Fat toads and bright red-spotted salamanders sat on the pond's edge, their eyes unblinking, waiting as if they sensed something important was about to happen.

"Watch," Máhí commanded, her voice carrying an edge of authority.

With a deft motion, she tossed a handful of gold sand across the pond. The grains dissolved in mid-air, shimmering as they touched the surface of the water before sinking below. For a heartbeat, there was nothing but the ripple of water—then a whirlpool began to form, spinning slowly, and from its depths, an image surfaced.

The water revealed a dark cavern, lit only by the eerie glow of green gems set into wall sconces and torches. The air around Sekowah seemed to grow colder as she peered into the image. She saw a stocky, brutish figure, a bald man cloaked in a cape made of rough snakeskin, his fingers wrapped tightly around a gnarled staff and a coiled whip dangling from his other hand. The staff was carved from petrified cedar, etched with strange symbols, and at the top was a fox's head sculpted from gold, its eyes gleaming with a sinister intelligence.

Sekowah's skin crawled as she took in the scene. Around the man were Moorigato: lizard-like humanoids, their eyes slitted like reptiles, tongues flicking in and out of lipless mouths. Behind him, a consort of Dasheahs followed—human-like figures with bat wings, draped in snakeskin capes—their heads bowed in twisted reverence. The brutish man strode through the cavern and retired to a shadowed chamber, a throne room where his seat was constructed from large bones, topped with the skulls of reptiles, each staring down with empty eye sockets.

The cavern walls rose high, formed from jagged stone, stacked with no apparent order, creating an oppressive, windowless space. Sconces in each corner cast a sickly green light that washed over the chamber, giving the air an eerie, unnatural glow. Bookcases lined the walls, filled with old manuals, manuscripts, talismans, and arcane objects. On the far wall, a bookcase swung inward, revealing a hidden shelf of cobalt glass jars, each crammed with strange, purple mushrooms sealed tightly within.

Attached to the throne was a steel chain, and at the end of it was a gray fox with unsettling, pale violet eyes. The man sat, legs sprawled, the staff between his knees, his face stern.

"*Zincubus,*" Máhí muttered, her tone dripping with contempt. Her eyes narrowed, blinking sideways in that strange, inhuman way. Her arms crossed over her chest, a fierce look of disgust settling across her face.

Sekowah turned away, a feeling of nausea bubbling up inside her. She wanted nothing more than to leave the image behind, to forget the man's cold, lifeless gaze. "I don't understand what this has to do with me," she said, her voice tinged with angst.

Máhí stepped into her path, grabbing her shoulders, turning her firmly back toward the pond. "He must be stopped. He steals the valley's gems, robbing us of our life force, our fertility. The balance of all life is in danger. The prophecy is our only hope."

The prophecy. Sekowah's mind spun. She could sense where this was going, and a prickling fear began to crawl up her spine. She shook her head, trying to back away.

"That's you," Jade said, her voice brimming with excitement.

Sekowah stumbled, looking from Jade to Máhí in disbelief. "*Me?* Oh, no. I don't know anything about a prophecy." Her breath caught, panic sticking in her throat like a stone. She felt as if invisible hands were squeezing her neck, cutting off her air. She glanced around wildly, a desperate urge to flee rising within her, though she had no idea where she would even run.

Máhí leaned close, holding Sekowah's gaze with an intensity that left no room for argument. Her voice was low, almost reverent. "When skies turn dark and river red, when many are among the dead, an emerald queen of mortal blood will rise to vanquish evil's flood."

Jade nodded, her eyes wide with expectation.

"The emerald queen? Evil's flood?" Sekowah repeated, her voice shaky. She pulled away from Máhí's grasp, stumbling backward.

As the words left her lips, the image in the pond shifted. Zincubus' head turned, his gaze piercing through the water as if he could see them, sense them in that very moment. His eyes locked onto Sekowah's, sending a chill that twisted down her spine.

Jade gasped, pointing, and Máhí quickly splashed her hand through the water, dissolving the image in a swirl of ripples. "All signs have come to pass. The Great Flood will be upon us before long."

Sekowah's face went pale, her stomach roiling. She pressed a trembling hand to her belly, fearing she would be sick again. "I want to go home," she whispered, her voice breaking. "My parents must be worried sick by now. *Take me home. Please.*"

Jade's expression hardened, her enthusiasm curdling into bitterness. "Oh, no. My time is up. That's *my* home, not yours. You belong here, and I'm going back."

Sekowah clutched Máhí's arm, her voice frantic. "Máhí! Take me back. I don't want to be here. Don't tell me anything else. *Please.*"

Jade, on the other side of Máhí, gripped her arm tightly. "You promised!" Her voice was edged with a childlike desperation, raw and pleading.

The two young women pulled on Máhí, tugging her in opposite directions, until she shook them both loose with a growl. Her gaze turned to Sekowah, fierce and unyielding. "We need you here, Sekowah. Zincubus can only be defeated by a royal of mortal blood. That's you. If you don't stay, he'll destroy everything. The people, the animals, the very land of Jasper Valley—*all will perish in the flood*."

Sekowah's eyes darted around, panic welling up within her. "Me? Defeat Zincubus? That's impossible! I can't do this—I don't know anything about it!" She pointed at Jade, her voice rising. "*She's* human, or mortal, or whatever!"

Jade scoffed. "I'm not a royal, and I'm the only other mortal in the valley." She glanced at Máhí, muttering, "Except Zincubus."

"He doesn't count," Máhí replied, her voice grim.

Behind them, in the looking pond, a dark shape slithered just below the surface—a snake, its head lifting ever so slightly, listening as they argued. Then, it slipped beneath the water, vanishing into the depths.

· · · · • ◯◯ • · · · ·

They returned to the cottage, Sekowah's face solemn, while Jade buzzed about in a manic rush, excitement making her hands quick and clumsy. She flitted from shelf to shelf, gathering tinctures and ointments, tying them up in bundles of twine and muttering last-minute instructions to Máhí.

"This one is for Allibaster," Jade said, setting aside a small vial filled with a murky green liquid. "Poor thing's got hoof-rot again." She reached up for a small pot of lemon salve, its lid slightly askew. "And this one is for Mr. Croody," she continued, her tone brisk but laced with affection. "His wife's wandering again. Can't keep a thought in her head anymore." Blowing a layer of dust off a copper flask, she wrinkled her nose. "Ugh, mouse poo."

Sekowah paced in anxious circles behind her, each step heavier than the last. Her fingers fidgeted at her sides, and every now and then, she cast pleading glances at Máhí. Her voice trembled as she spoke. "You can't leave me here. I don't know what to do."

Jade barely looked up, her voice absent, distracted. "You'll figure it out," she murmured, her attention locked on the jars she was stacking. In truth, her thoughts were already miles away—back in the mortal world, imagining the life she had dreamed of for so long. Her real parents, her real home, her real family. She hadn't dared hope it would happen, but now... "You can start by dusting this top shelf," she added. "It's revolting."

Sekowah watched her with an odd mix of frustration and awe.

Jade moved with a frantic sort of joy, a barely-contained exhilaration as she darted from task to task. Her thoughts wandered back to the many years she had spent here in the apothecary, hidden away under the guardianship of Daisy and Hackmere, two elder Nezkwah with a mastery of herbology and the botanical arts. They had taught her the secrets of roots, leaves, and flowers, had schooled her in the ancient Nezkwah ways of healing. But to Jade, those years had been a prison sentence. They had felt suffocating and unfair—she had longed to be a part of the celebrations, the harvest festivals, the laughter and companionship of the valley's people. And all the while, she had watched Sekowah from afar through the looking pond, living a life that should have been hers.

She knew exactly who to blame. She had raged at Máhí for years, resenting her for the swap, for stealing her life. Whenever Máhí visited the cottage, Jade had met her with cold silence or sharp words. But deep down, she knew the swap hadn't been Máhí's decision alone; it had been part of a larger plan, a prophecy beyond any of their control. *The Good of All,* Máhí would tell her in a soothing voice that only made Jade's anger burn hotter.

Jade straightened up and stood tall. She was *ready.* Ready for the life she had been denied. Ready to escape this world and claim the family that had unknowingly been hers all along. She shook with excitement, her fingers fumbling as she tied off the last bundle of herbs.

Joy. It flooded through her like sunlight, filling every dark corner that resentment had once occupied.

Sekowah watched her, helpless and frantic. Jade's casual confidence seemed only to make her panic grow. Sekowah's breath came in short, shallow bursts, her fingers playing with the fabric of her tunic. "Jade, please," she said, her voice small and trembling. "I don't know how to live here—I don't even know what I *am.*"

Máhí stepped forward, placing a firm hand on Sekowah's shoulder. "Don't worry," Máhí said softly. "I'll help you."

Sekowah turned on her, tears brimming in her eyes. "Máhí, please! You can't make me stay here!" Her voice broke as she looked at Máhí, desperate. "This is all wrong!"

Máhí didn't answer, her face impassive, but there was a hint of sadness in her eyes as she turned back to Jade. "Are we ready?" she asked, her tone brisk.

Jade took a deep, steadying breath, her excitement now tempered with a rare seriousness. She embraced Máhí tightly, closing her eyes as she inhaled the familiar scents of herbs, smoke, and earth. "Ready yesterday," she said, her voice firm. She kept her back to Sekowah, refusing to let her last memory here be her double's stricken, frightened face. Instead, she kept her gaze on Máhí, offering a final, tight-lipped smile before they turned toward the door.

Máhí nodded, placing a hand on Jade's shoulder, guiding her out of the cottage and down the front cobblestone path. The night air was thick with the scent of dew-soaked leaves, and in the distance, fireflies flickered between the trees. Sekowah followed them to the threshold, her heart pounding with each step they took farther away.

At the door, Máhí paused, turning back to Sekowah with a grave expression. "Stay inside. Do not open this door for anyone, no matter what you hear. Do you understand?"

Sekowah swallowed, gripping the doorframe tightly. Her stomach twisted with fear, her pulse a desperate drumbeat in her ears. She didn't answer at first, her mind racing with the impossibility of what was happening, the feeling of being left behind—abandoned in this strange world that made no sense.

"Sekowah. Do you understand?" Máhí's voice was unyielding, a note of warning threading through her words.

Sekowah nodded, unable to speak, her throat thick with unshed tears. Máhí's face softened, just for a moment, and then she turned, leading Jade away into the night. She collapsed to her knees, her body shaking with silent sobs. "No, no, no, no!" she whispered, her voice a broken whisper, her heart cracking open with despair. She watched them go, feeling the silence close in around her as their figures faded down the pine straw trail and into the shadows. She sat in a heap by the door long after they'd gone, listening to the soft hum of the forest, her mind whirling with confusion and panic.

Chapter Fourteen

An Unpleasant Visit

S ekowah sat alone in the dim cottage, the silence enveloping her. Outside, darkness cloaked the forest, thick and absolute, broken only by the occasional flicker of fireflies drifting past the windows. She hugged her knees to her chest, shivering—not from cold, but from a gnawing fear that twisted in her stomach. Every creak of the floorboards, every whisper of wind outside made her jump. She was acutely aware of her own heartbeat, loud and insistent in the stillness, as if to remind her she was truly alone.

In the ethereal light cast by the strange gemstone lamps on the walls, she took in her surroundings, searching for anything that might offer a sense of comfort. The lamps, clusters of uncut emeralds and amethysts, glowed softly, each with its own aura, bathing the room in shades of green and violet. She wondered how they worked—there was no flame, no cord, nothing she could recognize from the world she knew. When she leaned in close, she saw a soft, rhythmic pulsing within the stones, as if they held tiny hearts that beat in unison. The lights fascinated her and, for a brief moment, made her forget her fear. She traced her finger along the amethyst's edge, feeling an odd warmth radiate from it.

She turned her attention to the small, cluttered bookshelf near the hearth. There, amid ancient texts and dusty tomes, were familiar books—*her* books. She ran her fingers over their spines, touching each one with reverence, as if seeing them after a long separation. She pulled out *Where the Wild Things Are* and clutched it to her chest, a bittersweet ache settling over her. These weren't *Jade's* books—they were *hers*, taken from her life without her even realizing it.

Eventually, hunger crept in, interrupting her snooping. She moved over to the small kitchen area, searching the shelves for something to eat. Her fingers brushed over jars filled with dried herbs, clay pots with unidentifiable roots, bundles of mushrooms strung together like beads. She found a basket of small, bright red berries, but something about them seemed... off. She sniffed them, catching a pungent, sour odor, and quickly put them back. Who knew what might be safe to eat here? Her stomach grumbled in protest, but she ignored it, unwilling to risk it. Instead, she poured herself a small cup of water from the pump, sipping slowly as she waited, feeling the hours stretch into eternity.

Time passed—or at least she thought it did. It was hard to tell in this strange world where time itself seemed twisted. Every second felt like it stretched and elongated, her heart counting out each one as she waited alone in the dark cottage.

At long last, just as the first whispers of morning began to emerge, she heard footsteps approaching outside. She froze, clutching her cup. The door handle turned, and Máhí stepped inside—alone.

Sekowah's heart dropped. "Is she gone? Where did you take her?" she asked, her voice trembling. Hot tears ran down her cheeks as she imagined Jade back at home, sleeping in her bed, laughing with Robbie and her parents.

Máhí avoided her gaze, moving around the room as if in search of something. "She's where she belongs," she said shortly, picking up tincture bottles one by one and examining their labels. "Now, pay attention."

Sekowah felt her stomach twist with a mixture of anger and helplessness. "This isn't right, Máhí. Switching us like that... tricking us. She's not going to understand my world, just like I don't understand anything about yours."

Máhí paused, looking up at her with a hard, unyielding gaze. "She's ready," she said with a certainty that made Sekowah's blood run cold. "She's been watching you in the looking pond for twenty harvests. She knows the ways of your world." After a long thoughtful moment, she put the tincture bottles down and held her hand out to Sekowah. "Come on then."

Máhí led Sekowah out of the cottage and through the winding paths of the garden once again. The early dawn light filtered through the trees, casting a hazy glow over the cottage grounds, making everything feel otherworldly, more dream than reality. Sekowah followed her in silence, her heart pounding with questions she was too afraid to ask, a growing dread in her chest.

When they reached the looking pond, Máhí stopped, gesturing for her to sit by the water's edge. The pond lay perfectly still, its surface a dark, glassy mirror broken only by clusters of lotus blossoms and the occasional ripple of a fish below. Máhí reached into her pouch and pulled out a handful of shimmering gold dust, letting it trickle from her fingers and scatter across the pond's surface. As the dust settled, the water began to swirl, lightly at first, then more strongly, until a whirlpool formed at the center, pulling the dust into a spiral that glowed and shimmered.

Sekowah leaned forward, entranced, as the water cleared to reveal an image—the familiar, rocky ledge near the Whispering Falls, surrounded by trees. She recognized it instantly. *The lake,* she realized, her heart skipping a beat. Home. It was home, right there in front of her, so close she could almost reach through the water and touch it.

Máhí's voice was soft, almost reverent. "Watch closely. She'll be there soon."

Sekowah nodded, swallowing hard as she watched the scene unfold. The pond showed the waterfall first, mist rising from the pool as sunlight began to cut through the afternoon fog. The trees around it were drenched in the pale, golden light of sunset.

And then, with a soft shimmer, Jade appeared, surfacing slowly from beneath the waterfall. She rose through the clear water, her face breaking the surface, eyes wide, hair clinging to her face. She blinked against the light, as if dazed, as if the world she'd dreamed of for so long was suddenly too bright, too much. But then something shifted in her expression. A realization. A surge of joy.

Jade waded forward, her movements full of an excitement that Sekowah had rarely seen in herself. Jade lifted her arms, running her hands through her hair as she waded through the water, her eyes scanning the shoreline.

And there, standing on the bank, next to the waterfall was a panicked Robbie.

Sekowah's stomach tightened at the sight of him, standing there looking bewildered and more than a little alarmed. His clothes were soaked, his hair a mess, his eyes fixed on Jade as if he were staring at an apparition.

"Oh my God. Jade!" he called out, his voice cracking slightly. He took a hesitant step forward, his gaze flicking between her and the waterfall. Then his eyes rested on her body. Her clothes were missing. "What... what just happened? Where were you? Are you okay?"

Jade broke into a sprint, splashing through the lake water, laughing as she closed the distance between them. "Robbie!" she cried, her voice filled with an overwhelming joy. Without a second thought, she flung herself into his arms, wrapping her arms around his neck, as she buried her face in his shoulder, sobbing, a mix of joy and sadness combined together.

Robbie staggered back under the weight of her embrace, his eyes widening as he tried to process her sudden, inexplicable return. But before he could react, Jade pulled back just enough to look him in the eyes, her hands still clutching his shoulders. She looked at him with such intensity, such longing, that even Sekowah, watching from the looking pond, could feel it.

And then, in one swift, unhesitating motion, Jade leaned in and pressed her lips to his.

Sekowah gasped, her hand flying to her mouth as she watched the scene unfold. It was surreal, seeing her own face—her own body—kissing Robbie with such hunger, such fervor. Robbie, for his part, froze for a moment, clearly taken off guard. But then he melted into the kiss, his arms sliding around her waist, pulling her closer. He kissed her back, his fingers tangling in her wet hair, as if he were grounding himself in her, making sure she was really there.

Máhí glanced over at Sekowah, her expression compassionate. "She's waited a long time for this," she murmured softly. "To have what you had."

Sekowah barely heard her. She was too transfixed, too stunned, as she watched Jade pull back from Robbie, a beaming smile on her face, her eyes alight with a happiness Sekowah had never seen in herself. She touched his face, tracing his cheek with her thumb, as if she were memorizing every detail of him.

Robbie looked at her, his brow furrowing slightly. "Are you sure you're okay?" He searched her face. "What was that... that thing? That was nuts! It took you—" he pointed to the pool at the base of the waterfall "—into that underground cave. I saw you going in. I tried to swim down there, but it was too far. I had to come back," he stammered. "I called 911 and they sent a rescue team. They sent divers into that cave. You weren't in there!"

Sekowah's heart ached as she watched Robbie hold Jade close, her own face pressed into his shoulder, her laughter mingling with his nervous chatter. It was like looking into a mirror of a life she could no longer touch. Watching it now, from this strange world, she felt a pang of loss she hadn't anticipated—a yearning for the life she thought she wanted to escape.

Next to her, Máhí cleared her throat softly. "It's time to go, Sekowah," she said, her voice laced with something akin to sympathy.

Sekowah didn't move at first, her eyes glued to the pond's shifting surface as she saw Robbie shed his shirt, covering her up, his face animated as he gestured wildly at the sky, as if trying to explain something to her. Jade listened, nodding with a secretive smile that Sekowah knew all too well. It was the same smile she had when she was hiding something, when she was keeping a truth to herself. And as she watched them wait on the shore,

Sekowah realized that Jade would be okay, she would adjust to her new world just as she would eventually adjust to this one.

With a pang of resentment, Sekowah tore her gaze away from the pond, swallowing the knot in her throat as she looked up at Máhí.

"Come on," Máhí said gently, offering her hand.

Sekowah took it, her fingers cold and clammy, and Máhí pulled her to her feet. Together, they turned away from the looking pond. They walked back through the winding garden paths in silence, Sekowah's mind a tangled web of confusion and sorrow.

When they reached the cottage, Máhí held the door open, motioning for Sekowah to step inside.

Sekowah hesitated on the threshold, glancing back toward the direction of the pond. For a fleeting moment, she imagined running back, finding a way to reach through the water, to pull herself back into that world. But she knew it was impossible. And perhaps, deep down, she knew that the life she'd left behind wasn't really hers anymore.

With a resigned sigh, Sekowah stepped into the dimly lit cottage, letting the warmth of the still air wrap around her. The familiar scent of herbs and wildflowers filled her senses, grounding her in this new reality. Máhí closed the door behind her, the latch clicking softly, sealing them into the cozy confines of the cottage.

Sekowah sank onto the low wooden bench near the fireplace, resting her head in her hands. She felt Máhí's presence nearby, hovering in that way that reminded her of her mother, of someone wanting to comfort but not quite knowing how. After a moment, Máhí crouched down beside her, her gaze steady and gentle.

"I know this isn't easy," Máhí said softly, placing a hand on Sekowah's shoulder. "But this is where you belong. Jade may have your old life now, but you have a greater purpose here."

Sekowah looked up, her eyes shadowed with doubt. "I feel like I've been ripped out of one life and dropped into another against my will."

Máhí's expression softened. "Sometimes the choices that define us are the ones destiny makes for us."

Sekowah scoffed, looking away. "Destiny. Right." The word felt bitter on her tongue, hollow. She wasn't sure she believed in fate—she hadn't believed in much of anything, really, until she found herself in this strange place.

Máhí squeezed her shoulder, her touch warm and grounding. "You're stronger than you think," she murmured. "And you'll see, in time, why you were brought back here. The Jasper Valley needs you, Sekowah. I need you."

Sekowah blinked, surprised by the quiet vulnerability in Máhí's voice. For all her strength and sharp edges, there was something tender there too, something almost motherly. It softened Sekowah's anger, just a little, and she found herself nodding, though she still felt the ache of Robbie and her old life twisting inside her.

Máhí rose to her feet, brushing her hands on her tunic. "Now, we have work to do," she said briskly, the tenderness in her voice replaced by a more familiar sternness. She moved to one of the shelves, pulling down several small vials and arranging them in a line on the table.

Sekowah watched her, curiosity flickering through the haze of sadness. She had seen hints of magic already—the invisible threads of it woven through the cottage, the way the plants seemed to pulse with life. But now, with Jade gone, it felt more real, more urgent.

"Fine," she said, her voice quiet but steady.

Máhí gave her a small, approving nod. "We start with the basics," she said, handing Sekowah a vial filled with a silvery, shimmering liquid. "The first rule in the valley: respect. Every herb, every stone, every creature here has a spirit, a life force. If you want to work with it, you must first honor it." She handed her a small blue bottle, sealed with a cork. "This is for you. Blue is for change—shapeshift, animal likeness, disguise. We'll need this one." She slid a box out from under the shelves and rummaged through it until she found a leather belt, which she dusted off. "Stand."

Máhí reached around her and fashioned it tightly to Sekowah's waist. "Never take that off." Máhí stepped over to the next section of bottles, all various shades of green, and passed one to her. "Put it here." She slid the vial into a loop on the belt.

Sekowah removed the vial from her belt, examining it. "How do you remember them all?" Sekowah asked, turning it over in her hand, sliding her thumb along the smooth surface.

"Look on the bottom."

Sekowah turned the bottle over and found a symbol etched there. "I can't read your language." The written symbols were a mystery.

"Don't worry. We'll go over it again later." Máhí put a cobalt vial in her own belt.

Sekowah took the bottle, studying the strange liquid inside. *Shapeshift?* She didn't know if she wanted to drink something that would make her... change. She brushed her fingers over the bottle's smooth surface, resisting the urge to throw it back at Máhí in frustration. "What's going to happen to her?" she asked, thinking of Jade trying to navigate her life, her friends, her classes. *How could she possibly know everything about her life?* What about all the symbols of this new world for her? Next semester was calculus, and she was pretty sure, based on what she saw in the cottage, that Jade didn't know the first thing about math. She imagined her staring at the equations on the test, just like she was now staring at these strange symbols on the vials. It would be a disaster. She imagined Jade walking the campus, her head filled with confusion... but as she imagined it, her thoughts drifted, leaving her with only a milky image of a figure in an unknown place. *Who was she just thinking about?*

Máhí continued rummaging through her shelves. "The balance has been restored. All has been set right now. Good of All." She pulled out a bright green bottle and handed it to Sekowah. "Healing," she explained, then grabbed a small black vial, holding it close to her own chest.

Before Sekowah could inquire, there was a sharp knock at the front door.

Máhí stiffened, glancing sharply at Sekowah. "An odd hour for a visitor." She pressed a finger to her lips and whispered, "Remember, you're Jade."

Sekowah's shoulders slumped, and she gave the door a wary look. "Right," she muttered, trying to tamp down the anxiety that flared within her.

Máhí stepped over to the door and opened a small, round window set in its center. "Who comes?"

Through the window, an old man's face loomed close. His eyes were dark and piercing, and his voice, when he spoke, was a rough scrape, like stone grinding against stone. "'ere for me order," he muttered.

"It's quite late," Máhí said, feigning politeness. "Perhaps you could return tomorrow, before the sun has rested?"

The old man pressed closer, his gaze flicking over to Sekowah, who shrank back instinctively. "Can't wait. Me wife is ill. Tis a longer walk 'ere for an old man than a young one. 'Ave a bit a pity."

Máhí sighed and opened the door. The man hobbled inside, leaning heavily on a gnarled cane, his gaze never leaving Sekowah. He looked her up and down with a predatory curiosity that made her skin crawl.

"'Ello, Jade," he greeted her, his voice thick with something that felt like mockery.

"Hello…" Sekowah mumbled, stepping back, her hands clasped tightly together as if to shield herself from his scrutiny.

Máhí found a small package and handed it to him. "Croody, right? Was there anything else?"

The old man's eyes narrowed, and he leaned in toward Sekowah. "Jes' the usual," he said softly.

Sekowah cast an uneasy glance at Máhí. "The usual?" she echoed, voice barely above a whisper.

Máhí stepped between them, giving the old man a forced smile. "Jade's not feeling well this evening. A touch of the epizooty."

Sekowah coughed and tried to sniffle convincingly.

Máhí grabbed Sekowah by the arm and dragged her into the bedroom, shutting the door firmly behind her. Sekowah pressed her ear to the wood, listening as Máhí made her apologies in the main room.

"My apologies, Mr. Croody," she heard Máhí say. "A fever has taken her mind."

A low chuckle, full of something unkind, came in response. "Tsk. Sorry to 'ear it," he murmured.

Sekowah heard the rustle of soft paper and the clink of small bottles. She backed away from the door, feeling an uncomfortable shiver ripple down her spine. Finally, she heard the front door open and close, and a wave of relief washed over her.

But as she let out her breath, a shadow moved outside her window.

She turned, her heart stopping as she saw the old man's face peering in at her through the glass. His eyes met hers, and he grinned, showing teeth that were sharp and yellowed, a flash of something sinister in his gaze. He pulled his hood over his head and hobbled away, his soft chuckles echoing in the night.

Máhí entered the room, her face dark with worry. "That was worse than I could have imagined."

"This is impossible!" Sekowah burst out, her voice trembling. "I don't know anything here!"

Máhí sighed. "You can do more than you know. Cross your arms." She demonstrated. "Hold your earlobes. Touch your tongue to the roof of your mouth." Sekowah followed her instructions. "Exactly. Now hold your breath." Sekowah took in a deep inhale, holding it tightly in her chest, and Máhí waited as her image faded, leaving only a slight visual warp where her body had been. "You're a natural. Now exhale."

Sekowah reappeared, startled. She held her arms out in front of herself and watched as they re-materialized. She repeated the exercise and watched again as her legs re-materialized. "That's so crazy!"

"Use it when you need to disappear quickly, but only for a few minutes. Too long and you'll pass out. In time, you'll learn to hold your breath for a very long while."

She held her breath and crossed her arms again, delighted in this new-found talent. Invisible. Visible. Invisible. Visible. It didn't hurt or make her feel the least bit strange. "How is it possible? Can you do it, too?"

"No. I can't. But I can commune with the plants and trees. And fly. Which is way better than going invisible anyway." There was a hint of jealousy in her words. "Everyone has a gift or two. The rest you'll need to learn."

"The rest of what?"

Máhí's impatience was obvious. "Everything! Pay attention." She snagged a well-loved book off the bedroom end table. "Read this. Every word. Keep reading it until it's carved forever in your memory."

Sekowah held the book to her chest. Books had long been her friend, helping her escape into other worlds when she was lonely, and this book in particular felt heavy and perfect in her arms. The cover was made of a dense, soft material, woven from baby-fine roots and vines, and the pages, as she flipped through them, were light, the homemade paper mixed with flower petals. It even smelled delicious … like gardenias, only sweeter.

The next morning, outside the cottage, Tahgeet waited patiently, her eyes gleaming in the early dawn light. But next to her stood another creature, equally confounding and magnificent: Perrin. Taller than any horse Sekowah had ever seen, Perrin had the striped body of a tiger. His fur and feathers blended seamlessly, dark stripes cutting through soft, tawny feathers that grew thicker around his neck, like a mane. His wings—thick and sleek—were folded gracefully against his sides, the feathers tipped with russet and gold. But it was his eyes that captivated Sekowah most. Pure tangerine orange, with dark, intelligent centers, they seemed to peer directly into her soul.

Sekowah's heart swelled with awe. She stepped forward, her mouth opening in silent wonder. "Nice to meet you, Perrin," she murmured.

The pleasure is mine, Perrin's voice echoed in her mind, a low, warm rumble that seemed to vibrate through her whole body. It was as if he'd wrapped her in a telepathic embrace, a strange comfort that calmed her jitters and made her feel, just for a moment, like she belonged.

Sekowah grinned, a silly, joyful smile spreading across her face as she stared up at him. She wanted to say something witty, something that would make him think she was brave or clever, but the words got tangled on her tongue, leaving her smiling like a starstruck child.

Máhí chuckled softly, reaching over to place a simple necklace around Sekowah's neck. The pendant was a small, polished gold whistle, gleaming in the early light. "That's right," Máhí said. "You're his, and he's yours. You two can speak to each other with thoughts now. But," she added, raising a stern eyebrow, "if I'm around, it's rude, so don't. Understood?"

Sekowah nodded, still dazed, her hand brushing the whistle at her throat. She barely noticed as Máhí guided her to the side of Perrin, helping her place one foot in the stirrup and giving her a sturdy shove up into the saddle. The seat was covered in felt, soft and sturdy, and a marble saddle horn gleamed before her, smooth and solid.

Máhí hooked a strap from Sekowah's belt to the horn, securing her in place, then held her by the ankle, looking up at her with an intensity that made Sekowah's pulse quicken. "Tell me," Máhí said quietly, her voice serious. "Who are you?"

Sekowah stared down at her, heart pounding. She wanted to say "Jade," but that name felt like a borrowed coat now, ill-fitting and wrong. A memory—a faraway, flickering image of her reflection in the cottage mirror, her face unfamiliar yet strangely true—rose in her mind. She took a breath. "Your sister. Sekowah."

Máhí nodded, satisfaction gleaming in her eyes. "Good. And where were you born?"

Sekowah hesitated, uncertainty prickling at her thoughts. She opened her mouth, then closed it, feeling a flash of frustration. She didn't *know*. She'd spent her life thinking she was Jade, with parents in the mortal realm, and now... where did she truly belong?

Máhí's voice softened, a note of pride threading through it. "You are Sekowah of the Nezkwah, daughter of Jájá, born in the Jasper Valley on the night of the harvest moon."

Sekowah's chest filled with a warmth, an unexpected sense of rightness, as if she were slipping back into her true skin after a long, strange dream. "Yes," she murmured, nodding. "I was born in the Jasper Valley... on the night of the harvest moon."

"Excellent," Máhí said, smiling as she released Sekowah's ankle. "Now, don't be afraid of flying. Perrin won't let you fall. You're strapped in, and he's got you. Just hang on."

Sekowah's hands clutched the saddle horn instinctively. "Just... hang on?" she repeated, her voice a tad too high-pitched. Her stomach twisted at the thought of soaring into the sky on this magnificent, feathered beast.

Beside her, Máhí laughed and winked at Perrin. "Easy on her. No sharp turns or dives. At least not until she's ready."

Don't worry, Perrin's voice murmured in her mind, warm and reassuring. *I've got you.* He puffed up his feathers, dug his talons into the soft earth, then spread his enormous wings, sending a rush of air around them. With a powerful lunge, he lifted off, rising into the sky with a smooth, graceful motion that left Sekowah breathless.

The ground dropped away beneath them, the cottage shrinking rapidly as they rose higher, higher, until the canopy of trees lay far below, a dark green sea stretching out in every direction. Her stomach did a flip, and she tightened her grip on the saddle, pressing herself close to Perrin's warm, feathered back. "Whoooaaaa..."

The air felt different up here—cleaner, sharper, alive with possibility. As they cleared the treetops, Sekowah's eyes widened, taking in the sight of rolling hills and meadows below, dotted with splashes of wildflowers. The wind swept past her face, cool and invigorating, filling her lungs with the wild, earthy scents of the valley. Her heart raced, part exhilaration, part fear, her hands shaking as she held tightly to the saddle horn.

Above her, Máhí and Tahgeet soared, wings outstretched, silhouetted against the dawn. Máhí glanced back, meeting Sekowah's eyes, as she swooped into a steep dive, plummeting down before looping back up in a dizzying, graceful arc. "Whaaaaa-heeeeeee!" she whooped, her laughter carried back to Sekowah on the wind.

Sekowah's eyes went wide, a nervous laugh bubbling up in her chest.

Beside her, Perrin's voice purred in her mind, a low, gentle invitation. *Care to join?*

Sekowah took a shaky breath, feeling the wind tugging at her hair, the thrill of adventure sparking through her veins. She leaned forward, pressing herself close to Perrin's powerful neck, and whispered, "Ready."

With a silent nod, Perrin angled his wings, tilting them downward, and then they were plummeting, the ground rushing up to meet them as they sliced through the air. Sekowah held her breath, a mix of terror and exhilaration flooding her senses as they hurtled toward the treetops. Just as she thought they'd crash, Perrin pulled up, his wings flaring wide, and they soared up again, breaking through a patch of mist as he leveled out.

Sekowah threw her head back, laughing breathlessly, the wind carrying her joy into the open sky. She was flying—truly flying, not bound by the world below, free and wild as the creatures who lived among these hills. Perrin's steady presence anchored her, guiding her with surety and strength, and in that moment, she felt a connection to him that was deeper than words, a shared understanding that pulsed between them like a heartbeat.

They glided together, the valley unfolding beneath them in all its untamed beauty. And for the first time since leaving the mortal world behind, Sekowah felt a sense of belonging, a glimmer of purpose that whispered through her like the wind in her hair.

This was her world now.

CHAPTER FIFTEEN

A RAT IN PEREGRINE'S KEEP

The journey across Jasper Valley was, without question, Sekowah's favorite part of flying. As Perrin soared north, the heavy, humid air of the swamp lifted, replaced by a cool breeze that carried the scent of pine and distant rain. Below her, the valley sprawled in a patchwork of emerald forests and golden meadows, connected by silver threads of twisting creeks and foot-worn trails. The hills rolled away like waves, each one softer, gentler than the last.

As they dipped lower, gliding just above the canopy, Sekowah caught sight of movement below. A band of Zahnene swooped up from the treetops, joining her in the air. The tiny blue-skinned creatures darted around Perrin and Tahgeet like a swarm of curious fireflies, chittering and laughing, showing off their aerial prowess. They zipped up and down, looping and spinning in dizzying arcs, each trying to outdo the other. Now that they were so close, Sekowah could see that their eyes were huge, luminous, fringed by impossibly long lashes. They blew her tiny kisses and buzzed in, close enough to touch, their laughter bright and infectious. She wanted to wave back, to join in their joy, but she dared not let go of the saddle horn. Instead, she gave them her best smile, hoping it conveyed her delight.

As they approached the great stone wall that marked the valley's border, the Zahnene suddenly halted, hovering as if frozen in mid-air. They cast one last, wistful glance at her, then peeled away, diving back into the dense canopy and vanishing among the trees.

Beyond the wall, the landscape grew wilder as they followed a narrow dirt trail that led higher into the mountains. The lush valley gave way to a dense pine forest, its dark needles spackled with white birch and aspen, their trunks gleaming silver against the shadows. Within the forest, there were winding cobblestone trails connecting small stone structures with thatched rooftops to larger stone buildings that bustled with the activity of Lirian villagers.

Beyond the trees, rising like the spine of some ancient beast, was Peregrine's Keep—a towering fortress of stone, carved into the side of a granite mountain, with jagged cliffs plunging down into mist-filled chasms below. As they circled to land, Sekowah's heart pounded with a mix of awe and trepidation.

They touched down on a narrow, craggy ledge tucked just out of sight of the Lirian guards patrolling the castle grounds below. Máhí dismounted first, then offered Sekowah a hand, steadying her as she slid down from the saddle. From her bag, Máhí pulled a handful of seed pods, feeding them to Tahgeet and Perrin, who chuffed their thanks.

"Tell Perrin to wait for us near the Cave of Song," Máhí instructed, her voice a low murmur. "If all goes well, we'll meet him there when the sun sleeps. If not..." She hesitated, casting a cautious glance toward the towering stone walls. "Tell him to return to the valley. We'll send for him later."

Perrin unfurled his great wings, gave her a solemn nod, and leapt from the ledge, disappearing eastward in a flash of orange and tawny feathers.

Máhí, meanwhile, was rummaging in her belt, selecting a small blue vial. "Jájá is being held in the North Dungeon," she explained, her tone clipped and businesslike. "I'll keep my father occupied while you—"

"Oh, no," Sekowah cut her off, shaking her head furiously. "I'm not going anywhere without you."

Máhí sighed, exasperated but patient. "If I could do it myself, I would have done it already. But I can't turn invisible, and I can't change my form. You, however..." She held up the vial, the liquid inside a murky shade of brown. "You have that gift in your line. Let's find out."

Sekowah stared at the vial as though it were poison, recoiling. "I don't want to change my form, thank you very much!"

Máhí rolled her eyes and pressed the vial into her hand. "Here. Drink."

She unscrewed the cap reluctantly, peering into the thick, unpleasant-looking liquid. She sniffed it and wrinkled her nose. "It's brown. It smells like... moldy bread."

"It tastes like chocolate," Máhí assured her, though the glint in her eye suggested otherwise.

With a doubtful frown, Sekowah took a cautious sip. The liquid was thick, coating her tongue in a bitter sludge. "Ugh! It tastes like—"

"Rat," Máhí interrupted with a grin, stepping back as if preparing for a show.

The transformation hit fast. Sekowah felt her body shrink, her limbs contorting and changing. Her heart raced as her field of vision shifted, widening in strange, disorienting ways. She squeaked, high-pitched and startled, staring up at Máhí from a rat's-eye view, her tiny paws twitching against the stone.

Máhí clapped her hands in delight. "As we thought! Look at you. An adorable little pet!"

Sekowah squeaked in fury. *I'm a rat?!* She scampered in frantic circles, examining her small, clawed feet, her bald tail, her wiry fur. She could hardly breathe. Panic shot through her like lightning. *Turn me back! Now!* She launched herself at Máhí, clawing at her ankle in a fit of rage.

Máhí only laughed, lifting her foot to avoid Sekowah's furious little claws. "Oh, don't be so dramatic," she said, her voice still dripping with amusement. "You'll change back when it's safe." She reached down, attempting to pick up the squirming rat, only to be met with another flurry of tiny, angry claws. "Enough, you little terror! You have to go in my pocket. I won't have you ruining an important day with a tantrum."

Ignoring Sekowah's furious squeaks, Máhí dropped her into the deep pocket of her cloak and gathered Sekowah's clothes, now in a heap on the trail, and shoved them into her saddle bag. Sekowah thrashed and scratched at the fabric, but it was useless. She was trapped. She poked her nose out, glaring at the world with beady eyes. The indignity of it all was nearly unbearable.

As Máhí led Tahgeet along a narrow path toward Peregrine's Keep, Sekowah sulked in the darkness of the pocket, clutching the edge with her tiny claws. The forest grew denser, shadows thickening under the boughs of ancient pines and twisted birch trees. Every now and then, she would glance down at her own whiskers, twitching in rhythm with her breath, or at the tiny claws on her feet, and a wave of disgust would wash over her. It was unfair. Utterly unfair.

Máhí's voice floated down to her. "Once we're inside, I'll keep my father busy. You slip down the stone steps to the North Dungeon."

Just go down some steps? That's it? Sekowah's little heart pounded as she considered her mission. She was about to meet her mother—her *real* mother. The thought left her cold. Why had her mother sent her away? What would she look like? And then it hit her with sudden, stinging clarity: she didn't even know what she herself was supposed to look like. She'd been made to look like Jade, a stranger's face and form imposed on her in infancy. The truth of her own features, her own identity—lost, stolen before she'd ever had a chance to know it. It was a theft of a thing she didn't know could be stolen.

She slumped down, nestling into the depths of the pocket. Not for the first time, she felt a pang of resentment toward Máhí. A part of her wanted to lash out, to claw her way free and demand answers. But she was too small, too helpless, her tiny claws useless against the thick fabric that held her.

She closed her eyes. A fuzzy image of Mindy's face drifted into her consciousness but was obscured by black and white spots behind her eyelids that flashed and faded until she could no longer imagine what she was trying so hard to remember. All she knew was that in a short time, she would be meeting her real mother.

The iron gates of Peregrine's Keep loomed tall and foreboding, the stone walls draped in shadows cast by the late afternoon sun. Máhí approached with Tahgeet, her face set in a look of effortless command. Waiting at the gate were two Lirian guards, towering even above Máhí, their chests broad and imposing beneath leathered armor plates. Their brown-and-white-striped wings were folded tightly against their backs, and their faces were painted stark white, with a single brown stripe slashing across their keen, yellow eyes. Each held a bow in hand, with quivers strapped over their shoulders, the red-tipped arrows gleaming like embers. The polished steel knives and sheathed swords at their belts completed the picture of lethal elegance.

One guard stepped forward, extending a hand for the reins. "You know the rules."

Máhí shrugged, feigning indifference as she handed over Tahgeet's reins. "Have it your way, but put her in the clover field, will you? She's famished."

She kept her face impassive, but internally, she bristled. *Complete idiots,* she thought, eyeing the guard with a mix of disdain and pity. The Lirian, her kin by blood, were impulsive and unrefined, forever itching for battle and incapable of seeing beyond brute strength. They lacked the Nezkwah's reverence for balance, for harmony. They took and took from the valley, never giving back, and now they were paying the price—the lands were turning against them, drying up, falling to ruin. An old, familiar anger tightened in her chest, but she quelled it, rising above the impulse to strike them both dead on the spot. Her restraint, she mused, was perhaps the only Nezkwah trait she could consistently cl aim.

With a quick snap of her wings, she took flight, leaving a rush of wind in her wake that ruffled the guard's feathers and scattered small peacock feathers into the air. She saw the irritation in their eyes as they brushed the feathers away, and a sly smile crept to her lips. As one guard led Tahgeet toward the clover field, the other resumed her post, muttering as she plucked stray feathers from her hair.

Máhí soared up toward the castle entrance, her gaze passing over the grounds below. Once, this place had been a haven of life and beauty—a garden bursting with color, songbirds filling the air with music as she played with the other Lirian nestlings. Now, the gardens lay withered and abandoned, choked by ivy and overrun by thick, invasive tweedle weeds. The fountain was dry, its basin cracked and streaked with lichen, and the birdsong had been replaced by a grim silence.

The castle itself was no better. She entered the main hall, and the familiar ache of loss tugged at her heart. Dust clung to faded banners, each representing a Lirian king of the past. In the center hung Vesper's flag—a falcon in flight against a field of green ferns. But the statues of the Nezkwah queens, once proudly displayed in reverence, had been removed and replaced by suits of shiny Azurtanium armor. Her father's alliance with Zincubus was an abomination, all for the spoils of Azurtanium.

Máhí pursed her lips, trying to ignore the bitter taste in her mouth as she continued through the castle. She heard laughter nearby and guessed it came from the banquet hall. Quietly, she slipped a small blue vial from her belt, tucking it into the pocket of her cloak where her little rat sister waited, blinking up at her with wide, nervous eyes. "For Jájá," she whispered, her voice barely audible.

Sekowah took the vial in her tiny claws, her beady black eyes wide with apprehension. Máhí studied her for a moment, noting the tremor in her sister's paws. *Is she ready?* she wondered.

Passing the banquet hall, she glimpsed a small group of Lirian knights in Azurtanium chainmail, their mugs brimming with wine and mead. Zahnene servants flitted about, refilling drinks, their delicate wings a blur as they moved from one knight to the next. These tiny folk, once lively and mischievous, seemed drained, their usual spark dimmed to a weary, listless shuffle. The stone walls of the keep were no place for them; they belonged to the meadows, the lakes, watching over the crops and keeping the valley in balance. Here, they were nothing more than servants, and the sight of it made Máhí's hearts burn with anger.

One of the Zahnene servants caught her eye, and Máhí gave her a brief, encouraging nod. A silent promise: *Hold on. Change is coming.*

Once, the valley had been a place of bounty and endless abundance. The fields and orchards, tended with care by the Nezkwah and Zahnene, yielded perfect fruit every harvest. Berries were so plentiful they rotted on the ground, untouched. Máhí remembered those times well—the carefree days of swooping through orchards, filling herself with fruit, the trees bearing more than they could ever use. But that time was gone. Now, the crops had to be guarded, the lands patrolled, and yet the bounty grew thinner with each passing season. The Golds and Dokar tribes, their lands scorched and barren, raided the valley more and more frequently. The world was changing, becoming harsher, harder, impossibly segregated into those who had plenty and those who were forced to settle wit h less.

Máhí straightened her shoulders, took a deep breath, and strode toward her father's favorite room: the fencing arena. She could hear the familiar ring of swords clashing as she neared, and the sound stirred a bittersweet nostalgia within her. She stepped inside, where rows of Azurtanium weapons lined the walls—swords, spears, axes, all gleaming, ready for use. The air was thick with the scent of sweat and dust, and Máhí felt a pang of longing for the simpler days when she had trained here, when this place had felt like h ome.

Her father, Vesper, was sparring with Gavril, his top commander. Vesper moved with the grace of a much younger man, his long salt-and-pepper hair flowing from beneath his helmet. Tall and lean, he wielded his sword with an elegance that belied the hard lines of his face—a face shaped by countless battles and years of rule. Gavril, half his age but equally skilled, was a hulking figure, long black hair flowing over his broad shoulders and powerful wings marking him as a formidable warrior. Yet there was a gentleness to his face, a quiet intelligence that set him apart from the other knights.

They danced through the air, their wings churning the dust below them as they dodged and parried, each move precise, controlled. Máhí's anger softened as she watched, reminded of the deep skill and tradition that ran in her blood.

"Heyo!" Vesper called out, spotting her at the doorway. "Daughter! Watch and learn!" He lunged at Gavril, who dodged with a wry grin.

Gavril waved her over, laughing. "Distract him, will you? I'm down by two."

"You know better than to ask that of me, Gavril," Máhí replied, smirking.

Vesper laughed, feinting toward Gavril with a quick swipe. "Ha! Foiled by loyalty!"

As they continued their sparring, Máhí reached into her cloak pocket and gently set the tiny rat down on the dusty floor beside a table leg. She gave Sekowah a quick, meaningful look, then glanced toward the back door of the arena—the one that led to the stone steps descending to the dungeons.

"Aaahhh!" Gavril exclaimed as he took a blow to the chest plate. With theatrical flair, he collapsed to the floor, clutching at his chest. "See... what... you have done to me. Traitor!" He feigned a dramatic death, his wings spread out behind him as he fell. Lowering his head, he caught a glimpse of Sekowah, clutching the blue vial, scurrying along the wall toward the stairs.

"What rises must fall," Vesper intoned, landing gracefully on the slate floor, his eyes twinkling.

Gavril, rising from his exaggerated death pose, dusted himself off with a grin. "Aye, and all that falls rises anew, stronger than before." He cast a quick, knowing look at Máhí, his loyalty apparent. She met his eyes with a subtle nod. They shared a deep bond, built over years of trust and shared secrets—secrets that even her father knew nothing about.

Máhí approached Vesper and gave him a respectful nod, speaking to Gavril as she did. "You're lucky he's in a generous mood today. Usually, he takes my dignity along with my points."

Vesper chuckled, playfully slicing a single peacock feather from her head with his sword. It floated to the ground in a delicate spiral, and Máhí let out an exaggerated squawk. "Caaah! That takes me three full moons to grow out, you brute!"

Gavril laughed. "Always a pleasure seeing you, Máhí. Staying for the festivities tonight? We've planned quite the celebration for yesterday's victory."

"No." Máhí's voice held an edge. "This isn't a social call. I have urgent matters to discuss."

Chapter Sixteen

FRACTURED HEARTS

Carrying the blue vial in her tiny paws, Sekowah scurried down the winding stone steps of the north dungeon, her heart thudding wildly in her chest. Every step was a calculated risk—one slip, one misstep, and she'd send the precious vial tumbling down the stairs, shattering her mission in an instant. She clasped it tightly against her plump little belly, her claws trembling as she navigated the descent. Each step was its own small agony; she'd place the vial down, swivel her small rat body around, drop to the next step, and retrieve it again. The painstaking journey stretched on in what felt like an endless loop, her frustration mounting with every careful movement.

Why a rat? she grumbled inwardly. *Why didn't she turn me into a monkey?* Rats, she quickly realized, had paws that were entirely too small for the job. If she were a monkey—a little circus monkey with nimble fingers—she'd be bounding down these steps with ease. But Máhí had left her as she was, clinging to the vial like a lifeline with her awkward, clawed hands.

Finally, Sekowah reached the last step and set the vial down just long enough to shake out her tiny paws in relief. She gazed ahead at the north dungeon, bracing herself for whatever grim and dank chamber might await her. But as her rat eyes adjusted, the scene before her was nothing like she'd anticipated.

The dungeon was... beautiful.

Her nose twitched, her sensitive snout overwhelmed by the unexpected scents that swirled in the air—fresh herbs, lavender, even a subtle whiff of honey. The walls, carved from smooth stone, were lined with flourishing potted plants, their leaves lush and green, casting playful shadows across the floor. Iron-barred windows let in filtered shafts of light, softened by drapes of thick, golden velvet. Wisteria vines curled down from above, their purple blossoms swaying gently in the breeze that drifted through the bars. Statues of past queens—each elegant, each poised—stood solemnly in the corners, their feet garlanded with fresh flowers, while small marble fountains gurgled with crystal-clear water, filling the space with a gentle, soothing sound.

Sekowah's rat ears perked up, catching every detail, every sound: the buzzing of a bee somewhere near the wisteria, the rustling of felt slippers on stone, the soft murmur of voices further down the hall. She skittered along the wall, staying in the shadows, her tiny heart racing with anticipation as she approached the cell at the end of the hallway.

Then, through the bars, she saw her.

Sekowah rose onto her haunches, balancing herself on her long, slender tail as she gazed at the woman inside. Her mother.

Jájá stood by the barred window, draped in a deep purple robe embroidered with delicate gold threads that traced patterns of flowers and birds. Her figure was tall and regal, her dark skin luminous against the silk. Pointed ears peeked out from beneath braids adorned with ribbons, and her eyes—brilliant, curious yellow—gleamed with a light that spoke of both wisdom and strength. Black feathers, glossy and pristine, unfurled gracefully from her back, forming wings that seemed as natural as her own limbs. Most arresting of all was the crown of antlers that rose from her head, each point adorned with raw, uncut gemstones that shimmered in the filtered sunlight.

Sekowah's breath hitched, her tiny paws tightening around the vial. Her mother was… glorious. Magnificent, ethereal, and terrifyingly beautiful. In that moment, Sekowah felt like the tiniest creature in the universe.

Suddenly, Jájá's voice cut through the silence, directed at Tahgeet, who was outside, waiting patiently on the other side of the window bars. "A rat? Horrible! Poor thing. Máhí should know better."

Tahgeet's ears flicked toward Sekowah, and with a gentle nicker, the mare announced her presence.

Jájá turned, her face lighting up with warmth and wonder as she spotted Sekowah clutching the vial. "Oh! Come, come. Here at last. My little Sekowah!"

Sekowah's tiny heart fluttered at the words *my little Sekowah*. She skittered forward, squeezing through the bars with ease, and extended the vial toward Jájá with trembling paws. The sight of her mother up close was almost overwhelming; she seemed to radiate an aura of calm and power, her presence as grounding as the roots of an ancient tree. Sekowah felt a swell of emotion she couldn't name—awe, reverence, and something dangerously close to love.

Jájá knelt to the floor, took the vial from her, offering a gentle smile as she brushed Sekowah's tiny nose with a gentle swipe of her index finger. "Excellent. Out you go!" With a practiced gentleness, Jájá lifted her up and set her outside the window bars overlooking the clover fields.

Sekowah clung to the cold bars, peering in as her mother unscrewed the vial and took a delicate sip, her face contorting briefly in distaste. "Awful," Jájá murmured before setting the empty vial down. With a soft, controlled exhale, she turned in a tight circle, her body shimmering with a magical light. In an instant, she had transformed into a small owl, her feathers a soft blend of white and brown. The empty vial rolled to the floor as Jájá hooted softly, fluttering through the bars and out into the clover meadow.

Landing in the grass, Jájá gave a brief shake of her feathers and transformed back into herself, though missing her clothes, her antlers catching the sunlight as she beckoned Sekowah down. "Down you go. Carefully."

Sekowah stared down the wall, a dizzying drop from her precarious perch. Her little rat claws clutched the stone ledge as she surveyed the descent. Each groove and crevice in the stones offered a possible foothold, but the distance felt daunting. She began the descent tail first, letting her tail feel out the next foothold, one stone block at a time, zigzagging her way down until she was safely at the bottom, surrounded by clovers.

"Now you. Come on, come on. Quickly." Jájá instructed.

She took a tentative step, then froze, her tiny heart racing with panic. She turned in a small, pathetic circle, letting out a helpless squeak.

Jájá's laughter was warm, amused. "Darling. Just tell yourself 'Return to true form,' close your eyes and imagine yourself as yourself, and spin a circle. Go on, go on." She bent down, snatching Sekowah's little paw and giving it a comforting squeeze. Then she gently rotated her in a clockwise circle, her fingers light but firm. "Focus. Trust yourself."

Sekowah closed her eyes, a shiver running through her tiny body as she spun. *Return to true form. Return to true form.* She repeated it like a mantra, willing the transformation to take place. A strange tingling sensation began at the tip of her tail, spreading through her body, warming her like a fire from the inside out. Her whiskers faded, her fur receded, and she could feel her bones shifting, reshaping as her true form emerged.

But with the return of her human body came an overwhelming, unbearable itch. Sekowah scratched furiously at her arms and legs, desperate to relieve the prickling sensation that seemed to crawl under her skin. A wretched feeling rose in her stomach, then her throat. She coughed, once, twice, until a small hairball worked its way up, tumbling from her mouth and leaving stray rat hairs on her tongue.

Horrified, Sekowah spat out the clump of fur, wiping her mouth with the back of her hand, grimacing. Jájá chuckled, her eyes twinkling with mischief. "Naughty Máhí. Next time—choose bird." She plucked a stray downy feather from her nose and sneezed.

Finally returned to their human forms, Sekowah and Jájá stood in awkward silence, the rush of transformation still flowing through their veins. Sekowah glanced down at her own body, trying to reorient herself to her shape and skin. She hugged her arms across her chest, feeling strangely exposed and vulnerable without clothes. Her mother, Jájá, stood before her, unclothed and unselfconscious, her dark skin sleek and nothing like what Sekowah expected—no breasts, no navel. Just the smooth, streamlined planes of her chest, almost avian in their delicate strength.

Jájá's eyes were shining with emotion as she took in Sekowah's form, her gaze warm and intent. But then, as she looked closer, her expression shifted, a flicker of confusion and perhaps even disapproval surfacing. Her eyes drifted to Sekowah's breasts, lingering there as if trying to make sense of something that didn't belong.

"Your mortal form is... quite an oddity, isn't it?" Jájá murmured, her voice tinged with a trace of pity. "A shame," she added softly, almost to herself.

Sekowah stiffened, feeling her cheeks burn. Her arms tightened across her chest, an instinctual attempt to shield herself from that searching, bewildered gaze. She hadn't expected her mother's first words to be... that. *A shame.* The words felt like stones dropped into the well of her stomach, stirring something raw and resentful.

In that moment, she was painfully aware of their differences. The lines of her mother's body were foreign, striking in their grace and unfamiliarity. Where Sekowah's body felt warm and tender, Jájá's seemed sculpted, as if by ancient forces, without the maternal shape she'd once thought universal.

She could feel her mother's hands reaching out, clasping her own with a gentle but unyielding grip. "Welcome home, darling," Jájá said, her voice softening, a tremor of emotion breaking through. "My precious daughter. I've waited many harvests for this day."

The words should have been a balm, but to Sekowah, they felt distant, hollow. *My precious daughter.* She wanted to believe them, wanted to sink into her mother's arms and let herself be held, but instead, a swell of anger rose within her, surprising her with its force. *You sent me away,* she wanted to scream. *You kept me hidden. You left me to feel like a stranger in my own skin.*

But she held herself back, swallowing the bitterness as tears pricked at her eyes. She bit her lip, looking away, blinking hard as the warmth of Jájá's hands failed to reach the cold knot that had formed in her chest.

Instead, she stood in silence, feeling the ache of things left unsaid. The embrace she had longed for remained just out of reach, separated by the unbridgeable chasm of their differences—differences neither of them fully understood.

She yanked her hands free, her voice trembling with restrained fury. "You sent me away!? Why? Why would you do that to me?"

Jájá blinked, taken aback by the outburst. "Yes... oh. I see, I see." Her expression softened, a pained understanding flickering in her gaze. "Please, Sekowah. Don't hate me. I had to keep you safe. It was too dangerous here for you. Zincubus would have snuffed you out long ago once he figured out who you were."

The sound of footsteps echoed from the stairwell above, growing louder with each passing moment. Jájá's eyes widened, and she swiftly pulled Sekowah close, pressing them both against the stone wall beside the window. "Quiet," she whispered.

Sekowah held her breath as she heard a cell door swung open inside, the iron bars creaking on their hinges. "Alert Vesper!" a voice commanded.

Quick as a whisper, Jájá folded her arms over her chest and held her earlobes. "Do as I do," she mouthed, vanishing from sight in an instant. Sekowah followed suit, holding her own earlobes, pressing her tongue to the roof of her mouth. A strange wave of energy washed over her, and she vanished.

Just beyond the bars, Sekowah could see a pair of hands gripping the iron. Her heart raced, praying her invisibility would hold.

Another voice spoke up. "I'll secure the animal."

The hands released the bars, and the guards retreated, their footsteps fading as they made their way back up the stairs. Silence returned, heavy and suffocating.

· · · • ⟲ • · · ·

V esper and Gavril stood bent over a stretched map on the king's desk, their eyes scanning its scorched leather surface. Máhí, silent and simmering, held her ground on the opposite side of the desk. She pointed to a dark patch marked *Obsidia* just south of Mount Lira, her finger pressing down as though she could anchor her father's attention there by force. The map itself was crude, scarred with black burn marks instead of ink, a testament to the turbulent history it depicted—a map not of lands but of conflicts.

Vesper's chambers were a grotesque gallery of past conquests. The walls were cluttered with trophies—foxes, rabbits, and elk, each once noble, now reduced to relics of Vesper's need to dominate. Bright yellow citrine stones, embedded in the wall sconces, flooded the room with an amber glow that cast elongated shadows across the floor.

The king's desk, carved from heavy ebony, sat like a beast of its own. The legs were carved like horse legs, with hooves at the bottom, while horse heads adorned each corner, frozen in a perpetual stare. A single citrine lamp that seemed to pulse with an inner light, illuminated the desk. Next to it, a pheasant quill pen, a copper ink well, and a cluttered heap of scrolls.

Máhí knew there was nothing she could tell him that he didn't already know, but her ruse would be found out soon enough and she dreaded Vesper's wrath when he discovered Jájá's escape. *Good of All*, she reminded herself. He would eventually forgive her, though the tongue lashing she would receive would be unpleasant; that much was certain.

In a way, she believed herself to be righteous. It was Vesper after all who had broken the family pact not to do business with Zincubus, and in a fit of rage, locked her mother up in the dungeon to keep her from interfering. *Serves him right.* He had taken her mother away from her too soon. Had it not been for Gavril, she would have been lost to grief forever. The sting of that day still needled at Máhí's heart. She had been forced to live out the last two decades in service to her father, who behaved as though what she thought was of no consequence. *He deserved everything that was coming.* She felt a deep satisfaction in knowing that his control over her life was coming to an end, whether he liked it or not. *Soon. She would belong to herself once again, as would her mother.*

Vesper straightened, pushing the map aside as though dismissing her concerns with the same gesture. "His presence in Obsidia makes no difference to me," he said, his tone flat. "Zincubus keeps to himself."

Máhí resisted the urge to roll her eyes. Instead, she leaned over the desk, tapping her finger on a northern region beyond the mountains and the twin waterfalls. "He shows no respect for the balance—no respect for the lives ruined by his recklessness."

Vesper's brow furrowed. *I know you're right*, it seemed to say, *but I'll never admit it.*

"The valley will survive," he said, the words cold and final.

Máhí gritted her teeth, unwilling to let him shut her down so easily. "What of the Dokar?" she pressed, her voice steady and defiant. "We cannot hold them forever. Zincubus knows this. He keeps you distracted at the border while he takes the valley's lifeblood."

Vesper's gaze hardened, his irritation flashing. "Why this change of heart? You've always been supportive of the border."

Her eyes met his, a cold fire burning there. "I have been supportive of *you*."

Vesper let the words hang in the air for a brief moment. "As you should be," he said quietly, a threat woven into each syllable.

At that moment, a guard burst into the room, his armor clinking as he saluted hastily, Jájá's robes draped over his other arm. "The Queen. She's gone."

The blood drained from Vesper's face, and he turned to Máhí, fury sparking in his yellow eyes. He thrust a finger toward her, his voice a hiss. "Where is your loyalty?! I gave you free access to visit her, to see her at will, and this is how you repay me?" He turned to the guard. "Secure the gates. All doors and windows. When you find her, bring her to me."

Máhí steeled herself, squaring her shoulders. This was the confrontation she'd rehearsed countless times in her mind. She was ready. "Loyalty?!" she spat, her voice rising, filling the room. For the first time since she was a child, she raised her voice to her father. "You mine the Jasper Valley and trade our lives for weapons, as our valley falls to ruin. The network grows weaker every day without the emerald. You are so obsessed in your battle with the Dokar that you cannot see what you do to us all."

Vesper's face twisted with rage, his hand clenching as if he might strike her. "Without my armies, your valley would be overrun by the Dokar. You're a foolish girl—and I, a foolish father, for thinking you otherwise."

Máhí didn't flinch, but her pulse quickened. Vesper had never looked at her with such disdain. Before he could raise his hand further, Gavril, who had been watching with silent intensity, stepped between them.

"My King," Gavril said, his voice calm but firm. "You know where my loyalties lie. But Máhí speaks with reason. We cannot hold them at bay forever. Perhaps the time has come to reconsider our... arrangement with Jájá. To enlist her help."

"Arrangement?!" Máhí snorted, the bitter irony palpable. Her father had taken the valley by force, enslaving Nezkwah and Zahnene alike, stripping their land bare for his own gain. And now he had the audacity to speak of arrangements, as if it were a mutual agreement.

Vesper turned his wrath onto Gavril, the sting of betrayal simmering beneath his gaze. "You'd have the Dokar at our doorstep, then? You know as well as I do that the Nez cannot hold them back. We fight not only for our border, but for theirs as well—with little in return!"

Máhí pulled her shoulders back, unwilling to let Gavril carry the weight of this alone. "You take our most precious resources and leave us with scraps. Our crops on the western meadows, next to the mines, are failing. The signs have come to pass, yet you deny the Prophecy at our peril, as well as your own."

"*The Verses.*" Vesper's sneer deepened. "Superstitions, nothing more. There hasn't been a mortal in this realm for generations. There's nothing to fear but weakness. Sit down, daughter, lest I be forced to remind you of your place."

Máhí's wings unfurled behind her, a defiant blaze of shimmering iridescent blackness. She leaned in close, her face mere inches from his, her voice a low, dangerous growl. "Your arrogance will be your downfall. Just like your father's. Challenge me on this, and I'll have your head on a platter for this evening's feast."

The room fell deathly silent. The air between them crackled with tension, her words echoing off the stone walls, magnified in the thick stillness. For a single heartbeat, she relished the stunned look on his face, watching as his composure cracked, if only slightly.

Then she saw it. The tremor of shock in his eyes, quickly masked by an even deeper rage. Never, in all their comings and goings, had his daughter spoken to him in such a way.

Turning on her heel, she strode out of the chamber, her wings still unfurled, leaving Vesper standing in stunned silence. She didn't look back, not even once.

CHAPTER SEVENTEEN

THE BETRAYAL

J ájá sprinted through the tall grasses, Sekowah struggling to keep pace at her side. The horn sounded again from somewhere above, piercing the air with an urgent warning that rattled Sekowah to her bones. She stumbled through the thick vines and clover, her long legs not quite used to the uneven terrain, while her mother bounded forward with grace, using her wings to propel herself forward in powerful bursts.

"Wait!" Sekowah gasped, tripping over a clump of weeds. "I can't keep up!"

But Jájá was already at Tahgeet's side, pulling robes from the saddle bags for them both. "Put this on," she commanded, tightening the saddle straps with swift, practiced hands, her eyes darting toward the distant guard towers. They made quick work of dressing, but before they could mount, a guard emerged from the opposite direction, his armor clanking as he seized Tahgeet's reins.

The creature reared up, pawing at the air, its neigh slicing through the chaos. Above them, high in the castle watchtower, another guard drew an arrow, her sharp voice ringing out: "Halt! By order of King Vesper!"

Jájá froze, arms outstretched, her expression one of calm surrender. She glanced back at Sekowah and bowed her head in a silent command. Sekowah, her heart racing, copied her mother's stance, lifting her arms in kind.

"Lay down your weapons!" Jájá shouted to the guards above. Her voice was strong, unyielding. "I go willingly."

An arrow whistled through the air and thudded into the ground mere inches from Sekowah's feet. She gasped, her stomach clenching in fear. Jájá dropped to one knee, and with a peculiar calm, she reached into the grass, gathering clover blossoms by the handful and tucking them into the pockets of her robe. Without understanding why, Sekowah did the same, plucking the delicate green sprigs with trembling hands, the scent of clover filling her senses.

What is going to happen to us? Sekowah's mind raced with dark possibilities—captivity, servitude, execution. She'd failed her first mission. Tears stung her eyes, and her hands shook as she whispered, "I'm so sorry."

Oddly, Jájá turned and winked, an almost playful gleam in her eye. She seemed entirely untroubled, as if the guards' threats and the looming arrows were mere inconveniences.

· · · • ◯◯ • · · · ·

Vesper stood in the doorway of his chambers, his face hard as he surveyed the scene before him. Jájá and Sekowah, flanked by half a dozen guards, were brought into the room. Behind him, Máhí and Gavril held back, each watching with uneasy anticipation. The tension in the room was thick with fighting words, the silence heavy. Betrayal still hung in the air, and he pressed his lips together to keep from spilling more words into the room that he might later regret. An impetuous tongue was a trademark of both her age and gender, and he steeled his will to conceal his rage.

The words his daughter had thrown at him only moments ago still echoed in Vesper's mind, cutting deeper than he cared to admit. Máhí had always been a difficult nestling—rebellious, independent, impervious to advice or reason. She had a fire in her belly from her youth, and once she reached the age of flight, she would stir up trouble wherever she could find it. She had run away from the Keep before her first rites, and taken up residence in the valley, even building her own nest in the tallest of pines whilst others her age struggled with their flight lessons. Her fire had been a source of pride once, but now, that fire threatened to consume the last threads of loyalty she had left for him. And as he looked at Jájá, the wife who had betrayed him as well, Vesper felt his control slipping, his patience unraveling.

The first guard stepped forward. "Caught them trying to escape on Máhí's familiar."

Another guard presented a small blue vial. "Found this."

Vesper's gaze darkened as he glanced at Máhí. "I see." But his eyes shifted quickly to Sekowah, a newcomer. *Who was she?* She was too tall to be Zahnene or Nezkwah, and too solidly built to be Lirian—without wings, without the telltale markings of any tribe he recognized. A changeling, perhaps, but an unusually striking one, with none of the sickly pallor or frail limbs he'd expect. His suspicion grew as he took a step closer, brushing Sekowah's hair away from her ears, his eyes narrowing.

Gavril, standing a few steps behind, seemed equally transfixed. His gaze softened as he looked at Sekowah, his usually stoic face betraying a flicker of something unfamiliar—a kind of fascination, even admiration. Sekowah felt her cheeks flush under the weight of his stare, but she couldn't bring herself to look away.

Jájá interrupted, her voice breaking the silence. "Before you speak against us—"

"Silence, wife!" Vesper's voice cracked like a whip. He turned back to Sekowah, his eyes piercing. "What is your name?"

Sekowah looked to Máhí, silently pleading for guidance.

"She was—" Máhí began, but Vesper cut her off with a sharp gesture.

"I'll hear nothing from you," he snarled, his voice low and dangerous. He turned his full attention back to Sekowah, his face inches from hers. "Speak, intruder. Who are you?"

Swallowing hard, Sekowah stammered, "I'm J-Jade?"

Máhí's voice was soft but firm. "You can speak the truth here."

Vesper's mouth twisted in a sneer. "Yes. By all means, let's hear the truth. It would be a novelty."

"My name is Sekowah," she said, her voice trembling but growing steadier. "Daughter of Jájá. I was born in the Jasper Valley. I think you might be... are you my real father?"

The innocence of her question caught him off guard, and he felt a jolt of something uncomfortably close to sympathy. *Father?* Did she truly know so little? If he had fathered her, she would bear wings. His eyes darted over to Jájá, fury mingling with betrayal as he saw in his wife's gaze the truth of this changeling child.

"Most certainly not," he spat. "Where have you been hiding?"

Sekowah blinked, bewildered. "Hiding? No, I—I don't know, I—"

Jájá stepped closer, her tone defiant. "She was hidden in the mortal realm. Insurance against your stubbornness. I sent Máhí to retrieve her just two suns ago."

Vesper stared at his wife, the implications washing over him like a tidal wave. Conceived without his knowledge, hidden away in another world, brought back now as some kind of fulfillment of the Prophecy? He took Sekowah's hands, turning them over, examining her fingerprints. "You have mortal markings." The confirmation twisted his stomach.

Gavril's expression softened, a lopsided smile tugging at the corner of his mouth as he looked at Sekowah.

Máhí, sensing an opportunity, lifted her chin and declared, "Of royal line and mortal blood!"

The words hit Vesper like a blow, and he flinched. "I can see that for myself," he snapped, his voice tinged with resentment. He turned on Jájá and Máhí, his fury barely contained. "Tell me—what have I done to warrant the betrayal of both my wife and daughter?"

Jájá's gaze was unflinching, her voice calm but laced with venom. "I owe no allegiance to a husband who would keep me locked away for twenty harvests while he ravages my valley."

Vesper's control cracked, his hands shaking with barely suppressed rage. He stepped closer, looming over Jájá, his face twisted with contempt. "On that count, you are right. You have no allegiance to this family. You would turn our eldest daughter away—banish her, even—curse her with ugliness."

Jájá's eyes flashed, but she looked away, a flicker of pain crossing her face. "Faylen has proven herself unworthy of our loyalty. She cares for no one, not even you."

Máhí muttered under her breath, "Sneaky snake," her voice thick with bitterness.

Vesper's hands shook with rage. Faylen was a picture of loyalty, making the best of an exceptionally difficult situation, turning it to his advantage more than once. She had never wavered in her support of his campaigns against the Dokar, nor betrayed him in any way, ever. When the curse was cast upon her, Vesper had vowed to keep his wife imprisoned until the curse was lifted. It was Jájá's own stubbornness that kept her captive. Had she agreed to lift the curse, she would have been freed many harvests ago.

Vesper turned his attention to Máhí and Gavril. "Were it not for her, we would have no weapons to defend ourselves. The Dokar would have taken us all long ago."

"We can take care of ourselves, thank you very much." Máhí replied, her head high.

Their stubbornness did not surprise him, but the intensity with which they spoke, did. Vesper stood a moment to contemplate. *Were they all against him? Had he misjudged those closest to him?* Though he didn't like to entertain it, he contemplated his position. Even Gavril stood strong, his allegiance on this issue clear. He was alone. For the first time in many suns, he felt the need to consult with his Council, to weigh the opinions of those not so closely aligned to Jájá. With a swoop of his cape, Vesper turned away from his wife, and with quiet defeat in his voice, spoke to Gavril. "Fetch my advisors."

He then turned to Sekowah. "You." He motioned to the guards. "Take her down. Better yet. Take all three." *Best to keep them under guard while the Council debates,* he thought.

The guards gathered them together and marched them out of the room.

He turned a brief moment to address Gavril but found his hearts too heavy to utter a single word before he left him to convene his advisors.

···• ⌾ •····

D eep underground in Obsidia, in a small vault made of stone, Faylen stared at the emerald, encased in an iron cage. As a result of her mother's curse, she had skin with scales like that of a rattlesnake, reptilian eyes, and enormous bat wings, folded up and draped off her shoulders. She wore a cascade of obsidian necklaces and bracelets, and deep ruby gems hung from her ears. She wore her white hair in a tightly woven braided tower, a gold snake with emerald eyes coiling the length of it.

The emerald pulsed and glowed a deep green, the center of it dark. Strands of neon green emanated from its base out into a fine mesh of plant roots that led into the walls and crept through the cracks. The change in the emerald's intensity could only mean one thing: her mother's changeling had returned. *Máhí must have traveled the crossing between worlds and retrieved her,* she concluded.

Embedded in the walls, were hundreds of glowing gems of all colors and sizes. A window overlooked a cavern below, which was loaded with chili peppers, hanging ripe from vines. Black dragons grazed on them, tendrils of smoke rising from their nostrils. Bright amber citrine gems were suspended from the cave ceiling, giving nourishing light to the pepper crops.

Zincubus entered the vault, his cape floating behind him as he walked.

Faylen watched over the dragons. "Production is up," she said.

Zincubus kept his eyes on the emerald. "When did it grow brighter?"

"Two suns." Faylen's voice dropped to a hush. "She is here."

The pulsing of the emerald kept Zincubus in a hypnotic state. He reached out to caress it, but the emerald's glow diminished as his fingers neared it. He stepped away and turned to Faylen. "Yes. I'm aware. I've just returned from the apothecary. She's replaced Jade and is masquerading in her image."

Faylen ran her hands over Zincubus' chest, soaking in his powerful presence. "I am curious. Is she beautiful?"

Zincubus kissed her fingers. "I didn't notice."

This satisfied Faylen. It had taken many harvests in his world to appreciate him, to revel in his intellect and vast knowledge. Though he was cruel to most, he had graced her with his heart, truly, and she felt privileged to be at his side. She endured his outbursts, his violence, his disregard for her predicament. It was a better fate than any other in this pl ace.

Pleased, Faylen turned her eyes to the emerald. "She sends a titmouse to battle a dragon." Flattery, she knew, was his weakness.

Zincubus took her by the shoulders and kissed her passionately. When his lips met hers, she felt his nobility, his conviction, his deep yearning for what she knew she would never give him: her heart.

CHAPTER EIGHTEEN

VISIONS

The banquet hall emptied slowly as Gavril ushered the knights out, his face impassive. "The Council will meet at once," he declared, his tone brooking no argument. "All not on the Council will stand by." Half-drunk warriors and a few seasoned squadron leaders, honored to dine at the king's table, grumbled as they grabbed whatever scraps they could from their platters, shuffling toward the door with reluctant, heavy steps.

Gavril's outward calm belied the turmoil within. The upcoming council session loomed like a storm, full of unpredictable currents and sudden shifts. He and Máhí had spent countless hours scrutinizing the votes of each member, building lists and allies, yet several loyalties remained unsettlingly unclear. The introduction of a mortal changeling—a figure spoken of only in the oldest prophecies—would no doubt stoke the fires of skepticism and fear among the Council. But he prayed that it might kindle something else as well. Perhaps, a spark of unity.

He looked down the length of the great wooden table, now a battlefield of its own—a mess of pheasant bones, scraps of rabbit, half-drained mugs of mead, and bowls of porridge abandoned in disarray. The long-standing banquet tradition seemed profane against the task ahead, the chaos of feasting a harsh reminder of the chaos that awaited him in the council chamber. A colossal stone fireplace roared at one end of the hall, casting flickering shadows that animated the portraits lining the walls—kings of the past, staring down with silent judgment.

Above the table hung chandeliers fashioned from antlers and candles, their wax drippings sealing in place a collection of dusty wishbones left by warriors before battle. Each wishbone was a quiet reminder of the Lirian soldiers who had feasted here before their final marches, never to return and retrieve their tokens. To Gavril, those grim relics felt like silent witnesses, as if the spirits of the fallen were gathering, weighing his every decision. They had sworn loyalty to die before surrendering to the Dokar.

Would they, he wondered, now entertain an attempt at peace?

Brock, his thick red mustache drooping over his lips, paced anxiously at the entrance, puffing furiously on his pipe. His wings, broad and striped a dusty red, buzzed with barely-contained agitation. When Gavril approached, Brock leaned in, muttering around his pipe, "If you release her, you'll have madness on your hands. She'll interfere at every turn."

Gavril regarded him carefully. Brock had a reputation as a peacemaker, a man with an uncanny talent for brokering agreements even among bitter rivals. If there was to be a way forward, Gavril would need Brock's steady hand and sharp mind to sway the Council toward reconciliation. He held Brock's gaze, beseeching. "There's more at stake than you realize. We need your support, Brock. If we don't act now, we risk everything."

Brock's eyes narrowed, his face inscrutable as he puffed a cloud of fragrant smoke. "We'll hear the matter," he said at last, his tone guarded. "And I'll give it a just consideration. That's the best I can offer." He turned away, but not without a lingering glance—half suspicion, half curiosity.

Vesper gathered his band of advisors at the far end of the table as Gavril and Brock approached, taking their seats. "As you heard earlier, the escape horn was blown, as it appears my wife and daughter have concocted their own strategies for reconciliation with the valley by fostering the emergence of a changeling," the ruler said.

Brock's mustache twitched, a brief flicker of surprise crossing his face as he shot a questioning glance at Gavril.

"They have acted in accord with *the Verses*," Gavril explained calmly, "to bring a mortal of royal blood into the fold."

A hush fell over the room. The council members shifted uncomfortably, glancing at one another. The Lirian seldom paid heed to the Nezkwah prophecies, but there were a few among them—especially the elders like Brock—who had seen uncanny events unfold over the years, whispers from *the Verses* given form. And for some, the prophecies held a distant but profound respect.

Vesper's patience snapped. "Rubbish," he scoffed, dismissing Gavril's words with a wave of his hand. "This is nothing more than a ploy to distract us from Zincubus and his dealings, to pull us away from our campaign against the Dokar, so that they might seize control of the valley once more."

Servants swept through the hall, clearing plates and goblets, but their ears were sharp, and whispers rippled among them as they listened to the heated debate.

Brock puffed thoughtfully on his pipe, his brows drawn low. Though he was Lirian, his long years had given him a grudging respect for Nezkwah intuition. He'd watched events play out that defied all logic, saw prophecies take root and grow wild. If even a sliver of *the Verses* were true, the presence of a mortal changeling was not a matter to be dismissed lightly.

· · · · • ◯◯ • · · · ·

I n the dungeon, Jájá and Sekowah stood at the barred window, looking out as the sun dipped below the horizon, casting the sky in an explosion of amber and turquoise. A soft halo crowned the sun, its fading light illuminating the meadow beyond with a surreal, dreamlike glow. Sekowah gazed at the sky, enraptured. She had never seen colors so intense, and for a fleeting moment, she felt a calm wash over her—a fragile peace in the eye of a gathering storm.

Máhí paced restlessly by the cell gates, her feathers rustling with irritation. She yanked one from her plumage and toyed with it absentmindedly, flicking it between her fingers.

Jájá watched her agitated daughter and then turned to Sekowah, her eyes softening with regret. "Please forgive me," she whispered. "It wasn't always this way." Her gaze drifted over Sekowah, her expression proud yet haunted. "Such desperate times..."

She pulled a handful of clovers from her robe pocket and chewed them, then handed some to Sekowah. "Here. Chew slowly, then let it rest under your tongue."

Sekowah took the clover leaves hesitantly. "What happened to create all of this, this... anger?" she asked, her mind swirling with questions.

Máhí stopped her pacing, tossing the feather into the air and watching it drift slowly to the floor. "Faylen happened," she interjected, bitterness in her eyes.

After the argument in Vesper's chambers, it was clear that this family plotted and schemed against one another, even lied to one another. It was the first she had learned of another sister as well. *How many sisters do I have?* Sekowah wondered.

Sekowah glanced back at Jájá. "You're her mother. Can't you reason with her?"

Máhí let out a harsh laugh and stomped over, grabbing more clover from Jájá with a scowl. She chewed, grimacing at the taste. "See? Even here, the fields are bitter."

"A little luck on the breath is better than nothing," Jájá murmured, giving Sekowah another handful of clover. "Chew."

Sekowah chewed obediently, her mind drifting to a lesson her parents had taught her in the mortal world: that disagreements should always be settled before bedtime, that family conflicts required both respect and compromise. How could things here have soured so deeply, so irreversibly? She searched for the right words. "Resolution requires respect and compromise," she said softly, the words sounding strangely small and naïve in the cold dungeon air.

Máhí's gaze darkened. "Never," she hissed. She stopped, her eyes locking onto Sekowah with a haunted intensity. "You don't know what you're talking about. Faylen stole the emerald from the Cave of Song. She set the Dasheahs loose on our pear orchards—"

Jájá's face tightened, her voice barely a whisper. "The sacred birthplace of our nestlings..." She shared a painful glance with Máhí, a shadow passing between them. "We don't speak of that time."

Máhí's wings rustled with frustration. "How will she learn? She needs to understand everything."

Jájá held her hands out to Sekowah, pulling her close and gently covering her eyes. "Come. See with my eyes." A golden thread of magic spiraled around Sekowah's head, shimmering softly as Jájá sang a single, resonant note that hung in the air, vibrating the air around them both.

A vision blossomed behind Sekowah's closed eyes—she saw the valley, bright and alive, filled with laughter, butterflies dancing in the air. "I see it," she whispered, wonder in her voice.

Máhí's voice came soft and steady. "She has the gift of shared visions. Tell us what you see."

Sekowah's breath quickened. She saw Nezkwah youngsters playing among the pear trees, laughter filling the orchard as butterflies flitted around them. The trees were heavy with fruit, and from their branches hung nests woven with ribbons, cradling eggs the size of pears. As she watched, the eggs began to crack open, revealing tiny newborns, each perfect and radiant. "Babies," she murmured, a mix of awe and sorrow. "I see the babies..."

Jájá's hand stroked Sekowah's golden hair. "Yes, love. You were one of them."

Sekowah felt an ache deep in her chest, a memory not entirely her own. She watched as Jájá cradled a dark-haired infant, holding her close with tears in her eyes. A part of her heart she hadn't known was missing, filled with warmth, but then—shadows fell. Bat-winged creatures with red eyes and dark cloaks descended upon the orchard. "I see... bat people."

"Dasheahs," Jájá whispered, her voice tight with pain.

The vision shifted, the golden thread around Sekowah's head flaring crimson. She saw the Dasheahs sweeping through the orchard, their cruel laughter filling the air, snatching up the Nezkwah infants in rough sacks. Only one child was spared—her. Protected by the midwives, she lay nestled at a young Máhí's feet as Jájá battled fiercely, her white gown turning crimson in the fray.

When the vision faded, Sekowah was left trembling, her face wet with tears. She looked at Jájá, her voice choked. "I see now..."

Jájá tooks her hands in her. "Faylen set the Dasheahs loose on the orchard, and we lost our nestlings. We still don't know what's become of them. I fear the worst. If I hadn't sent you away, they would have returned for you. It was an unforgiveable act. So, I cursed her with ugliness, such that no creature would see her and be deceived again." Tears fell as Jájá recalled the events. "She took the emerald from its place in the Cave of Song as revenge. Now she trades our precious gems with Vesper for the spoils of Obsidia."

Máhí's face hardened. "There can be no reconciliation."

A heavy silence fell. Sekowah grappled with the weight of it all, with the knowledge that her existence had cost her family so much. She swallowed, her heart aching with guilt and confusion.

"Why is the emerald so important?" Sekowah asked quietly. "And the Cave of Song?"

"The emerald binds life to this valley," Jájá explained, her voice laced with sadness. "Without it, our world fades. The Cave of Song is its sanctuary—a place of pure energy, the heart of our world. Without the emerald, that energy stagnates, weakens."

Sekowah's mind reeled, struggling to grasp the enormity of it. "And Vesper... he did this?"

Jájá's eyes darkened. "No. It is Zincubus who unleashed his wrath on the valley. Vesper thinks he has saved us from him, by keeping the peace. But he has only made things worse. He trades the valley's life force for weapons. He punishes me. For banishing his daughter. He keeps me here so that I won't interfere in his trade agreement with Faylen and Zincubus. He's forsaken his sacred oath to me, to protect the land."

Máhí chimed in. "He's blind to all but victory with the Dokar, and the occupation of the valley."

Jájá nodded. "What kind of husband locks his wife away in a dungeon?"

Vesper stepped out of the shadows into the light outside the cell for them to see, his face anguished. "What kind of mother curses her own daughter and sends another away to be raised by mortals?"

His presence startled them. Jájá turned, her face still wet with tears. "What kind of daughter betrays her family, betrays her own people?"

"A loyal daughter. One who would act in good faith, sparing me the ugliness of your actions, leaving herself to suffer alone in darkness." Vesper obviously had a totally different take on the events of the past. He glared at Máhí, who turned away with revulsion. "The advisors have agreed to hear your case, given the—" he gestured at Sekowah, frustrated, "—current change in circumstance."

He opened the cell door, entered the room and pulled a leather harness off the wall.

He placed the harness over Jájá's shoulders, strapping her wings down. He pulled a second harness off the wall, and repeated the procedure with Máhí, who kept her head held high but allowed it.

He stared at Sekowah, a mix of pity and regret in his eyes. Sekowah didn't like his expression. It looked as though he was about to do something he didn't want to do.

"After you." He corralled them together and escorted them back up the steps.

Sekowah climbed the marble steps. With each step, she felt her apprehension rise, as the unknown, once again, confronted her. She didn't like seeing the harnesses on her mother and sister, and now that she knew more of their story—her story—she felt both admiration and pity for them.

They had saved her life, not abandoned her.

CHAPTER NINETEEN

LUCK ON THE BREATH

In Vesper's dimly lit chambers, the captives stood under the scrutiny of the Council, enduring a rigorous inquisition led by Brock and several other advisors. The tension in the room was thick, almost palpable. Feathers rustled as the Lirian nobles shifted and fidgeted, exchanging sharp looks and whispers. To Sekowah, they were a proud bunch, but they were unnecessarily arrogant, all jockeying for dominance over the conversation, their voices cutting over one another in a chorus of irritation and indignation.

Brock, flushed and fuming, was pacing in tight, agitated circles, his pipe lodged firmly between his teeth. Each time he opened his mouth to speak, he seemed to stop short, as if caught off guard by the enormity of what was unfolding. Finally, he could hold back no longer.

"Crossings are forbidden!" he roared...

But it wasn't Brock's words that lingered in the chamber; it was Sekowah's wide-eyed silence. Her stillness. Her obvious lack of wings.

Whispers broke loose like a dam behind the council dais. Several nobles leaned forward to get a better look, their brows pinched in distaste or disbelief. One noblewoman—a councilor draped in sun-burnished feathers—tilted her head and sniffed audibly, as though testing the air for mortal scent. Another narrowed his eyes, murmuring a protection verse under his breath as he recoiled ever so slightly.

"She has no wings," came a voice from the sidelines, sharp and astonished. "No plume, no aura. She is... unfinished."

"A changeling, born of shadow," muttered another, eyes wide, almost reverent, horrified.

Gavril remained silent, watching the reactions with calculated calm. But his gaze flickered toward Sekowah, and his fingers clenched around the hilt of his belt dagger—not out of fear, but instinct, as though bracing for the storm of centuries-old prejudice now unleashed in the room.

Old Councilor Trevah, whose wings bore the ash-silver stripes of a warrior past his prime, paced uneasily. "We've not allowed a mortal through the Cove since the Revolution. *The Verses* warned us, long ago. Mortal blood carries echoes of destruction."

"And yet," said Jájá, her voice low and smoking with warning, "*the Verses* also foretold the return of a bridge between worlds. You'd best remember your sacred texts before you drown in ignorance."

Sekowah felt every eye on her. Some stares seared with contempt; others, with the hollow fascination one might give a relic unearthed from a forbidden tomb. She straightened her back despite herself.

"The Cove is sealed!" Brock roared again, his voice echoing off the stone walls. "It's been locked long before you," he spat, pointing an accusatory finger at Jájá, "or you," another jab at Máhí, "were more than a whisper on the lips of your father. What lies beyond those gates will destroy us all. It's... a mirror with bad memory. Doesn't go where you *want* it to—it goes where you *believe* it goes. Big difference." He tapped his temple. "That's why the elders locked it. Thought alone makes a bridge—but not all thoughts are safe to follow, nor are they easily controlled." His eyes darted to Vesper, suspicion flaring. "You knew?"

Vesper stiffened, visibly insulted. He held Brock's gaze, his voice low and dangerous. "Do you know me to be a king who keeps secrets from his council?" He turned to his wife, disbelief burning within his gaze. "Explain yourself."

Jájá's eyes flickered, her fingers lifting unconsciously to the fine gold chain around her neck. She caught herself and dropped her hand, meeting Brock's stare with cool composure.

"The key was given freely," she replied, her voice measured.

"The key was melted," Vesper hissed, his shock rising to anger.

A hint of a smile played on Jájá's lips. "Not so," she said, almost wistfully. "It was spared. I have it still—safeguarded."

A stunned silence fell over the room. Vesper's face twisted with emotion as he drew in a long, controlled breath, and then let it out slowly. "You'll give it to me at once," he commanded, his voice hard.

"I will not." Jájá's tone was unyielding, her eyes blazing with defiance. "It was never yours, nor your father's. It belongs in the valley, as it always has and always will."

Gavril, who had remained silent until now, watched her intently, his eyes darting to Sekowah every so often. She could feel his gaze like a warm weight on her, and it made her pulse quicken, though she tried to keep her focus on the conversation. The words being exchanged were half-understood, fragments of old resentments and secrets that she couldn't quite grasp, but the tension in the room was clear. This was more than a family quarrel; it was a reckoning.

Brock stoved his pipe at a steady speed, filling the room with the scent of cloves. Jájá and Máhí, oddly, breathed in the air and opened their mouths ever so slightly to exhale. Sekowah wasn't sure why, but she instinctively followed suit, and breathed in deep, letting her breath slowly slip from her lips, focusing on Gavril, the only kind face in the room.

Gavril broke the silence, his tone calm but edged with amusement. "I'll give it to you, Jájá," he said. "This is a bold plan."

"If there is any truth to the Prophecy," Vesper muttered, skepticism coloring his voice.

At the mention of the Prophecy, Sekowah's ears perked up, a surge of protectiveness flaring in her chest. She had no reason to believe in the Prophecy, no personal connection to it, yet hearing it dismissed so casually stung. What was this Prophecy, really? Who had woven its words, and for what purpose?

"Has *the Verses* ever been wrong?" Jájá's voice softened, becoming almost musical, seductive.

"Interpret them as you will," Vesper replied, crossing his arms and narrowing his eyes. "They are the incoherent ramblings of an outcast, from long before the reign of King Marin."

Jájá stepped closer to him, her voice a low, throaty murmur as she exhaled clover-scented breath. "A prophet and mystic," she whispered, her eyes locking with his, "who foretold your father's fall from grace."

That one stung. Sekowah saw Vesper's eyes flash, a flicker of pain crossing his face before he could hide it.

"Bah!" Vesper snapped, waving her away dismissively. "His end was inevitable. A rock could have predicted it."

But Gavril, standing close to Máhí, appeared intrigued. He kept his gaze on Sekowah, a flicker of something—hope? curiosity?—in his eyes. "I'm inclined to agree with the queen," he said. "If what she says is true, if the emerald is restored... the valley's crops would flourish again. We'd have enough land to broker a truce with the Dokar."

Máhí's posture relaxed slightly, though her expression remained skeptical. "You'd need more than luck to convince Faylen," she muttered.

Vesper's brow furrowed, but he seemed to soften, an idea forming. He turned back to Jájá, his gaze calculating. "If the curse were lifted," he mused, "perhaps Faylen would concede. And I... I might, as well."

Jájá, seeing her opening, exhaled another waft of clover essence into the air, the invisible tendrils wafting toward Vesper. "Go on."

Vesper's eyes glazed over, his voice dropping to a mumble. "If the curse were lifted, and she brought us the emerald... we could restore the land, strike a deal with the Dokar..." His fingers drummed absently on his desk, the gears of his mind turning.

Sekowah, watching in fascination, felt her own breath catch. The clover-scented air had softened the room, the hostility ebbing away, replaced by a strange, quiet introspection. She looked around; Jájá and Máhí had closed in around Vesper, their expressions intense but serene. Gavril seemed unaffected, yet his watchful gaze stayed on Sekowah, and Brock, ever astute, observed it all with a wry smile, his pipe smoke wreathing his head like a crown.

Brock circled Vesper and Gavril, curiosity evident in his posture. "A truce, eh?" he scoffed, raising an eyebrow. "Are ye daft? The Dokar will have our throats in a day."

Sekowah, emboldened by the clovers, spoke up, her voice steady. "Perhaps a temporary truce is possible?"

Brock looked at her, his eyes narrow. "Temporary, you say?" He tilted his head, as though weighing her words. "Nay, but... what about slave camps, eh? We rescue them from the giants and give them work, food, shelter..." His voice trailed off, thoughtful.

Trevah, standing on the outer edges of the group, furrowed his brow. "Let's not forget Faylen's treasons." He gave Jájá a nod of respect. "No offense to the family of course."

The queen lifted her chin and blinked: *no offense taken.*

Vesper, his eyes half-lidded, looked out the window at his lands, desolate and scarred by neglect. "Slave camps..." he murmured. He swayed slightly, appearing almost drunk. "It could be an equitable compromise. We save them from the giants, and in return..." His gaze sharpened as he turned to Jájá. "I'll restore your valley. And in exchange, you give me my daughter back, and bring an end to your senseless feud."

Gavril, stepping forward, asked the question that had been on everyone's mind. "What of Zincubus?" he said. "He won't stand idly by. He'll fight us."

A tight smile crossed Vesper's lips, his arrogance returning. "Zincubus?" he scoffed. "He's a fly in my father's tomb. He is one. We are many."

Jájá chewed another handful of clover, swallowing as the others gathered by the window, their faces illuminated by the dying light. "I would consider your offer," she said finally, her voice calm but laced with authority. "But only with conditions."

Vesper turned back to her, interest gleaming in his eyes. "Conditions?"

"We will have an equal voice on the Council," Jájá said, her tone leaving no room for argument. "A new Council that brings us together—the Nezkwah, the Lirian..." Her gaze flickered to Brock, acknowledging him with a slight nod, "and the elder fathers. I believe they should have several seats given their help during the Revolution."

Brock, his pipe clamped in his mouth, raised an eyebrow, clearly pleased. "Kind of ye to remember," he murmured.

Jájá's gaze was unyielding. "And the Zahnene will be freed from servitude. At once."

Then, she took Vesper's hands in her own, her clover-scented breath drifting across his lips as she leaned in, her voice soft but firm. "And the gem web—restored in full. Every single one."

Vesper blinked, his resolve crumbling in her presence. "Done."

Sekowah was astonished. Her mother's expert persuasion had turned the snarling wolf into a harmless pup. She fought to keep her excitement hidden, bowing her head in what she hoped was respectful acquiescence.

Jájá turned her back to Vesper, and he moved with surprising tenderness, unfastening the harness from her shoulders. Gavril followed suit, unbuckling Máhí's restraints. For a moment, they all stood in quiet understanding—a fragile truce forged from the whispers of old grudges.

Vesper handed the harness to Jájá, his voice softened. "I'll send word to Faylen," he said. "She'll resume her place here, with us. And you," he turned to Máhí, "will see that she is... accommodated."

Máhí gave a curt nod. "You have my word." She took Sekowah by the elbow, her grip firm but warm, guiding her toward the door.

As they left the room, shaking out their wings and whispering in soft, triumphant murmurs, Sekowah lingered just out of sight, listening. She heard Vesper's voice, taut with confusion and wonder. "Can someone explain to me what just happened?"

Brock's rumbling chuckle followed. "Ya made a wise decision, eh? Yah. A very wise one indeed."

Brock emerged, nearly bumping into Sekowah in the hallway. He grinned, his eyes twinkling as he tipped an imaginary hat to her. "Pardon me, Princess," he said with a smirk, before shaking his head in bemusement and trailing after the others.

Sekowah stood for a moment, her heart racing, feeling the weight of what had just been set in motion. In that dim corridor, she felt the strange pull of destiny, winding tighter around her, drawing her toward a path that was as exhilarating as it was terrifying.

Chapter Twenty

OBSIDIA

In the shadowed depths of the Pine Bogs, where sunlight was all but a myth, Vesper and Jájá dismounted their familiars in a small clearing just beyond the meadow's edge. The sky here was a brooding swirl of storm clouds, an oppressive darkness above them, as though Zincubus himself had wound the heavens into this churning darkness. The forest loomed ahead, its ancient trees cloaked in heavy strands of Shade Bane moss. Rain dripped endlessly from their branches, pooling in the rich black soil below.

The familiars shifted uneasily, ears flicking back as they surveyed the forest. Even they sensed the sinister energy here; a place where nature herself seemed haunted, cursed by the darkness Zincubus had cast over the land. The animals refused to set foot in the forest, backing away from the tree line with nervous whinnies and shudders. Vesper and Jájá were left to proceed on foot, crossing the threshold into the oppressive gloom of Obsidia, a region known now only in whispers.

Jájá hesitated as they stepped into the shadows, her hearts pounding. Twenty harvests had passed since she last ventured out of her captivity, and the rumors about Obsidia—the dreadful transformations wrought upon it since Zincubus claimed it—were enough to make even the bravest heart falter. Once called the Healers Wood, this place had been a haven, a thriving ecosystem of rare herbs and healing plants tended by the Nezkwah healers. But now, it felt like something ancient and sacred had been violated, twisted into a hollow parody of its former self.

They moved carefully through the bog's uneven terrain, their steps muffled by the thick layer of wet moss underfoot. The forest floor was a lush but treacherous landscape of mushrooms—black-capped amanitas, and glowing green toadstools—sprouting from the base of boulders slick with slime. Scattered about in bunches, horsetail reeds rose from the bog, like arrows, ready to slice the soles of the unfortunate. Vesper, always impatient, pushed ahead, paying little attention to the toxic beauty around them. Jájá, however, could not help but linger over every strange new specimen she encountered, her eyes wide with fascination even as a quiet dread settled over her. She stooped to pluck a purple mushroom with fluorescent green dots growing from the side of a fallen log, careful to wrap it in cloth before stashing it in her satchel.

"Indigo Maginasius," she murmured to Vesper, a touch of excitement in her voice. "I thought it was gone forever."

Vesper barely glanced at her, his impatience seeping through his every movement. "You can forage on the way back," he snapped. His voice was tight, almost brittle, as if he could feel the weight of the darkness pressing in on them, just as she could.

Around them, the forest pulsed with an eerie life. In the absence of sunlight, the ecosystem had shifted in strange, almost sinister ways. Fireflies darted through the shadows in dense clusters, their glow casting a ghostly, stuttering light that illuminated the hollow eye sockets of tree trunks and the glistening scales of enormous centipedes coiled around branches. Owls, bats, and other nocturnal creatures flitted silently through the darkness, their eyes gleaming like scattered gems in the underbrush.

As they followed a narrow, winding trail deeper into the bog, Jájá could feel the heavy, sticky spores clinging to her skin, filling the air with a musky, decaying scent. She covered her face with a black flaxen scarf, leaving only her eyes exposed, giving her an air of an outlaw—an apt disguise, she thought, for someone trespassing in Zincubus' kingdom. Vesper did the same, though he was more focused on the path ahead than the choking atmosphere around them.

They finally arrived at the edge of a clearing where two towering obelisk statues marked the entrance to the obsidian caves. Each was hewn from polished black stone, streaked with rainbows of color that shimmered in the dim light, giving off a deep, humming energy. The sight unsettled Jájá; these statues hadn't been here when she was last here. She could feel the buzz of some otherworldly magic vibrating through her bones, a frequency just on the edge of her perception.

Between the statues was a heavy steel gate, set with thick iron bars that gleamed with oil. Beyond it, standing like a figure carved from shadow, was Faylen. Beside her, a winged black panther with glinting yellow eyes watched them with an intelligence that sent a chill down Jájá's spine. The panther was enormous, standing taller than a horse, its sleek body adorned with black and silver leopard spots that shifted as it paced in front of Faylen, ever ready to protect her.

Faylen's gaze locked onto Vesper. "Hello, Father," she said, her voice cold, hollow. She didn't spare any effort on her mother.

Jájá's hearts twisted at the sight of her daughter, changed beyond recognition. Beneath the fierce anger in her face, Jájá saw a glimmer of the child she had once adored—a bright, fearless girl, now encased in bitterness and hurt. A pang of regret surged through her. Had she been too harsh, too quick to judge, when she'd cast the curse upon her all those years ago? She searched Faylen's face for a trace of forgiveness, but all she saw was the deep red aura of anger and betrayal emanating from her.

Vesper stepped forward, his hand reaching instinctively for Jájá's as though to steady himself. "Your mother and I have discussed—" he began, but Faylen cut him off with a snarl, her eyes flashing.

"I'm not interested in favors," she hissed, her gaze finally lingering on Jájá.

Jájá swallowed her rising anger, forcing herself to stay calm. She managed a smile, though it wavered. "Darling. I mean you no harm," she said softly, willing herself to remember the child she had loved, the girl she had once cradled in her arms. Somewhere, under all that bitterness, she hoped her Faylen was still there.

Vesper's voice was gentler now, paternal. "Don't be stubborn, daughter. Your mother has come a long way to offer her hand in peace."

Jájá bowed her head. "Can we come in?" she asked, voice barely above a whisper.

Faylen tilted her head, the movement sharp and reptilian. "Well," she sneered, "I can't come out, can I?"

Her bitterness was stronger than Jájá had anticipated. What had Zincubus done to her? What poison had he planted in her mind over these twenty seasons? Jájá took a deep breath, trying to steady her nerves. "We must return the emerald to the Cave of Song," she implored, hoping to find some common ground. "The valley is dying without it. The crops are failing."

Faylen's face remained impassive. "We need it here," she said, her tone ice-cold, devoid of empathy.

"Faylen, you know as well as I that if the valley dies, all of us will suffer," Jájá said, a note of desperation creeping into her voice.

Faylen's lip curled, her tone laced with disdain. "Your confidence is naïve," she replied. "If the valley dies, we will survive here. We will create a new balance."

Desperate, Jájá extended a hand through the bars, reaching out to her daughter. "Don't you want to come home?" she whispered. "We miss you."

A flicker of something—perhaps regret—crossed Faylen's face. Her reptilian eyelids blinked, slow and deliberate. "There is nothing for me at Peregrine's Keep," she murmured, voice barely audible.

Jájá's hearts sank. Despite her anger, despite her flaws, she had hoped against hope that time would heal this rift. But the pain in her daughter's eyes was a wound too deep, too infected with bitterness. She wondered if they would ever find peace.

Vesper stepped forward, his voice softer now, more coaxing. "A new council has formed, Faylen," he said. "A seat at the table will be yours."

Jájá rummaged in her satchel and withdrew a small blue vial. "With Máhí's blessing," she added, hoping this offering would soften her daughter's heart.

Faylen held out her hand for the vial, but Jájá kept it just out of reach. After a long, tense moment, Faylen unlocked the gate with a cold, defiant stare and stepped back, allowing them to enter. Her familiar growled as Jájá crossed the threshold, his yellow eyes gleaming with suspicion.

"Do you have the emerald?" Jájá asked, her voice barely concealing the urgency beneath her calm facade.

"First things first," Faylen replied, standing firm, eyes narrowed.

Vesper gave Jájá a small nod, urging her forward. With a sense of reluctance, Jájá handed over the vial. Faylen took it greedily, pulling the cork free and drinking it down in one gulp. Jájá watched, a shudder of revulsion passing through her at her daughter's eagerness, her feral hunger.

Jájá was repulsed by her demeanor but knew that the curse was at work deep within her. Her ugliness was not simply skin deep. Her hearts had grown dark, and her vision was altered by the change as well. With the snakeskin, had come a reptilian nature: cold, calculating, emotionally dull. Jájá reached into her pockets, anxious to see her daughter return to true form, to be released from her torture. She pulled gold sand from her robe pockets and scattered it in the air around her. "Where once were scales, return to flesh," the enchantress spoke. "Blood of snake, heart of stone. Return to softness, silk and bone."

The gold dust transformed into moths, and covered Faylen's entire body, their wings fluttering ... and after several moments, they flew off and down a corridor, leaving her transformed. Her scales gone, her snake eyes gone, her Lirian eyes now a vibrant gold—she was flawless. Her skin turned a milky brown with deep undertones. Her bat wings disappeared, leaving in their place the dark tan and grey speckled wings of her former time.

As Faylen scooped up her cape off the floor to cover herself, Jájá tenderly helped her, pulling her cape around her shoulders with a soft whisper. "There she is."

Vesper's eyes filled with tears as he moved to embrace her, overwhelmed by her restored beauty. For a brief, fragile moment, Faylen's face softened, a glimmer of the daughter he remembered. She returned his embrace, and then turned to Jájá, a tight smile on her lips.

"Wait here," she said softly, slipping away into the shadows beyond the gate.

As Jájá and Vesper waited, a cautious hope flickered in Jájá's heart. Perhaps, just perhaps, the curse had not entirely taken her daughter from her. But the forest around them seemed to breathe with a dark anticipation, as if Zincubus himself were watching from the shadows, waiting for the moment when their fragile peace would splinter once again.

Chapter Twenty-One

THE KISS

In her new chambers at Peregrine's Keep, Sekowah stood before an ornate mirror, watching Máhí fuss over the finishing touches of her gown. The fabric, a fine mint chiffon, shimmered in the dim candlelight, draping off her shoulders and cinching elegantly at the waist, where clusters of pearls caught the light and gleamed softly. Emerald lace traced a delicate pattern across the bodice, curling around her arms and spilling down the sides of the floor-length skirt. Máhí was currently threading the back with feathers—white and soft, too fine and fragile to be mistaken for real wings, yet they gave her an ethereal appearance. The feathers were anchored with silvery thread that Máhí wove skillfully into the fabric.

Sekowah felt both awe and trepidation as she studied her reflection. The canopy bed behind her was dressed in deep blue velvet, its heavy curtains tied back to reveal pillows of burgundy and gold. Rich woolen rugs covered the stone floor in intricate patterns, and the dark wood bookcases—some crammed with books, others with strange glass trinkets—stood like silent guardians against the walls. She felt as if she'd stepped into a world that didn't belong to her, and she wondered, uneasily, if she'd ever truly belong to it.

Máhí worked quickly, attaching the last feather with a deft flick of her needle. She studied her half-sister's reflection in the mirror, a hint of mischief playing at the corners of her mouth. "There. Fit for a queen," she said, though her tone held a trace of amusement, as if the whole charade tickled her more than she let on.

Sekowah's gaze dropped, her fingers brushing the chiffon of her skirt. "Do you stay here?" she asked quietly, unsure if she wanted to hear the answer.

Máhí let out a soft laugh. "No, no, no. I have a nest in the valley. But I won't abandon you. Not yet." She tugged a silvery thread into place and then glanced up, meeting

Sekowah's eyes in the mirror. There was a warmth there, a silent promise. Yet it was laced with something else—a reluctance, perhaps, or a knowledge of things unsaid.

"Why not you?" Sekowah asked, her voice barely above a whisper. "You're the oldest. It should be you."

Máhí snorted, a playful gleam in her eye. "I'm no mortal. No offense." She twisted Sekowah's hair, fastening it with a lotus flower she'd plucked from the Moon Garden. "Besides, do I look like a queen?" She laughed, the sound light but carrying an edge, as if she found the idea both absurd and distasteful.

Sekowah looked down, her fingers tightening around the fabric of her gown. "What if I can't?" The words came out in a rush, betraying a fear she hadn't meant to voice.

Máhí's expression softened, and she placed a reassuring hand on Sekowah's shoulder. "You can. Trust me." She stepped back, taking in her handiwork with a satisfied nod. "Elegant. Regal. You're a natural."

Sekowah gave her a tentative smile, though the weight of the dress seemed heavier than before. She wanted to believe her sister, but the doubt gnawed at her, a quiet, insistent whisper at the back of her mind.

· · · • ⟨⟨⟩⟩ • · · · ·

Out on a stone balcony overlooking the Moon Garden, Gavril stood alone, dressed in a leather suit that caught the moonlight, his dark hair pulled back into tight braids. Potted ferns and ivy spilled over the edges of the balustrade, mingling with climbing roses that tangled in delicate abandon. The flowers had been placed there after Jájá's return to the upper castle, a part of her relentless quest to restore beauty to every corner of Peregrine's Keep. The air was thick with the fragrance of blooms, the heady scent of lilac and rose: a reminder of how different the Keep had become in just a few suns.

Sekowah caught sight of him from the hallway as she left her chambers, pausing when she saw his silhouette against the night sky. Cleaned up for the banquet, dressed in finery, he looked majestic—his face softened in thought, his profile illuminated by the glow of the rose-tinted moon. She hesitated, her heart pounding with a strange mix of excitement and unease. He seemed so self-contained, so lost in his own world, and for a moment she wondered if she dared disturb him.

She took a step onto the balcony, her silk-clad feet soundless against the stone. "So many stars," she murmured, her voice breaking the stillness.

He turned to her, surprise flashing briefly in his eyes before they softened. Their gazes locked, and in that instant, a flicker of recognition passed between them—something deeper than familiarity, an echo of something half-remembered, as though they had shared a lifetime together in another world, another time. The feeling left her breathless, vulnerable.

"Stars?" he asked, an innocence to his voice.

Sekowah found herself holding her breath, unsure if the information she knew about the night sky would be troubling for him to hear. How do you explain planets, galaxies and an infinite universe to someone in a sentence, in a word? "Yes. Those little dots of light. We call them stars." She saved her revelations for another day, another night perhaps, when the weight of the evening was lighter.

"I see only one star tonight," he replied, his voice soft as he held her gaze. His words sent a rush of warmth through her, and she looked away, flustered, her cheeks flushing.

She moved to stand beside him, their shoulders almost touching, and they gazed out in silence over the Moon Garden and the mountain range beyond. Small fires dotted the upper ridge, where the Lirian encampments nestled, casting a warm glow that mingled with the starlight. Beyond the fires, far into the distance, twin waterfalls shimmered under the moon's gaze, their silver threads cutting through the dark rock like veins of light.

Sekowah could feel his eyes on her, a steady weight that both thrilled and unsettled her. She gripped the cold marble of the rail, searching for words, anything to break the silence that had grown thick with possibility. "What do you think about the slave camps?" she asked, her voice catching slightly. The thought had haunted her since she'd first heard of the plan. The idea that her suggestion for peace could result in such suffering turned her stomach.

Gavril's expression darkened, his wings ruffling as he looked away. "Barbaric," he said flatly. "We'll trade a war at the border for one within our own walls."

"Why can't they just live here... with everyone else?" She didn't know where the words came from; they were out before she could stop herself.

He shook his head, a sadness shadowing his face. "We've been at war for too long. Old grudges don't simply die. It would only be a matter of time before those old wounds festered, leaving us vulnerable." He paused, then offered her a small, regretful smile. "But it's not something you should worry about. Not tonight. This is your night."

"Yeah. My night. Whoohoo." She forced a small, self-conscious laugh and gave him a "thumbs up" in a mock celebration.

Gavril looked at her in confusion, his brows drawing together. "What is that?" he asked, tilting his head.

"What?"

"Your thumb... in the air." He gave her a puzzled smile. "Is that some kind of spell?"

Sekowah glanced at her own thumb, startled, as if it belonged to someone else. The gesture felt natural, yet strange, like a fragment of a memory from a life half-forgotten. "I... I think it just means I agree." The answer came out awkward, but it felt right.

"If you say so." He gave a bemused chuckle.

They fell silent again, and her gaze drifted down to the garden below, where trellises of flowering vines arched over a circular maze, its pathways lined with lanterns. She imagined herself running through it with Gavril, her hand in his, their laughter echoing in the night. The image was so vivid, so real, that she could almost feel his fingers entwined with hers, his breath against her cheek. She didn't know if it was a memory, a dream, or simply a wish.

Lost in her thoughts, she barely noticed when he reached out and took her hand. The warmth of his skin startled her, and she looked up to find his face close to hers, his eyes intense. Her heart raced, and instinct took over; she let go of his hand, crossed her arms tightly, held her earlobes, closing her eyes and holding her breath, leaving only a shimmer of herself in his presence.

Gavril chuckled softly, his voice tinged with amusement. "I see someone's been teaching you a few tricks," he murmured, his tone playful but warm.

She let herself reappear behind him, tapping him on the shoulder with a mischievous grin. He turned, laughter dancing in his eyes. "And you've inherited your mother's mischief as well," he said, and before she could react, he reached out, cradling her face in his hands. His touch was gentle, hesitant, as though he feared she might vanish again if he held her too tightly. Then he leaned in, brushing his lips against hers, a kiss both tender and electric.

For a moment, time slipped away. The fears and doubts that had haunted her melted, replaced by the simple, undeniable warmth of his embrace.

· · · · ● ⬭ ● · · · ·

Deep in the vault, the emerald glowed, its green light pulsing with newfound energy. Faylen held a small fox-fur blanket in her arms, her gaze fixed on the gem. She knew what it meant. Sekowah's presence, her growing connection to the land, was reviving the valley's life force. The emerald, responding to her energy, pulsed with an almost feral intensity.

A bitter smile curled on Faylen's lips. The plan she and Zincubus had woven in secret had begun to unfold, and though she had once felt conviction, now a flicker of doubt gnawed at her. Her true form, restored by her mother's spell, had unearthed old loyalties she had buried deep. But loyalty was a double-edged sword, and her loyalty to Zincubus had sharpened with years of bitterness.

She shook the feelings away. What had to be done, would be done.

"You haven't said a word about my new look," she remarked coolly, as Zincubus approached and removed the emerald from its pedestal, placing it carefully in her arms.

He smirked, his gaze lingering on her, appraising her. "I preferred the bad-girl look, to be honest," he sneered, the words slicing through her pride.

Faylen swallowed her anger, forcing herself to meet his eyes with a mask of indifference. She hid her revulsion and contempt for the man that she had shared her life with for the last two dozen harvests and wrapped the emerald in the blanket. *Does he ever have a kind word for me?*

"But I wouldn't turn you away on a dark night," he added, pulling her into a possessive embrace.

Disgust stirred within her, but she hid it well, suppressing the urge to recoil. "I'll see you tomorrow night," she murmured, extricating herself with grace.

With a swish of her new wings, she vanished into the darkness, carrying the emerald wrapped in fur: a precious offering for the game they had set in motion, the weight of old grievances and fresh wounds heavy in her heart.

CHAPTER TWENTY-TWO

RETURN OF TWO DAUGHTERS

A t one time, the celebration room had been the heart of Peregrine's Keep, before Vesper had taken control of the valley and consigned Jájá to the dungeon. Grand feasts had once filled this space, honoring births, harvests, rites of passage, and the mating ceremonies that bonded generations of Lirian and Nezkwah alike. Máhí could still remember her own first rites here, where she'd been given the choice that had felt both liberating and inevitable: to join the nesters or vow her loyalty to the king's fleet. Her decision had been as swift as it was fierce—there had been no calling greater than the warrior's path, a path she'd watched her father train for tirelessly in the arena when she was just a nestling.

Her mother's face had been drawn and silent that day, unable to mask her disappointment. Jájá had wanted a different life for her eldest, one grounded in roots rather than swords. But Máhí had only felt a hunger for the thrill of the fight, the sharp clarity that came with risking life and limb. It was a life she had embraced without hesitation. Warriors were forbidden from mating, but that restriction hadn't mattered to her. She'd never felt love's stirring—at least, not in the way it seemed to stir in others. The warriors kept their distance from her, the king's daughter, treating her with reverence and a hint of wariness. She'd preferred it that way, her life a clean, ordered thing: duty, combat, loyalty, nothing more.

Now, as she paraded herself through the gathering crowd, Máhí marveled at the transformation of the celebration room. It had once been left to dust, reduced to little more than an unorganized armory. But after days of supervising workers who polished, dusted, and scrubbed every inch, the space sparkled with new life. It pleased her to see it reclaimed from decay, though the pride she felt surprised her; she'd always believed her true loyalty lay outside these walls, in the valley's wild forests. And yet, seeing the room glow again, its stones restored to life, stirred something deep within her.

Along the back wall, tables were piled high with all manner of delicacies: pear tarts, chee-chee dumplings, violet snaps, and pitchers of lilac wine, contributions from the Nezkwah and Zahnene in celebration of tonight's truce. The Lirian had prepared their own offerings as well—rabbit stew and roasted boar. Máhí filled a small oak bowl with violet snaps, savoring the earthy crunch as she wove her way through the crowd, nodding to familiar faces.

The atmosphere was jovial but tense all the same. Lirian guards, once commissioned to patrol the outskirts of the valley, mingled with Nezkwah, who were none too pleased to have conversation with such heartless sorts. For their part, the Lirian were apprehensive, as rumor had already spread that the new council would include more Nezkwah, and they feared retribution, she imagined. *Good*, thought Máhí, *let them revisit their crimes. It will be good for them.*

She glanced up at the chandeliers, where a small gathering of Zahnene had taken up their usual perch. They pointed and giggled from above, gossiping as they observed each new guest from their vantage point near the ceiling. One of them, a daring youngling, waved and pointed insistently toward a figure in the crowd, but from her vantage, Máhí couldn't see who or what had caught their attention. Probably some poorly dressed noble, she thought, amused.

The floor beneath her feet was a mosaic of colorful tiles, restored to their original vibrancy. The arched stained-glass windows framed sweeping portraits of kings and queens from long ago, their gazes watching over the gathering with a regal, stoic pride. Máhí lingered in front of the portrait of King Marin, her grandfather. Her memories of him were faint now, but she could still recall his warm laughter, the way he'd lifted her into the air as a child, her tiny wings beating against his chest. He had led the rebellion that had freed the valley from the tyrannical rule of Ragjoy and Camelia, bringing balance and prosperity to the land. *It is a shame*, she thought, *that his legacy was so quickly forgotten by her father.*

Máhí shook her head, pulling herself from the past. Politics, she thought. The eternal pendulum. She wanted no part of it. That was why, despite her mother's pleas, she'd refused to take her place in line for the throne. That duty, they had agreed, would fall to

Sekowah. And tonight, Máhí prayed they had made the right choice. The future of the valley hung in the balance.

Overhead, the ceiling had been painted in swirling patterns of gold and silver, with arched beams that soared to dizzying heights. Iron chains held chandeliers strung with an array of colored gems, casting a rainbow of light that shimmered across the stone walls, turning the room into a kaleidoscope of color. Festive. Joyful.

At the front of the room, a marble platform held a group of Nezkwah minstrels and a Zahnene dance troupe. Drums, flutes, mandolins, and chimes filled the air with their haunting, lilting melodies, weaving a rich tapestry of sound that made the stone walls hum. The celebration room had come alive, its echoes full of laughter, music, and the murmur of voices.

At the long table along the western wall sat Vesper, Brock, Gavril, Jájá, Sekowah, and Faylen, each dressed in their finest attire. Guests approached the table to offer gifts to Sekowah, who accepted them with a grace and confidence that seemed to surprise even her. She looked every bit the young queen, radiant and poised. Jájá glowed with pride as she watched her daughter, and Máhí felt a flicker of satisfaction herself. Sekowah had come a long way, and perhaps, just perhaps, she would be strong enough for the role ahead.

Máhí, as was her custom, arrived last, acknowledging each at the table with a nod before taking her place beside her mother. Jájá stood, lifting a glass of wine, waiting for the room to quiet.

"Tonight, we celebrate the return of two daughters!" she announced, her voice ringing out clear and strong. She gestured toward Sekowah and Faylen, who both rose to scattered applause.

Nezkwah and Zahnene chittered and hissed as they glared at Faylen. Old grudges and gossip do not simply fade away at the first sign of peace. Máhí knew Faylen would have to prove herself, not only to the valley, but to her as well. She suspended her suspicions, fearing it was temporary but holding out a small bit of hope that she had changed.

Vesper stood beside Jájá, raising his glass. "Friends, tonight we end the occupation of the valley and come together in peace, to strengthen our position against the Dokar," he declared, his voice steady but cautious. "We have much work ahead."

A heckler shouted something from the back of the room. Vesper put his glass down and searched the crowd. "Come forward coward," he shouted.

At the rear of the room, Croody mingled among the Lirian. He lowered his hood. The Zahnene, still hovering near the chandelier, pointed at him again. Máhí searched the crowd, but could not understand who or what they were pointing out to her.

One of the warriors, his speech slurred from having drunk more than his share of mead prior to the party, seized the opportunity, and staggered to the front, anxious to be heard. "Nezkwah have no place on the Council!" His words inspired a chorus of foot stomping and grumbles among the Lirian. Máhí seethed. *No place. I'll show you no place. I'll send you into the Big Dark!*

"Trickery!" A voice rose above the rest. "We know their motives. They cannot fight." Other Lirian joined in, jeering and shouting. Máhí began to stand but felt a firm grip on her knee by her mother.

Old Man Croody yelled from the back, "a changeling no less!" A silence struck the room on the word 'changeling,' and Máhí watched Croody disappear behind a pillar. Hushed whispers traveled among the crowd as all eyes were on Sekowah.

Enough, thought Máhí. *This must be settled or there will be no peace on the Council going forward.* She shook off her mother's grip and stood, left the table and stomped to the center of the room. "I will fight any here."

The Lirian burst into laughter.

The mockery stung, but she embraced the anger, let it fuel her. She was the king's daughter. She had nothing to prove, and yet—she wanted to remind them, all of them, who she was.

One of the warriors, staggering from too much mead, rose to the challenge. "Winner takes Máhí's place on the Council!"

She knew him—Evoch, a soldier she had bested in combat seasons ago. His grudge was no secret. *Challenge me, you drunken idiot? A pleasure!* she thought. Máhí let out a cold laugh, her voice carrying across the room. "Challenge accepted."

She spread her massive wings and rose into the air, holding a petrified wood staff above her head. "Choose your champion!" she shouted, her eyes flashing with defiance.

As she expected, Evoch backed up. Máhí scanned the room, finding the largest among them. She pointed her staff at him. "You."

The warriors shoved Tourik forward. He was, by far, the biggest Lirian in the ranks, with massive shoulders, a thick neck, and braids to his waist. It was rumored that his father was a Kudlah, but none could prove it, and none dared ask.

Guests exchanged bets with small gems and gold coins. Zahnene chittered and shook their heads at Máhí in warning.

The crowd cheered their champion on, "Tourik! Tourik! Tourik!"

Máhí lowered herself to the floor and squared off with her impressive opponent. "We play by the rules of the battlefield," she announced. Which basically meant no rules. Máhí, both a warrior and a skilled user of magic, knew this would be to her advantage.

Vesper left the table, and acted as referee, in the center of the room. He pulled her aside. "Your pride is greater than your might, daughter. Tourik is undefeated. Even in our ranks."

"I know who he is," Máhí said with confidence, pulling her shoulders back, undeterred. Her father's arrogance was his most unflattering weakness, and she was tired of protecting his vanity. "You doubt my training?" she asked. "You think your victories against me were honest wins?"

Vesper raised his eyebrows in mock surprise and exchanged a concerned glance with Jájá but stepped away. "As you wish."

Faylen fixed her sights on Máhí, giddy with delight, anxious to see her sister humiliated. *Watch and learn, little sister*, Máhí thought as she returned the glare. *While you have been squandering your time with Zincubus, I have been preparing. This first blow will be for you.*

Brock, amused, took a swig of his wine and turned to Jájá. "Size doesn't matter," he said. "Wager two bits on Máhí."

Jájá spurned his gamble with stone silence and tight lips.

Tourik stomped over to the eastern wall and removed an iron sword. A small group of Nezkwah flittered along the wall, choosing a sword for Máhí.

Not necessary. I have all I need in my hands and belt, she assured herself.

Máhí waved them off and held to her staff as she and Tourik rushed toward one another, and the crowd backed away to give them space. They both opened their wings and lifted into the air. Tourik's brute swings were powerful, but slow. Máhí flew above and around him with agile avoidance, annoying Tourik's fans, one of whom grabbed on to her foot, giving Tourik a clear shot.

SHHIIIING!

Jájá leaped from the table to aid her but was held back by Vesper.

The sword came down, slicing across Máhí's wing, spraying feathers over the audience. The crowd gasped. Her wing sliced, burning, Máhí dropped to the floor, unable to keep herself aloft. *A nasty trick. He will pay,* she thought.

Máhí jabbed her staff at the warrior who had grabbed her foot, knocking him off balance, then turned swiftly, and struck Tourik with it. A flash of yellow crackled across his chest, stunning him. He faltered, nearly falling, but managed to regain his balance.

Was he immune to magic? Máhí wondered. If so, she would be done before she started.

The Lirian cheered him on as he pulled his wings in close and rushed toward her. They exchanged blows again, Máhí using all her strength to block his mighty swings but was brought to her knees, nonetheless. She would not win this fight by might.

Jájá wrestled herself away from Vesper and called out, "Stop it at once!"

While the crowd was distracted by Jájá's declaration, Máhí reached into her belt and retrieved a green vial, drinking it all. She wiped her mouth, gathered her strength and stood, determination across her face. *He cannot be immune to all magic,* she thought. There was one spell that had never failed her, and she searched her belt for the pink vial.

Evoch pointed at her and turned to Vesper, "Trickery!" he shouted.

Vesper watched his daughter shake off the injury as her wing repaired itself, and he held angry bystanders at bay. "Rules of battle," he reminded everyone. "All is allowed."

"Shake this off, ya kudlah!" Máhí yelled as she flew over Tourik, spreading her wings, and circling him, just out of reach. He thrust his sword into the empty air, as she taunted him, angry now. She pulled the pink vial out and hurled it at the floor.

Jájá, relieved, sat down with a grin and gave Brock a pat on the knee.

The vial shattered, a pink cloud rising from the floor, enveloping Tourik. Confused, he descended to the floor, stumbled about, waiting for what horrible fate awaited him ... then gradually, he began to chuckle. The chuckle turned into laughter, and the laughter became unstoppable. He fell to his knees, holding his sides, tears flowing from his eyes, his bellows both contagious but disturbing all at once.

The audience stared at Tourik as he was tickled by an unseen force. After rolling about on the floor for some time, barely able to breathe, he finally let out a moan and yelled, "Stop! Stop! I concede!"

Máhí lowered herself to the floor, meeting the angry glances from the Lirian. "What's so funny?" The pink vapor spread into the crowd, taking more victim, as they too, collapsed into fits of giggles.

"Take him away," Máhí commanded. "Feed him stinging nettle tea ... he'll return to normal before the moon rises." Máhí commanded.

Nezkwah and Zahnene applauded and nodded their heads, laughing and pointing as the afflicted were helped out of the celebration room.

Máhí returned to her seat at the table and picked at her feathers as bets were settled and music rose into the air.

· · · · • ◯◯ • · · · ·

Gavril, seated beside Sekowah, leaned over with a quiet chuckle. "The Cloud of Laughing. Brilliant."

Sekowah felt her cheeks flush, both horrified and thrilled by Máhí's antics. She was beginning to realize just how much she still didn't understand about this world, its magic, its dangers. When she clinked her glass with Gavril's, a strange warmth tingled through her arm, and she felt the air between them charged with electricity.

Faylen's voice cut through the haze. "Máhí's not known for fighting fair."

Sekowah, emboldened by the lilac wine, looked at her with a cool gaze. "Funny, I've heard the same about you."

Gavril laughed, a rich sound that echoed through the hall. "Careful, Faylen. She may be quiet, but she misses nothing." He winked at Sekowah before rising. "If you'll excuse me, I have a bet to settle." He chuckled once more to himself, gave Faylen an almost imperceptible glance, as though he wasn't quite sure if he should leave Sekowah unattended, then relaxed and left for the main floor.

Faylen picked at what remained on her plate. "He's got his eyes on you, doesn't he?" she asked her half-sister.

Sekowah blushed and Faylen leaned in, refilling her goblet. "Pairing ceremonies are around the corner, and you could do worse. Much worse." She had a mischievous glint to her eyes. "What do you know about the ceremonies?"

Sekowah shifted in her seat. She knew nothing. But it sounded like sex to her, a subject she was not exactly jumping to discuss with a new acquaintance. "I've heard of them. But nobody's explained much to me, I mean, not about that."

"Of course they haven't. They only see things from their perspective and that doesn't include pairing ceremony jitters, which, I will tell you from firsthand experience, is a real thing. They don't think about that at all, do they? Máhí is with the fleet now, and Jájá is far beyond the time of pairing. But I, on the other hand, know everything." She put a reassuring hand on her knee and whispered, "And there's a lot to know."

Sekowah relaxed in her presence, feeling something akin to sisterhood, if even briefly. It was a pleasant break from the lectures that seemed to stream from Máhí's mouth. "I'd like that."

CHAPTER TWENTY-THREE

THE MOON GARDEN

S ekowah lay awake in her new quarters, her mind restless as moonlight spilled in through the window, casting an silver glow across the thick rugs. The evening had left her exhausted, yet sleep remained elusive. The events of the night played over in her mind—a tangle of names, faces, laughter, and whispers, all of them woven with hidden motives she was too new to discern. Everyone in Peregrine's Keep seemed to carry secrets, like precious stones tucked away in dark pockets. She had the sense that each interaction, each lingering look, held layers beyond her comprehension.

Sekowah lay there, drifting in and out of that haunted space between waking and sleep, her thoughts becoming a hazy parade of images and half-formed memories. She found herself envisioning the pairing ceremony Faylen had described earlier—bells and ribbons, candles flickering, couples weaving in dance under a canopy of stars. In her mind's eye, she saw herself there, with Gavril's hand steady around her waist, the warmth of his palm grounding her as they turned together. She could almost feel the weight of his arm, the unspoken promise of safety in his quiet gaze.

Then, as if bubbling up from some forgotten place, a different memory surfaced—a birthday party, the warm smell of candles and cake, the feel of a puppy's soft fur under her fingers. A man and woman laughing beside her, the woman's gentle kiss on her forehead. Sekowah closed her eyes, trying to hold onto the memory, to conjure the scent of the man's cologne, earthy and familiar. The memory comforted her, briefly—but it left a hollow ache in its wake, and she felt an unexpected pang of loss for those people—*who were they?*—they felt like family, but now, she wasn't sure.

She shifted restlessly in bed, trying to find a position that would lull her to sleep. She was on the verge of surrendering to the unease that curled around her thoughts when the door creaked open, pulling her sharply into the present. A shadow stretched across the far wall, gliding closer to her bed, and her body went still, tense with apprehension. Her first thought was Gavril. But as the figure drew nearer, she saw the shape resolve into a familiar silhouette.

Faylen.

Her half-sister sat softly on the edge of her bed, her expression mischievous in the dim light. Sekowah felt her pulse quicken. She hadn't yet settled on how she felt about Faylen. The warmth between them earlier had surprised her; Faylen was lively, charming even, her laughter infectious. Yet Máhí and Jájá's warnings lingered like a sour taste. Could she trust her?

"Shhhhh," Faylen whispered, placing a hand on Sekowah's shoulder, her touch cool and feather-light. "I want to show you something." She tossed a silk robe onto the bed, and Sekowah, curiosity stirring in spite of herself, slipped it over her nightdress, its fabric whispering against her skin.

"Where are we going?" she asked, voice barely above a murmur. She spied a satchel Faylen carried under her cloak, which glowed a bright green. "What's that?"

Faylen smiled, a glint of mischief in her eyes. She took Sekowah's hand in hers. "I thought you'd like to see the Moon Garden. To smell the lucklace. It only blooms under the full moon." Her tone softened, her expression almost vulnerable. "Mother's pride and joy."

Then, unexpectedly, Faylen pulled her into a hug, and the tension in Sekowah's shoulders melted. The embrace was brief, but genuine, and it left Sekowah feeling unsteady. "I'm so glad to finally have a sister I can trust," Faylen murmured, the words wrapping around Sekowah like a warm blanket.

As they made their way down the quiet corridors, Sekowah felt like a child sneaking out for a forbidden adventure. The castle was still, moonlight pooling in the alcoves and staining the stone walls with shades of blue and green as it filtered through the stained-glass windows. Shadows shifted and danced as they descended the staircase, and Sekowah couldn't help but feel a thrill of excitement. The castle felt alive tonight, like it was watching them, its ancient eyes blinking open after centuries of slumber.

· · · · ◯◯ · · · ·

F aylen led Sekowah into the Moon Garden, her hand warm and firm as she guided her through statues of royal ancestors and past stone benches weathered by
time. They followed a winding pebble path into the hedge maze, turning corner after
corner, hushed laughter bubbling from their lips as they navigated the labyrinthine
paths. The cool night air carried the subtle scent of distant flowers, mingling with
the thrill of secrecy that hung between them.

At the center of the maze, they reached a trellis dripping with vines. White
blossoms hung in clusters, their petals unfurling in the moonlight, releasing a scent
that was rich with delicacy. Faylen plucked one of the blooms, its delicate petals
glowing under the moon's gaze. "Smell." She lifted it to Sekowah's nose and let her
breathe in the scent.

It was sweet. Intoxicating. She inhaled, her eyes fluttering.

"Oooh," she murmured, half in wonder, half in confusion. "I feel... strange."

The world seemed to shift around her, the garden tilting gently, the sky swirling
with stars that pulsed and spun. A warm, tingling sensation spread through her
fingers and toes, and she let out a soft, breathless giggle, stumbling slightly as the
ground beneath her feet seemed to ripple.

Faylen caught her arm, steadying her, her eyes glittering as she watched Sekowah.
Behind the trellis, a shadow moved, and a figure emerged, stepping into the silvery
light.

Zincubus.

He moved with a grace that was both elegant and predatory, his dark gaze fixed
on Sekowah. He held a bouquet of lilies of the valley, their tiny white bells trembling.
Sekowah swayed on her feet, struggling to focus as her mind swam with fragments
of memory and sensation.

"Oh," she said, blinking at him, her voice light and girlish, almost a whisper.
"Hello. I don't believe we've met. I'm Sekowah. I'm... a princess." She gave a clumsy
curtsy, the gesture strangely innocent, almost absurdly so. Her eyelids fluttered, and
she batted her lashes, her smile hazy.

"So I hear," he replied, his tone edged with something dangerous. "I've brought
you a gift."

He extended the lilies, his dark eyes never leaving her face. There was something
unsettling about the way he looked at her, as though he were sizing her up, peeling
back her skin in his mind to see what lay hidden underneath.

A flicker of recognition sparked in Sekowah's dazed mind—a memory, sharp and clear, of a face in the looking pond. The same dark eyes, the same cruel, watchful expression.

"Wait," she mumbled, taking a stumbling step back. "I... I know you. I saw you in the looking pond." She turned to Faylen, her face a mixture of hurt and confusion. The realization crept over her slowly, like ink bleeding into water. "Faylen...?"

But Faylen's expression remained cool, calm even. She took the bouquet from Zincubus, her fingers grazing the silver bells of the flowers as she gave them a small shake. The bells chimed softly, a lullaby that seemed to reach into Sekowah's mind, wrapping around her thoughts and pulling them down, down, into a dark, soothing void.

"Sleep," Faylen whispered, her voice soft, almost tender.

Sekowah's vision blurred, the world around her slipping into a haze. Her mind spun, her thoughts scattering like leaves in a windstorm, drifting just out of reach. She felt herself sinking, her limbs heavy, as though the earth itself were drawing her into its embrace.

"Or was that... someone else?" she murmured, her voice slurring, barely audible. "I... can't remember..."

She yawned, the simple motion feeling like an immense, impossible task. Her knees buckled, and she sank to the ground, her body folding in on itself as the weight of sleep pressed down on her. Zincubus knelt behind her, his hands cold as they wrapped around her shoulders, catching her before she could fully collapse.

"That's my girl," he murmured, his voice a low, possessive purr as he cradled her limp form in his arms. The moonlight cast long shadows over them, making his face a mask of darkness. Without another word, he turned, carrying Sekowah's unconscious form into the shadows of the Moon Garden, his figure melting into the darkness.

Chapter Twenty-Four

BLOOD AND LIES

In the dim chill of the early morning, Peregrine's Keep was alive with frantic voices echoing through the ancient corridors. Doors slammed. Footsteps thundered. Servants and guards shouted Sekowah's name, their voices rising in urgency, reverberating through the empty spaces.

On the back balcony, Vesper stood rigid, hands gripping the marble railing as he looked out over the shadowy maze. His face was drawn in anger.

Behind him, the doors flew open with a bang, and Máhí burst onto the balcony, out of breath, her cheeks flushed and streaked with tears. She held a single Lucklace bloom in her hand, its white petals trembling, luminous in the morning light. She shoved it in Vesper's face, her voice thick with rage.

"This is your fault," she hissed. Faylen and the emerald were missing, and the bloom—a flower that only blossomed under the full moon, was plucked from the vine—it could mean only one thing. Sekowah had been taken. Her sister had betrayed them all.

Vesper's chest heaved, his gaze unwavering, refusing to meet Máhí's eyes. He seemed to be somewhere else.

Jájá appeared behind Máhí, her face tense as she pulled her daughter back into Sekowah's sleeping quarters. "Don't alienate him," she murmured sharply. "We'll need his help."

Máhí yanked her arm from her mother's grip, her eyes blazing. "Need his help to clean up a disaster he created?" Her voice broke, bitterness twisting her words. "He was warned. I told him, you told him. We both knew what she was capable of, and he still—"

Vesper joined them, his face drained, his voice raw. "She's right." The words fell heavily, as if dredged from some deep, hidden well of guilt. "I let my hope cloud my judgment." His voice softened, barely a whisper. "Blood alone does not a family make."

· · · · ◉ · · · ·

D eep underground, in the cold silence of the emerald vault, Sekowah's eyelids fluttered, her senses sluggish as consciousness trickled back. She shifted, trying to move her arms, but leather ties dug into her wrists, biting into her skin. Her mind struggled to piece together the fragments of her memory. She remembered Faylen, the Lucklace blossom, the sweet, drowsy scent... and then... nothing.

As her vision sharpened, she saw Faylen standing near her, pulling something gleaming and green from a satchel—the emerald, pulsing with an ominous light. Realization struck like ice through her veins. She had been taken. Betrayed. Fear clawed up her throat, and she twisted against her bindings, her heart pounding.

Zincubus stepped into view, a twisted smile spreading across his face as he watched her struggle. His eyes were dark pits, glinting with sadistic pleasure as he drank in her terror. "Don't worry, little mouse," he crooned, his voice sickly sweet. "We just need a few drops of blood." He chuckled.

The look in Zincubus' eyes terrified her. His pupils were fully dilated, turning his eyes black. Sekowah's breath caught in her throat, her pulse racing. *Blood?* The word pulsed in her mind, heavy and terrifying. *What were they going to do? Where was Máhí?* Desperation surged, and she yanked at the ties binding her wrists, finding her voice. "Help! Máhí! I'm in here! Help me!"

Zincubus laughed, a deep, hollow sound. He leaned closer, his breath rancid, and seized her foot as she tried to kick him away. "Go on," he whispered mockingly. "Yell all you want, cupcake."

The sound of his voice, his twisted mockery, sent a flood of memories crashing over her. *Cupcakes. Lemon Icing. A dog named Ningo. School. Robbie.* Everything, her entire childhood, was cascading into a pool of lost memories, newly found. For a moment, it was all clear again. *The cottage. The looking pond. The warnings.* Sekowah narrowed her eyes at him. He was revolting. She looked Zincubus in the eyes, her voice steady with defiance. "You're a horrible, horrible man."

Zincubus' smile only widened, his eyes glinting with dark amusement. "Why, thank you," he replied, his voice dripping with mock sincerity. He tilted his head, feigning disappointment. "Why the hate? I haven't done anything to you," he murmured, leaning in so close she could see the oily sheen of his skin, smell the sickly, musty scent of decay that clung to his cloak.

Sekowah's voice trembled, her defiance mixed with fear. "You tricked me. Kidnapped me." Her voice faltered, the words tumbling out in a desperate rush. "You belong in jail."

Zincubus threw his head back and laughed, a deep, bellowing sound that echoed off the stone walls. "Jail." His laughter bellowed. "Yes. Call the police! Hello? 9-1-1? I've been kidnapped by an evil wizard." He wiped tears from his eyes as his laughter finally subsided.

Faylen, who had been watching silently, shifted uncomfortably. "What's a police?" she asked, her confusion breaking the dark tension for a brief moment.

Zincubus ignored her, his gaze fixed on Sekowah, his voice dropping to a dangerous whisper. "Living among the mortals," he said, his tone playful. "All this time. Tsk. Tsk. Bad girl."

Sekowah's heart pounded, but she lifted her chin defiantly. "I was just a child," she spat.

Zincubus leaned in closer, his breath hot and foul against her cheek. "You're still a child," he murmured, his voice oily and soft, almost coaxing. "Still don't know much of anything, do you?"

Sekowah closed her eyes, willing herself to disappear, to wake up somewhere far, far from this nightmare. But when she opened them, Zincubus was still there, leering at her, his fingers brushing her cheek as if she were a prized possession.

With a nod, he gestured to Faylen, who stepped forward, a small blade glinting in her hand. Before Sekowah could react, Faylen seized her hand and sliced a shallow cut across her finger. Sekowah gasped as pain flared, hot and sharp. Blood welled from the wound, dripping sluggishly into a small azurtanium bowl that Faylen held beneath her hand.

The sight of her own blood, pooling dark and viscous, made Sekowah's stomach churn. She stared at Faylen, betrayal and hurt twisting her voice. "Why are you doing this to me? You should be ashamed."

Faylen looked away, her face a mask, her voice flat. "You know nothing, sister."

Sekowah's blood dripped into the bowl, each drop sapping her strength, leaving her light-headed and pale. She could feel something slipping away from her, something precious. Her voice was barely a whisper as she glared at Faylen. "I know the difference between right and wrong."

Faylen gave a bitter laugh, tipping the bowl to pour Sekowah's blood onto the roots of the emerald. "Right and wrong," she sneered. "Such simple ideas. Maybe there is no right or wrong. Maybe there's only power and survival." She turned to Sekowah, her gaze cold. "Did you know Máhí was stealing your memories, dosing your food with ginkgo berries? You're nothing but a pawn in their game, a flag in a battle you don't even understand."

Sekowah's chest tightened, tears blurring her vision. They had all betrayed her, in their own ways, even the ones she'd trusted most. She felt hollow, adrift, as if she no longer knew herself.

The blood soaked into the roots of the emerald, and its green light flared, brighter and brighter, filling the chamber with an eerie, pulsating glow. Faylen's face was bathed in the light, but there was no triumph there—only a strange, haunted sorrow. Sekowah stared at her, wondering if somewhere deep within, Faylen regretted what she'd become.

Sekowah was horrified. *What were they doing?* She fixed her eyes on the emerald. She could feel a connection to it somehow, as though it were a part of her. An urge rose up in her chest... to sing. So powerful was the urge, that it wouldn't be stopped. She lifted her chin, and drawing in the air, she let the urge overtake her. A low note vibrated in her throat... unearthly and steady. That note was followed by another and another, each more distinct than the last, until finally, she hit it. A haunting, full note full of vibration and power. She could see the effect of the note on Zincubus as his aura shifted with the sound waves from deep orange to a electric green. And Faylen's as well, turned from a murky grey and green to deep blue.

Then, to her surprise, the emerald lost its glow and grew darker ... darker ... darker ... until it was entirely black. The roots fizzled out and threw small green sparks about that died on the stone floor. Sekowah felt a rush of hope. Had she caused the emerald to go dark? She continued to hold her focus on the gem and kept singing. Small pebbles dislodged from the walls and bounced on the stone floor in front of her.

Zincubus shoved Faylen back to Sekowah's side of the room. "Cut her again! Silence her!" he shouted.

Faylen did as she was told, and cut Sekowah's thumb, this time much deeper. The pain was excruciating, and Sekowah's song faltered, the melody slipping from her grasp as blood dripped from her hand. She stood with dignity nonetheless, her eyes burning with resolve.

Blood ran out of her again, filling the bowl. Faylen ran promptly back over to the emerald and poured its contents over it. The roots shrank away, withered, and disappeared from beneath it.

Sekowah breathed relief. Whatever her connection was to this gem, was magical, timeless, and sacred. She could feel it. "The emerald does not serve the wicked," she announced.

The new tone to her voice took Zincubus unaware. His face twisted with rage, and he took a step back, momentarily thrown off balance. Faylen, shaken, looked at the lifeless emerald, the weight of her choices visible in her eyes.

In a sudden burst of clarity, Faylen dropped the bowl and turned to Zincubus, her face a mixture of defiance and despair. "I betrayed my family... for this?" she whispered, her voice breaking. "You've ruined everything."

Zincubus paced. "And I have allowed you to dissuade me long enough," he said. "We must move operations into the valley."

Faylen's face hardened. She stepped forward, blocking his path to Sekowah. "No. I won't let you desecrate our land."

Zincubus laughed, a low, dangerous sound. "Stand aside, Faylen," he warned, his hand reaching for his dagger.

In a desperate move, Faylen unfastened Sekowah's bonds and shoved her toward the door. "Run!" she whispered fiercely, her voice a broken plea. "Warn them. Go."

Sekowah hesitated between the doorway and the unfolding violence. But then she heard Zincubus' dagger hiss through the air. Faylen cried out, a soft, broken sound, as she staggered back, blood blooming across her chest.

She dropped to the floor, gasping for breath. He stood over her as blood oozed out onto the granite floor as she tried in vain to pull the dagger out.

Sekowah backed away, shocked. She watched as Faylen writhed in pain on the floor. She wanted to rush in and help but found herself frozen in fear, unable to move, so dreadful was the sight of her.

"You know better than that, my love," he hissed at her.

"Your day will arrive." She moaned, pulling at the dagger.

"Thankfully, that day is not today. Today ... my petal, is your day." He pulled the dagger from her chest, stabbing her again and again, anguish across his face. Sekowah could see that it pained him to do it, but he let the dagger sink into her one last time.

Faylen took her last breath. It was more of a heaving, desperate gasp.

Immediately overcome with grief and regret, Zincubus leaned over her body and enveloped her, pulling her close, her head falling unnaturally to the side as he clutched her tightly in his arms. As he held to her lifeless body, he turned his gaze to Sekowah. His grief vanished, leaving only blind hate in his eyes.

With a shuddering breath, Sekowah crossed her arms, held her earlobes, vanished from sight, and ran for her life.

CHAPTER TWENTY-FIVE

LABYRINTH

At the gates of Peregrine's Keep, the rescue party gathered in a tense huddle, winged steeds shuffling impatiently in their harnesses as warriors tightened their saddles and checked their weapon belts. The morning mist clung low to the ground, turning the world to shades of gray. Vesper, Jájá, Gavril and Máhí all prepared to scout the territory for their missing Sekowah. A small band of Lirian warriors mounted horses, and Vesper's elite squadron gathered ahead of the rest to lead the team.

Vesper noted the dark, churning skies over Obsidia as he cinched his saddle belt tight with a grunt. "We haven't the resources to penetrate the bogs," he said.

Beside him, Jájá adjusted her cloak, her eyes distant but steely with resolve. "We'll negotiate if we have to," she said, a glint of determination in her eyes. "They want something."

Vesper looked at her, a shadow of pain crossing his face as he reached out to place a hand on her shoulder. His voice was softer, almost hesitant. "They want to rid themselves of any threat—"

"If that were the case," Jájá interrupted, her tone fierce, "why not kill her in her sleep? Why not drain her blood and return with only the emerald?" Her eyes burned with conviction as she held his gaze. "No, Vesper. This is more than mere elimination. They want us there for a reason."

He considered her words, an uneasy silence settling between them. "Are you suggesting it's a trap?"

She took his hand in hers, a brief, tender touch. Her eyes softened, carrying an apology she couldn't bring herself to say aloud. "I have faith enough for us both. Trust me. They're being driven by forces even they don't understand. There are forces at hand working in the darkness."

Vesper held her gaze for a moment, searching her face as though hoping to find reassurance there. But he said nothing more, only gave a curt nod, his silence a fragile truce.

A few steps away, Máhí pretended not to listen, though her ears missed nothing. Her fingers worked deftly, securing vials in her belt—Gravity, Itch, and the precious Dasheah whistle, her only real defense against Zincubus' legion of winged specters. Her hands trembled slightly as she secured the whistle, the reality of their mission gnawing at her composure. She knew better than to voice her thoughts aloud, but she was certain Zincubus had read *the Verses*. He knew what Sekowah was meant to become, why she had been brought back. He didn't want her dead—he wanted her enslaved, her powers twisted to serve his will. The thought made her stomach churn. What else he might have at his disposal, she was unsure. It had been many harvests since she had seen or heard news of his operations in Obsidia. The Moorigato did not concern her as much, as her advantage would be striking from the air. And how they would get through the Pine Bogs to find her … was also unknown. They'd had no time to prepare, plan, to scout, or to take inventory of the threats.

With a final glance at her mother, Máhí mounted her steed, hiding her turmoil behind a mask of cool resolve. She nodded at Jájá, and then, with a sweep of their wings, they were airborne, lifting off in unison as the castle fell away below them.

D eep within the labyrinth of Obsidia, Sekowah shimmered into view, her breath coming in gasps as her lungs fought to draw in the dank, stale air. She was in a narrow stone passage, the walls close, damp, and heavy with the scent of earth and rot. Moss clung to the stones, slick and cold, and tendrils of root reached out from the walls like fingers, blind but searching.

She moved to the center of the passageway to avoid them, but a lightning-quick root caught her scent and lunged forward, snagging her ankle. It wrapped itself around her leg, pulling her toward the wall, where the other roots waited to capture her arms and neck. Desperate, Sekowah tugged at it, to no avail. She swatted at the other roots as they reached for her neck and kicked at the root to release her.

Her hands flew to her belt, fingers closing around the hilt of her small dagger. She slashed at the root, her strokes frantic, desperate. The blade bit into the fibrous tendril but barely made a mark. Her heart thundered. In a surge of strength, she planted her foot on the root, holding it down as she drove the dagger beneath it, cutting with all her might. *Svvvtt!* The root severed, and the end flailed wildly, spraying a dark, bitter-smelling sap that sizzled as it splattered across her wrists and ankles, leaving blistering burns. She used her silk robe to wipe away what she could, but the damage had been done. The spots turned bubbly and black on her wrists and ankles. Sekowah sprang to her feet, and ran down the length of the passageway, not knowing whether she was going deeper into the caverns or toward a possible exit.

She rounded a corner, finding herself in front of a small cavern, made of rainbow obsidian. The colorful walls shimmered as the light emanating from a pile of gems glistened against the smooth surface. On top of the pile of gems sat an intimidating green dragon, surrounded by smaller, baby dragons. Newly hatched, the little ones nestled under her chest making puttering, crackling sounds, like firecrackers. Broken eggshells and baskets of fresh chili peppers littered the base of the gem mound.

A dragon! Sekowah stood transfixed, her fear forgotten as she took in the dragon's terrifying beauty, the ancient power radiating from its coiled muscles, the lethal glint of its spear-tipped tail, which, she imagined, might slice through her without stopping.

The thought of it frightened her and she let out a small gasp.

The dragon's head snapped toward her, its red eyes blazing, and before Sekowah could move, it unleashed a torrent of flame. She ducked back behind the wall, heat licking at her as the fire roared past, illuminating the passage in a flash of orange and gold. Somewhere deep inside the labyrinth of tunnels, Sekowah could hear the echoes of voices shouting, chains clanking, and Dasheahs shrieking. The hair stood up on her neck and arms.

She fled away from the ominous sounds, and down an adjacent passage, continuing cautiously, listening carefully and taking corners slower. More rattling, clanking, and snapping echoed nearby. Another turn. Another narrow corridor. The walls pressed in, slick with slime, the air thick with an acrid, peppery scent that burned her eyes and nose. She tried to orient herself, to remember the path, but the passages twisted endlessly, each corner bringing her back to familiar landmarks. She felt trapped, as if the tunnels were folding in on themselves, leading her nowhere. *Have I gone in a circle?* She recognized an archway with crimson gems flanking the door ... *that path goes back to the emerald vault. Should I return to the vault and try to retrieve the emerald?*

No, she decided. *Too dangerous.*

As she paused to consider her direction, she heard the sound of heavy, sloppy footsteps, jogging in her direction. She vanished, holding her breath, and took the left passage away from the sounds. Behind her, two Moorigato guards appeared at the end of the tunnel, searching. One took the right passage, but the other slowed his pace, and walked quietly toward her, not seeing her warped shimmer. He was tall, though hunched over, with arms that hung to his knees. His scaly skin, a rough shimmer of grey and green, covered his entire body and face, and across the top of his head, like a mohawk, was a jagged fin, that ran from his forehead to the base of his neck. He wore a waist band made of leather, with metal loops every inch or so. His large feet, with webbed toes, slapped against the slate floors as he approached.

Sekowah could feel herself getting dizzy. *Move along! Keep going.* She prayed he would pick up his pace. As the guard shuffled slowly by her, his long tongue flicked in and out of his mouth, as he smelled the air. He stopped, trying to locate the source of the scent.

She could feel her fingertips going numb. Her lungs felt as though they might collapse in a spasm, leaving her gasping for air. She tiptoed away, ever so slowly, going back the way she had come in. When she turned the corner, she released her breath, and bent over, regaining her composure. She peered down the passage to see the guard swipe suspiciously at the air, then proceed further down the tunnel.

The new passage turned from earth and moss to obsidian again, and she made her way soundlessly along it until she arrived at an enormous cavern, with balconies, made of wrought iron, running along its entire perimeter. She held her breath and vanished before stepping inside.

There she saw Dasheahs in black cloaks with long whips, flying overhead screeching and snapping. Their cries were deafening, making her ears ring and skin crawl. She covered her ears, as their shrieks and harsh clicking noises began to make her feel nauseated and disoriented. Like flying ghosts, the Dasheahs whipped through the air, their batwings adept at sharp turns and unexpected dives. They were more horrifying than anything she had seen yet, and that included a fire breathing dragon. In between their ear-splitting cries, they spoke to each other in muffled, hoarse whispers that blended together and echoed off the walls, further confusing her.

Sekowah searched for a hiding spot and found a pillar of obsidian to duck behind and release her breath. She trembled with fatigue and fear. Getting out of this hellish place was proving far more difficult than she imagined. She had no memory of arriving, and no clues about where to go, or even if there was an exit she could use. But if there was a way in, there had to be a way out.

Watch, listen, follow, gather clues, she told herself. *Stay calm.*

"*Calm yourself down. You're okay*". An orphan memory pushed its way into her consciousness, the sound of the distant voice echoing in her ears. *She was a child. Wearing white shoes with rainbow laces. A kind woman sitting next to her in a dentist chair, was showing her how to relax herself through breathing.* "*Breathe in. Count to Five. Breathe out. Count to five*". She closed her eyes briefly and let her body relax, taking her time, slowly regaining her head. The memory vanished as quickly as it had arrived, leaving her feeling disoriented.

After recovering, she vanished again and peered out from behind the pillar to see the floor of the cavern, covered by fields of chili peppers. These were the largest peppers she had ever seen: more the size of eggplants than peppers. Large citrine gems hung from the ceiling, providing light over the fields. She could feel the warm glow on her face. It was a nourishing, rejuvenating, pleasant light. She took a moment to bask in it but was quickly pulled from the pleasure by the sound of Dasheahs snapping their whips at the workers in the fields, who harvested the peppers.

The workers were the lizard humanoids, like the guards, who went about their work begrudgingly, occasionally hissing at the Dasheahs overhead. This was the first time they were enslaved and forced to bend to the will of anyone. They did not take to it willingly.

Sekowah marveled at the activity below. In small caves along the lower perimeter, were red, green and purple dragons, lined up to feed on the baskets of peppers. Sekowah was unsure how to feel about these creatures. They were fierce, and yet, she felt an attachment to them she did not understand, empathy for their plight perhaps. They were enslaved as well, wearing glowing green metal collars, their wings sewn together across their backs with strips of leather.

After feeding on the peppers for a brief time, the Dasheahs would screech at them to keep moving. They shuffled along in single file, to an exit at the back of the cavern. One stubborn red dragon refused to move away from its basket, and a fight broke out between that one and another red dragon. Dasheahs swooped in to break it up, hurling their whips at their faces and screeching. Finally, the offending dragon dropped his head, and marched in line with the rest, but let out a streak of fire in the direction of the Dasheah squad for good measure before ducking away into the exit.

Sekowah counted multiple exits from the upper perimeter. Where they led, she hadn't a clue. *Could one of them be a way out?*

She ducked into the passage nearest her, feeling quite dizzy, and losing her breath again. She hid momentarily while recovering. It was damp here and getting enough oxygen to recover was difficult. The air was thin, but the humidity thick and hot. Her nostrils burned, her eyes watered, and her nose ran from the chili pepper mist in the air. She spied a center passage over the dragon's exit, feeling pulled toward it. But the perimeter was long, and she wasn't sure she could hold her breath for that long.

Just run, she thought. *Run, and don't look back.*

Chapter Twenty-Six

THE WALLS HAVE EYES

Sekowah pressed herself against the cool stone wall, her lungs straining as she sucked in deep, shuddering breaths. She crossed her arms over her chest, vanished, and bolted from her hiding place, weaving around pillars and ducking beneath the dark-winged Dasheahs as they swept close, their red eyes glinting in the smoky gloom. She kept her movements light, her feet barely touching the ground as she sprinted along the perimeter of the cavern toward the center passage.

The cavern was thick with the sharp stench of melting metal and scorched rock. The smoke clawed at her lungs, making her want to cough, but she stifled the urge, pressing her nightshirt over her mouth to muffle any sound. Her eyes watered as she slipped through the cavern and found a shadowed alcove behind a pillar. She doubled over, hands braced on her knees, heaving for air.

I made it, she thought, relief flooding through her. *I'm getting better. Just like Máhí said.* Each time she vanished, she felt her lungs grow a little stronger, a little more capable of withstanding the strain. She scanned the room, assessing her surroundings. Below her, dragons of all sizes and colors were chained to enormous vats, their scales glinting in the dim light as they exhaled great streams of fire, melting chunks of rock into shimmering molten metal. The thick, iridescent liquid oozed like lava, pooling in black molds that lined a conveyor belt, slowly solidifying as it moved further down the line.

Weapons, she realized, her eyes narrowing. *They're making weapons.*

Swords, spears, and armor plates took shape on the belt, and she glimpsed what looked like parts of larger machines—perhaps even pieces of a rocket or some other war engine. Her gaze traveled along the assembly line, following the conveyor belt as it disappeared into another cavern. Beyond that tunnel, through a narrow gap, she saw something that made her heart skip—a warm, golden glow. Sunlight.

Sunlight!

There's an exit, she thought, hope rising within her. But the gap was small, barely large enough to see through, let alone crawl through, and the belt itself was searing hot from the freshly molded metal.

She scanned the room again, her mind racing for another way out. Her eyes darted to an upper ledge where she spotted a thin trail leading toward what looked like a passage, perhaps another exit. She would need to get closer.

But then her heart sank. Standing near the edge of the ledge, his eyes cold and calculating, was Zincubus. His staff glowed with an eerie green light as he surveyed the operation below. Beside him was a Dasheah—unlike the others, this one wore a crown of twisted steel snakes, each one gleaming like the blade of a dagger. Her eyes burned with an unnatural red light, scanning the cavern below.

Sekowah's stomach twisted with fear, her skin prickling as she hugged the wall, praying they wouldn't notice her. Her pulse thundered as the Dasheah commanded a squad of her underlings, who immediately took flight, screeching as they disappeared into one of the side passages. Zincubus followed, his dark figure vanishing into the shadows. Sekowah exhaled slowly, feeling the tension drain from her muscles.

She didn't dare stay in the vat room any longer. She ducked into the nearest passage, pressing herself against the damp, cold walls to escape the suffocating smoke. Her sense of direction was muddled, every twisting corridor blending into the next. After a few turns, she found herself at a fork, each path leading deeper into the warren of tunnels. Her heart pounded as she hesitated, the damp chill seeping through her nightdress and silk robe, which was now frayed and filthy.

Then, as she stood there paralyzed by indecision, she noticed something horrifying. Tiny black eyes embedded in the stone walls blinked open, singular and glistening, like beads of polished obsidian. They stared at her, unblinking, watching. She stumbled backward, revulsion tightening her throat.

Get out. Move.

She chose the right-hand passage, sprinting forward blindly, desperate to escape the accusing stares. The hem of her robe caught on a jagged rock, tripping her. She fell hard, scraping her palms against the rough stone. Frustrated, she tore the robe from her shoulders, leaving it in a crumpled heap on the floor as she continued down the passage in only her nightdress and belt.

· · · · ◯◯ · · · ·

In an observatory high above the vat room, Zincubus watched the scene unfold through a narrow window, his eyes gleaming with amusement. Sekowah had slipped his grasp for now, but he knew her escape was temporary. The labyrinthine tunnels of Obsidia were a prison in themselves, their shifting walls and echoing passageways designed to lead intruders in endless circles. She was his little titmouse, darting and flitting through his domain, unaware that the cat already had her scent.

He ran his fingers over the surface of his desk, brushing aside dusty scrolls and alchemical texts. In the center of the table stood a line of crystal skulls, each one etched with ancient runes. Zincubus picked up the skull in the middle, cradling it in his hands. With a murmured incantation, an image swirled into view—a vision of Sekowah, her face pale with fear, fleeing down a dark passage.

He chuckled softly, his fingers caressing the crystal surface. "Run, little mouse, run," he whispered.

Just then, a Moorigato soldier, towering and muscled, entered the observatory, clutching a tattered scrap of white silk. He knelt, presenting the garment to Zincubus.

"Found this in the corridor near the vats," he reported, his voice a low rumble.

Zincubus' eyes glinted with satisfaction as he took the robe, holding it up to his nose and inhaling deeply. The trace of her scent lingered—fear mingled with something innocent, something untouched. He felt a flicker of something like pity, but it vanished as quickly as it had come, replaced by a twisted delight.

She is making this too easy, he thought. Perhaps he would keep her, he mused. A new pet, a little plaything to replace Faylen. She could sing to the emerald, soothe its restless power. And when she tired of him, when she began to show defiance, he would crush her spirit just as he had crushed Faylen's.

"Send for Oreta," he commanded, tossing the robe to the ground.

The soldier bowed and exited, leaving Zincubus alone with his thoughts. He returned to the skull, watching Sekowah's terrified face as she stumbled through the maze. "Yes," he murmured to himself. "I think I will keep you."

Moments later, Oreta entered the room, flanked by her cohort of Dasheahs. She was a grotesque sight—her bat-like face stretched into a grin, her cloak of snake skin sweeping the floor as she moved. Her eyes, the color of congealed blood, narrowed as she took in the shredded remains of Sekowah's robe.

Zincubus sneered, pointing at the remnants of silk. "See to it she doesn't leave the bogs."

Oreta's lips twisted into a smile. "Bring her to you?"

"Yes," he replied, his voice laced with dark amusement. "Have a little fun with her if you like. But bring her back alive."

Oreta gathered up the silk from the floor and held it to her nose, inhaling deeply, her eyes gleaming with malicious glee. "Mmmm. Princess. My favorite."

With a swish of her cloak, she signaled her Dasheahs, and they vanished into the passageways, their screeches echoing through the corridors as they set off in pursuit.

· · · · · ◯◯ · · · · ·

Sekowah pressed herself against a doorway, the cold stone biting into her back as she struggled to quiet her breathing. A line of Moorigato guards marched past, their webbed feet slapping wetly against the stone, their tongues flicking in and out, testing the air. She closed her eyes, willing herself to disappear completely, even beyond the shimmer of her vanished form. *I'm not here,* she thought. *Please, I'm not here.*

The guards passed, their gazes sliding over her without a second glance. She waited until their footsteps faded before exhaling, her legs trembling as she fumbled for the door handle behind her. She slipped inside, closing it quietly.

The room was dimly lit, the air thick with the scent of old paper and dust. She looked around, heart pounding as she took in the surroundings. In the center of the room was a stone throne, surrounded by towering bookcases filled with ancient tomes, some so aged their spines had crumbled away. There were no windows, no visible escape.

A strange, musical whisper drifted through the air: *"Inal silana wi, adazuyguna wi, Sekowah."*

The voice was gentle, melodic, filled with an ancient wisdom that resonated deep within her bones. Sekowah's eyes widened as a small shape stepped out from behind the throne—a fox, slender and grey, with delicate, pointed ears tipped in white. Its eyes were luminous violet, and as it watched her, a swirl of colors emanated from its heart, bathing the room in a soft, ethereal glow.

The fox tilted its head, gazing at her with a curiosity that seemed almost human. Sekowah felt a wave of calm wash over her, her fear receding as the creature's presence filled the room with a sense of peace.

The fox's violet eyes held her gaze, a silent understanding passing between them. It did not speak again, but in its eyes, she saw something—a reflection of herself, a reminder of her purpose, her strength. She felt the walls of the room press in around her, the weight of her fear lifting.

CHAPTER TWENTY-SEVEN

A GREY FOX

Sekowah's heart hammered in her chest as she stared at the fox, trying to steady her breath. The creature's violet eyes glowed with an intelligence that felt ancient, powerful, and entirely unknowable.

I am Inanna, the fox's voice echoed in her mind, soft and certain. *Untie me, and I'll set you free.*

She took a hesitant step forward, uncertain. There was something unsettling about this fox, even as her presence radiated a calm authority. She glanced at the thick metal collar locked around Inanna's neck and the chain that tethered her to the floor.

"How do I know I can trust you?" she whispered, her voice barely audible.

You can't. Inanna swished her tail, eyes fixed unflinchingly on Sekowah. *But you must.*

The words felt like a command. Sekowah bristled at the presumption. *Must trust you?* She narrowed her eyes, assessing. Trust had been a precious and fragile thing in her life lately.

You are in no position to question me, Inanna replied, a flicker of impatience flashing in her violet eyes. *Zincubus is on his way.*

Sekowah's heart skipped, her stomach lurching at the mention of him. The fox—Inanna—was watching her with a calm, steady gaze that seemed to see through the layers of her thoughts, reading her doubts and fears as easily as one might read a page of text.

You can hear my thoughts? Sekowah's question echoed in her mind, tentative and startled.

I can hear everything, Inanna replied smoothly, pawing at the air. Her eyes flickered over to the doorway, her ears pricking up, as the sound of footsteps and low voices drifted down the corridor outside.

Disappear yourself, Inanna instructed with silent urgency. *Hide behind the throne.*

Sekowah didn't need to be told twice. She scurried behind the massive stone throne, pulling herself into a tight ball, arms wrapped around her knees, and held her breath. She willed herself to vanish, feeling the familiar tingling sensation as her form shimmered out of sight. The footsteps grew louder, and she pressed her back against the cold stone, willing herself to become invisible in every way.

The door creaked open. She could hear the shuffling of Zincubus' cloak, then the muted clink of jars on a nearby shelf. Sekowah stole a peek around the edge of the throne, her stomach twisting as she glimpsed his tall, imposing figure. He moved with a kind of feverish impatience, his hands twitching as he rummaged through a shelf cluttered with glass jars. His fingers found a lid, and he struggled with it, his hands shaking. When he finally popped it open with a sharp suction sound, Inanna's eyes opened lazily, as if waking from sleep, and she lifted her head to greet him.

Zincubus reached into the jar, pulled out a shriveled purple mushroom flecked with green, and popped it into his mouth, closing his eyes as he savored it. His whole body seemed to shudder, his hands steadying, his expression slackening as though the mushroom's effects calmed some inner turbulence. Sekowah watched him with mingled horror and fascination. *What kind of power lies in those mushrooms?* she wondered.

Inanna, still chained, trotted over to Zincubus' side, rubbing against his legs like a cat. She whined, her eyes wide and pleading as she nudged him, demanding a mushroom. Zincubus reached down, feeding her one with an absent gesture before turning back toward the throne. Sekowah felt her muscles tense, a new wave of panic rising.

But Inanna leaped up, placing her paws on his leg, whining louder, demanding his attention with a persistence that bordered on desperation. Was she distracting him? Or was her hunger for those mushrooms as intense as his?

Zincubus growled, brushing her away. "I haven't the time for this," he muttered, shoving several more mushrooms into his cloak pocket before storming out of the room.

The moment his footsteps faded, Sekowah exhaled, bringing her form back into being. Inanna's entire demeanor changed. She looked to Sekowah with fierce determination in her violet gaze. *Untie me. Feed me three mushrooms.*

Sekowah felt a prickle of doubt but forced herself to push it aside. She crept to the shelf, her movements careful and silent. Opening the jar, she counted out three mushrooms, her fingers brushing over their leathery texture. She lifted one, offering it to Inanna.

Untie me first, she insisted. *Unbuckle my collar.*

Sekowah hesitated, her eyes locking with the fox's. Those violet eyes were mesmerizing, a strange blend of warmth and urgency, as if they held centuries of knowledge and the weight of forgotten worlds. Compelled, she reached forward and unbuckled the collar. It clinked heavily to the floor, and Inanna's entire posture shifted—she stretched her neck, the hint of a smile touching her mouth.

Without hesitation, Sekowah fed her the mushrooms, one by one, watching as the fox devoured them with growing energy. After the last one was swallowed, Inanna took a deep breath, closed her eyes, and began to move her lips. Her sounds were a barely audible low hum, but Sekowah could feel their power rippling through the air, making the hairs on her arms stand on end.

The fox began to spin, faster and faster, a blur of color and light, her form shimmering as if caught between worlds. The colors coalesced, a glowing spiral of greens and silvers, until the shape of a woman emerged from the light.

Sekowah took a step back, her eyes widening. The woman before her was flawless, her silver hair cascading in thick, curly braids. Her skin was a rich but delicate mahogany, her wings a soft shimmer of silver, delicate yet unmistakably strong. Her aura sparkled a bright white with shimmering violet around the edges. A strange symbol was tattooed on the front of her chest: a circle inside a circle, with eight points, like stars, on the outer circle. As with Jájá, she bore no navel, no breasts, only a sleek body of fine, downy feathers. She was neither young nor old; her age seemed to exist outside time. And her violet eyes held the same intensity, the same mesmerizing pull, but now they were larger, filled with both warmth and fierce intelligence.

Inanna wasted no time. She swept her gaze over the room, and finding a small trunk on the bottom shelf, she pulled a sage flaxen robe from it and put it on. She grabbed mushrooms from the shelves and stuffed them into her pockets. *Eat as many as you can,* she commanded, her tone leaving no room for argument.

Sekowah hesitated, but the urge to obey was overwhelming. She took a handful of mushrooms, shoving them into her mouth. The taste was unlike anything she'd ever known—rich, like dark chocolate with a floral undercurrent, and a warmth that spread through her, from her tongue to her fingertips, making her feel both light and strong, as though she could fly.

They slipped out of the chamber, moving swiftly down the corridor, Inanna leading with an air of effortless grace. Every step seemed calculated, deliberate. Sekowah struggled to keep up, her feet feeling clumsy beside Inanna's long, fluid strides. She watched, entranced, as Inanna waved her hand at the walls, and the embedded eyes blinked shut, the prying gaze of the stone receding under her command. Tendrils of roots that reached out to snag them withered under her glare, curling back like frightened snakes.

At a distance from the main corridors, Inanna paused and turned to Sekowah, studying her with an intense, searching gaze. *You're Nezkwah?* Her voice in Sekowah's mind was layered, textured, each word heavy with unspoken questions.

Sekowah shifted under her scrutiny. "Yes. I am the daughter of Jájá. I was born in the valley."

But you have no wings, Inanna noted, reaching forward and tracing a line down Sekowah's spine, her fingers probing, pressing, as if searching for something unseen. She circled Sekowah, examining her from every angle, her face growing troubled.

Sekowah's mind raced. It was true—she had no wings, a fact she had never questioned but now seemed glaringly obvious under Inanna's intense scrutiny. *Why don't I have wings?* she thought, the question lingering bitterly in her mind.

Inanna took Sekowah's hands, examining her fingers as if they held the secrets she sought. Her eyes widened, and a shadow of something dark passed over her face. *You're mortal,* she said, the words thick with disbelief and something else—concern, perhaps. She inspected Sekowah's ears, the hair on her arms, even poked a finger in her mouth, feeling her teeth as if Sekowah were a strange specimen.

Are you from another place? Inanna's voice was quiet, but her tone held an edge that Sekowah couldn't quite read.

Sekowah felt her throat tighten. A surge of memories—fuzzy and disjointed—flashed through her mind. The world she had come from, the home she had left behind... She tried to suppress the thoughts, not wanting to reveal them, but Inanna's piercing gaze left her mind defenseless.

Inanna's expression hardened, her tone shifting to something fierce, almost urgent. *That world is gone. You're never to speak of it here. Of the things you know... in this place. Do you understand?* Her grip on Sekowah's hands was firm, grounding, and Sekowah nodded, though confusion churned within her.

Inanna let go, her face softening just slightly, before she spun around, leading Sekowah to a cavern overlooking a large tunnel. Below them, dragons were marching, carrying heavy metal crates down the path, flanked by snarling Dasheahs. Inanna's gaze fell on a black dragon with violet eyes and a glinting metal collar. Her eyes filled with unshed tears.

Follow the blue light, she communicated to Sekowah, her tone thick with something that almost sounded like sorrow. *It will lead you out.*

Sekowah pointed toward the tunnel flooded with sunlight. "But ... I can see the light! That's the way out, isn't it?"

Inanna's grip tightened painfully on her arm, and her eyes bore into Sekowah's with a vehemence that left no room for argument. *Never go through that tunnel. Follow the blue lights into the Healers Wood. I will come for you again. We have more to discuss.*

Sekowah's heart sank, her instinct urging her to stay at Inanna's side. But Inanna released her with a soft smile, a warmth in her gaze that melted Sekowah's resistance.

Go.

With one last look, Sekowah turned toward the passage lit with blue sconces, her heart pounding. She had barely taken a step before the cavern erupted in chaos behind her. Dragons reared, flames roaring as Dasheahs shrieked and scattered, whips snapping uselessly in the smoky air. The ground trembled, the very walls shaking as though the mountain itself were tearing apart.

KABOOOOOOM!

An explosion reverberated through the tunnels, the shockwave throwing Sekowah to the ground. Dust and stone rained down, and she scrambled to her feet, coughing, disoriented. Her eyes stung with smoke, but she found the glow of the blue sconces and stumbled forward, pushing herself through the dense haze until—

She reached a small cavern, and beyond it: trees.

Chapter Twenty-Eight

THE FIRST SKIRMISH

Sekowah stumbled through the dim cavern, her breaths coming in short, panicked gasps. The jagged rocks sliced into her bare feet, each step leaving behind a smear of crimson on the cold stone floor. But she pushed on, the only thought in her mind to escape, to reach the Healer's Wood and whatever sanctuary it might offer.

Ahead, the exit appeared, framed by the twisted silhouettes of ancient, crooked trees. Thick masses of Shade Bane moss draped over the overhang, their long, slimy tendrils swaying slightly in the damp, dense air. She pulled herself up through the gap, her shoulder brushing against a green tendril. A sizzling pain flared as the ooze seeped into her skin, leaving a dark stain and an unbearable itch that made her hand scratch reflexively. She forced herself to pull it back, afraid that scratching would only spread the poison.

Half-crawling, half-stumbling, she ducked under the moss and staggered into the forest beyond. Above her, the dense canopy of the Healer's Wood loomed, the trees twisting in unnatural patterns, their branches knotted and reaching, like skeletal hands clawing at the sky. The forest floor was a tangled mat of moss and rotting leaves, its spongey black soil sucking at her feet with each step.

She barely felt the cold, wet earth beneath her raw feet as she bolted forward, slipping and stumbling in her thin white nightdress. Her lungs burned, her heart a frantic drum in her chest. Somewhere above, the eerie shrieks of Dasheahs sliced through the air, and she knew they were close. Too close. The deep amber sky had turned to black, thick with the swarming forms of vampire bats, all chittering and circling, sniffing her blood, sensing her fear. She was exposed, a pale figure against the shadows, far too easy to see.

Her hands trembled as she fought the rising panic. She darted between tree trunks, her eyes scanning frantically for a place to hide. But everywhere she turned, Shade Bane hung in bunches, blocking her path, toxic droplets seeping into the soft moss, burning her bare feet. The rocks were slick with slime, making it impossible to run without stumbling, and the ground itself was treacherous—pockets of bog lurked beneath the moss, waiting to swallow her whole.

· · · · • ◯◯ • · · · ·

On the edge of the Healers Wood, Vesper's search party landed in the windswept Daylight Meadow. Tall grasses and wildflowers bent over in waves beneath the cold gusts that howled out from the dark forest. Jájá's gaze was drawn immediately to a swirling black cloud above the forest canopy—Dasheahs, and countless bats, circling with fevered intensity.

"Vesper! Look!" Jájá's voice was sharp with urgency as she pointed to the ominous gathering in the sky. Vesper's eyes narrowed, and he quickly loaded his bow with an arrow, Gavril following his lead. Both took aim, ready for the fight that awaited them.

· · · · • ◯◯ • · · · ·

Sekowah's desperate eyes caught sight of a hollow tree, its trunk wide and dark, promising some small shelter. She scrambled toward it, practically diving into the opening and curling up inside, pulling her knees to her chest as she tried to calm her racing heart. *Don't be afraid. Don't be afraid. I cannot be afraid.* She repeated the words to herself like a prayer, willing herself to believe them.

In her mind, she saw Inanna's violet eyes, heard her reassuring voice echoing, *I'll be back for you.* She clung to that promise, allowing it to settle her frayed nerves, and gradually, her breathing slowed. Her own energy seemed to respond, shifting from a raw, panicked red to a deep, calming blue. She closed her eyes and let the color wash over her, feeling her muscles release their tension, if only for a moment.

But then the chittering of bats filled the air outside her hiding place. They had picked up the scent of her blood on the moss, and their high-pitched squeaks formed an urgent chorus. Sekowah froze, holding her breath as the sound grew louder, nearer. She heard Oreta's chilling whisper from somewhere nearby: "She's close."

Sekowah's heart skipped a beat as she peered out from her hiding spot. She could make out the dark, hulking form of Oreta hovering above the bog, her snakeskin cape drawn close as she drifted just above the ground, undeterred by the treacherous terrain. The bats clustered around her, sniffing out Sekowah's path with feverish excitement.

Panic seized her once more, and her energy flickered from orange to red, betraying her fear. She remembered her belt and began fumbling through the vials, her fingers shaking as she turned each bottle to look at the symbols etched on the bottom. Máhí's voice drifted to her from a memory: *Green for healing. Blue for shapeshift.* But the symbols were a mystery, and her mind raced, unable to focus.

The bats drew closer, their squeaks piercing through the forest's thick silence. Sekowah's eyes darted between the vials in her belt, trying to make a choice. Finally, she pulled out a blue vial with what appeared to be a bat symbol etched on the bottom. Inside, the liquid was black, like ink, and its sharp, acrid smell made her gag. She brought it to her lips, pinched her nose, and choked it down.

· · · · • ⬭ • · · · ·

Near the Daylight Meadow, Máhí soared above the Healer's Wood astride Tahgeet, her sharp eyes scanning the canopy below. She spotted a frenzy of bats swirling in one spot, their shrieks unmistakable, as they hunted something—or someone. A chill ran through her. She knew it had to be Sekowah.

She dug into her saddlebag, pulling out a handful of red dust, and signaled Tahgeet to dive lower. But as soon as the massive steed caught sight of the Shade Bane draping the forest, he reared back, refusing to dip below the dangerous canopy.

"MAAAAAHOOOOOOOOOO!" Máhí's battle cry echoed through the air, sharp and fierce. A squad of Dasheahs rose from the trees, followed by a stream of bats. They hovered just below her, their ghastly faces twisted in mocking jeers, daring her to come closer.

Máhí flung the red dust at them, scattering it like a crimson cloud. "Down!" she commanded.

The Dasheahs laughed, their cackles cutting through the air as they flapped their wings to dispel the dust. But some were close enough to be caught by the dust's enchantment, and they spiraled, disoriented, while others gathered themselves and lunged toward her. Five of them tore at her cloak, their sharp claws grabbing hold of her feathers and cape, pulling her from her saddle.

Tahgeet bucked and twisted, flailing his hooves and tail to shake off the attackers, but they clung tight, their claws digging deep. Máhí wrestled against them, feathers flying as she struggled to free herself.

· · · · • ◯◯ • · · · ·

B elow, the bats continued following Sekowah's blood trail, their frenzied squeaks echoing through the woods as they arrived at the hollow tree where she'd hidden. They swooped inside, only to find her belt and nightdress lying in the darkness. Oreta sneered in frustration. "Keep going," she hissed, commanding the bats onward, sniffing out her scent.

Unseen among them, a small bat with shimmering green eyes flew alongside the swarm, imitating their frantic search. Sekowah's new form was slight and unsteady, and the other bats paid her little attention. She struggled to maintain her composure as the swarm moved toward the edge of the woods, her instincts battling with her fear.

Oreta urged the swarm on, her voice slicing through the air. "Guard the border!"

The bats poured out of the forest and into the Daylight Meadow, where they were met with a storm of arrows. Vesper, Jájá, and Gavril fired arrow after arrow, their aim swift and true, piercing the swarm as it burst into the open sky.

ZZZZZTTTTTT!

Sekowah flinched as an arrow whizzed past her, so close she felt its wind ruffle her fur. The bat next to her spun in mid-air, struck, and fell lifeless to the ground.

· · · · • ◯◯ • · · · ·

J ájá, seeing Máhí struggling with the Dasheahs, pulled out a whistle from her cloak and raised it to her lips. The piercing, high-pitched sound cut through the air, sending waves of disorientation through the Dasheahs and the bats alike. Máhí joined her, adding the sharp whistle of her own, creating a dual siren that drove their enemies into a panicked retreat.

The Dasheahs clutched their ears, screeching in agony as they veered back toward the canopy. Oreta, furious, flung herself into the air, snatching a Lirian warrior from his horse and dragging him over the border into a snarling mass of Shade Bane. His screams echoed as he became ensnared in the deadly tendrils, until finally, his voice went silent.

Sekowah, caught in the siren's grip, felt the world spin around her. Her small bat body quaked, her wings flapping uncontrollably as she spiraled toward the earth. She managed a brief, clumsy glide, but the ground rushed up to meet her, and she tumbled through the air, her senses reeling.

A Lirian warrior spotted her struggling form and aimed his bow. He released the arrow with precision, and it struck her wing, searing pain shooting through her small body. She veered right, losing altitude rapidly, her wings folding as she careened down into the meadow.

J ájá and Máhí rejoined the ground troop and surveyed the meadow in front of them. Downed bats, dozens, flipflopped in the grasses, struck down by arrows and disorientation. Among the fallen, Sekowah flopped and squeaked, the search team very near. She heard them talking but was helpless to do much of anything except utter small, pathetic chirps for help.

Vesper put his arrows back in his quiver. "We need nets, and a stronger sky team," he said. "We'll return tomorrow better prepared."

Jájá dismounted from her familiar and scoured the forest with her eyes. "No. She's in there. We'll go on foot."

Máhí picked at her feathers ... torn, broken, bald in places. "Agree," she replied. She kneeled, placing a hand on the meadow floor. She closed her eyes and listened while the group waited. "She is very near."

Tahgeet neighed and stomped in disagreement, backing up.

Gavril dismounted. "I'm in," he said.

Unable to stand, let alone spin, Sekowah continued to flail in the grass, her green eyes round with fright, while the group debated. She drew in a great breath and heaved out a strong yelp.

Jájá's head whipped around, her eyes narrowing as she caught sight of her. She hurried through the grasses, her hearts lurching as she knelt and gently scooped the trembling bat into her hands. Sekowah clung to her fingers with her tiny claws, pressing her small nose into Jájá's palm, exhausted and bleeding. When Jájá's eyes met her daughter's, she heaved a sigh of relief and shouted to the others, "Here! She's here!"

Wrapping her daughter carefully in her cloak, Jájá mounted her familiar, cradling Sekowah close. They lifted into the air, heading back toward Mount Lira, with the rest of the search team following in tight formation.

In the comforting darkness of Jájá's cloak, Sekowah could hear the steady beat of her mother's hearts, a familiar, soothing rhythm that calmed the last of her fear. Thump-thump. Thump-thump. She nestled closer, breathing in Jájá's scent, earthy and warm, letting the heartbeat lull her into the safety of sleep.

CHAPTER TWENTY-NINE

PAINFUL TRUTHS

S ekowah awoke slowly, every inch of her body aching as if she had been shattered and pieced back together. Her head throbbed, a relentless, punishing rhythm that seemed to echo the deeper hurt buried somewhere in her chest. Blinking against the dim light, she became aware of Jájá seated beside her in her bed chamber.

Jájá's hands moved over her, steady and tender, applying a cool blue salve to her wounded shoulder. The paste stung where it touched her burns, and Sekowah let out a soft, involuntary moan, unable to keep the discomfort contained.

Gavril stood just inside the doorway, his arms folded tightly across his chest, his usually calm face drawn and tense. He flinched at her pain, and Sekowah caught a flicker of something fierce and vengeful in his eyes.

Sekowah's thoughts flashed to Zincubus—the cruel twist of his smile, the way he had looked at her, taunting, as if her pain were a mere amusement. She shivered, the memory almost more painful than the wounds themselves. Her stomach churned, and her mouth felt dry. She wanted to speak, to tell Jájá what had happened, about Faylen's final moments, but the words lodged in her throat like stones. It was as if the horror of it had turned to ash inside her, impossible to voice.

"They cut me," she whispered finally, her voice small and broken, her fingers twitching against the flaxen sheets.

Jájá's eyes narrowed, her lips pressed into a thin, grim line as she inspected the deep slices on Sekowah's fingertips. Rage simmered beneath her calm exterior, an intensity that made Sekowah's skin prickle. Jájá continued applying the salve, but her fingers trembled, betraying her carefully held composure.

"It won't happen again," Jájá said softly, a promise woven into each word. "Máhí will bring more healing potion soon," she added, turning to Gavril. "Please fetch her. She mustn't delay."

With a short nod, Gavril turned and left, his steps heavy and reluctant, as though he hated to leave Sekowah unguarded, even for a moment.

As Jájá worked, she began to hum a low, soothing melody—a lullaby, familiar and foreign all at once. The sound of it, a gentle rhythm, wrapped around Sekowah like a blanket. She closed her eyes, letting the melody wash over her. It felt like a veil lifting, as though some barrier between her present self and her past were dissolving, a feeling she had begun to notice not long after eating the mushrooms with Inanna, and for the briefest moment, she was adrift, floating in a realm that was neither here nor there.

She stared blankly out the small window at the tawny sky, watching the clouds shift and mingle, their shapes morphing and twisting. In the drifting clouds, she saw a face—soft, comforting, yet achingly distant. It looked like Inanna's face, then as the wind rose, changing it again, the new face in the cloud rattled a memory somewhere deep inside her. Her vision blurred, and in the morphing clouds, another face appeared, flickering through her mind like a half-remembered dream. The face was kind, warm, familiar in a way that sent a pang of longing through her chest. And then, a voice—quiet and clear, inside her mind: *This woman is not my mother.*

The thought jolted her. She turned her gaze back to Jájá, who was humming as she applied salve to Sekowah's burns. The Queen's eyelids blinked in that strange sideways motion, her magnificent wings shifting slightly as she leaned over her daughter. For the first time, Sekowah noticed the sheer strangeness of Jájá's form—so close to her own, yet undeniably different. She had no wings. And hadn't Inanna, too, found that fact... unsettling?

She lifted her hand, examining it as if seeing it anew. Her fingertips were bandaged, but she could still make out the wounds beneath, the evidence of her ordeal. A memory surfaced—a memory of falling off a slide as a child, of breaking her wrist and being cradled by a woman with soft hands and a warm, lavender scent. The woman had wiped her tears away with gentle strokes, whispering reassurances. Who was that woman? And why did the memory feel so real, so vivid, yet utterly out of place in this world?

Silent tears traced paths down Sekowah's cheeks as she lay there, limp and exhausted, the weight of everything pressing down on her. She remembered Faylen's parting words, her voice laced with bitterness: *You see only what they want you to see. You're nothing but a flag in a game you know nothing about.*

It was true, wasn't it? She was a pawn, a tool, a symbol they had summoned back to fulfill some prophecy or purpose she couldn't begin to understand. And for what? For *their* needs, *their* desires. The realization ignited a small, smoldering flame of anger deep within her.

"You've been through quite a lot," Jájá murmured, as if reading the turmoil in her expression. She held Sekowah's hand gently, her eyes filled with what seemed like tenderness, but Sekowah wasn't sure if it was real.

She turned her face away, the bitterness rising to the surface. The anger she had suppressed for so long was bubbling up, a dark and tangled knot in her chest, and she could hold it back no longer. Was Jájá her mother? She no longer trusted a word from any of them. Her insides churned. The pounding in her head got louder. She wanted to scream at her, throw something, break something, but she only stared out the window, seething. After a long silence, she forced herself to sit up, her injured arm protesting the movement, and fixed her gaze on Jájá.

"You're using me," she said, her voice barely above a whisper, but sharp as a blade.

Jájá didn't flinch. Her expression remained calm, almost indifferent. "I did what I thought was best," she replied, each word measured, devoid of warmth.

The hollowness of her tone cut deeper than Sekowah expected, and the knot in her chest tightened. How could she not see? How could she be so oblivious to the pain she had caused? She swallowed, not wanting to be weak, but the tears came anyway.

"You don't care about me," Sekowah choked out, her voice trembling. "None of you do. You only care about what you want—what I can do for you. You took me from my family, from everything I knew, just to serve *your* purposes."

Jájá's eyes sharpened, and for the first time, Sekowah saw something like sadness flicker across her mother's face. "You remember, then?" she asked softly.

Sekowah nodded, her throat tight. "Yes, of course I remember."

An uncomfortable silence settled over them, heavy and suffocating. Jájá glanced over at Máhí, who was lingering just outside the door, and gave a slight nod. She turned back to Sekowah, her expression softer, but still guarded.

"What do you want, darling?" Jájá asked, her voice almost tender, as if the question held the weight of an apology but stopped just shy of one.

Sekowah stared at her, taken aback by the question. *What do I want? I want this nightmare to be over.* She could still feel the memory of Whispering Falls, the life she'd had before all of this—the innocence of it, the simplicity. She longed for it, but as quickly as the thought surfaced, she dismissed it. That life was gone. She didn't belong in that world anymore, and she didn't belong in this one, either.

Before she could answer, Máhí stepped inside, with Gavril following close behind. The familiar sight of them only deepened her sense of displacement.

"I don't want to fight," Sekowah muttered, almost to herself. *This is not my battle,* she thought. *It's your battle. You fight.*

Máhí's expression softened. "If you don't want to fight, then don't," she said gently. "We'll find another way."

Sekowah shook her head, her mind flashing back to Zincubus, his sneering face, his words echoing in her mind: *Cut her again.* Her stomach churned, the fear and revulsion rising. "I don't want to fight him," she whispered, her voice taut with remembered terror.

Jájá lowered her head, a touch of regret shadowing her gaze. "I see," she murmured. "He is... intimidating. It was wrong of me to assume."

Sekowah let out a heaving sigh, the frustration and confusion swirling together. "What makes you think I can do anything for you? I'm just a person." She could feel herself unraveling, the threads of her carefully held composure slipping from her grasp. *Did you really think you could stash me away in another world, and bring me back as though nothing had changed?*

The Queen's voice softened, almost as if she were trying to soothe a frightened animal. "You're a person, yes. A hut-dweller. A mortal. But you're also Nezkwah," she said, her tone laced with an intensity Sekowah couldn't quite understand. "Never forget that."

Sekowah's frustration spilled over. "That doesn't mean anything!" she yelled, the words echoing in the chamber.

Gavril stepped forward, his gaze fixed on Jájá, his respect evident but his tone firm. "She's not been prepared for this. Is it any wonder she's afraid to fight?" he said, his voice carrying a weight of reproach. "We train all our warriors for years. None would think it wise to send one out to battle without proper training. So why should Sekowah be any different?"

Jájá looked down, her fingers twisting around a scrap of bandage in her lap. For the first time, the queen looked weary, vulnerable. "Perhaps I have not done my part to prepare her," she admitted quietly. "She deserves nothing less than the training my other daughters received."

Sekowah's anger softened, replaced by a flicker of pity. *Other daughters,* she thought, the words twisting in her mind. And with that thought, a pang of guilt surged within her. How do you tell any mother that one of her daughters is dead? She took a shaky breath, bracing herself. "I need to tell you something."

Jájá stilled, her gaze sharpening. "Yes?"

Sekowah met her eyes, her own brimming with sorrow. "It's about Faylen."

Jájá stopped wringing the cloth, her fingers stilling as she took in Sekowah's words. For a moment, the steady calm that always cloaked her fell away, leaving her eyes bare and vulnerable. "I'm sorry for her as well," she murmured, almost to herself. Her voice was a strained whisper, a single note of regret echoing in the dim room. "We shouldn't have allowed her—"

"No." Sekowah cut her off, reaching out and placing her hand over Jájá's, unsure whether she sought to comfort or restrain. Her voice trembled, not from fear but from the weight of what she had to say. "She wasn't just acting out of selfishness. Faylen... she was trying to help you. She made a deal with Zincubus—to keep him from the valley. To keep him in Obsidia." Her throat tightened. "He wanted to take over the valley, so she took the emerald to Obsidia, thinking she could protect us. To keep him away."

A sharp, disbelieving sound escaped Máhí's lips. Her foot stomped against the slate floor, sending a shiver through the room. "What?! What do you mean, she betrayed the family! She—"

Sekowah shook her head, her voice barely audible, a fragile wisp hanging in the silence. "You don't have to hate her anymore." The words were almost too painful to say. "She's... she's gone."

The room seemed to stop breathing. Jájá's face went deathly still, her hand frozen beneath Sekowah's. "What do you mean, gone?" Her voice was thin, stretched, as if dreading the answer.

"The emerald... it went dark," Sekowah whispered, fighting to keep her voice steady. Her gaze dropped, unable to meet the dawning horror in Jájá's eyes. "They argued. And then he... he stabbed her. I'm so sorry."

Jájá leapt to her feet, her entire form vibrating with sudden energy, as if the grief had woken something primal within her. "Killed her?! Dark? Máhí!" Her voice cracked like thunder. "Get your father."

Máhí, momentarily stunned, didn't move. She stared, her mouth open as if she had forgotten how to breathe. But Jájá's command shattered the spell, and Máhí turned, darting from the room in silence.

With the door left open, a chill breeze swept in, unsettling the heavy air. Jájá remained standing, her gaze lost in some distant horror, her hands trembling as she clutched at her robes. The grief seeped into her bones, a visible agony that seemed to hollow her from the inside out.

Sekowah reached out, her own hand shaking as she gently touched her mother's arm. "I'm sorry," she whispered again, feeling the inadequacy of the words, like offering a raindrop to quench a wildfire.

"Oh, it makes sense," Jájá muttered, her voice hollow and faraway, as if she were speaking from the depths of some cavernous place within herself. "It makes perfect sense. How did I not see?" She began pacing, clutching at her robes, her movements erratic, like a wounded animal circling itself, unable to escape.

Sekowah's guilt twisted deeper. She had watched Faylen die, paralyzed, unable to intervene. Her own inaction gnawed at her. She found herself whispering, as if confessing to the air, "She saved me."

Jájá paused mid-step, her face snapping to attention. "She did?"

Sekowah nodded, a dull ache spreading in her chest. "Yes, and she paid with her life." She closed her eyes, feeling the weight of her own failures crushing down. "It's my fault. I don't know this world, or its rules. I'm not whoever or whatever you think I am." Her voice broke. "I can't help you."

The admission hung between them, stark and raw. Sekowah turned her face away, too ashamed to meet Jájá's gaze. She rolled onto her side, retreating into the bed's folds as if they could shield her from this world's demands. The hope they had placed in her, the expectations, felt like a crushing weight she could no longer bear.

Jájá crumpled to the floor, her sobs erupting like a dam breaking. She covered her face, her shoulders shaking as her grief spilled out, unchecked and consuming.

It was then that Vesper entered, his stride urgent, with Máhí close behind. He took one look at Jájá's collapsed form and knelt beside her, gathering her into his arms. The queen melted into him, hiding her face in the crook of his neck, her anguish muffled as she clung to him.

"Forgive me," she whispered, her voice barely audible. Her fingers twisted into the fabric of his tunic, anchoring herself to him as though he were the last steady thing in a world slipping from her grasp.

The Keep was cloaked in a heavy silence over the days that followed, as if every stone, every shadow, mourned with the family. Faylen's death settled over them like a dark cloud, casting a pall over even the smallest acts of daily life. Servants moved quietly through the halls, their eyes downcast, as they worked to prepare for the funeral rites. They braided grapevines to create a nest, placing it at the center of the Keep, and lined it with soft rose petals, each one a silent tribute.

White lilies filled the corridors, their ghostly petals lending an almost otherworldly beauty to the somber setting. Jájá drifted among them, her expression vacant, her gaze distant. She moved as if in a trance, overseeing every detail with a numb focus that seemed more ritual than intention.

Sekowah stayed out of sight, feeling as though she were intruding on a grief she had no right to share. She spent most of her time in solitude, the weight of guilt pressing her further into herself. One evening, she caught sight of Máhí standing alone on the balcony, her face turned toward the maze below, her usually serious face softened, touched with sorrow. But when she noticed Sekowah watching, Máhí's expression hardened, and she vanished back into the shadows.

Vesper had taken Gavril and journeyed to Obsidia, seeking... vengeance, perhaps, though no one spoke it aloud. Sekowah overheard whispers at supper, fragments of dark rumors about the desecration of Faylen's body—the Dasheahs leaving her lifeless body exposed in the Daylight Meadow for wild beasts to devour. It was a declaration of war, they said, a provocation meant to strip them of honor.

The rumors were confirmed when they returned with the remains of her corpse, wrapped in colorful silk blankets.

The day of the funeral arrived with an oppressive stillness, as if even the wind dared not disturb the gravity of the occasion. The procession began at the Keep, a solemn line of family and friends winding down the mountain path, their voices lifting in song.

The music was a haunting blend of sorrow and grace, notes carrying the weight of lives intertwined, and the bittersweet ache of farewell. Jájá and Vesper walked at the head of the procession, their faces carved from stone, each step a testament to their dignity and pain.

Sekowah followed, garbed in a silken gown of deep indigo, the fabric flowing around her like water. As they sang, she felt her own voice rise, unexpected and clear, threading through the others. Though she had barely known Faylen, the loss had carved a hollow ache within her. Guilt and regret colored every note she sang, transforming her voice into something fierce and fragile.

When they reached the valley's center, they entered a stone circle, crafted from boulders arranged in a spiral that wound toward the middle. At the center stood a great stone tablet, flanked by four cone-shaped rocks, each one towering like ancient sentinels. The procession slowed as they approached, and one by one, they followed the spiral path until they stood around the stone.

Faylen's nest, her wrapped body nestled inside and swathed in ribbons of silk, was lifted gently from the wagon and placed upon the stone tablet. Sekowah watched as her mother, Vesper, and Máhí each took their place by one of the cone-shaped stones, leaving the last for her. She approached it with trepidation. At her feet, was a round rock, perfectly smooth. She picked it up, as the others did, unsure why.

The congregation fell silent, the songs fading into the quiet of the valley. Holding the stone firmly, Jájá raised hers and struck it gently against the cone-shaped rock. A clear, resonant note rang out, soft and pure. Vesper and Máhí followed, each adding their own tone, creating a harmony that vibrated through the air, rich and layered, as if the rocks themselves mourned.

The stone Sekowah held in her hand felt oddly warm, vibrating slightly as if it were attuned to the song of grief surrounding them. She could feel the resonance in her bones, a deep, ancient hum that seemed to echo up from the earth beneath her feet. Following the others' lead, she lifted the stone and struck it against the hollow cone before her. The sound that rang out was deep, bell-like, a low, resonant tone that settled in her chest and vibrated through her ribcage.

As the music of the rocks grew stronger, the congregation joined, their voices blending with the tones to form a haunting chorus. The valley pulsed with an unearthly orchestra, a living heartbeat, an ancient song of farewell. The congregation began to sing, their voices melding with the tones of the stones, creating a melody that was haunting and ethereal. Sekowah could feel the power of it, a vast river of sorrow and remembrance flowing through her, carrying with it the grief and the strength of every person gathered here. Though she had barely known Faylen, the loss cut her deeply; it was as if she were mourning something larger than one life—perhaps the sister she might have known, or the childhood she had lost, or the innocence she would never regain.

She closed her eyes, letting herself be swept up in the music, her own voice rising to join the others. She sang without words, without conscious thought, letting the song pour from her in a raw, unfiltered stream. Her voice trembled but held, and as she sang, she felt a strange sort of peace settle over her—a fragile, bittersweet calm, like the quiet that comes just after a snowfall.

As the sounds grew louder, and they all continued to strike the rocks, Faylen's nest lifted into the air... and began to spin, bursting into flame. The flames in the nest leapt higher, the rose petals spinning a web around it, the flames swirling up into the air in a furious cyclone of red. The petals spun faster, caught in some unseen current, creating a whirlwind of color against the darkening sky. Then, as if ignited by their own momentum, the petals caught fire, bursting into flame one by one until the entire tornado was ablaze. The valley was cast in white hot light, and Sekowah could feel the heat intensifying, pressing against her skin, as ash was carried away on the currents, lifting Faylen into the heavens.

The procession began to wind back up the mountain, the congregation moving in quiet lines, their voices subdued, their faces etched with sorrow and reverence. Jájá and Vesper led the way, their shoulders set, their steps slow and deliberate. Sekowah fell into step behind them, the scent of smoke and roses clinging to her skin, the memory of Faylen's final moments still fresh in her mind.

As they climbed the rough trail back to Peregrine's Keep, the sky darkened, and stars began to appear, one by one, flickering against the vastness of the night. Sekowah glanced up, her heart aching, and for a moment, she imagined one of those stars was Faylen, watching over them, guiding them through the darkness.

When they finally reached the Keep, Sekowah lingered at the edge of the crowd, reluctant to step back into the confines of stone and walls. She felt raw, exposed, as if the ritual had stripped away some essential layer of protection, leaving her bare to the cold wind and the vast, endless sky.

Her eyes found Jájá, who stood alone now, gazing out over the valley, her face illuminated by the stars. There was an emptiness in her mother's expression, a grief that was alien in its intensity. Sekowah watched her, feeling a strange pull—a mixture of pity, anger, and something else, something she couldn't name.

In that moment, she wanted to reach out, to bridge the gap between them, to say something that would make sense of the tangled web of duty, family, and loss that bound them to one another. But the words died in her throat, and instead, she turned away, slipping into the shadows of the Keep, leaving her mother to grieve alone.

As she moved down the stone corridors toward her quarters, her mind returned to Faylen's last words: *You're nothing but a flag in a game you know nothing about.*

The thought lingered like a splinter in her mind, sharp and unyielding. Now, she questioned everything—the stories, the prophecies, the expectations they had all heaped upon her shoulders. She felt the weight of it pressing down, a crushing inevitability that made her long for the simple life she'd left behind, even as she knew there was no going b ack.

Reaching her quarters, Sekowah collapsed onto her bed, her body heavy with exhaustion, her heart hollowed out by grief. She closed her eyes, letting the quiet settle around her, but sleep did not come easily. Instead, she lay awake, haunted by visions of fire and ashes, of Faylen's face in the flames, and of the cold, unyielding truths that lay just beyond her reach.

As dawn began to creep over the horizon, Sekowah felt a stirring deep within her, a quiet resolve that took root in the dark soil of her doubt. Whatever lay ahead, she would face it—not because it was expected of her, or because it was foretold, but because, somehow, she knew she owed it to herself. And perhaps, in some small way, to Faylen.

With that thought, she finally drifted into a fitful sleep, her mind filled with visions of fire, of stars, and of the long, uncertain path that stretched out before her.

CHAPTER THIRTY

RETURN OF THE GREEN DRAGON

On the high balcony of the Keep, Vesper and Jájá stood side by side, watching as Máhí and Sekowah moved through the twisting paths of the maze below. It had been years—decades, even—since the king and queen had stood together like this, silently aligned.

In the maze, Sekowah stood at the entrance, listening to Máhí's instructions with a look that was half-attentive, half-distracted. Vesper observed this with a furrowed brow, murmuring, "It feels strange, doesn't it? They're both grown, yet it's as if she's only now learning to walk." His voice was quiet, touched by a hint of sorrow.

Jájá tilted her head slightly, eyes never leaving the two figures below. "She was never given the simplest lessons as a nestling. What she did learn—her mortal skills—are of little use here. Let her play. Let her have this week of games. It will mend her heart, and perhaps sharpen the basics." There was a wistful note in her tone, a recognition of all the years lost.

The maze below was an intricate tapestry of trails, canopied trees, and flowering vines woven in spirals and twists. From their high vantage point, Vesper and Jájá could see the lavender flags, tied like ribbons to various branches, fluttering in the breeze. At the maze's center stood a trellis draped in delicate Lucklace, its tendrils glistening like silver under the midday sun. Beneath the trellis, almost daringly out in the open, was a single white flag.

On the ground near the maze's entrance, Gavril leaned casually against a tree, chewing on Sleeproot, his keen gaze fixed on Sekowah. She and Máhí stood at the entrance—two trees with branches entwined to form an archway: the silent threshold of the maze.

Máhí's voice held a hint of mischief as she explained the rules. "It's a game," she said. "Simple, really. Your task is to find the white flag and bring it back here to the start."

Sekowah glanced down the path ahead, memories flashing before her eyes—the night of her capture, Faylen's laughter echoing through these very trails. Her emotions were tangled, her mind torn between anger and understanding.

"Are you even listening?" Máhí's voice cut through her thoughts, sharp with irritation.

Sekowah blinked, refocusing. "Yes. I'm listening. Get the white flag."

Máhí's lips curled into a wry smile. "There's another part to the game," she continued. "I'm going to try and stop you from getting that flag."

Sekowah's eyes narrowed. "Hardly seems fair. You have wings."

Máhí raised an eyebrow, her smirk widening. "I won't use them. Today."

Sekowah's gaze shifted to Gavril. "And what about him?"

Gavril stepped forward with a roguish grin, his eyes glinting with excitement. "I'm your secret weapon," he said, bowing slightly. "You can use me however you like. Except—" he cast a sidelong glance at Máhí—"I can't engage with Máhí physically."

Sekowah took a moment to think. "Any other rules?" she asked, a spark of cunning lighting her gaze.

Máhí shrugged. "Nope. That's it. I'll give you a head start, and then... I'll find you. And to be fair, you may use invisibility."

Sekowah gave a small, defiant smile. "I have my own ideas."

There was something mischievous in her expression, something that hadn't been there before. She stepped close to Gavril, leaning in to whisper her plan. His face lit up with approval, and he gave her a quick nod. "That'll work," he said, grinning even wider. He looked over to Máhí. "Proceed."

Máhí turned her back, and closed her eyes.

Up on the balcony, Vesper leaned forward, intrigued as he watched Sekowah and Gavril dart through the arched entrance and disappear into the maze's leafy depths. He murmured to Jájá, "Máhí's not an easy opponent. I almost feel sorry for Sekowah. But, as you say, it will—"

But he fell silent, his words fading as he saw Gavril rise from the maze canopy, carrying Sekowah in his arms beneath his massive wings. Together, they soared toward the center, Gavril descending over the trellis as Sekowah stretched out her arm and snatched the white flag.

Jájá, catching sight of this, burst into laughter—an unrestrained, joyous sound that seemed to chase the shadows from her face. Her voice carried across the air as she called down to Máhí, who had just opened her eyes, ready to begin, "The best has been bested!"

Máhí's expression, as she opened her eyes to find Sekowah and Gavril standing victoriously with the white flag in hand, was a mixture of disbelief and frustration. "Impossible!" she sputtered, her pride clearly stung.

Above, Vesper took Jájá's hand, a rare gesture of warmth that softened the edges of his usual stoic demeanor. "It seems," he said with a smile, "You underestimated your opponent."

"But how?!" Máhí demanded, looking from Sekowah to Gavril in exasperation.

Vesper chuckled, calling down, "You know the rules, Máhí. Strategies belong to the victor!" He winked at Sekowah, who was clearly taking this secret to her grave.

Máhí turned to Sekowah, her gaze steely. She knew better than to press for answers. "Fine," she muttered. And then, without warning, she shoved Sekowah to the ground.

Sekowah stumbled, landing hard on the packed earth, surprise flashing across her face. "Ow!" She pushed herself up onto her elbows, glaring up at Máhí. "What was that for?"

Máhí crossed her arms, her stance unyielding. "Now get up."

Sekowah climbed to her feet, brushing dirt off her tunic, only to have Máhí knock her down again. Her annoyance flared into anger. "Stop it!" she snapped, scrambling to her feet once more. *If she wants me to hate her, it's working*, she thought bitterly.

Máhí held up her hand, demonstrating her own stance. "Next lesson. Stand like this." She placed one foot forward, one back, her posture solid and grounded. "Start with how you hold yourself. You're only as strong as you believe yourself to be."

Sekowah mimicked her stance, planting her feet with determination. Máhí gave her another shove, but this time, Sekowah managed to hold her ground, though just barely.

Gavril called up to the balcony. "Claim your ground!" he shouted, his voice ringing with encouragement.

Vesper and Jájá watched, their expressions softened with amusement as Máhí delivered a quick punch to Sekowah's arm. Vesper chuckled. "What lesson is that supposed to teach?"

"I haven't a clue," Jájá replied, laughing.

Sekowah winced, rubbing her arm. "What was that for?"

Máhí handed the flag back to her with a smirk. "That, was for making me come all the way down here and play for nothing," she said. "I missed my berrywine biscuits." She turned on her heels and strode back toward the castle, her head held high, as though she hadn't just been bested in her own game.

Sekowah watched her go, a sense of triumph simmering just below her bruised frustration. *I won,* she thought, standing a little taller as she began to follow. *I can do this. I can learn.*

Jájá leapt gracefully from the balcony and swooped down to meet them, her face alight with pride. "You're brilliant," she said, embracing Sekowah warmly.

Sekowah returned the hug, a new confidence swelling within her. "Thank you." She glanced over at Gavril, who was grinning with approval. "I know I have a long way to go... but I believe I can learn."

"Excellent," Jájá declared, her voice bright with enthusiasm. "Tonight, we'll feast! Blueberry snippets and forever beans!" She held her head high as they made their way back to the castle, her voice brimming with anticipation.

Sekowah took a deep breath, savoring the warmth of the morning sun. The light cast a halo around the castle, and for a moment, she felt truly at peace, as though she had finally found a place in this strange, beautiful world. "I think Inanna would be proud of me," she said quietly.

Jájá froze mid-step, her face shifting from warmth to shock. "What did you say?"

Máhí's eyes widened, exchanging a look with her mother. Her voice trembled as she asked, "Inanna... you saw her?"

Sekowah shifted, feeling their intense gazes. "Yes. I saw her in Obsidia," she admitted. She hadn't expected such a reaction. "She was chained to Zincubus' throne. She looked like a fox... a grey fox with violet eyes. I freed her, and she helped me escape. Without her, I'd still be down there... or worse."

The color drained from Jájá's face. She reached out, clutching Sekowah's arm. "Come inside," she whispered, her tone both reverent and urgent. "Tell me everything."

T he clash of swords echoed through the high-walled arena, each clang reverberating against the stones. Sekowah, weighed down in azurtanium chainmail, struggled to keep her balance as she squared off against Máhí. The chainmail, though marvelously crafted, felt like an anchor dragging her down. Every movement was laborious, each swing of her sword a battle against the thick links pulling on her shoulders. The leather boots cut into her ankles, and the weight pressing on her collarbones made her knees feel as though they might buckle.

Across from her, Máhí moved like liquid steel—swift, precise, almost mocking in her effortless grace. Vesper and Gavril observed from the sidelines, their voices occasionally cutting through the sounds of combat with words of encouragement.

"Your greatest defense—" Máhí murmured as she sidestepped Sekowah's clumsy thrust. "—evade." She thrust her sword towards Sekowah, who stumbled back, just narrowly avoiding the blow. "Good. You're improving."

It didn't feel like improvement. Sekowah could feel sweat soaking through the tunic beneath the chainmail, her breath coming in short, shallow gasps. Her arms quivered from the weight of the sword, and the rough edges of the chainmail dug into her pointy ears, causing a dull, throbbing pain. She gritted her teeth, feeling her frustration rise. *Máhí made it look so easy!*

Before she had a chance to catch her breath, Gavril stepped in, taking Máhí's place with a playful, almost dangerous gleam in his eye. "Anticipate," he said as he raised his sword high above her. Sekowah tracked the blade, stepping aside just as Máhí had taught her—but a sharp pain stabbed into her ribs as his other hand, unseen, brought a practice dagger in from the side.

"Distract," Gavril explained, his voice almost amused.

A dirty trick, she thought. Sekowah scowled, stung not just by the impact but by the embarrassment. She felt the simmering heat of frustration flare into anger. *They're ganging up on me,* she thought bitterly. It's like they're enjoying this. She wanted to scream, to toss aside the heavy armor and walk out.

"Oh, forget it," she muttered, throwing her sword to the floor with a clatter. She watched as it skidded across the stone, stopping beneath a table. Her arms ached from the exertion, and her spirit felt bruised.

Gavril's face softened. He picked up her sword and handed it back to her with a reassuring smile. "Don't worry," he said gently. "You'll get better with practice. We've been at this for many harvests."

A bell rang out from the far corner of the arena, the deep, echoing chime a welcome interruption. "That's us," Vesper called, clapping his hands together as he approached.

He placed a hand on Sekowah's shoulder, leaning in close to whisper, "Just between you and me, it took Máhí twice as long to reach this level. Well done."

Máhí snorted as she left the room, but there was a smirk on her face. "I heard that!"

···· • ⟨⟨ • ····

Later, in the dim, firelit confines of Vesper's private chambers, a more somber atmosphere settled over the gathering. The room was rich with the smell of smoke from Brock's pipe, an earthy scent that mingled with the aroma of ancient parchment and leather-bound tomes. Vesper didn't sit at his desk as he normally would; instead, he reclined in a high-backed chair draped with a white, shaggy animal skin, gesturing for Sekowah to take the chair beside him.

They watched her with expectant eyes—Máhí, standing tall and plucking absently at her feathers; Gavril, serious and attentive; Brock, wrinkled and frowning; and Jájá, her gaze fixed intently on Sekowah as if searching for signs of a secret she already knew.

Máhí leaned forward. "Tell him what you told me," she urged, her voice barely masking her impatience.

Sekowah hesitated, feeling the weight of their attention settle heavily on her shoulders. But she began, her voice steady, despite the nervous flutter in her stomach. "I saw dragons."

A collective silence followed, tense and unbroken until Máhí, eyes gleaming, prompted her, "Tell them what color."

Sekowah took a breath, watching their faces. "Red, green, black, and purple."

Brock choked, coughing on his pipe smoke. He recovered with a violent shake of his head, his wrinkled face contorting as if he'd just heard an obscenity. "Nay. Not possible, ya know." He shook his head violently and screwed up his face, as if his expression alone might ward off evil or change the truth of it.

Sekowah held her ground. "I saw them. In small caves. Big ones, small ones... even babies."

Gavril's expression darkened, and he exchanged a look with Vesper. "He's breeding them?" he asked, his voice barely a whisper, as if the question itself were dangerous.

Sekowah nodded slowly. "I think so. Yes."

Brock shuffled closer to Vesper, lowering his voice as he muttered, "We nay seen a green dragon for ten reigns. Ya can't conjure something out of nothing, eh."

In the dim light, Jájá's face turned pale. She whispered, "With his fire, the dark shall scatter, the land reborn in ash and light..."

Vesper waved her off, his voice sharp with impatience. "Go on."

"Slaves," Sekowah continued, watching the flicker of horror cross their faces as she added, "who looked like lizards, working."

Vesper's mouth set in a hard line. "Moorigato," he murmured. "How many?"

Sekowah shook her head, struggling to convey the sheer scale. "Hundreds. Building... guns."

The room held its breath. Brock took a step forward, his brow furrowed. "Guns? What're ya about, child?"

Sekowah's voice was tight with urgency. "Guns. You know. Guns. Bang, bang?" She shot an imaginary gun with her finger. She could tell from their expressions that they hadn't the slightest idea what she was talking about. "They're metal things ... that shoot bullets." Vesper furrowed his brow at her in confusion. "Bullets are like, little balls that shoot out of the end of it."

They looked at her, bewildered.

"Fast enough to go right through you," she said, feeling their disbelief like a wall she had to climb over. "They're more dangerous than swords. You don't even need to get close to kill someone."

The laughter that followed was low and uneasy. They chuckled, their amusement forced, the echo of it uncomfortable.

"Absurd," Vesper spat.

Sekowah didn't laugh. She leaned forward, intent, her eyes locked on Vesper's. "It's not absurd. One bullet could kill a warrior from a distance. It's faster than anything you've ever seen. So fast you don't see it." She paused, feeling the need to break through their skepticism. "May I?" She gestured toward his desk, where quills and ink waited.

Vesper bowed his head, granting her permission.

Sekowah picked up a quill and dipped it in berry ink, drawing a crude outline of a gun. The shapes were familiar from old films, from passing glances in a world that now felt impossibly far away. She finished the drawing and held it up. "Here. There's a trigger, here. You hold the gun like this, pull the trigger, and it... it explodes inside, sending the bullet out."

They stared, transfixed, as if she'd just revealed the existence of some dark magic. Vesper examined her drawing, his face drawn with tension. "You can show us how to make this?"

She shook her head. "No. I don't know how they're made. I've only seen pictures." She looked to Jájá, noticing the pallor in her mother's face, the way she avoided Máhí's eyes. "Where is Zincubus from?"

Jájá spoke up. "He's mortal, so of course, he travels between worlds." She addressed Vesper, defensively. "I have no knowledge nor have I helped him in any way. He cannot use the cove gates, as I have had the key."

Vesper shot her a quick glance, then turned back to Sekowah. "Continue."

She nodded. "They're more dangerous than anything I know of... except maybe bombs."

Vesper's eyes darkened. "Bombs?"

She nodded, searching for words to make them understand. "They're like... a giant bullet. They explode. Pieces fly in all directions, killing anyone close. It's... like a hundred guns going off at once."

A tense silence filled the room, stretching, thickening. And then, as if released by a spell, the Council broke into urgent whispers, their voices colliding in a frantic chorus.

"He must be stopped."

"Mortal weapons, in our realm—"

"He violates every treaty."

Brock addressed Vesper, angry now. "I warned of this, ya know."

"We cannot fight a war on two fronts." Gavril's face was lined with worry as he paced, his steps heavy with dread.

Sekowah raised her hand, her voice barely above a whisper. "Excuse me."

They ignored her, the protests rising again.

"Excuse me!" she repeated, louder this time.

Máhí silenced them with a sharp gesture. ""Tihile si!" Let her speak."

Sekowah took a deep breath. "There's an army of Dokar on the other side of that mountain. They know how to fight. Why can't we ask for their help?"

Brock scoffed, throwing up his hands. "The Dokar? Barbarians, the lot!"

Gavril interrupted, "A ruthless enemy turned ally. It would end our border war and sever our alliance with Zincubus."

They all turned to Vesper, awaiting his judgment. He looked out over the hills, considering. Finally, he shook his head. "If we do... we drive him away, yes. But at what cost? The Dokar will demand resettlement privileges. The valley would be overrun."

"Then we must do more than drive him away," Jájá argued, her voice firm.

Brock frowned, loading his pipe. "Ye forget, he has the Keeper's protection. Should he perish at our hand—"

Vesper interrupted him, annoyed with his quotes from *the Verses*. "Lies. The Keeper has planted fear in the hearts of our people for too long. That will be enough."

"'From the Pine Bogs to the Great Blue, all will be turned to sand,'" Gavril finished Brock's sentence. "We cannot risk it."

The room went silent, and Máhí, her gaze steady on Sekowah, said, "But she can."

Brock laughed bitterly. "Ayyooo! That'll be the day."

Sekowah glared at him. *For a little man, he sure was confident.* She felt a sudden urge to kick him in the shins but resisted.

Jájá cleared her throat and addressed Brock. "Inanna is alive. As is Krag, her black dragon. The same black dragon that Zincubus once claimed to have slaughtered. Both were enslaved by him. His protection extends only to our kind. Not mortals. Thus, the Prophecy reveals the path."

The room stilled, stunned into silence.

Vesper was the first to speak. His voice softened, hope glimmering in his eyes. "Inanna... is alive?"

Sekowah rose from her chair, feeling proud. Important. She had something to contribute after all. "Yes," she announced. "She is very much alive. I met her myself. During my time in the underground—I set her free, and she showed me the way out. I would not be here now if it wasn't for her."

Jájá lifted her chin in triumph and turned to Vesper. "Why do you never listen to me? I told you I suspected her presence here. Now it is confirmed. You mustn't deny *the Verses* any longer."

Gavril pulled Jájá aside and whispered in her ear and they both glanced over at Sekowah. Sekowah tried to hear their conversation but was unable.

CHAPTER THIRTY-ONE

A COMMON ENEMY

The quiet of the forest weighed heavily as Vesper guided his troop along the narrow, rock-strewn trail, the slope steep and unforgiving beneath their horses' hooves. They moved under the cover of darkness, a silent procession through the towering pines of Mount Lira, their path lit only by thin threads of moonlight slipping between branches. Vesper kept his gaze forward, lost in his own thoughts. Beneath the leather and chainmail, his skin prickled with sweat, yet his fingertips were numb from the night chill at this elevation.

The only sounds were the soft clinking of armor and the occasional clatter of stones tumbling down the mountainside. Behind him, Gavril's voice rose in low, casual conversation with Faro, the lead of the squad—a jovial tone that grated against Vesper's nerves. He couldn't understand how anyone could speak lightly after all they had lost.

He never imagined Gavril, his steadfast friend and ally, capable of keeping secrets from him. Though he knew the man well enough to trust his intentions, it still stung. Secrets, however well-meant, were dangerous currency in times like these. *You want a truce with the Dokar? You can negotiate it yourself*, he thought, his mind a roiling sea of doubts and mistrust.

His black gelding picked its way carefully down the rocky path, muscles shifting beneath Vesper as the winged horse navigated the loose stones. Vesper loosened his grip on the reins, giving the animal room to find its balance, his attention returning to the distant glow of fires flickering between the trees ahead. The sounds of camp life grew closer—the murmur of voices, the crackle of flames, the clank of pots and armor. It was a weary, subdued sort of noise, heavy with the knowledge of another day's bloodshed.

As they approached the encampment, the sight that greeted him was familiar yet no less grim. Along the edge of the clearing, wagons lined up like silent sentinels, each one bearing the bodies of fallen Lirian warriors, their faces shrouded by dirty flax sheets. Vesper's chest tightened at the sight. They were running out of warriors, and he knew it. Too many were gone, and those who remained were young, unseasoned, pushed through training with brutal haste. They had been born into this war, taught to hate the Dokar with every fiber of their being, and he was about to ask them to ally with those very enemies.

As he rode past a cluster of warriors huddled around a fire, Vesper caught a few nods of acknowledgment, but most kept their eyes down, staring into the flames or at the ground. He could feel their exhaustion, their doubt radiating from them like heat from the embers. It was a disquieting sensation, the kind that sat in the stomach like a stone. These were warriors who had given everything, who had seen friends and kin fall, who had known nothing but this endless struggle against the Dokar. Now he would ask them to cast aside years of hatred, to join hands with their sworn enemies for a new, unknown fight. He doubted their loyalty to such a cause, and worse, he doubted his own.

Vesper's mind drifted to Sekowah's revelation of Inanna, alive and held captive in Obsidia. A ghost from their past, returned to haunt them. He'd long thought her gone—dead or vanished. But now, her presence was a whisper of prophecy, a warning of change. If Sekowah spoke true, if Inanna had indeed been a prisoner of Zincubus all this time, then everything he'd thought he knew was a lie. It made him sick to think of it, the bitter taste of betrayal souring his mouth. He shifted uncomfortably in his saddle, grappling with questions that had no answers.

Ahead, the camp commander, Horato, emerged from a large tent near the center of the clearing. A man built like a mountain, with broad shoulders and a jaw carved from granite, Horato moved with a quiet authority. He had risen to command through sheer grit and skill, his reputation cemented by feats both on the battlefield and in the Games, where he had once been a champion javelin thrower. Horato approached, gripping Vesper's hand in greeting with a hearty smile.

"Your timing is good," he said, his voice a warm rumble. "We pushed the line back a great distance today."

Vesper did not return the smile, his expression weary. Instead, he placed a hand on Horato's elbow, guiding him back toward the tent with a quiet urgency. "There's been a change in strategy," he said. "We need to speak privately."

· · · · ⬭ · · · ·

The early morning air bit into Gavril's skin as he sat by the campfire, his breath mingling with the rising steam from his mug of pine-needle tea. Around him, the small patches of snow clung stubbornly to the forest floor, sparkling in the dawn light. The bitter cold nipped at his fingertips, though the tea offered a momentary warmth, and the sun, just beginning to crest over the twin waterfalls in the distance, promised more. The waterfalls glistened in the first rays of sunlight, an ethereal rainbow halo forming where the mist met the light. For a brief moment, Gavril felt a sense of peace—a reminder of what they fought to protect.

He swallowed a spoonful of rabbit porridge, the coarse texture and earthy taste familiar, grounding. Beside him, a few other warriors warmed their hands over the fire, their faces drawn and wary. The wear of endless battle was etched into their expressions, the fine lines around their eyes, the way their shoulders sagged under the weight of armor and unspoken grief.

One of the warriors, a broad-shouldered man with a scar trailing from his temple to his jaw, glanced toward Vesper, who stood in the distance preparing the horses with Horato. The warrior nodded in their direction and spoke quietly. "Word is, we may be negotiating a truce. On what grounds and conditions, do you know?" His voice was low but carried a note of desperation—a hunger for clarity, for some anchor amid the shifting tides of war.

Gavril set down his mug, choosing his words carefully, conscious of the weight they would carry. "We've held the border for longer than most would dare," he began, his voice calm, steady. "You've all gone above and beyond to protect our land, to defend your homes. But... we're losing ground." He didn't sugarcoat it. These warriors deserved the truth, and they would detect any hint of false hope. They understood the language of sacrifice.

A murmur ran through the group, and another warrior, his face hardened with grief and rage, spoke up. "Aye, but we've lost too many to give up now."

Gavril took a sip of his tea and nodded in agreement. "It may appear as though we are giving up, but we have a far bigger threat now," he confessed. This got their attention. *A common enemy. Keep them focused on winning the war, not the battle*, he thought. "We've been distracted with our northern border, but Zincubus has been busy. He's secretly been preparing to take over Mount Lira and advance into the valley."

The murmurs grew louder, tinged with disbelief and anger. The news hit them like a hammer blow; it was as if he'd spoken a foreign language. For years, Zincubus had been their benefactor, their ally against the Dokar, the one who supplied them with the resources they needed to hold the line. To suggest that he was anything other than a friend felt like blasphemy.

One of the older warriors stood abruptly, his face contorted in anger. "Zincubus has provided us with all we needed to fight the Dokar! This is nonsense," he spat, looking around at his comrades for support. Others nodded, their faces shadowed with doubt.

Gavril took a deep breath, calming the fire that flickered within him. They were blindsided; of course, they would resist. He met the fighter's gaze, letting the silence stretch until it commanded their full attention. "It's true. I believed it myself. But, as we have learned, it was no more than a strategy to keep us busy, decrease our numbers, and weaken our position against him. While we are killing each other, he has waited patiently for the right time to declare his true intentions. That time is now upon us. He has taken the life of the king's daughter Faylen, thrown her body into a meadow to be eaten by beasts, and cut off all trade. These are acts of war. We suspect he plans to advance from the south with mortal weapons. None that has been seen before, things we know nothing about. His army is the Moorigato and his arrival is imminent."

A shiver ran through the group, a ripple of shock and fury. Gavril's words hung heavy, the betrayal sharp and raw. He could see it in their faces, the way realization dawned slowly, painfully. The bonds of trust that had tethered them to Zincubus were unraveling, snapping like threads under tension.

One of the younger warriors, his voice quiet but resolute, spoke up. "If he has these... mortal weapons, as you say, how can we fight against that?"

Gavril nodded in agreement. "We can't, not alone. That's why we need the Dokar. They have numbers, strength. And with them, we can stand a chance against Zincubus and whatever he brings from the mortal world. This alliance—it's not surrender. It's survival."

The fire crackled, casting flickering shadows over the warriors' faces as they absorbed his words. They had fought their whole lives against the Dokar, lost friends and family to their spears and blades.

Vesper's voice cut through the murmur of voices, steady and commanding as he approached the small group. "We'll know more soon enough. We have a long day ahead of us." He raised his hands, quieting their questions. "Let us see what we can accomplish today. There will be time for answers."

The tension eased, if only slightly, as Vesper moved away. The men watched him go, uncertain but swayed by his authority, by the resolve etched in his posture. But not all were satisfied. A young recruit, his face twisted with anger, hurled his metal cup into the fire and stormed off, muttering curses. Gavril watched him go, feeling a pang of understanding. For those who had lost the most, this alliance was a bitter pill.

Gavril stood, addressing the rest of the group. "Your allegiance is not required," he said, his voice quiet but firm. "But I hope you'll join us. This is the fight that will determine our future. Alone, we face a dark and certain end. Together, we may have a chance."

The warriors exchanged uneasy glances, but none spoke against him. Their loyalty to Gavril was strong, their respect hard-earned. Slowly, one by one, they nodded, the beginnings of acceptance flickering in their eyes.

He joined Vesper and the expedition, their path taking them down a narrow, winding trail through the thicket, the underbrush dense and unforgiving. Behind them, he could hear the warriors debating among themselves, the air thick with tension and doubt.

The peace party advanced cautiously toward the final ridge before the twin water-falls. This was the edge of Lirian territory, the last strip of land before the border with the Dokar. From their vantage point, they could see the Dokarian warriors stationed behind trees, their figures dark and foreboding against the gray mist of morning. Their armor was dull steel, wrapped in fur capes that billowed slightly in the cold breeze, their boots thick and crude, perfect for trudging through the mud and snow. Bows were drawn, spears ready—each warrior a coiled spring, waiting for the first sign of hostility.

At the front, Horato raised his arm, signaling the group to halt. Vesper reined in his horse and dismounted; his eyes scanned the tree line. The silent threat was palpable, the air thick with the tension of hundreds of unspoken promises of violence. This was either the end of a war—or the beginning of a massacre.

Vesper took a deep breath and reached into his saddlebag, pulling out a small, twisted horn carved from the horns of a prairie ram. Lifting it to his lips, he blew a high, piercing note. The sound echoed lightly, not the deep, thunderous call of the Horn of War, but something gentler, almost hesitant—a request rather than a command.

Across the ridge, the Dokar warriors stiffened, their hands tightening on their weapons. Arrows were notched, aimed, their eyes tracking every movement.

"We come in peace!" Vesper shouted, his voice carrying over the sound of rushing water. Horato unfurled a purple flag, waving it overhead in slow, deliberate motions, a gesture of goodwill.

"Come no farther!" a voice barked from behind a nearby tree, rough and edged with distrust.

Vesper stepped into the open, hands spread to show he was unarmed. "We wish a meeting with Mardig," he called out, his tone steady, commanding.

For a tense, breathless moment, silence hung between them, a stillness that stretched to the breaking point. Vesper half-expected the familiar whistling of arrows slicing through the mist toward him, the inevitable betrayal.

The air remained quiet.

Finally, a runner emerged from the trees, his fur cloak whipping around him as he sprinted back toward the Dokarian encampment. Vesper's eyes tracked him, his muscles tense, every instinct telling him to prepare for an ambush. Yet he remained rooted, calm on the outside, while his mind calculated and recalculated the risks.

He waiting an eternity, his breath filling the chilled air with tendrils of mist.

Finally, the runner returned, relaying a message from the Dokar: "You may send only one."

Vesper huffed. *One? They wanted to draw him in, unguarded?* The arrogance—and the insult—was unmistakable. He would not send his top commander into enemy territory alone. His voice, cold and authoritative, sliced through the air as he responded. "Tell Mardig that I will send my top commander with two guards. If they do not return by nightfall, we will advance across the waters without mercy."

The ultimatum hung heavy, a blunt reminder of the stakes. The runner nodded and disappeared back into the trees, leaving the Lirians to wait, their breaths visible in the cold morning air. Vesper scanned his men, his eyes hard, unwavering. If this gambit failed, the path to peace would be sealed in blood. But if they succeeded...

· · · · • ◯◯ • · · · ·

Gavril entered Mardig's tent flanked by his two guards, the warmth from the central fire rushing over him like a sudden wave. The tent, fashioned from animal hides stitched with sinew, felt oppressive and close, the earthy scent of leather and smoke filling the air. He kept his eyes down, resisting the temptation to look around, though he could feel the weight of hostile gazes pressing in from every side.

At the entrance, two Dokarian guards, hulking brutes with cold eyes, waited like stone sentinels. One of them moved forward, shoving Gavril to his knees. Pain flared at the base of his neck as the guard wrapped his braid around a brutish fist, twisting and yanking it back sharply, forcing Gavril's face upward. The humiliation burned, almost as much as the sharp sting radiating from his scalp, but he swallowed his pride, focusing on the task that had brought him here. He would endure this—*must* endure it—if he wanted any hope of securing an alliance.

The guard dug a knee into Gavril's back, keeping him pinned, as the Dokarian leaders watched with cool amusement. Mardig, the king, sat on a plush mound of furs near the fire, his imposing figure half-draped in shadow. He was young by their standards, perhaps three hundred harvests, yet his face bore the hard lines of someone who had seen too much. A mohawk of thick black hair crowned his head, while tattoos twisted along the sides of his skull, curling down his neck and vanishing beneath his fur cloak.

Beside him, his sister Ylva watched Gavril with dark, penetrating eyes that sparkled with a feral intelligence. Her own mohawk, a mirror to her brother's, was braided back, black hair falling to her waist. Unlike Mardig, she wore a mischievous smile, one that hinted at dangerous amusement. In her hand, she held a knife with a blade that caught the firelight, flickering through the shadows. Gavril recognized it instantly—azurtanium, the distinctive gleam of metal unmistakable. He didn't need to wonder where she'd acquired it; the Lirian's own armor was made from the rare mineral, and the knowledge that one of their own had likely died for that blade soured his stomach.

The guard wrenched Gavril's head back further, forcing his eyes toward the tent's smoky ceiling. Gavril's shoulders tensed as he fought to hold back a grimace. One of Gavril's guards took a step forward, hand moving to his weapon, but Gavril managed a slight shake of his head. This was not the time for heroics.

Mardig let out a soft chuckle, his voice rough and low, clearly enjoying Gavril's discomfort. "Release him. He is harmless here." The command came with a casual wave of his hand, as though Gavril were nothing more than a passing nuisance. The guard loosened his grip, letting Gavril's braid fall back along his back, as he retreated to his post at the tent's entrance.

Ylva stood, the knife glinting in her hand, her smile widening as she regarded Gavril like a wolf sizing up prey. "You're just in time," she murmured, circling him slowly, her eyes never leaving his face. She tilted the knife, letting the firelight dance along its edge, taunting him. He kept his eyes down, muscles tight, resisting every instinct to meet her gaze, to challenge her. This was their game, and he knew better than to rise to their bait.

She leaned close, her breath hot against his ear. "The equinox is calling." Her tone was mocking, and from behind him came the coarse laughter of the Dokarian guards. An inside joke, it seemed, one meant to further humiliate him. He remained still, though every nerve in his body screamed to react.

Mardig, clearly savoring the display, rose from his seat, his movements slow and deliberate. He reached over, pulling Ylva back with a smirk. "Let him speak. Then you can have him." His words were half-joking, half-serious, and they drew a fresh round of laughter from the tent's occupants.

Ylva's eyes glinted with mischief as she moved back behind Gavril, seizing a handful of his hair once more. With a swift, brutal motion, she sliced off his braid, holding the severed length up before him with a wicked smile. She raised it to her nose, inhaling mockingly, before tossing it into the fire. The scent of burning hair filled the tent, acrid and sharp. Gavril forced himself to keep his gaze steady, even as the indignity of it seared his pride.

Mardig grinned, patting Gavril on the shoulder with a condescending familiarity, his crotch level with Gavril's face. "Speak," he commanded, voice dripping with amusement.

Gavril straightened his back, ignoring the burning scent of his own hair, ignoring the eyes on him, the sneers, the barely concealed hatred. He spoke with a tone both firm and conciliatory, holding onto his dignity with every syllable. "Vesper wishes to offer a truce."

The tent erupted into laughter once more. Gavril felt the sting of humiliation rise, the laughter clawing at his composure. *Let them have their moment,* he reminded himself. The Dokar would agree to nothing unless they felt that they held the upper hand. He breathed in, steadying himself, and continued in a louder, unwavering voice.

"Please, listen to me," he urged. "We are all in peril as Zincubus gathers an army of Moorigato and prepares to march. He will spare no one. His forces outnumber us. If he succeeds, both Mount Lira and the valley will fall under his control. He has dragons, green dragons among them, and they are fully under his command."

A heavy silence fell over the tent, the Dokarians' laughter fading into a tense stillness. Ylva's dark eyes narrowed, her gaze flickering to her brother with something between skepticism and curiosity. She let out a low, dangerous snarl, addressing Mardig in a voice laced with contempt. "I smell trickery," she muttered.

CHAPTER THIRTY-TWO

CLAIM YOUR GROUND

The rich scent of ground flax meal and wildflowers filled the air in the cooking quarters at Peregrine's Keep, circulating with the warm, earthy aroma of baking bread and dried herbs. The grand kitchen was a marvel of stone and fire, the walls hewn from rough blocks of mountain rock and punctuated by freestanding ovens with polished granite fronts and cast iron doors. Iron pots and pans hung like armor along the walls, glinting in the firelight, while baskets brimming with fresh and dried herbs lined every shelf.

At one of the long tables, Jájá worked deftly with Sekowah at her side, shaping delicate pastry sheets into the likeness of roses. Her hands moved with effortless grace, folding the thin dough around a bright yellow cream, pressing each petal into place with a precision that spoke of years of practice. Next to her, Sekowah struggled to mimic the shape, her own dough collapsing into a messy lump. The disheveled pastry brought a quiet smile to her lips, and she glanced sideways at her mother, feeling a strange, unexpected warmth in this simple act of cooking together.

As she worked, Jájá's eyes sparkled with a mischief that was rarely absent. "He's beautiful, is he not?" she asked, her voice soft but sly. The question, unexpected, startled Sekowah, and her cheeks flushed a deep crimson.

"Yes," Sekowah admitted, fumbling with the pastry as the image of Gavril filled her mind—his intense gaze, the quiet strength in his posture, the way he moved through the world as if he belonged to it more than anyone else. Her stomach did a small, involuntary flip just thinking of him. She hadn't known feelings like this before; her attraction to Robbie was dull in comparison. Gavril's presence had a gravity to it, a pull that left her unsteady, breathless.

Jájá observed her with knowing smile, flattening Sekowah's failed pastry with a marble rolling pin. "The trick is not to make it too thin," she advised, pressing down slowly. "If it's too delicate, it won't hold its shape in the oven. But too thick, and it will turn soggy."

Sekowah tried again, focusing intently, though her mind remained half-distracted by thoughts of Gavril. Her attempt came out better this time, but the shape was still more dumpling than rose. A stray puff of flax meal tickled her nose, and she sneezed, quickly covering her face with her apron.

Jájá tilted her head, curious. "Why do you cover your face like that?" she asked.

Sekowah paused, caught off-guard by the question. She remembered Mindy, ever the kitchen supervisor back home, warning her never to sneeze on food. "I don't want to get anyone sick," she explained, lowering the apron cautiously.

Jájá laughed, a rich sound that seemed to fill the whole kitchen. "We have no sickness here, dear. The Nezkwah eradicated disease long ago. You needn't worry about such things." Her tone was casual, but there was pride beneath it—a reminder of the strange and formidable nature of the world Sekowah now inhabited.

"Oh?" Sekowah felt a wave of relief, mixed with amazement. She was often sick back in the mortal realm, where colds and fevers seemed to come and go with the seasons. The idea of a life free from illness was almost too good to be true. "That's... wonderful."

Jájá reached for a small blue flower from a nearby dish and held it out to her, the petals bright and fragile, glistening as if dusted with morning dew. "Here," she said with a slight smirk. "Try one. They're sweet."

Sekowah eyed the flower warily, catching the glint in her mother's eye. It was a look she'd come to recognize in the Nezkwah—a glimmer of deception, of secrets hidden behind casual words. Food in this world was rarely just food, she was learning. Everything here held some latent magic, some hidden purpose. Remembering her last encounter with enchanted food at the cottage, stealing her memories, she shook her head, smiling. "No, thank you."

Jájá's grin widened, her amusement evident. "You're learning," she remarked approvingly.

Sekowah wiped her hands on her apron and pushed her lopsided pastry across the table toward Jájá. "If Gavril wants to date me, he can ask me himself," she said with a defiant smile. She plucked a grape from a bowl nearby and popped it into her mouth, savoring its familiar sweetness as she turned and left the kitchen, feeling an unexpected lightness in her step. *From now on, I make my own choices,* she thought with quiet resolve.

· · · ·  · · · ·

Máhí landed lightly in the apothecary's garden, Tahgeet's hooves barely making a sound on the soft earth. Behind her, three additional winged horses, their saddlebags empty, touched down as well, their nostrils flaring as they sniffed the air, sensing her tension. She had come here to gather supplies for the battles ahead with Zincubus, hoping to load the bags with potions and salves.

But something felt wrong.

She dismounted, moving cautiously, her eyes scanning the garden. One of the fences was down, the plants around it trampled as though a heavy creature had crashed through. She knelt, pressing her palm to the cold earth, reaching out with her senses, connecting with the root network below. *What happened here?* she asked silently.

The trees shivered in response, sending vibrations through their roots. *You are alone now,* they answered in a voice that was neither sound nor thought, but something deeper, something primal.

She rose, troubled. Jade had been gone for some time, leaving the place vulnerable. Máhí had heard rumors of rogue Nezkwah, mischievous outcasts who took pleasure in theft and vandalism, but she doubted even they would dare to attack the apothecary. The destruction here seemed mindless, violent in a way that unsettled her.

Cautiously, she approached the cottage. The front door lay splintered on the ground, torn from its hinges and thrown aside like a child's toy. Shutters hung askew, one swinging loosely in the cold breeze. The weight of unease grew heavier with each step. This was no petty theft.

With her staff held high, Máhí crept to the back entrance, every sense alert. She peered inside, her eyes adjusting to the dim light filtering through the broken windows.

"Hee-yo! Ini kiwane?" she called, her voice firm and clear, but only silence answered.

The interior was a wasteland of shattered glass and splintered wood. Shelves had been swept clean, every vial and herb gone, stolen or destroyed. She picked her way through the debris, her boots crunching on shards of broken jars, taking in the scene. The walls were lined with claw marks, and every surface bore the signs of a brutal, methodical ransacking.

Máhí's gaze fell on the remnants of Jade's work—the fragments of carefully bound books, their pages torn and scattered across the floor. She picked up a page, its edges jagged and curling, the botanical notes rendered useless. This was no simple act of thievery. Whoever had done this wanted to erase the knowledge housed here, to strip the apothecary of its power.

She moved into the small bedroom, the only part of the cottage that seemed untouched. As she turned to leave, something caught her eye—a shred of dark material, caught on the doorframe. She took it down and examined it carefully, her fingers tracing the familiar texture: snakeskin.

Máhí's eyes narrowed as she lifted the scrap to her nose, inhaling the foul scent. Not rogues. This was something far more sinister.

Dasheahs.

Chapter Thirty-Three

A Fragile Truce

The journey down Mount Lira was quiet and tense, each footstep laden with suspicion and unspoken history. Accompanied by Vesper's chosen expedition team and a small retinue of guards, Ylva and Mardig moved through Vesper's territory for the first time, their eyes roving over the land with a mixture of admiration and calculation. The mountainous path was steep, littered with loose stones that skittered down the trail with each step.

The air held a chill, even under the full light of the afternoon sun, though here, further south, the winters were gentler and the summers stretched longer. Ylva, shedding her fur cape in the warmth, took a moment to survey the surrounding landscape with an expression that hovered between approval and suspicion. The meadows below stretched wide and green, framed by dense forests of fir and pine. To the far west, a line of rugged snow-capped peaks stood in solemn silhouette, with jagged summits.

They followed the narrow trail in silence, alert to every sound as they approached Peregrine's Keep. The fortress emerged from the hillside with quiet authority—its stone walls weathered but solid, its towers sharp against the grey sky. Ylva's eyes widened as she took in the scale and precision of its construction, a blend of elegance and military strength. She cast a glance at Mardig, who had gone tense beside her, his jaw tightening as his gaze locked on the sentries above. Lirian guards tracked their approach with cool, appraising eyes. The group dismounted without a word and climbed the worn stone steps that led to the highest turret, where the wind tugged at their cloaks and the full sweep of the contested valley stretched out before them.

Vesper gestured toward the distant peaks. "From here to the Seven Devils," he said, his voice calm but firm. "Yours."

Ylva's gaze shifted to the east, where the glint of a river caught the sunlight as it meandered through the Jasper Valley. She raised her chin defiantly. "We want access to the river," she said, each word laced with conviction.

Vesper's face remained impassive. "That is not mine to give," he replied, a hard edge to his voice. The river, with its vital access to fertile lands and fresh water, was too valuable a prize to concede. But Ylva's expression darkened, her eyes narrowing with the knowledge of what her people had lost and the bitterness of needing to ask for what should have been theirs.

Beside her, Mardig looked away. "What use is land without water?" he muttered, his tone dripping with disdain.

Gavril, sensing the rising tension, stepped forward, his voice smooth as he addressed Mardig directly. "Jájá will make arrangements for water. We can provide a labor force to help with well-digging," he explained, offering a practical solution. "There are caverns beneath the Seven Devils with pristine reserves, more than enough to irrigate the land."

Mardig's eyes flickered, processing this new information. "Half my forces," he countered, testing the waters of negotiation.

"No," Vesper said sharply, his tone unyielding. "We'll need every able soldier."

Mardig's eyes turned icy, but Gavril intervened, softening the blow. "With the combined armies of Lira, Dokar and the Nezkwah, we can push Zincubus back," he said. "It's our only chance."

Ylva snorted derisively. "The Nezkwah? An army of Dugandi birds, fluttering about?" She laughed, the sound hollow and mocking, echoing off the stone walls of the guard tower as if to remind them all of the precariousness of this alliance.

Vesper ignored her scorn and moved to the edge of the tower, gazing out over the northern region where his own people had lost so much. Beyond the twin waterfalls, the valleys lay decimated by the ravage of giants. He felt a pang of sympathy for the Dokar—their desperation, their need to push outward for survival. He, too, would have fought for his people in the same way, had circumstances demanded it. But the Dokar had not come to negotiate peacefully or with humility. They had come with fire and blade, leaving him with uncountable losses.

A surge of anger bubbled up, but he forced it down. Now was not the time for pride or grudges. "You're in no position to decline assistance from anyone willing to help you," he said, his voice low and unyielding. "You know as well as I that you won't survive another winter at the border."

Mardig cast a glance at Ylva, who met his gaze with steely defiance but did not contradict him. The two moved a few steps away, heads bowed together as they spoke in murmurs just out of Vesper's earshot. Gavril caught Vesper's eye and gave a small, reassuring nod. "So far so good," he whispered.

Vesper allowed himself a rare smile. "They have no other choice," he murmured back. "Once they're settled, they'll be at a safe distance from Peregrine's Keep. And if they grow restless or rebellious, it will be easy enough to drive them westward—straight into Gold territory." The thought pleased him; the Golds guarded their land with a ferocity that bordered on myth, and the Dokar would stand little chance if they overstepped their bounds.

As Mardig and Ylva returned, Gavril's hand moved instinctively to the hilt of his dagger, catching Ylva's eye. She chuckled, pulling her own blade—a slender, lethal-looking azurtanium knife—from her belt. The sunlight glinted off its edge as she held it up. "Relax, Commander," she said, a smirk twisting her lips. "King Vesper can keep hair."

Despite himself, Gavril chuckled, letting his hand fall away from his weapon.

But Ylva's gaze remained on the blade in her hand, her expression shifting to something more appraising. "We don't have such weapons," she said, testing the weight of the knife thoughtfully. "You will provide us?"

Vesper's face tightened. The thought of sharing their limited supply of azurtanium weapons—already barely enough to arm his own forces—filled him with dread. And with the looming knowledge of Zincubus' superior weaponry, the request seemed almost absurd. "Our weapons come from Obsidia, forged by Zincubus himself," he replied, unable to keep the bitterness from his voice. "But he has ceased trade with us. We understand he now possesses weapons unknown to us, devices from the mortal realm. We'll need shields that can deflect 'flying balls,' if you will."

Mardig's face twisted with distaste. "You ask us to fight war against army throwing flying balls?" he scoffed, as if the words themselves were an insult.

"Something like that," Gavril interjected, trying to conceal his own unease. "We've begun work on shields that might withstand such attacks, but it will be a challenge. That's why we need your forces as much as you need land."

Ylva stared at him, her brows drawn together in suspicion. "I don't like this," Ylva stared at them both. "I don't know what you mean, flying balls. What's flying balls?"

"We have drawings, from a reliable source. I can explain more in detail later, but I admit, it will be most challenging, which is why we have laid down arms and offered you resettlement here in exchange for your help. We cannot win against him, but with your help, we may overpower him in numbers," Vesper explained.

Gavril met her gaze. "If we do nothing, Zincubus will take this land regardless," he said. "And he won't stop there. Once he's through with us, the Dokar will be next. He will conquer without mercy. Better to unite against him at the outset than face extinction alone."

A heavy silence fell as the implications sank in. Finally, Vesper spoke, his voice carrying the weight of command. "This will take everything we have. Anything less, and we are all doomed."

Mardig pulled a copper flask from his belt and held it out for Vesper to take. "Mah-ho," he cheered. Vesper did not take it, so he took a swig himself. "All our warriors. If we succeed, we take here to Seven Devils and you give us well diggers, enough supplies to seed crops, and team of Nezkwah to oversee first harvest."

"We share weapons," Ylva reminded.

A reasonable offer. Well diggers and seeds were easy to spare, Vesper thought. He took the flask from Mardig and drank. "Mah-ho," he agreed. He passed it over to Gavril who downed a shot and handed it to Ylva.

Ylva drank as well. "We have celebration on equinox. I take your Commander to seed first nestling of birthing season," she said, nodding at Gavril.

Gavril returned the nod. "You can try, but I doubt you will meet with much success," he retorted.

Vesper raised his eyebrows at the exchange. *What had happened in that tent?* Gavril, once again surprised him with his ability to make quick friends with even the most stubborn of adversaries. "I'll sacrifice my second in command, Brock," he offered. "He has no companions."

They all laughed then, and the discussion turned to the details of how to break down the camps and lead their people out of the mountains.

Unseen by all, a murder of large crows circled overhead. As the group convened their meeting and disappeared into the stone turret stairway, the flock gathered together in the air and headed south.

Chapter Thirty-Four

PREPARATIONS

The journey to the Jasper Valley had been quiet, each of them lost in thought as they prepared for the delicate task ahead. Sekowah followed Máhí down a narrow trail that cut through fields of wildflowers dancing in the afternoon breeze. Sunlight filtered through the trees, casting dappled patterns on the ground and filling the valley with a soft, golden light. For all its beauty, though, there was tension in the air—a feeling that something wicked was at their doorstep.

As they entered the valley's heart, a group of Zahnene, normally elusive and secretive, revealed themselves one by one. They emerged from behind trees and popped up from within the wildflower fields, their expressions wary as they observed the two visitors. Máhí had told Sekowah to dress in her brown tunic and work boots, and as the Nezkwah gathered around her, she understood why. They examined her closely, their fingers brushing over her hands to study her fingerprints. Soft, quiet gasps and murmurs rose from the crowd as they fussed over her hair, pushing it back to reveal her Nezkwah ears. A murmur of approval rippled through the group.

Nearby, wooly llama-like creatures stood patiently with baskets clamped in their teeth, carrying bundles of herbs, seeds, and flowers. These creatures, half the size of mortal llamas and far more docile, watched the scene with mild curiosity. Sekowah felt an immediate fondness for them, their large eyes and gentle demeanor oddly comforting in the midst of all this attention. She wanted to reach out, pet one, maybe even take one home, but resisted. Pets were unheard of in this world; the creatures here were respected partners rather than possessions.

From a distance, an elder Zahnene watched them with thinly veiled displeasure. Elo, with his long, graying beard and stern eyes shaded beneath a straw hat, held himself apart from the gathering. His double wings twitched as he observed the crowd surrounding

Sekowah, his mouth set in a grim line. When the crowd began to disperse, he strode over, his arms shaking as he gestured at Máhí with an air of restrained panic.

Máhí translated his gestures for Sekowah, her voice calm though a trace of irritation flickered beneath. "He says that an early flower harvest will ruin the migration," she relayed. "There'll be no food harvest. No harvest, no seeds. The colonies—" He closed his eyes and let his shoulders and arms go limp. Máhí continued. "They'll starve during the dormant suns with no honey." Elo punctuated her words with a sharp stomp, his arms crossed over his chest as he turned to scold a young Nezkwah maiden gathering wildflowers nearby.

"We don't want the honey, just the blooms," Máhí replied firmly, making a decisive gesture, her fingers blooming outward in a delicate sign. But Elo was unmoved. His scowl deepened, and he mirrored her gesture in reverse, as if the flower were wilting.

"He says they can't make honey without the wildflowers. This is true," Máhí muttered to Sekowah, a weary sigh escaping her. She pulled a small vial from her belt and thrust it toward Elo, her tone edged with frustration. "No wildflowers, no potions. No potions—no peace." She nodded to Rhye, a young Nezkwah standing by, who looked equally tense, awaiting instruction.

Sekowah, feeling a surge of determination, interjected, "Perhaps we can save some seeds now?" Her voice carried a newfound confidence, the hint of leadership that was beginning to awaken in her.

Elo turned to Máhí for translation, grunting as he signed in response. Máhí's face fell slightly as she relayed the message. "The seeds are not due for another sixty suns. And they need the pollen now."

"If you have a better suggestion, then let's hear it," Máhí snapped, her patience wearing thin. "The apothecary was destroyed, and all our stores have been depleted. We have no choice."

Behind them, Gavril arrived on horseback, the thud of hooves muffled by the soft earth. In his hand, he held a modest bouquet of wildflowers, their colors muted in the dimming afternoon light. Elo, spotting the bouquet, threw his arms up in exasperation and limped away, muttering under his breath. A small swarm of bees buzzed angrily around Sekowah's head, then flitted off after Elo, trailing behind him like a dark cloud.

"Trouble with Elo, I see," Gavril remarked dryly as he dismounted. He extended the bouquet toward Sekowah with a small bow.

Sekowah accepted it, feeling her cheeks warm. "I don't see any blue snippets," she observed with a shy smile.

Gavril gave a slight nod, his gaze warm and steady. "I wouldn't think of it," he replied.

Sekowah inhaled the delicate scent of the flowers—lilies and baby's breath, soft and gentle in her hands. "They're lovely," she murmured.

Máhí gave Gavril a knowing wink. "I'll be in the root cave when you're ready," she said, leaving them alone with a mischievous smile.

Gavril's eyes followed Elo, watching as the elder harassed a young Zahnene gathering flowers nearby. "He may have a point," he said, his tone contemplative. "I wouldn't dismiss him so quickly. Elo knows every detail of the harvest schedule; he understands the balance we must keep."

Sekowah nodded, though her thoughts were elsewhere, on the suitor standing beside her, on the unspoken question that seemed to hang in the air between them. After a moment, Gavril turned to her with a hesitant smile. "Care to take a walk with me?" he asked. "There's something I'd like to ask you."

Sekowah's heart fluttered, though she tried to appear nonchalant. "Oh?" she replied, feigning ignorance. It was hardly a secret that a mating proposal might be forthcoming. She felt a thrill at the thought, tempered by a flicker of uncertainty.

They walked side by side along a narrow path winding through the orchard, hands clasped as they made small talk. The air was thick with the scent of ripening fruit, and a golden pear tree stood ahead, its branches heavy with sun-warmed fruit. Gavril reached up, plucking a pear from a low branch, presenting it to her with a warm smile. She bit into it, savoring the sweetness, juice trickling down her chin as she laughed, feeling, for a moment, as though all her troubles had melted away.

Gavril turned to face her, his expression serious now, as if he had reached some decision within himself. He glanced around, ensuring they were alone, then lifted her hand to his lips and pressed a soft kiss to her fingertips. The warmth of his breath against her skin caused Sekowah's pulse to quicken, her heart pounding against her ribs.

From the shadows, unseen by the pair, Nezkwah and Zahnene peeked out from behind trees and over logs, watching with barely concealed curiosity. Sekowah was dimly aware of their presence, yet in that moment, they might as well have been miles away. As Gavril leaned in, his face close to hers, she felt the now-familiar wave of warmth wash over her, the feeling both exhilarating and terrifying. She leaned in, meeting his kiss, a soft and gentle connection that sent a shiver through her.

When she pulled back, her mind was racing, torn between the tenderness of the moment and a nagging sense of unease. She was a stranger here still, caught between two worlds, and the thought of binding herself to someone in this place filled her with equal parts excitement and dread. An intimate relationship was not something she'd ever considered seriously in her mortal life. Here, it was not a casual affair, but a commitment steeped in ritual, expectation, and the weight of destiny. Did she really want this? Or was she merely being swept along by forces she could not control?

They walked in silence for a moment, Gavril seemingly content, though she could feel his watchful gaze on her. Finally, he spoke, his tone soft, almost tentative. "I know things here are ... different. It's not my wish to pressure you, Sekowah. I would like nothing more than to stand by you, as your mate, but only if that's what you want."

She looked down, her fingers tracing patterns on the stem of the bouquet he'd given her. "Máhí and Jájá have already been planning, you know," she said with a wry smile. "The dress, the flowers, the feast. It seems that everyone has decided my fate before I've had a say in it."

Gavril nodded, understanding in his eyes. "Then let it be our decision. Not theirs."

Sekowah met his gaze, finding a steady reassurance there, a kindness that felt like an anchor in the storm of uncertainty around her. She took a deep breath, feeling the weight of her decision, yet a warmth blossomed in her chest at the thought of being with him—not because of tradition or obligation, but because she wanted to.

Still, the doubts lingered, the sense of not quite belonging. She glanced back down the path, where Máhí had disappeared toward the root cave, and then into the shadows of the orchard, where the hidden eyes of the Nezkwah and Zahnene glimmered like stars.

"I ... I need time," she whispered, her voice barely audible. "To understand my place here. To understand myself."

Gavril's hand tightened around hers, a silent promise. "Then I will wait," he said, his voice soft, unwavering. "As long as you need."

Sekowah held Gavril's hand as they strolled through the orchard, their steps slow and unhurried, as though neither wanted to break the fragile moment between them. But beneath her calm expression, her thoughts twisted with uncertainty. She had grown to care for him, to trust him. He made her feel safe, his presence a comfort she hadn't known she was missing. And yet, even as they walked together in silence, a shadow lingered in her mind—an uneasy question of whether he felt the same, or if she was just another piece on the board, a pawn of royal blood to be paired off, her choices little more than illusion.

She glanced around the orchard, taking in the light filtering through the branches, dappling the ground with patches of gold. She tried to focus on the beauty surrounding her, the peace of the valley in the quiet hour before dusk. "I love these orchards," she said softly, her voice almost swallowed by the stillness. "They're beautiful."

Gavril inhaled deeply, as if the weight of his next words needed gathering. "This would make a fine place for a pairing ceremony," he said, his tone almost too casual.

Sekowah's heart stumbled. *Pairing ceremony?* The term echoed in her mind, laced with mystery and a sense of dread. Though she had discussed it in hushed conversations with Faylen, she had never truly understood what it entailed. Only vague, half-formed imaginings came to mind—scenes of rituals she couldn't comprehend, bound by customs she barely understood.

Gavril must have sensed her hesitation, for he turned to her with a gentle smile. "You have questions," he said, his tone inviting, open. It was something she admired about him—his ability to read her thoughts even when she couldn't find the words to voice them.

She gave a nervous laugh, embarrassed by her ignorance. "I do. I feel like I don't know anything about... well, *anything* here."

He nodded, understanding. "I imagine it must be difficult for you, being here, surrounded by customs that are unfamiliar. It's how I would feel in the mortal realm, I'm sure."

The mortal realm. When he said it, memories stirred like fleeting shadows at the edge of her mind. Echoes of a life that felt distant and intangible. She could remember flashes—faces, places, a few scattered details—but nothing solid. It was as though her past was a puzzle missing half its pieces, the fragments slipping through her fingers whenever she tried to piece them together. "I don't know if I remember enough now to tell you much," she admitted, a twinge of sadness in her voice.

He studied her for a moment, then gave a slight nod, his gaze shifting to the valley stretching out before them. "You're here now," he murmured, a quiet intensity in his voice. "That's what matters to me."

There was something in the way he said it, something that sent warmth blooming in her chest, erasing the world around them. She felt her cheeks flush, the words faltering on her tongue. But a question lingered.

"What... what happens at the pairing ceremony?" she asked, trying to keep her tone light, though the question felt heavy. "And who decides who gets paired?"

Gavril's expression softened, and he leaned in, his voice low and reassuring. "For the royals, it is the queen's choice," he explained. "But even so, we must agree. If you wished to pair with someone else, that choice would be yours. But..." He hesitated, his fingers tightening around hers. "I hope you'll choose me. Am I not what you want? Do you not think we would make beautiful nestlings?"

The word *nestlings* landed like a stone in her chest, and she dropped his hands, stepping back. Did he not know? Did Máhí not tell him what she had told her... that she, with her mortal body, did not have the ability to reproduce? She was silent, her mind racing with a mix of emotions she could barely sort through—embarrassment, frustration, and something deeper, a pang of sorrow that she hadn't been prepared for.

Gavril's brow furrowed, sensing the shift in her mood, but before he could ask, she forced a smile and changed the subject, steering the conversation away from her own tangled thoughts. "I don't know about that," she said, brushing her hair back with a feigned casualness, "but I do have another question for you, if you'll indulge me."

His brow relaxed, though a hint of curiosity lingered in his eyes. "Of course."

"*The Verses*," she began, her voice steady but her heart pounding. "You've read them? All of them?"

"Many times," he assured her.

"And you're convinced I'm... needed?" she asked, her voice barely above a whisper. "That Jájá's plan to use me against Zincubus... that I'm actually capable of it?" The words came out faster than she'd intended, each one laced with doubt. Speaking it aloud made it feel real, a burden pressing down on her shoulders. The idea that she, of all people, was meant to stand against a being as powerful as Zincubus seemed absurd. She hadn't been able to stand against him in Obsidia; she had barely managed to escape. She had been weak, helpless, a lost girl saved only by luck and the intervention of Inanna.

Gavril was silent for a long moment, his gaze drifting upward as though searching the sky for answers. Finally, he looked back at her, a glint of understanding in his eyes. "They've not shared *the Verses* with you, then?" he asked, his tone gentle, almost apologetic.

"No!" Sekowah exclaimed, her frustration spilling over. "They teach me what they want me to know, and nothing more. It's annoying." She folded her arms across her chest, her glare challenging him to defend the secrecy she had come to despise.

To her surprise, Gavril chuckled, a look of relief softening his features. "I see. That is easily remedied. When we return, I'll share my copy with you." He paused, a thoughtful expression on his face. "In fact... I'd like to be your teacher, if you'll let me. Elo taught me *the Verses*, and it would be an honor."

Sekowah's face softened, a spark of hope flickering within her. "Good," she said, though her tone was more grateful than commanding. "And I'd like to speak with Elo as well. There are things I need to understand."

Gavril nodded, a hint of pride in his gaze. "As you like. It will be your valley soon enough, and you must establish yourself here. But," he added, a hint of caution in his tone, "you'll need a translator. Elo is... particular, and he does not trust easily."

Sekowah surveyed the rolling fields, the wildflowers swaying in the breeze. She felt a strange sense of ownership growing within her, a pride she hadn't expected. "Then perhaps the best way to gain his trust is to learn his language," she declared, a determination in her voice that surprised even her.

Gavril's smile widened, his admiration clear. "Ambitious," he said, a hint of teasing in his tone. "But if anyone can do it, it's you."

Together, they crossed the field toward Elo, who sat on a tree stump, his back turned to them as he grumbled to himself. Sekowah knelt beside him, her expression earnest, and offered him the bouquet Gavril had given her—a small peace offering. She could sense the weight of Gavril's gaze as he signed her words to the elder, who watched her with narrowed eyes, his suspicion evident.

Elo glanced from Sekowah to the bouquet, then back again. For a moment, Sekowah feared he would reject her gesture, that her intentions would go unrecognized. But slowly, his fingers reached out, trembling as they took the flowers from her hand.

Gavril translated her words as she spoke, his gestures measured and respectful. "Tell him," she said, her voice steady, "that I wish to learn. That I want to understand... to earn a place here, not merely inherit it."

Elo's gaze softened, just slightly, as he studied her face. There was a flicker of approval, hidden beneath his wary expression, and he nodded once, a single, solemn acknowledgment.

CHAPTER THIRTY-FIVE

PAST AND FUTURE

Gavril's chambers were a surprising mix of the familiar and the strange, a place both intimate and unknowable. The walls were lined with mismatched bookshelves, each crowded with volumes bound in deep greens and earth-tones, their titles scrawled in the looping script of the Nezkwah. Above them hung intricate mandalas made from feathers of every imaginable color—crimson, teal, gold—each one woven together with delicate threads to form radiant circles that seemed to pulse with a quiet, sacred energy. Tapestries of fine silk draped from ceiling to floor, depicting lush forest scenes and shadowed creatures with eyes that followed her as she moved.

In the center of it all, Gavril's bed sat low to the ground, a simple nest of fur blankets piled on an overstuffed mattress, its frame little more than a wooden platform. The casual, almost haphazard arrangement felt warm and inviting, entirely unlike the formal, ornamental bed she slept in. Sekowah felt an urge to sink into it, to bury herself in those furs, and the thought sent a rush of heat to her cheeks and throat. She quickly turned away, hoping Gavril hadn't noticed.

If he did, he gave no sign, preoccupied as he was with a drawer beside his bed. He rummaged for a moment, then withdrew a book, which he cradled carefully in both hands. It was unlike any book Sekowah had ever seen—handcrafted, delicate yet sturdy, and almost alive in its texture. When he placed it in her hands, she felt a thrill of surprise; it was unexpectedly heavy. She ran her fingers over the cover, feeling the smooth, warm grain of birch bark under her thumb. Hardened sap traced intricate patterns along the spine, catching the light with an amber glow.

Sekowah inhaled deeply, and the scent of the book filled her senses: lavender with an undercurrent of loamy earth, damp leaves, and something wilder, sharper, like the smell of deep forest humus. She pressed the book to her chest, and a strange energy seemed to pulse from its pages, quickening her heartbeat, raising goosebumps along her arms. She'd never felt this way holding a book before—as if it were both artifact and oracle, whispering secrets to her, secrets she wasn't yet ready to hear.

"There are only seven copies," Gavril said, his voice quiet but intense, as if he too felt the power of the object in her hands. "This one is the sixth, and it belongs to the valley. It's... well, it's meant to be yours, for now."

Sekowah felt a jolt at his words, her grip tightening on the book. *Mine?* The idea unsettled her, as though *the Verses* were a responsibility she hadn't asked for but could not refuse. She fumbled with the brass clasp along the edge, finally managing to unfasten it, and opened the cover. The first page contained an illustration, inked with perfection, and was a complex work in which many things revealed themselves slowly to her as she scanned the image: animals, mushrooms, feathers, trees, insects, birds. The pages were soft and thick, each one infused with tiny flecks of flower petals, ferns, and fragments of moss. The more she looked, the more details emerged, as if the images were shifting, revealing layers upon layers of hidden meaning.

"Who wrote it?" she asked, her voice hushed, unwilling to break the stillness of the room.

"No one knows," Gavril replied, a reverent edge to his tone. "*The Verses* have been passed down for thousands of harvests. Before they were written, they were shared in story circles, passed from elder to nestling. It's... it's not just a book, you understand. It's a record of our history, our struggles, our dreams." He turned the book upside down, then opened it from the back. Each page had text on one side, and upside-down text on the other, creating two parallel paths through the book—one in each direction.

Sekowah tilted her head, laughing softly at the strange construction. "I don't get it," she admitted, shaking her head. "Why would anyone make a book this way?"

Gavril's face grew solemn, his gaze unwavering. "Read it once front to back, and you will understand the past," he said, his voice dropping to a whisper, as if he were confiding a secret. "Turn it round, read it again, from back to front, and you will understand the future. Those are the prophecies."

The word *prophecy* struck her with a small shock, like touching a blanket filled with static electricity. Prophecy. They had been using that word since she arrived, dangling it in front of her like a sword over her head, a destiny she hadn't chosen. Now, with *the Verses* in her hands, she felt its weight—an obligation, a demand. Her belly tightened, and she fought the urge to hurl the book across the room. Instead, she settled for sarcasm, her voice laced with skepticism.

"And how exactly does anyone know the future?" she asked, trying to keep her tone light, though the question cut deep.

Gavril looked at her thoughtfully, his eyes clouding with something she couldn't quite read—pity, perhaps, or understanding. He turned toward the window, drawing back the silk curtains to reveal the mountains in the distance, their peaks brushed with the last golden light of the setting sun. His profile against the fading light looked almost like something from one of *the Verses* themselves—strong, shadowed, ancient.

"It's a fair question," he admitted. "The only ones who truly *see* the future are the keepers. They are a lineage of seers, living in the northern territory, far from here. They receive visions, glimpses of what is to come. And while we cannot be certain they are always correct... as time passes, and we watch their prophecies unfold, the truth becomes undeniable. Those who have lived long enough to see their predictions come to pass believe. And those who choose to close their eyes... well," he gestured vaguely out the window, toward the distant guards patrolling the perimeter, "they live in darkness, fearing what they do not understand."

Sekowah pursed her lips, suppressing a sigh. It all felt maddeningly similar to the rigid doctrines she'd grown up with—demands for faith without evidence. She kept her thoughts to herself, though; something in Gavril's expression told her he would not appreciate her skepticism. Instead, she glanced down at the book, flipping the pages idly. She tried to make sense of the symbols that filled the upside-down pages, but they were a strange alphabet, indecipherable to her.

Gavril leaned over, closing the book gently. "You must know the history first," he said. "It is the only way to understand the future."

He opened the book right-side-up again, guiding her to the first page. But even these pages were a bewildering array of symbols and illustrations, a beautiful chaos of shapes that hinted at meaning just out of reach. She traced a finger over the strange letters, her frustration growing. She had always been quick with languages, proud of her ability to understand and translate. But this... this was something else entirely.

"I can speak Nezkwah," she confessed, her voice tinged with embarrassment, "but I don't know how to read this."

Gavril's eyes sparkled with amusement, a warmth that softened his serious expression. "Then our first lesson will be to teach you," he said, his tone playful.

· · · · • ⦾ • · · · ·

Over the next several suns, Gavril and Máhí took turns guiding her through the maze, where each stone, carefully etched with a symbol from the Nezkwah alphabet, became a step in her learning. Sekowah's initial frustration gave way to fascination; she found herself absorbed in the earthy, resonant language, with its thirty-three distinct symbols, each one carrying a sound that felt rooted in the natural world. The language seemed to grow from the land itself, as if each word were a leaf or root, shaped by wind a nd soil.

"Os sigada wi ataileni," Gavril arranged the stones in a line before her, watching as she sounded out the words. It translated to *I love the forest*. The syllables rolled off her tongue, unfamiliar but satisfying, like a song remembered from childhood.

She met his gaze, feeling a spark of mischief, and rearranged the stones into her own message. "Mel ilmina ri may adlaymim lihie nesoma," she pronounced slowly, looking him squarely in the eye. *May we never fight or hate one another.*

For a moment, they stood in silence, the meaning of her words hanging heavy in the air. Gavril looked at her, his expression softening, and a warmth kindled in his eyes, something that went beyond admiration. He reached out, gently tracing a line along her jaw with his thumb, his touch sending a shiver through her. There was an intimacy in his gaze, something deeper than words could capture, something that made her heart pound in her chest. "Mel silami gu am," he said, a deep affection in his tone. *May our spirits be one.*

Sekowah swallowed, suddenly unsure of herself. She had come to learn, to decipher the language of the Nezkwah. But in this quiet moment, surrounded by stones and symbols, she felt as though she was learning something far more profound—a language spoken not with words but with glances, touches, silences.

Chapter Thirty-Six

A Mountain Temple

After days spent devouring *the Verses*, Sekowah found herself with more questions than answers. The text, with its layers of meaning and lyrical complexity, had entranced her, yet the experience had left her feeling as though she were adrift, with no land in sight. The most startling discovery, however, lay near the end: the prophecy that foretold her existence, her role in saving the valley from Zincubus, was only a handful of verses. The realization unnerved her. It was as if her entire purpose here was something approaching its end—and beyond that, a dark unknown. The prophecies written after hers, told of ferocious giants and an end to the valley and the Nezkwah way of life. If the prophecies were to be trusted, then what lie ahead was very dark.

She and Gavril spent hours discussing *the Verses*, yet their conversations seemed to spiral in circles. Every time she posed a question about the prophecies—especially about what lay ahead—Gavril's answers grew vague, abstract, as if he himself were trying to make sense of it as well. The historical verses, however, were different. On those, he was clear, his explanations rich with context and meaning. Sekowah absorbed stories of the Nezkwah's struggles and triumphs, their unwavering love for community, for the land and the stars. She read about ancient illnesses that once plagued the valley and were now vanquished, the sacrifices of kings and queens, the reverence for dragons—creatures both feared and adored. Each story felt like a thread in the tapestry of who the Nezkwah were.

But the prophecies were maddeningly cryptic, full of symbols and riddles. They could be twisted to mean nearly anything, their interpretations shifting like shadows depending on the light. Sekowah couldn't help but think of Vesper, whose skepticism had been palpable when he spoke of *the Verses*. She began to understand his cynicism. How easy it would be to dismiss the prophecies as convenient myths that only gained meaning after events had come to pass.

Her frustration grew until, at last, she resolved to seek the answers herself. *I'll go to the Keeper*, she decided. The Keeper, it was said, was the only one who truly saw beyond the present, the one who could interpret the prophecies with clarity.

Gavril, hesitant at first, was eventually convinced. A quiet conversation with Jájá had tipped the scales; the Queen, whose faith never seemed to waver, had told him simply, "It unfolds as it should." She had even given her blessing, pressing a small leather-wrapped item into Gavril's hands. She instructed him to hand it privately to the Keeper when the time was right, but under no circumstances was he to open it himself, nor to reveal it to Sekowah.

And so, with Gavril by her side, Sekowah set out for the northern territory, leaving the valley behind as dawn painted the sky in hues of amber and rose.

T he journey north was breathtaking. As they flew over the dense forests, the terrain changed dramatically. The gentle slopes of the valley and foothills of Mount Lira gave way to towering, rugged peaks shrouded in mist. From above, Sekowah could see narrow rivers winding like silver threads through the hills, glistening lakes nestled in the hollows, and waterfalls that cascaded down cliffsides like ribbons. It was a land untouched, untamed, where nature reigned unchallenged.

The sky here was alive with strange, prehistoric-looking birds that wheeled on thermal drafts, their wings leathery and vast, casting long shadows over the pines below. They were silent as they glided, their elongated, beak-like jaws snapping at the air in search of prey. Some perched on the tallest branches, their clawed wings folding awkwardly against narrow, muscled bodies, while vivid feather-like crests crowned their heads, shimmering in the morning light. Occasionally, one let out a piercing shriek, its cry echoing through the valleys. Sekowah shivered. These creatures belonged to a world far older than her own, a world of myth and legend.

Perrin proved tireless as he carried them through the skies. The journey spanned three days in total, with brief pauses to rest and eat. Each morning, they set off at dawn, the mist still clinging to the trees, and each night they landed under a canopy of stars, the silence of the wilderness wrapping around them like a cloak.

On the third day, as the sun dipped low in the sky, they descended toward a narrow clearing along a winding riverbank. The air smelled of wet stone and pine. Gavril helped Sekowah down from the saddle, his movements uncharacteristically cautious. He surveyed the sky before speaking.

"Are we there?" Sekowah asked, unable to hide her eagerness.

"Almost," Gavril replied, his voice barely above a whisper. "We're in sky dragon territory now. Perrin will wait here. We'll go the rest of the way on foot."

He removed an oaken shield from their packs, strapping it to his arm, and handed Sekowah a sheathed knife. She raised an eyebrow.

"What's that for? Should I be worried?"

We're fine," he assured her, though his eyes darted to the treetops with a flicker of unease. "Just keep your eyes on the sky. And stay close."

They set off along the sandy riverbank, the murmur of the water their only companion. The forest here felt different, thicker, the trees twisted and ancient, their branches tangled as if trying to protect those below.

· · · · ● ◯◯ ● · · · ·

As they climbed higher into the mountains, the terrain grew treacherous. Sharp inclines forced them to clamber over rocks, their hands digging into the rough stone for balance. Gavril tied a rope around Sekowah's waist, a precaution she was grateful for as her legs began to tremble with the strain. The air was thin, each breath harsh and dry, and the path ahead was narrow, a thin band of earth clinging to the mountainside.

The silence was oppressive, broken only by the shuffle of leaves beneath their boots. Every so often, Sekowah would glance up at the large birds circling above, feeling their predatory gaze upon her.

Finally, they reached a softer trail carpeted in pine needles, a reprieve from the thick undergrowth. Sekowah noticed small, strange birds perched on the twisted branches above them. They were slender, almost skeletal, with delicate feathers that shimmered in the light. Their sharp, toothy beaks snapped at passing insects, and clawed forelimbs stretched out like miniature wings, suited more for gliding than true flight. The birds tilted their heads as they watched the pair, their beady eyes gleaming with a curious intelligence.

One of the birds let out a chirping call—a sound like stone tapped against stone—that echoed through the forest. Another answered from deeper within the trees, and Sekowah felt a chill run down her spine.

"There." Gavril pointed to a cliff in the distance, half-hidden by a shroud of mist. As they drew closer, Sekowah saw their destination: a stone temple, camouflaged by the surrounding rock, its weathered stones woven with vines. The closer they got, the more details she could make out—a sprawling garden of wild rose hedges, meticulously tended vegetable patches, and delicate fruit trees, their branches heavy with blossoms.

They passed through the gardens, where several Nezkwah, faces lined with age and wisdom, worked in silence. One of them, an elder with silver braids woven with beads, approached Gavril, a stern look in her eye.

"You're late," she said, her voice gentle but firm. She led them up a winding path toward the temple's rear entrance. Sekowah marveled at the temple itself. Each stone block, perfectly smooth and almost glassy, glistened under her fingers as she touched them. They were not the same granite as the cliffside; these stones had been brought from somewhere far away, a deliberate choice. The air here felt different—crisp, sharp, and oddly refreshing. With each breath, Sekowah felt her mind clear, her senses sharpen.

They entered through a heavy iron gate, passing into a dim passageway lit by torches set with amethyst crystals. The violet glow cast strange shadows on the walls, which were carved with intricate scenes of the valley, its rivers, its mountains, its people. A sense of tranquility pervaded the temple, a subtle energy humming through the stones themselves.

Sekowah found herself drawn forward, her steps light, her heart quiet. There was no fear here—only a profound sense of stillness. She glanced at Gavril, who offered a small, reassuring smile.

As they entered the inner chamber, Sekowah felt a tingling sensation rise from the base of her spine, spreading upward, through her chest and into her scalp, where it lingered, warm and bright. The air was thick with the scent of jasmine, a sweetness that enveloped her, calming her heart. The chamber was a circular room of polished stone, the center marked by a large silk rug woven in the shape of the sun, its vibrant colors a stark contrast against the muted stone.

Around the rug were hammered copper bowls filled with colorful water, each containing petals of a different flower, each petal casting a soft glow that illuminated the chamber in a rainbow of soft light. Tapestries adorned the walls, each depicting an aspect of nature: forest, meadow, sky, lake, mountain, fire. Sekowah could feel the room's heartbeat, as the steady rhythm matched her own pulse.

At the center of the rug, sitting cross-legged in absolute stillness, was the Keeper.

Sekowah held her breath. She had come here with so many questions, so many doubts. But now, standing before the Keeper, all those questions fell silent.

CHAPTER THIRTY-SEVEN

THE KEEPER

The Keeper remained motionless, a still figure draped in the circle's glow, eyes resting on Sekowah as though seeing through to the very marrow of her being. Their voice, when they spoke, was soft yet commanding, with an odd cadence that reminded her of running water over smooth stones. "Welcome, Sekowah." The Keeper bowed their head toward Gavril, who, after a respectful nod, was waved away.

"You may enjoy the gardens if you wish," the Keeper added, their tone gentle but absolute.

Gavril's hand lingered in Sekowah's for a moment before he released it, offering her a small, reassuring smile as he backed out of the chamber, his gaze holding hers until the very last second. The door shut with a quiet finality, leaving Sekowah alone with the Keeper.

She felt the full weight of the Keeper's gaze then, eyes like polished glass—a shimmering mix of green and gold, catching the light in a way that made them seem nearly translucent. She could not discern a gender, as everything about this soul was without definition, without boundary, unassuming and plain. They were a seamless blend of both the feminine and the masculine, and perhaps something beyond those definitions altogether. Their robe, woven from fine white silk, caught and held the light, and their skin was smooth, ageless and curiously marked with faint green designs—like the veins of a leaf—which twisted and coiled under the surface. The most striking feature, however, were the soft, downy wings folded across their shoulders and back, a pale grey like that of a cygnet's down, adding an air of something not entirely earthly.

For what felt like an eternity, they simply regarded one another, a deep silence settling between them. The quiet wasn't awkward, but rather charged, as though they were both drinking in the essence of the other. Sekowah felt as though the Keeper was unraveling her, bit by bit, yet strangely, she didn't feel exposed. She felt seen—perhaps for the first time since she had arrived in this world.

At last, unable to bear the silence any longer, Sekowah cleared her throat. "I have questions," she announced, her voice a tremor in the stillness.

The Keeper's lips curled into a grin, one that seemed both ancient and childlike. "Questions and answers are one and the same," they replied, as though this was the most obvious truth in the world.

Sekowah took a cautious step forward, feeling like she was crossing an invisible threshold. She gestured to the circular rug at the center of the chamber. "May I?"

The Keeper's eyes sparkled with something that might have been amusement. "I don't know. Can you?"

She smirked, recognizing the game, and settled herself cross-legged across from them, mirroring their posture. The rug was softer than she'd expected, its colors vibrant under her hands, threads of gold and indigo interwoven in swirling patterns that seemed to pulse with a subtle energy.

"What is your name?" she ventured first, almost reflexively.

The Keeper tilted their head slightly, a hint of mischief flickering across their face. "What is a name but a thing that separates? You are Sekowah. I am Sekowah. We are all Sekowah," they answered.

Odd, Sekowah thought. She leaned forward, pressing on with her most important question. "Who writes the prophecies?"

"Prophecies are footprints in the sand. The past writes the history and the future writes our dreams," the Keeper answered, their voice like a thread of wind winding through a canyon.

Sekowah shifted, frustration curling inside her. "I mean... who actually writes them down? On paper?"

The Keeper's gaze turned contemplative. "Whomever hears from the future, tells the Keeper."

Now we're getting somewhere, she thought. "So, you write them down," she deduced.

"If you wish," they replied, a playful gleam returning to their eyes. "The future speaks to us all."

It was like trying to grasp smoke. Every question she posed seemed to turn into something else in the Keeper's hands. "But how do I know the prophecies are true?" she pressed, a note of exasperation slipping into her tone.

The Keeper locked their eyes into hers, their gaze feather-light yet grounding. "Truth is found in the heart of the seeker. Only you can understand your truth." Their smile was warm, and she felt a strange current pass through her, a gentle wave that stilled the whirl of thoughts in her mind.

Sekowah sighed, her shoulders drooping. She hadn't come all this way for riddles. But the Keeper's presence brought a comfort she hadn't anticipated, a quiet calm that spread through her even as her mind continued to churn. "Why do the prophecies stop... shortly after mine?" she asked, her voice softer now, almost uncertain.

"The prophecies never stop," the Keeper replied, gesturing gracefully to the copper bowls that circled the room. They rose then, fluid as a shadow, and extended a hand to help her up. Without a word, they guided her to the first of the twelve bowls, watching her intently as she leaned over its surface.

Sekowah peered into the water, which was a soft shade of turquoise, petals of blue and green flowers drifting on its surface. She inhaled deeply, and a subtle scent wafted up—first roses, then lemon, as if the fragrance itself were shifting with each breath. She leaned in closer, hoping for a revelation.

"Relax," the Keeper whispered, their voice like a lullaby. "What do you see?"

Sekowah closed her eyes, willing herself to relax. She had seen "looking ponds" used before; they often required incantations or rituals, spells and symbols. But here, she simply let herself fall into the quiet, allowing her thoughts to dissipate. Slowly, something began to emerge within her—not a vision, but a feeling. A blend of hope and apprehension swelled in her chest, and she realized, with a start, that she was thinking of Gavril. The feeling was tender, a longing that caught her off guard, and she felt it rise up, thickening in her throat, bringing tears to her eyes.

She opened her eyes, and a single tear fell into the bowl. As it rippled across the water's surface, an image formed: herself, standing before a mirror in a dress of soft pink silk, her reflection smiling back at her. Two pairs of hands—whose, she could not tell—placed a crown of daisies on her head. She saw her own face, radiant, almost unrecognizable in its calm.

The image faded, leaving Sekowah smiling despite herself.

The Keeper watched her with that inscrutable gaze, as if savoring the shift in her emotions. "You feel deeply," they murmured approvingly.

Sekowah felt a flicker of pride. "Was that... the future?" she asked, hesitant.

The Keeper tilted their head to the side. "Only you know that answer, of course. I cannot see what you see, nor feel what you feel. Does it feel like the future to you?"

Sekowah considered this, and nodded. "Yes. It feels like the future."

"You are the path and the path is you."

She found herself warming to this strange game. She moved to the next bowl, casting a mischievous glance at the Keeper. This bowl was filled with crimson water, dark and rich, like diluted blood, with red rose petals floating along the edges. Sekowah closed her eyes again, allowing her mind to drift. Almost immediately, a deep ache rose within her, a yearning so intense it was as though she were starving for something unnamed, her hands clutching at emptiness. Her breaths grew shallow, the feeling filling her until it felt like she might burst.

She opened her eyes, desperate to see what this yearning would reveal. In the water, she saw herself sitting in a garden beneath a trellis draped with white blossoms. At her feet was a golden bucket brimming with purple mushrooms—the same ones she had tasted in Obsidia. She watched as her image reached for one, her fingers grazing its surface just as the image faded.

The longing in her chest receded, replaced by a sharp pang of disappointment. She'd wanted more.

The Keeper seemed to sense this and offered her a gentle smile. "I'm sorry you did not get what you wanted," they said, sympathy in their voice. "Wanting and getting... it is a trap, is it not?"

Sekowah nodded, uncertain how to respond. Wanting and *not* getting did feel like a trap in that moment, an emptiness that left her restless.

She took a step toward the third bowl, curiosity sparking in her once more, but the Keeper stepped into her path, their presence firm yet gentle. "It is time for my garden song," they announced, as if this were the most natural thing in the world. "I hope you'll visit me again."

Before she could protest, they took her hands, pulling her into an embrace that felt both warm and ethereal, like being held by a summer breeze. "I am pleased with you," they whispered, and then, with a graceful sweep, they moved away, disappearing down a corridor.

Sekowah followed, unable to shake the feeling that their meeting was somehow incomplete. She drifted through the archway into the garden, where the scent of jasmine hung thick in the air. Somewhere within the garden, she could hear the Keeper's voice, light and playful, singing a melody that seemed to flow like water over stones, bright and full of wonder. She wound her way through the foliage, trying to catch glimpses of them between the branches, but they remained elusive.

Turning a corner, she found herself before a bench beneath a trellis of enormous white blooms, their petals the size of dinner plates. Her heart skipped a beat—this was the garden from her vision. And there, at her feet, was the golden bucket brimming with purple mushrooms.

A thrill of recognition surged through her as she reached down, drawn to the mushrooms. Just as her fingers brushed one, a gentle but firm hand intercepted hers. Sekowah looked up to see the groundskeeper, an amused glint in her eye. She pulled the bucket away from Sekowah. "These are not for you," she said with a knowing smile, and then she was gone, leaving Sekowah alone in the fragrant silence.

· · · · • ⊙ • · · · ·

While Sekowah wandered the gardens, Gavril seized his moment. He approached the Keeper, his expression both reverent and determined as he produced a small, leather-wrapped parcel from his satchel. He handed it over with both hands, watching as the Keeper untied the straps, revealing a slim, dark glass rectangle within.

The Keeper turned the object over in their hands, examining it with an expression of mild curiosity. They murmured softly to themselves, tilting the odd thing to catch the light.

Gavril nodded. "From Jájá. I confess I don't understand how it works. She hoped you might know."

Sekowah, having just returned from her encounter under the trellis, overheard and approached them, recognizing the object immediately. "It's a cell phone," she said, smiling at their puzzled expressions. She took the device, pressing the side button out of habit, though she knew it was pointless. "It's... well, it's dead. No power."

"Dead?" Gavril asked, concern flickering in his eyes.

Sekowah laughed, realizing her phrasing was lost on them. "Not *that* kind of dead. It just... doesn't work here. No power. It needs electricity and a signal. It's broken."

The Keeper's expression softened with understanding, though a hint of wonder remained. "It holds no power here," they announced, with a tone of finality. They tucked the item into a robe pocket and shuffled soundlessly away and back into the temple's sanctuary.

Chapter Thirty-Eight

OLD GRUDGES

Jájá paced along the balcony of Peregrine's Keep, her footsteps as restless as her thoughts. The winds played with her feathers, stirring them in delicate ripples, but she paid them no mind, her gaze fixed on the horizon. Finally, she spotted movement through the thinning mists: the first wave of figures emerging from the wilderness, a long line snaking through the clover fields, led by two familiar figures—Vesper and Mardig, shoulder to shoulder, their ranks marching in uneasy harmony behind them. Her spirit lifted, a tremor of relief spreading through her chest.

They've done it, she thought, unable to suppress a smile. *They've struck a truce.*

Down below, the weary warriors trudged alongside their equally fatigued mounts, each step a testament to the strain of the journey and the hard-won peace. The winged horses, laden with tents and provisions, were too burdened to fly, and the armies—though united in purpose—were clearly divided in spirit. Lirian troops marched ahead, their ranks taut and disciplined, while the Dokar warriors followed at a distance, watchful, silent, their wary eyes scanning the unfamiliar terrain. The Dokar had their own rhythm, a looser, more fluid cadence that made them seem like shadows slipping through the field rather than conquerors marching across it.

As the Dokar stragglers passed, Jájá noted a motley assortment of creatures—Utdaga and Kudlah from the north, nomads bristling with travel dust, guiding their badgers along the fringes of the group. Refugees, she realized, their habitats lost to the giants and shifting lands. The northern regions had grown increasingly unstable, forcing even the most stubborn clans to seek shelter further south. *The world itself is changing,* she thought, a chill creeping into her bones, despite the warmth of the sun.

The clover fields stretched out beneath her, vibrant and green, but she knew they wouldn't remain so for long. Soon, tents and makeshift camps would litter the fields, the once-untouched landscape transformed into a temporary home for thousands of displaced souls. *A small sacrifice,* she told herself, though the thought stung. *Better to lose some land to trampled clover than everything to Zincubus.*

With a deep breath, she spread her wings, her feathers catching the sunlight as she lifted herself from the balcony, descending in a graceful arc to meet Vesper and Mardig in the fields below. Her wings cast shadows over the clover, and as she landed, soldiers and warriors alike turned to watch her, their expressions a mix of curiosity, respect, and—on the Dokar faces—unhidden suspicion. Jájá met their gazes without flinching, her own face a mask of dignified resolve.

The valley would welcome them, but respect was something they would need to earn.

Vesper and Mardig were close now, the weight of their journey etched into their faces. Vesper's gaze lingered on her, weary but resolute. She could see the toll this truce had taken on him—the concessions, the bartered land, the grudging acceptance of the Dokar. This alliance was born of necessity, not desire. She knew the fires of vengeance still smoldered within them, a quiet fury that would only be quenched by Zincubus' defeat.

"Victory always demands sacrifice," she murmured to herself as she approached Vesper, her voice low but resonant, as if the land were listening.

Her arrival caught the attention of both leaders, and she nodded to each of them in turn, her expression a blend of warmth and solemnity. With deliberate grace, she folded her wings behind her back, the gesture both regal and respectful. She knew that, in these times, every movement, every word carried weight.

"The apothecary has been raided," she reported without preamble, her tone grave. "All the potions, gone."

Vesper's face darkened, a flicker of something dangerous in his eyes. He turned to a Lirian guard nearby, his voice curt and commanding. "Give her access to the armory," he ordered. His gaze drifted towards the horizon, where an ominous cloud hung over Obsidia. "Though I doubt a laughing fit will do much against an army of green dragons," he added grimly.

Jájá bowed her head, acknowledging the point. She knew the potency of their potions, but even the most potent Nezkwah concoctions would be feeble against Zincubus' forces. The army they now faced was unlike any they'd encountered before, and both she and Vesper understood that. "True," she agreed, though a smile tugged at her lips as she watched the eastern meadows. "But perhaps... a pairing ceremony will."

Her gaze drifted to where Gavril was returning with Sekowah beside him on Perrin. The sight brought warmth to Jájá's heart, a momentary reprieve from the weight of impending battle. If anything could bring their people together, it would be a celebration.

· · · · • ⊙ • · · · ·

F ar below Peregine's Keep, in the dark, damp corridors of Obsidia, the emerald lay abandoned in its iron cage on the cold stone floor of Zincubus' chambers. It flickered erratically, weak pulses of light spilling into the shadowed room, casting brief glimpses of color against the grey walls. The once-brilliant gem now seemed like a caged creature, its light dimming with each passing moment, as though it could sense the malice gathering in the corridors outside.

Obsidia itself was unusually quiet, though an attentive ear might catch the echoes: the clink of iron, the distant scrape of scales against stone, the occasional low groan that reverberated like an underground tremor. A sense of anticipation hung in the stale, fetid air—a stillness that was not peace, but a held breath, waiting to unleash itself.

At the iron gates of Obsidia, Zincubus stood with his army assembled behind him, a monstrous horde stretching as far back as the darkness would allow. His chest swelled as he looked over them, satisfaction gleaming in his eyes. He wore full azurtanium armor beneath his tattered cloak, the iridescent sheen catching the light. His gnarled wooden staff was gripped tightly in his hand, a weapon and a symbol of his dominion. Beneath his helmet, his eyes burned with a fierce, unrestrained ambition.

This was the moment he had prepared for, the culmination of years of plotting and biding his time. Faylen's meddling had been a nuisance, but now that she was gone, he felt the weight of destiny pressing against his chest, urging him forward. The valley would fall. Vesper, Jájá, and the rest of them would grovel before him or perish. He let his mind wander to the image of himself standing on the balcony at Peregrine's Keep, overlooking a crowd of his own making, a people brought to heel under his reign. He remembered the day he had first stood there, side by side with King Marin, the crowd's adulation like a heady wine.

They will celebrate me again, he thought, his lips curving into a twisted smile. *This time, as their rightful ruler.*

Behind him, his army writhed and seethed, a chaotic mass of swamp dwellers, slaves, and zealots. The Moorigato—lizard-like creatures with scaled skin and narrow, vicious eyes—stood at attention. The Dasheahs, fierce and silent, skulked in the shadows, their tongues flickering in and out as they tasted the air. Vampiric bats clung to the edges of the cavern, their beady eyes glinting red in the gloom, while spiders the size of small dogs clambered over each other.

And then, there were the dragons. Massive, armored beasts corralled by the Dasheahs, their scales a noble green that shimmered with an unnatural sheen. Most of them were mounted by Moorigato riders, who held onto leather reins with practiced ease, the dragons snorting plumes of sulfurous smoke as they stamped their clawed feet in impatience. Zincubus had spared no expense in outfitting his army, his arsenal of twisted creatures and unholy alliances—a testament to his unyielding ambition.

He strode forward and mounted his own emerald dragon, a particularly vicious specimen with eyes that glowed a venomous yellow. The beast snorted, expelling a burst of flame that singed the stones at its feet. Zincubus tucked his staff into a holster at his side and drew a coiled whip from his cloak, snapping it in the air. The dragon responded with a guttural roar, its wings flexing, muscles rippling beneath scales as hard as stone.

This valley was meant to be mine, he thought as he clipped himself to the saddle, his grip firm on the reins. *Your time is over, Vesper. Your kingdom, your family, your precious little valley—all of it belongs to me. It has always belonged to me.*

With a final, triumphant howl, Zincubus spurred his dragon forward, the great beast lurching into motion, leading the horde out of Obsidia and toward the valley's shadowed embrace. The ground trembled beneath their weight, a low rumble spreading through the earth as the army advanced.

S ekowah's room had been transformed into a vision of elegance and anticipation, draped with strands of berry-stained silk and adorned with white lotus blossoms soaking in bowls of copper. The sunset's golden light spilled through the tall arched windows, casting the space in a warm, sacred glow. On the window ledge, an egg-shaped crystal balanced on a delicate gold stand, catching the light's last rays and scattering

rainbow prisms across the walls. For a fleeting moment, the room pulsed with a serene ma
gic.

With the help of Máhí and Jájá, Sekowah slipped into the pink silk gown—a gift of exquisite softness against her skin—and felt a strange dissonance within her. The dress was beautiful, the lace-lined bell sleeves brushing her wrists with a delicate touch, and yet, it felt like a costume, a garment for someone else's role. But as she turned to face the mirror, a gasp escaped her lips.

"It's the future!" she whispered, her voice trembling. "I'm in the future!"

Máhí paused, eyebrow raised as she adjusted the drape of Sekowah's dress. "What did you give her?" she muttered, half in jest, half in suspicion.

Jájá only laughed, a knowing smile playing on her lips. "She's been to see the Keeper, haven't you, Sekowah?"

Sekowah nodded, her fingers tracing the silver headpiece woven with fresh daisies, just as it had been in her vision. The feeling was both wondrous and unsettling.

"Look at you," Jájá exclaimed as she brushed Sekowah's hair, her voice rich with pride and affection. "A dress fitting for a Queen. What a pleasure you are."

Máhí smiled and continued to poke and prod at Sekowah's dress, but Sekowah continued to stare at her reflection. It was an odd, horrible, glorious and unexpected feeling. She couldn't have imagined that everything was orchestrated for a purpose outside of her control. She stepped in closer to examine herself, touching the crown of daisies, remembering the image in the bowl. It didn't make sense.

Máhí grumbled, adjusting the dress again and pinning it with more force than neces-sary. Sekowah winced as a sharp prick bit into her skin.

"Hey!" she protested, batting Máhí's hands away.

Máhí offered a sly smile through the mirror. "Oh, sorry," she said, not sounding sorry at all.

Jájá looked them both over. "Perhaps Máhí has her eye on Gavril instead?"

Máhí snorted, folding her arms. "In his dreams," she retorted.

Sekowah grinned. "Doubtful," she teased, and just as she said it, Máhí gave her another jab with the pin, earning a yelp.

"Ow! Would you stop that?" Sekowah exclaimed, rubbing the sore spot and shooting a pleading look at Jájá.

But at that moment, Máhí froze, her ears perking up, her face falling into a sudden seriousness. She held up a hand, urging silence. The shift was instant, an electric charge in the air that made Sekowah's heart lurch. Máhí darted to the window, flinging it open with such urgency that the curtains billowed in the evening breeze. Her gaze locked on something in the far-off southern sky, her eyes narrowing as she scanned the horizon.

"He's coming," Máhí whispered, her voice taut with dread. "I see it—there, above the Healer's Wood."

Jájá abandoned her careful primping, hurrying to join Máhí at the window. Sekowah followed, and there, in the distance, they saw it: a vast, dark cloud, writhing and shifting, blotting out the last light of day. It moved with an unnatural momentum, alive with a pounding malice. Bats, Dasheahs, creatures of darkness swarmed within it, like a plague spilling over the horizon, consuming everything in its path.

Jájá's hands flew to her mouth, horror etched into her face. "He'll reach the border of the Daylight Meadow by dawn," Máhí murmured, her voice brittle.

Sekowah felt the chill of fear coil around her spine, her throat tightening. "What about the ceremony?" she whispered, almost to herself, the question hanging like a fragile thing in the air.

"We have no time for celebrations now," Jájá said, her tone hollow, her eyes wide with the weight of their new reality. She placed a steadying hand on Máhí's shoulder. "Alert your father. Blow the horn of war!"

Without another word, Máhí dashed from the room, her panicked footsteps pounding down the hall. Jájá turned back to Sekowah, her expression hardening, the playful warmth replaced with fierce determination. She moved swiftly, unpinning Sekowah's gown with deft fingers, her movements urgent but tender. "No party tonight, Sekowah. We've underestimated him." She crossed the room to the wardrobe and yanked open the doors, pulling out a chainmail suit and tossing it onto the bed. "Put this on."

In a swirl of silk and feathers, Jájá disappeared down the corridor, leaving Sekowah alone in the dimly lit room. The weight of silence pressed down on her, the warmth of the setting sun suddenly feeling cold against her skin. She turned slowly to face the mirror, staring at the reflection of the empty gown draped across her shoulders, now slipping off in rumpled folds. Her eyes were wide, filled with a quiet terror she couldn't hide, her face pale against the darkening room.

Locking eyes with her mirrored image, Sekowah saw fear flickering back at her. Alone, in her room, she felt the chill of death swirling about her. *Will this be my end?* She edged closer to the window, not wanting to look, but unable to stop herself. Above the dark cloud churning over the Healer's Wood, she could see a fleet of black dragons rise above the rest.

Do not be afraid.

She heard Inanna's words in her ears, as if she were in the room with her. But she couldn't help but be afraid. The moving mass of destruction terrified her, and it wasn't just coming—*it was coming for her.*

She was unprepared, untrained, a fledgling in both skill and spirit. Her lessons with Máhí and Gavril had been no more than rudimentary drills, enough to sharpen her instincts but far from the depth of strength she sensed she would need. Her hand brushed the soft silk of the dress, then recoiled as if burned. Everything she'd thought she was ready to face seemed to vanish like mist, replaced by a gaping abyss of doubt.

What if the prophecy is wrong? she thought, her mind spinning. *What if I'm the wrong person?*

Trembling, she let the gown fall to the floor, stepping out of its folds as though shedding a layer of herself. She donned a tunic and tights, then lifted the chainmail, and stepped into it, feeling its cold weight settle over her, grounding her in the reality of what was to come. Its heaviness was oddly comforting, a solidness she could cling to in the face of her rising panic.

Her fingers brushed against the worn cover of *the Verses* on her nightstand. Without hesitation, she opened it, flipping to the passage that spoke of her role, her destiny. She read the words over and over, her lips forming silent prayers, seeking a strength she was not sure she possessed.

A single ray of light caught her eye, piercing through the gathering dusk. It slanted across the room, refracted through the crystal egg on the window ledge, bathing her in a shimmering prism that rested on her forehead. She closed her eyes as warmth spread from that point, a tingling that seemed to wrap around her skull, sinking into her heart and spiraling outward. Her pulse quickened as the heat filled her, flooding her veins with a power that was both fierce and gentle, a fire that held neither rage nor fear.

Then, from a place both deep within her marrow and far beyond the reaches of time and self, a vision took root in Sekowah's mind's eye. It shimmered there—fragile at first, like mist curling through the branches of her memory—then sharpened into something undeniable. She held her breath as it bloomed with impossible clarity, as if the universe had momentarily bent inward to whisper a secret meant only for her.

Her pulse quieted. Her doubt drained away.

This is my family. This is my home. This is my valley.

The words resounded not as thought but as truth—an inheritance passed not through blood, but purpose. She felt the weight of generations settle on her shoulders, not as a burden, but as a mantle.

CHAPTER THIRTY-NINE

SILVER DRAGONS

Under the cold, unflinching gaze of the moon, the Lirian and Dokar gathered in tense readiness, their bodies and spirits taut as bowstrings. Commanders barked orders over the clamor of clanking armor and hastily drawn weapons, their voices swallowed by the murmuring chaos that rolled across the field like a dark sea. Vesper and Gavril, stationed at the head of the Lirian forces, exchanged grim nods as they shouted commands, their eyes surveying their soldiers with a practiced, assessing gaze. Nearby, Mardig and Ylva moved among their own ranks, the unfamiliar terrain and hastily assembled defenses settling uneasily on the Dokar warriors' shoulders like cloaks woven from doubt and mistrust.

For all of them, this was an unforgiving hour. Only eight suns had passed since they had descended from their high mountain stations, and none of them had expected to raise their arms so soon. The suddenness of it gnawed at their nerves, a raw edge cutting through the ranks. For the Dokar, the sense of disquiet was even more pronounced. They knew nothing of this land's hidden paths and unseen dangers, and the hastily constructed shields strapped to their arms—a poor attempt at defense against the mysterious flying balls Zincubus' forces might wield—felt as flimsy as leaves in a storm. Mardig, standing like a boulder amidst the shifting currents of his warriors, spoke with a voice that sought to steady the tide.

"Vesper is no fool," he assured his commanders, the words steady and clipped. "He would not lead us here if he had meant to trap us. Trust in his strategy."

A grizzled Dokarian warrior stepped forward, his face carved with old scars, eyes sharp with suspicion. "How do we know we have not walked willingly to our own deaths?"

Ylva shot him a look that could have frozen the sun. "If they wanted an ambush, we would have seen it already. Look around you." She gestured at the mingling troops, at the disarray that mirrored their own. "They are as unprepared as we."

Her fierce certainty was enough to quiet the dissent, and the warrior dipped his head, picking up his gear with a gruff nod, and led his comrades to ready their horses. But even with Ylva's words ringing in their ears, an uneasy tension hung in the air, a collective breath that refused to release.

Near the front, Máhí moved quickly through the gathered ranks, overseeing the Zahnene as they distributed glowing gem torches to the commanders, their blue and green light casting ghostly shadows over the armor and faces around them. She clasped Tahgeet's reins, her sharp eyes sweeping the grounds. *Where is Sekowah?* she wondered, a nagging worry twisting through her thoughts. Was she hiding? Would she, even now, choose flight over the prophecy that awaited her?

Without her, we have no hope, Máhí reminded herself. Sekowah's mere presence, her connection to the prophecy, was believed to be a key to their survival. That she had been touched by Inanna, helped and guided out of Obsidia—that alone was proof to Máhí of Sekowah's destiny. But she knew Sekowah's training had been barely adequate; her sister was raw, untested. Would she flee now, when they needed her the most?

She narrowed her eyes, catching sight of Sekowah's darkened window in the distance. *If I have to, I will drag her out myself.*

"Wait here," she muttered to Tahgeet, dropping the reins as she strode toward the stone steps of the Keep, her body a taut line of impatience. But before she could reach the top, the double steel doors creaked open, and Sekowah stepped out onto the threshold.

The sight of her stopped Máhí in her tracks.

Sekowah stood bathed in moonlight, clad in chainmail that beamed under the stars. A belt crisscrossed over her chest, each pocket loaded with the last remaining potions from the apothecary. Her face seemed older, sharper, her eyes blazing with a fierce determination that sent a thrill through Máhí's hearts. The energy field around her was bright, a shimmering white that danced with flecks of radiant gold, as if her very soul were aflame.

Máhí stopped on the steps, delightfully awestruck.

Sekowah's shoulders held high, she looked down at Máhí. She met her gaze with a defiant gleam, pulling a small silver whistle from inside her tunic. She blew on it, the sound sharp and clear, cutting through the din like a signal to the stars. As the sound faded, she moved down the steps with steady grace, nodding to Máhí.

"Battle's that way," she chided.

From the edge of the chaotic scene, Perrin descended in a flurry of feathers, his eyes fixed on Sekowah as he knelt to allow her to mount. She approached him with calm reverence, whispering soft words to him as she stroked his neck, her fingers brushing over the chainmail that draped his sturdy body.

Sekowah lifted her foot into the iron stirrup and swung herself onto Perrin's back with a practiced ease, her body melding to his. Máhí watched, fiercely proud, but aware of the hollow pit of fear gnawing at her stomach. Sekowah had come far, yet she had so much further to go. *Can she withstand the storm that's coming?* Máhí thought. But then she silenced her doubt, reminded herself of the prophecy's words.

Who am I to question the Verses?

Raising her staff high above her head, Máhí shouted, "Maaa-ho!" Her voice carried over the field, a rallying cry, a surrender to the currents of fate. She turned expectantly to Sekowah, nodding for her to repeat the ancient phrase.

Sekowah lifted her sword, though her voice lacked the conviction of Máhí's. "Maaa-ho." Her tone was respectful, but shadows of uncertainty clung to the edges of her words.

Satisfied, Máhí squeezed Tahgeet's sides with her thighs, signaling her to take flight. She cast one last look at Sekowah, hoping her command would be enough to keep her close. "Stay in the air," she instructed sternly. "It's our only advantage. Do as I do, and stay by my side."

Sekowah gave a solemn nod, gripping her saddle tighter. Her fingers trembled ever so slightly, but she steadied herself, breathing in the cool night air and steeling her heart. She would be the only one in the sky without wings of her own. She lashed herself into the saddle with leather straps, pulling on the knotted ends to be certain she was secure.

They took to the air, rising above the field of warriors, their shadows cast long and dark over the ground below. As they soared higher, the deep, sonorous blast of the war horn echoed from the castle turret, its sound rolling like thunder across the valley. It was a sound that stirred both fear and strength in the hearts of those who heard it, vibrating in their chests, a reminder that the time for reckoning had arrived.

Below, the field gates of Peregrine's Keep swung open, and Vesper, Gavril, Mardig, and Ylva marched out, leading the combined forces across the moonlit fields. A swarm of

Nezkwah warriors, mounted on their own familiars, joined them, their wings shimmering as they rose above the marching mass. The ground trembled as Kudlah and Utdaga from the northern forests emerged, their ranks adding to the formidable presence. Fireflies, in a sparkling procession, gathered at the front line, casting a soft glow that illuminated the path ahead, a strange, ethereal light that danced upon the determined faces of those prepared to fight.

Máhí angled closer to Sekowah, her expression grim but focused. "Stay close," she reminded, her voice a low command.

Sekowah swallowed hard, but nodded, tightening her grip on the saddle and adjusting her chainmail. She was acutely aware that every eye was on her—Máhí's fierce gaze, Gavril's unspoken hopes, the soldiers below looking up to her, all of them seeing not a foreigner, but a symbol, a promise. She could feel the weight of it pressing against her chest, mingling with her own fear.

As the army moved forward, the valley around them stilled in the darkness, waiting. Shadows slithered and stretched in the moonlight, and the fireflies hovered like tiny stars.

Sekowah took a steadying breath, feeling the energy of the valley pulsing beneath her, an ancient strength rising from the earth itself. She wasn't ready, not in the way she should be, but the valley was, and it surged up through her, filling the hollows of her uncertainty with a fierce, unbreakable resolve.

And then, with a final nod to Máhí, she lurched Perrin into motion, following her into the night as the horn of war bellowed once more, sending a shiver through the gathered masses. They were bound for battle, for blood, for a destiny that felt both inevitable and terrifying.

Under the stark light of a clear moon, the Lirian, Nezkwah, Zahnene and Dokar armies moved forward as a single, pulsing mass. Aware that their strength lay in conserving energy for the battle to come, the Lirian warriors remained grounded, marching through the shadowed valleys and hills, side by side with the Dokar, while their winged familiars soared overhead, casting shifting shadows that melded with the landscape. It was a strange sight, seeing warriors who had once been enemies now marching in unison. The moon cast everything in shades of silver and gray, smoothing rough edges, cloaking old scars—making them look, for once, like a united army.

And yet, in this charged quiet, a murmur of camaraderie began to rise. Sekowah, perched atop Perrin as he glided through the crisp air above, could hear it: quiet laughter, whispered stories, the occasional raucous cheer as a brave soul told a tale that sparked amusement even in their hardened ranks. Tenuous friendships were being forged in the flickering moonlight, bonds made in the thin, uncertain hours before dawn. The sound of it made her heart ache, both hopeful and hollow, as if the peace of these small moments was too fragile to last.

Perrin flew low, skimming just above the marching soldiers, his wings silent as he followed Tahgeet's lead. Sekowah kept close to Máhí's side, feeling the rhythm of his flight synchronize with her own heartbeat. She could feel Inanna's presence, too—a whisper on the wind, a gentle weight on her shoulders. It was a strange sensation, this ghostly reassurance, as though every doubt in her mind was met with an invisible, calming hand. Her fears didn't disappear entirely, but they dulled, soothed by an energy that was neither hers nor wholly of this world.

Occasionally, Jájá would sweep back from the front, hovering beside her with a stern, confident gaze. Jájá's expression was one of fierce pride mixed with silent determination, and though neither of them spoke, Sekowah felt the strength radiating from her mother like a protective shield. They didn't need words; Jájá knew that Inanna was with them, and Sekowah saw in her mother's eyes that she, too, could feel the silent blessings woven into the night.

At dawn, the army reached the edge of the Healer's Wood, a dark line of trees silhouetted against the first light of morning. They climbed the final hillside, cresting it to overlook the Daylight Meadow—now filled with a writhing, ominous mass of Zincubus' forces, waiting like a black storm on the horizon.

A grotesque assortment of creatures swarmed along the forest's border: winged panthers prowled restlessly, their sharp growls sending shivers down the spines of even the bravest warriors. Above them, vampire bats hung from twisted branches, their eyes gleaming red in the half-light, while flocks of them darted through the air, scouting for signs of weakness. Mounted dragons snorted smoke and flame, kept barely in check by their Moorigato riders. The dragons lunged forward, as though desperate to unleash their fury, only held back by the steely grip of their masters.

At the sight, Jájá brought her fleet to a halt mid-air, lifting her hand in a silent command. Silence swept over their own ranks as all armies—Lirian, Dokar, Zahnene and Nezkwah—stared across the meadow. The whoosh of wings and the occasional clank of armor was the only sound as the two forces sized each other up in the tense stillness.

As the sun rose over the mountains, casting long beams of light across the valley, dust from the meadow rose into the air, catching the sun's first rays. It was like watching embers float through the sky, each particle glinting with a fiery promise. The sky itself seemed to ignite, the dawn blending with the remnants of night into a surreal, crimson expanse. The clouds above the Healer's Wood churned ominously, swirling in a deep, otherworldly red. The very atmosphere crackled with impending violence, and Sekowah felt her pulse quicken, her mouth dry as ash.

Then, from the shadows of the trees, Zincubus emerged.

Draped in dark armor that gleamed with an unnatural shine, he rode atop a massive green dragon, his whip lashing through the air. With a single flick, he spurred his army forward, his voice a dark thunder that rolled across the field.

"Leave none standing!" he bellowed, his voice filled with ferocious ambition.

The effect was immediate. His forces surged forward in a massive, chaotic tide—Dasheahs, Moorigato, bats, and dragons alike bursting from the trees. The ground shook as azurtanium-clad warriors charged, automatic rifles in hand. The staccato rattle of gunfire shattered the dawn's stillness, and the roar of Zincubus' dragon shook the heavens.

On the front lines, Brock caught sight of silver tanks rolling out of the trees—hulking metal beasts, fitted with cannons that gleamed in the dawn light. His face paled as he murmured, "Silver dragons," his voice barely audible.

Gavril, nearby, struggled to control his skittish mount, his eyes wide with horror as he took in the sight of the tanks, the unfamiliar machinery flashing in the early light. His steed reared at the sound of gunfire, eyes wild, but Gavril held his ground, his face set with grim determination. He glanced over his troops, seeing the terror in their eyes—the panic as they tried to make sense of the strange flashes and the sudden, deadly bursts that felled their comrades with a speed and violence they could not comprehend.

Vesper took in the advancing forces with cold calculation, noting the immense size of Zincubus' army. They were outnumbered, badly. Even with the Dokar by their side, they were dwarfed by the massive, monstrous force pouring from the forest. But he did not hesitate. Lifting his bow high, he roared, "For freedom from darkness!"

Jájá, hovering above, took up the cry. Her voice cut through the noise, clear and unwavering. "To reclaim what has been taken!" she called, rallying her Nezkwah fleet.

With a mighty war cry, the two armies charged toward each other, the meadow erupting into a cacophony of clashing metal, flying arrows, and explosions. The rattle of gunfire became a deadly rhythm, cutting through the sounds of battle with cold efficiency. Warriors fell by the dozens, some cut down mid-stride, their bodies collapsing before they even registered the pain. The ground was soon littered with the fallen, blood soaking into the earth.

The elite Lirian squadron, brave and trained as they were, was the first to fall. Caught off guard by the sheer speed of the bullets, most of them didn't have a chance to raise their weapons before they were struck. Their cries filled the air, cut short as metal tore through flesh, bone, and muscle. Above, Dasheahs descended in a black swarm, attacking the Nezkwah with relentless savagery. Claws raked wings, teeth snapped at throats, and the sky filled with torn feathers as Nezkwah fell, some spiraling to their deaths, others crashing to the ground only to be trampled by the battle below.

On the western edge, a group of Dasheahs dragged a net of Shade Bane over a small cluster of Nezkwah, the heavy, fibrous plants tangling in their wings and sending them plummeting to the ground. With gleeful yowls, the Dasheahs threw red dust into the air—poisonous spores that turned Nezkwah wings brittle, sending them into frantic, fatal freefalls. The Dasheahs celebrated each victory with cruel yips and laughter.

Máhí, hovering on the outskirts, fought to maintain her focus as her people screamed for help. Every instinct in her screamed to fly to them, to fight, but she held herself back, knowing she had one duty above all else: to keep Sekowah safe. She lobbed laughing bombs and itch potions into the fray, creating small pockets of chaos, but they were a small reprieve in a storm of bloodshed.

On the ground, the Dokar and Lirian fought shoulder to shoulder, their makeshift wooden shields raised against the relentless machine-gun fire. Kudlah and Utdaga hurled boulders from the rear, but even their strength was not enough to halt the advance. Trapped by unfamiliar weapons, with friends falling on every side, the soldiers formed a desperate, circular barricade on the ground, raising shields in a last stand against the invisible storm of bullets raining down on them.

Gavril fought like a warrior possessed, his arrows flying, but they glanced harmlessly off the armor of the Moorigato. Around him, confusion spread like wildfire; they were outmatched, their weapons ineffective. Warriors fled into the bordering woods, fear overcoming even the strongest of hearts as the silver tanks rolled forward, crushing everything in their path.

Amidst the chaos, Máhí turned to check on Sekowah—only to find her gone. Panic jolted through her veins, cold and sharp. *Where is she?* She scanned the sky, the ground, every shadow, but saw nothing.

"Sekowah!" she cried, her voice swallowed by the roar of battle. No answer came.

The nightmare played on, relentless, unforgiving. Nezkwah and winged steeds plummeted from the sky. Lirian and Dokar warriors fell in waves, their bodies broken underfoot or riddled with bullets. The Kudlah, valiant to the last, abandoned their posts, retreating into the cover of the forest. The meadow, so full of life just moments before, had become a graveyard.

Máhí's hearts pounded, her breath shallow as her eyes darted across the battlefield. She scanned every inch of the chaos, every fallen soldier, every fleeing figure.

But Sekowah was nowhere to be found.

In the carnage, the prophecy that had carried them here—the hope of salvation Sekowah embodied—slipped through her fingers like dust.

CHAPTER FORTY

FORETOLD

Máhí felt her hearts hammering as she steered Tahgeet upward to evade the incoming net of Shade Bane. Below her, Oleta and her Dasheah squadron lumbered clumsily through the air, their weight and the unwieldy net slowing their pursuit. Máhí's eyes flashed with fury as she twisted sharply to the left, her body pressing tight against Tahgeet's sleek, muscular form. The cool dawn air whipped at her face, and the sun, newly risen, cast a sharp golden light across the battlefield below. The meadow, once peaceful, had been transformed into a hellscape of blood and smoke, scattered with fallen bodies and shattered armor. The early morning brilliance only sharpened the horror, making every scream, every fallen comrade, unbearably vivid.

Máhí's chest tightened, rage boiling within her at the devastation Zincubus had wrought. Her people, her valley, her family—it was all in jeopardy, under threat from this monstrous army and its soulless, deadly machines. The silver dragons rolled mercilessly across the field, cannon fire roaring and shattering the earth beneath them. The machine guns, with their cold, relentless staccato, mowed down warriors in swathes, their bodies crumpling to the ground before they even registered the fatal blow. For an instant, Máhí felt despair licking at the edges of her resolve.

Then, from somewhere behind her, a strange and overpowering sound emerged, breaking through the cacophony of battle—a deep, rising buzz, a living storm.

Máhí turned, her breath stalling at the sight of a dark, pulsating cloud sweeping in from the eastern sky. It was dense, massive, a roiling wave that darkened the horizon as it grew closer. For a breathless moment, everything on the battlefield stilled—the gunfire stopped, the shouts faded, and every head turned toward the approaching swarm, stunned by the unnatural sound that filled the air.

At the front of this black storm was Sekowah, astride Perrin, with Elo at her side. The sight of her sister—bold and radiant, leading a swarm of vengeance—struck Máhí with both awe and relief. She felt a fierce pride swell in her chest, a thrill of admiration mixed with the sting of envy. *Why hadn't I thought of this?* she wondered, marveling at the audacity and brilliance of Sekowah's plan. There, behind her, was a seething army of hornets, yellow jackets, and wasps: a furious, buzzing tempest of venom and rage. Behind the army of insects, was a small fleet of Zahnene, carrying brown sacks in their delicate hands.

Máhí watched in astonishment as Sekowah raised her sword high, her voice ringing clear across the battlefield. "Now!" she commanded.

The hornets descended like dark rain, hurtling toward Zincubus' forces with terrifying precision. The swarm swept over the Moorigato soldiers in waves, slipping past armor, crawling beneath helmets, burrowing into boots. The hornets found every crack, every gap, and surged through, their stings a fiery, unrelenting assault. Moorigato fighters flailed and thrashed, screaming in agony as the wasps invaded their eyes, their noses, their mouths. They dropped their guns in panic, swatting desperately at the stinging invaders, their shrieks of pain echoing across the meadow.

The chaos was instant and absolute. Moorigato soldiers tore off their helmets, their armor, anything that trapped the hornets against their skin. Some fell to the ground, writhing and scratching, while others staggered blindly, clawing at their faces as the hornets relentlessly attacked. The tanks, those hulking monsters of metal, were not spared. Swarms flooded the open hatches and cannon barrels, driving the operators to abandon their posts, leaping out and running, swatting at their bodies as they fell under the hornets' assault.

"Advance!" Sekowah's voice soared above the battlefield, a rallying cry that jolted Vesper's troops from their shock.

The Lirian and Dokar warriors surged forward, seizing the unexpected opportunity. They dropped their shields and arrows, and charged, their spears glinting in the morning light. Those who had abandoned the field in fear now returned, emboldened by the chaos Sekowah had sown. The Kudlah and Utdaga, who had taken refuge in the forest, returned in full force, flanking the enemy and smashing the disarmed Moorigato to the ground, adding their brute strength to the fray.

The buzzing grew louder, a thunderous hum that filled the air, vibrating through bone and blood. It was a sound both terrible and triumphant, the sound of nature's fury unleashed. The swarm moved as a single, dark wave over the battlefield, an unstoppable force that drove Zincubus' army into frenzied retreat. The Moorigato and Dasheah, overwhelmed and outmatched, fled back toward the bogs, desperate to find safety in the swamps, while the silver tanks lay abandoned.

The agile Zahnene, holding their sacks, flew toward Zincubus. He leveled his machine gun and fired, but they swerved and dodged expertly, closing in on him. They neared the dragons, each flying within close range, and opened their sacks, revealing polished diamonds, rubies, and sapphires. The dragons—overcome with greed as was their wont—lunged at them, as the dragon-charmers coaxed them away from the battlefield, leading them into the neighboring forests.

· · · · • ◯◯ • · · · ·

A midst the retreating horde, one figure remained—a single, furious flame of resistance: Zincubus.

Astride his green dragon, he watched the destruction with blazing eyes. He plunged his dagger into the eyes of his dragon, blinding it to the temptations of the Zahnene. His grip tightened on his machine gun as he surveyed the carnage below. His soldiers were scattered, his precious army in ruins, reduced to a ragged, fleeing mass. *Beware the meek.* Zincubus recalled the words of the Keeper, many harvests ago, when he had traveled deep into the mountains to seek out the oracle. He had dismissed the warning, had scoffed at the notion of a mortal girl posing any threat to his plans. But now, watching Sekowah rally her people, the bitter truth gnawed at him.

If I can't have what I want, he thought, his face twisting with rage, *neither can she.*

He scanned the battlefield, searching for a target, and his gaze fell on Gavril. There, in the midst of the melee, Gavril rode through the carnage, his spear a blur as he took down the remaining Moorigato with unrelenting ferocity. A surge of hatred filled Zincubus, dark and seething. He lifted his machine gun, aimed it at Gavril, and fired a furious spray of bullets.

Gavril's mount reared, struck by the gunfire, and Gavril tumbled from the saddle, landing hard on the blood-soaked ground. His armor was punctured, blood seeping from the wounds as he writhed in pain. Sekowah, high above, caught sight of the attack and felt a cold fist tighten around her heart. Their eyes met, his gaze filled with pain, and a primal fury surged through her, eclipsing every other thought.

She pointed toward Zincubus, her voice a thunderous command. "Take him!" she shouted to the swarm.

The hornets obeyed, swarming toward Zincubus in a dense tidal wave, their furious buzzing filling the air around him. But Zincubus was ready. He leveled his machine gun at Sekowah, his eyes narrowing with deadly intent. She barely had time to react, nudging Perrin to veer to the side—but it was a moment too late.

The bullets tore through the air, hitting Perrin in the wing. He screeched, his powerful body faltering as blood sprayed from the wound. Sekowah leaned in, ducking behind Perrin's head, clutched at the saddle, her heart pounding as she felt Perrin's strength waver beneath her. His wing flapped frantically, struggling to keep them airborne, but the damage was too great. With a final, heroic effort, Perrin angled his body to shield her, his claws stretching forward in a desperate attempt to soften their landing.

They plummeted, hurtling toward the ground in a blur of feathers and blood. Sekowah clung to the saddle, her body pressed tight against Perrin's, as they crashed into the meadow with bone-jarring force. She felt the earth slam against her, the shock of impact radiating through her bones.

Breathless, Sekowah's body lay motionless in the blood-soaked earth.

Satisfied, Zincubus turned his dragon away and forced it from the battle as the maddening swarm of hornets licked at his heels.

Sekowah regained consciousness, and eased herself out from beneath Perrin's battered wing, her legs shaking as she took in the quiet devastation spread across the meadow. The silence was jarring, broken only by the soft groans of the wounded and the low, mournful moan of wind through trampled grass. The clamor of battle had faded, leaving in its wake an eerie stillness. She glanced around, pulling healing potions from her belt, her mind a blur of faces she'd seen fall, of bodies she hoped were still breathing.

"Gavril!" Her voice cracked as she stumbled over the fallen, her gaze darting from one warrior to the next, desperately scanning for him. Her breath halted as she spotted his familiar form sprawled on the ground, unmoving, his armor smeared with blood and dirt. She dropped to her knees beside him, her fingers trembling as she tilted his head back and placed three drops of healing oil on his tongue.

"Please," she whispered, her voice choked with tears. "Please don't be gone."

For a few agonizing moments, nothing happened. But then his eyes fluttered open, hazy and unfocused, a ghost of a smile tugging at his bloodied lips.

"Your plan..." he murmured, voice thin but laced with admiration. "Brilliant."

He gave her a weak thumbs up, and she couldn't help but grin, her voice filled with relief as she clutched his hand. "Elo—he organized the swarm. The honeybees are not too fond of the yellow jackets, you know. It took some convincing."

Gavril's eyelids drooped, exhaustion overtaking him, but there was a quiet pride in his gaze as he watched her. She kissed him gently before standing, her resolve hardening. There were others who needed her.

She moved from one fallen warrior to the next, her fingers slick with healing potion as she poured precious drops into open mouths, hoping to coax the life back into them. Nearby, a Nezkwah warrior hesitated over a wounded Dasheah, a look of distaste on his face as the creature writhed in agony, her flesh pierced with hornet stings. The Dasheah let out a guttural cry, clawing at her face as yellow jackets continued to torment her.

Sekowah approached, holding up her hand. "Enough," she buzzed at the yellow jackets, and they pulled back obediently, dispersing into the air. She knelt beside the Dasheah, meeting her frightened, desperate gaze.

"Help me," the Dasheah whimpered, her voice thick with pain and disbelief.

Sekowah unscrewed a green vial and lifted the creature's head gently, letting a few drops trickle between her lips. The Dasheah's shuddering breaths began to steady, and Sekowah nodded to the Nezkwah soldier standing by, his face a mask of conflicted emotions.

"Good of All," she said, her words as much an order as they were an invocation. She watched as he swallowed, his stance solid, but after a moment, he removed a vial from his belt and moved to help another wounded Dasheah.

Across the battlefield, warriors began to mirror her actions. Nezkwah aiding Dasheah, Dokar aiding Moorigato. The phrase passed from mouth to mouth like a chant, like a balm for the wounds that went deeper than flesh. *Good of All*. It was a promise, a covenant being renewed.

Elo, hovering above, watched Sekowah with quiet pride. He signaled to the swarm, gathering the hornets, wasps, and yellow jackets. With one final buzz, they lifted as a cloud and began to drift eastward, their task complete.

The battlefield was left to the living.

As Sekowah worked her way through the wounded, Máhí landed Tahgeet nearby, her expression one of awe and disbelief as she took in the scene. Warriors from every faction, every clan, were kneeling side by side, offering healing to friend and foe alike. She saw Sekowah tending to a fallen Moorigato commander, his face swollen from venom. As Sekowah applied the healing oil, the commander's eyes fluttered open, and gratitude softened his battered features.

"Let me help," he rasped, extending a hand. Sekowah handed him a vial, watching as he knelt beside a Dokarian warrior.

"Three drops," she instructed softly, and he nodded, his fingers trembling as he followed her guidance.

Across the battlefield, healing potions changed hands, moving from one warrior to the next, a wave of resurrection sweeping through the fallen. Hope rose like a fragile dawn over the valley, a promise stitched together by the acts of mercy unfolding in the blood-streaked grass.

But the supply of potions was nearing an end. Not all could be saved.

Máhí, in the midst of helping a wounded Nezkwah, caught sight of a familiar figure sprawled in the grass. She recognized Jájá, her body curled beneath Vesper, his hand clasped tightly in hers, her aura flickering a deep crimson. Vesper, wounded but alive, lay clutching his wife's fading body. She abandoned her charge and sprinted to her mother's side, sinking to her knees.

"Sekowah!" Máhí's voice was raw as she looked up, her eyes wide with desperation. "Come! Quickly!"

Sekowah hurried to her, the remaining vial clutched in her trembling fingers. She dropped to her knees beside Jájá, who blinked open her eyes, the light in them dim but determined.

"Did you kill him?" Jájá whispered, her voice barely audible.

Sekowah and Máhí exchanged a short glance. Máhí looked away. "A coward in the end," she spat. "He abandoned the fight and fled."

"Which direction?" Jájá's voice grew frantic, her breath shallow as her fingers gripped Sekowah's hand with surprising strength.

"North," Sekowah said, pointing to the distant hills where Zincubus had vanished.

Jájá's face twisted in pain, her hand pressing against the wound at her side, blood seeping through her fingers. She pulled Sekowah close, her voice a desperate whisper. "He must be stopped... the Great Flood..." Her words broke off in a fit of coughing, her body trembling as she clutched at Sekowah's arm. With a final, shuddering breath, she yanked a ruby pendant from around her neck, pressing it into Sekowah's hand.

Máhí's eyes widened in horror. "No!" she cried, reaching to snatch it back. "Mother, it's yours! You can't—"

But Jájá silenced her with a look, her gaze softening as she met her eldest daughter's eyes. "My first," she murmured, her voice threaded with love. "My bravest. You will lead the Council in times of war, and she"—she looked to Sekowah—"in times of peace."

"I don't care about the Council!" Máhí's voice cracked as she brought the healing vial to her mother's lips. "Take it! I command you. Please..." Her voice wavered, desperate.

Jájá turned her head to accept the healing oil, but only one final drop rested on her tongue. She drew in a long breath, and slowly exhaled, accepting her fate.

Sekowah knelt in the grass, cradling the ruby pendant in her hands, its crimson surface stained with the blood of her mother. Her heart thudded with a quiet, unbreakable certainty. This was not a mantle she had sought, nor a title she had dreamed of. But as she looked down at the pendant, as she felt the weight of her mother's final blessing settle over her, she knew it was hers.

Sekowah's voice, soft and steady, broke the quiet. She placed her mother's hand over her own eyes, "show me my father."

For a brief moment, Jájá's spirit lingered, her gaze soft with infinite tenderness. "I cannot," she whispered, her voice like the last light of the setting sun. She brushed her hand over Sekowah's brow in a final blessing, and then her presence faded, leaving only the ruby pendant, warm against Sekowah's skin.

Máhí, her face streaked with tears, gave what remained of her vial to Vesper, stroking his hair as color returned to his face. Then, she took the necklace from Sekowah's hands, lifting it over her sister's head, securing it around her neck. "Now you are Queen," she said, her voice breaking, but laced with a fierce pride. She adjusted the pendant, then stepped back, her eyes meeting Sekowah's with a look that spoke of both grief and unwavering loyalty.

Sekowah tucked the ruby pendant beneath her tunic, feeling its warmth press against her heart. An overwhelming sense of responsibility, of fierce and abiding love for the valley, took root within her. She had been given more than a title, more than a duty. She had been given a charge—to protect, to heal, to lead her people toward a future where the horrors of this day might one day be nothing more than a dark memory.

The valley was her home now. Her heart swelled with resolve, with a quiet, unyielding promise. She would be the queen her mother had believed she could be. And as long as the valley called to her, she would answer, with every ounce of strength she had.

For the Good of All.

· · · · ● ⊚ ● · · · ·

Z incubus' dragon—faltering, blind, in the air and near exhaustion—flew over the River of Tears, the twin waterfalls nearing. Enraged at his defeat, he lashed it mercilessly, as it blew fire on the boulders of the twin waterfalls, turning the rock to molten lava.

He whipped the dragon once more, urging it to unleash a final torrent of flame on the rocks surrounding the twin waterfalls. The flame licked hungrily at the stone, and as the rocks softened, they began to collapse, disintegrating under the immense pressure of the churning water behind them. Finally, with a sound like thunder cracking the very bones of the earth, the waterfalls shattered. Water poured forth in an unbroken wave, a tsunami roaring over the cliffs and down into the valley below, tearing through everything in its path.

Zincubus smiled, a twisted joy radiating through him as he saw the devastation spread. *Let them weep,* he thought, filled with dark triumph. *Let them mourn their precious valley.*

As the torrent surged forward, trees were uprooted and tossed about like twigs. Entire swaths of the lush valley were swallowed whole, turning into a swirling sea of mud, rocks, and broken boughs. The elder Nezkwah, who had stayed behind to guard the villages, halted their work, their faces pale as they realized what was coming.

"To the sky! Everyone, up!" an elder shouted, his voice slicing through the mounting panic.

The remaining Nezkwah scrambled, fleeing from the encroaching flood. They shot up from treetops, burst out of root cellars, and emerged from hillside mounds, hovering over their crumbling world. From above, they watched in horror as the flood washed away the orchards, leaving nothing but a murky wasteland in its wake. The wildflower fields, the beating heart of the valley, were swallowed whole. Root cellars—filled with carefully stored food, seeds, and medicinal herbs—vanished beneath the deluge. The very foundation of their lives was being swept away before their eyes.

Hovering among his kin, Elo stared down in shock as the waves overtook his beloved bee sanctuary. Hive after hive tumbled into the churning water, their delicate structures crushed under the relentless current. His face twisted with sorrow, and he clutched his chest, watching helplessly as everything he had nurtured and protected disappeared beneath the raging flood. Zincubus' face came to mind, and he cursed the man with every fiber of his being. *You soulless fiend,* he thought. *May your heart never know peace.*

The smaller animals of the valley were caught in the rising waters, their frantic, darting movements tragic in their futility. Nezkwah and Zahnene darted down to rescue as many as they could, scooping up rabbits, squirrels, and field mice, carrying them to the safety of the high cliffs. Yet, for every creature saved, countless others were lost, their cries swallowed by the roar of the river.

· · · •  • · · · ·

Hovering above it all, Zincubus delighted in his triumph. He watched as the valley, once vibrant and full of life, was reduced to a chaotic mire. He listened to the cries of the villagers, relishing each note of anguish, each sob of despair. His work was done, and with grim satisfaction, he lashed his dragon one last time, directing it toward the southern horizon and the distant shimmer of the ocean. He had no intention of waiting for any vengeance to find him here; he would escape, and leave them with nothing but ru ins.

Let them choke on their precious prophecies, he thought, sneering. *The valley is mine no longer, but neither is it theirs.*

· · · •  • · · · ·

In the Daylight Meadow, Sekowah and Máhí moved through the remnants of the battlefield, the echoes of their victory bittersweet as they tended to the wounded. Smoke drifted from craters left by the tank fire, the lingering scent circulating with the unholy stench of blood and earth. As they covered the dead in meadow grasses and comforted the injured, a distant sound reached their ears—a low, thunderous rumble that seemed to rise from the bones of the mountain.

Máhí froze, her face paling as the realization dawned. "Sekowah... do you hear that?"

Sekowah turned, her heart dropping as she recognized the dreadful, growing roar. She had read the stories—the ancient warnings in *the Verses*—but never had she thought she'd witness it. They scrambled onto Tahgeet, leaving Perrin behind with a pained, sympathetic glance. His broken wing still unfurled, he stood stoically, refusing the healing potion so others could be saved. "Stay safe, my friend," Sekowah whispered as Tahgeet lifted them into the sky.

As they approached the twin waterfalls, the horrifying truth lay before them. The rocks had collapsed, giving way to a monstrous wave of water that thundered down the mountainside, a cataclysm that engulfed the valley. Máhí's eyes widened in panic as she scanned the devastation below.

"We must open the cove gates!" she shouted over the roaring flood.

"The cove gates?" Sekowah echoed, struggling to keep her voice steady.

"Near the pyramids!" Máhí shouted. She pulled Tahgeet into a sharp turn, following the floodwaters southward, toward the sea. "After the revolution, the gates were sealed to protect the valley. But if we don't open them now, the entire valley will drown. The water needs a way out!"

Sekowah nodded, her pulse pounding as they soared over the torrent, the devastation below ripping at her heart. All around her, her homeland—her people's legacy—was unraveling, the land itself succumbing to the fury of the unleashed waters. Máhí's cheeks were streaked with silent tears, glistening in the morning light as they rushed over the flooded fields and villages.

They had fought so hard to protect this place. They had rallied warriors, sworn alliances, sacrificed their very lives—and for what? The prophecy had been their guide, their promise of survival, yet the valley lay drowning, just as it had warned. It was no longer a question of stopping the Great Flood.

Despite their valiant efforts, it had come anyway.

CHAPTER FORTY-ONE

THE COVE OF CROSSING

The air turned salty and humid as Tahgeet neared the sea, and Sekowah could feel the spray of ocean mist on her face. They had finally reached the coastline, but there was no peace to be found here—only the relentless, jagged beauty of the sea and the primal intensity of the waves crashing below.

Sharp rocks jutted out into the surf, black and glistening in the sun, while three black pyramid-shaped islands loomed just offshore, casting long shadows over the water. Their sides were perfectly smooth and dark, made from a strange, glossy metal that seemed to absorb the sunlight rather than reflect it. Running in waves along the outer walls were tendrils of silver light which pulsed and flickered as if by some electrical source, creating vines of illumination.

The Cove itself was a natural marvel—a massive cavern carved out over millennia by the pounding sea, with smooth granite walls that curved like the folds of a shell. The water in the Cove was a pure, crystalline turquoise.

A steep cliff surrounded the Cove, at least a hundred feet high on both sides. Ocean water rushed into it, filling the cavern nearly to the top, as waves crashed in and out.

Máhí shook her head. "The tides are not in our favor," she said.

They landed at the top of the cliff to survey the area. Máhí and Sekowah dismounted, and Sekowah stood at the cliff top, the wind pulling at her hair. She could hear the waves crashing inside the Cove, birds ca-cawing from the sky, circling over her. The hair on her arms stood at attention, and her gut clenched as she imagined herself climbing down the cliff.

Behind her, a shadow shifted.

She turned, her heart lurching, and there he was: perched on his dragon, battered and barely holding on, his eyes fixed on her with a feral intensity. His face was twisted with rage, exhaustion, and something close to desperation. His machine gun dangled uselessly at his side, empty. Zincubus looked as though he had been to the edges of hell and returned, and now his entire purpose was distilled into a single focus—her.

Sekowah's hand went to her belt of potions, her fingers shaking as she fumbled for anything that might help her. She had nothing left but a few vials, none of which would save her from him. She was cornered, trapped between the cliff's edge and the monster who had terrorized her people, destroyed her home, and murdered her family.

Máhí, her face set with fierce determination, positioned herself between Sekowah and Zincubus, her staff raised, her knuckles white. "Keep moving, Sekowah," she hissed, her eyes never leaving him. "Get to the Cove. I'll hold him off."

Zincubus calmly stepped down from his dragon with his hands in the air. "The gates cannot be opened. Not even by me," he announced.

He stepped toward Sekowah.

She instinctively backed away from him, heart pounding as she turned and scrambled down the cliff face. The rocks scraped at her hands, and loose stones tumbled beneath her feet, crashing onto the beach far below. She fought to keep her balance, her breaths coming fast and shallow as she descended the treacherous cliff face one anguished step at a time, one hand hold at a time, each motion an uncertain agony. She kept her focus on the granite inches from her face, never looking up, never looking down, every cell in her body alert to the smallest of changes in the architecture of the stones she used for balance. She encouraged herself with quiet whispers as the wind took the soft words from her mouth and scattered them.

She finally reached the bottom, her boots sinking into the wet sand, her legs and arms trembling from the effort, and without looking back, she ran toward the Cove entrance, where the ocean surged in and out with each wave, the roar of water filling her ears.

Behind her, she heard Máhí's defiant shout. "Hey-yo!" Her sister's voice rang out, strong and fearless, challenging Zincubus. She heard the whoosh of fire—a final, desperate burst from Zincubus' dragon as it tried to muster one last wall of flame. But it was weak, pitiful, the dragon's strength nearly spent. Sekowah swallowed hard and forced herself to keep moving, ducking as another wave crashed against the rocks, spraying her with icy seawater.

The entrance to the Cove loomed before her, dark and foreboding, filled with churning water that slapped against jagged rocks just inside the cavern. With trembling fingers, she unhooked her chainmail and let it fall to the sand. She yanked on her damp boots, tossing them aside.

She took one last, shuddering breath, and then plunged into the water. The shock of the cold hit her like a slap, and she fought to keep her head above the frothing waves as she made her way through the entrance. Every fiber of her body screamed at her to turn back, to flee from this dark, powerful place. But she pressed on, ducking beneath the surface, her limbs moving with a fierce, desperate rhythm. A wave moved in, tossing her into the churning brine. The water pushed and pulled at her, but beneath the surface, the currents were calmer, manageable.

You can do this, she told herself, though her heart hammered with fear.

· · · · • ⦵ • · · · ·

Máhí faced Zincubus at the edge of the cliff, her breath coming in short, sharp bursts as she tightened her grip on her staff. The fading sunlight painted the jagged rocks in hues of crimson and gold, a battlefield bathed in an ominous glow. Zincubus stood still, a predator savoring the moment, his lips curling into a sneer that dripped with contempt.

Máhí's gaze locked onto his. Beneath her searing hatred, there was resolve—a quiet, unyielding strength that even he could not dismiss. She shifted her stance, ready for his move, ready for anything.

Or so she thought.

Zincubus reached into his cloak and pulled out a small satchel. With a flick of his wrist, he scattered its contents onto the ground between them. Tiny pods burst open, releasing an unnatural hissing sound. Máhí barely had time to react before dozens of black, writhing spiders spilled forth, their bodies shimmering with an eerie bioluminescence. The creatures scuttled toward her in a living wave, their legs scurrying along the rocks. They were too fast, too coordinated. She swung her staff, striking several of the arachnids, their bodies crunching under the force. But for every one she crushed, more surged forward, relentless in their advance.

The first spider reached her leg, its tiny mouth pincher digging into her skin through her leggings. Then another, and another. They climbed her body with terrifying precision, leaving thin, glistening trails of silk in their wake. Máhí thrashed, trying to brush them away, but they were everywhere—her arms, her chest, her neck. She could feel the webbing tighten around her ribs, pulling her arms against her sides.

Her breath hitched as panic clawed at her mind. The spiders were weaving a cocoon around her, layer by suffocating layer. She staggered backward, her feet skidding dangerously close to the edge of the cliff.

Zincubus laughed, the sound cold and hollow, devoid of joy, and yet brimming with cruelty.

"How does it feel?" he sneered, stepping closer, his dark eyes glinting with malice. "To know that your strength, your courage, means nothing? You are a relic of the past, Máhí, and like all relics, you will crumble to dust."

Máhí's voice was muffled as she struggled against the sticky threads that bound her. She could feel the spiders skittering across her face, their legs brushing against her lips and eyelids. Her staff, her lifeline, slipped from her fingers and clattered to the ground.

The world began to blur, her vision narrowing to a pinprick of light as the web constricted her chest, squeezing the air from her lungs.

Sekowah struggled forward through the waves, clinging to the wall of the cavern as the ocean surged around her. Her arms ached, her body battered from the rocks, but she kept pushing on, deeper and deeper into the Cove. Each breath she managed to take was a victory, each movement forward a triumph over the panic that threatened to consume her. She reached the back of the cavern, where a strange glimmer caught her eye beneath the surface of the water.

Taking a deep breath, she dove, her fingers stretching toward the glinting object. Her eyes stung from the salt, but she forced herself to look, to see. There, beneath the churning water, stood a golden gate, covered in mysterious hieroglyphs. It was beautiful and terrible, an immovable force that blocked her path. And behind it, pressed against the gate with all the weight of the floodwaters, was a massive wall of muddy water, churning with debris, straining to break free.

The gates moaned and creaked, as the pressure behind them begged for release. *Open the cove gates,* she repeated to herself, like a mantra. She pulled desperately on the gates, but they didn't budge. She searched for a handle, a lever, anything, that might give her a clue about how to open them. She found nothing. Worse, she knew if she were successful in opening the gates, the mass of water and flood debris would explode, taking her with it

It was a horrifying dilemma.

Was this it? she thought, panic rising once again in her throat. *Was I created solely to open these gates to save the valley, sacrificing my life in the process? Was this why the prophecies came to an end shortly after her verse?*

She surfaced, taking a wave in the face, gulping for more air, then dove back down to continue searching. *There must be a way.* She repeated this half a dozen times, each time, coming up without an answer.

She dove back down, determined to figure it out. She ran her fingers along the symbols, pushing, pulling, examining them, one by one, attempting to interpret the instructions, but this was not the Nezkwah language she had learned to read. This was something entirely different: ancient and unknowable.

She wasn't sure why, but on the final resurface, through tears of frustration, she called out: "Inannaaaaaaaaaaaaa!!!!"

Her cry echoed through the cavern, bouncing off the walls and fading into silence. But in that silence, something changed. The water around her shimmered, and a figure appeared—a creature with blue skin and golden, fish-like eyes, her hair woven with glowing seaweed that floated around her like a halo. She was mounted on a massive, sand colored dappled ray, her gaze calm and ancient as she looked upon Sekowah with a wisdom that seemed older than the ocean itself.

After climbing down the cliff to the shoreline, Zincubus lounged on a boulder on the edge of the shore, near the cove entrance. He removed his boots and dangled

his feet into the cool water, then splashed his face and neck. The pristine water was clear to the bottom. Shells and colorful rocks lined the coast, creating an impressionistic painting beneath the shallow waves.

He let the sun bask him in late afternoon light as he waited.

He raised an eyebrow as Sekowah emerged from the cavern, looking horribly spent, defeated. She fought the current on her way across the rocks, finally dropping to her hands and knees in the sand.

He chuckled at her desperate expression.

She lifted her head to the sound of the laughter. She looked to the cliff's top, hoping to see some sign of Máhí, but the air was still, the cliff's edge empty. She set her angry gaze on her pile of chainmail, and the belt next to it. Between the arduous swim inside the cavern and the bashing she took on the rocks, she doubted she had the energy to even pick up the chainmail, let alone fight him in it.

Never before had she felt the desire to fight someone, to kill them. The intensity of her rage startled her, and she felt a knot in her stomach as she met his gaze. She had known humiliation before, but not like this. This was humiliation twisted in on itself and balled up with fire. This was pure hatred. She could feel it in every cell in her body. Pure, revolting, all-consuming, murderous hate.

He met her gaze and let out a final, bitter chuckle. "Go ahead," he said. "Put it on. I wouldn't feel right killing you so easily anyway. I do have my dignity to consider. It is, after all, the only thing I've got left."

Sekowah rose from her shaky knees and walked by the chainmail and belt. She dragged herself toward him, her crimson pendant sparkling in the sun. The fire that burned inside her now would not let her surrender. Not to this vile man. If he wanted to kill her, she would make him work for it.

His eyes focused in on the pendant around her neck, and his expression turned from contemptuous to something she hadn't seen in him before—almost friendly.

Out of breath, she stopped only a few paces from him, and sat on a flat rock. She took note of his sudden attention on her pendant. She gathered herself, recovered her breath, and observed him. It was then that the thought hit her, like a punch to the gut. She could feel the tears come as the possibility crept into her mind. Her throat tightened, and her stomach churned with disgust, but she had to know.

Chapter Forty-Two

THE KEY

Sekowah's question hung in the air, a raw, open wound. "Are you my father?" she asked, holding her breath, waiting for his answer.

Zincubus took his time, his gaze drifting out to the endless expanse of ocean as if the answer lay somewhere within its depths. When he finally turned back to her, his face was a mask of disdain, but something flickered in his eyes—a vulnerability she hadn't seen before. "And if I was?" he asked, his voice low.

Sekowah felt as if the ground beneath her was slipping away. Her heart thudded painfully against her ribs, her mind spiraling with questions she hadn't dared ask herself until now. *Did my mother create me from him? Was I born only to destroy him?* The thought was absurd, horrifying even, but it felt like everything in this world defied logic, like each piece of her life had been turned upside down and shaken free of meaning. She was choking on disbelief, anger, and a deep, festering sadness.

Zincubus bent down, picked up a smooth stone from the beach, and turned toward a small eddy, water pooling peacefully within it. With a practiced flick of his wrist, he sent it skipping across the surface—just as her father had once taught her at Lake Jocassee. Sekowah's stomach twisted as she watched the stone skim the surface, skipping a dozen times before sinking. The similarity between them sickened her.

He stretched his arms out, as if presenting himself to her. "I am the father of millions," he said, a smirk tugging at his lips.

She blinked back tears, her frustration spilling over. "That's ridiculous!" she shouted, her voice rising over the crash of the waves.

Zincubus chuckled, a dry, humorless sound. "I almost feel sorry for you," he said, his gaze still fixed on the distant horizon. "You really don't have a clue, do you?" His eyes drifted toward the pyramids that loomed off the shore, dark and foreboding. "You can't even begin to understand who I am. Let's leave it at that."

The arrogance in his tone, the utter dismissal of her, only fueled the rage building within her. "Tell me how to open the gates!" she demanded, her voice cracking with desperation. She was losing control, but she didn't care. She was exhausted, wounded, and trapped, and he was toying with her. Every answer he gave was a riddle, every gesture shrouded in secrets, and she was done with it.

Zincubus let out a long sigh, a mocking echo of her plea. "Ah, yes... the gates," he murmured. "The one thing we can agree on." He looked at her with an expression she couldn't place—a strange mixture of pity and resentment. "Believe me," he said slowly, "I want those gates open far more than you do."

She stared at him, stunned. This was the last thing she'd expected to hear. "What?"

He turned to face her fully, his voice softening, almost vulnerable. "Look at me. I have nothing now. You've taken everything from me," he said, the bitterness in his tone evident. "There's a world beyond those gates where I still have something. Where everything that was stolen from me can be regained."

"There's nothing behind those gates except mud and water," she replied, her voice trembling. She had seen it herself—the churning floodwaters, the debris pressing against the golden bars.

"If you say so," he replied. "You can have this world," he continued, his voice low and almost tender. "I don't want it anymore." He picked up a broken shell and tossed it into the surf. "But only you can open those gates, and only I know how you can do it. We're a team now, Sekowah. Take it or leave it."

Sekowah's heart pounded as she looked into his eyes. His expression was a twisted mixture of desperation, rage, and something that almost resembled... sincerity. She didn't trust him, and yet there was a brutal honesty in his gaze. He had done terrible things—unspeakable things—and yet he had not lied to her. In a twisted way, that seemed like his only redeeming quality.

"What do you want?" she asked, her voice barely a whisper. She felt like she was on the edge of a precipice, and that with a single misstep, she would fall.

He spread his hands, palms open. "We go in. I show you how to open the gates. You save the valley—and I return to my home." His voice hardened, and his eyes blazed with anger. "You owe me that much. You drove me to kill my only love. You destroyed the only means I had to travel between worlds. Open the gates, and I'll leave you here to do whatever you please. You have my word... for whatever it's worth to you."

Sekowah's gaze flickered to the cove entrance, the dark mouth of the cavern where the waves pounded relentlessly against the rocks. She thought of her mother, her sister, the valley. "Behind the gates is a portal that leads to your world?"

"Yes," he replied, his eyes gleaming. "Many worlds. Infinite worlds. Including yours, my dear. *Your* home." He paused, his voice softening as he watched her. "Once the gates are open, you can cross through if you like. Go back to the life that was taken from you. You hold nothing over me there. In your world, any talk of this place will get you locked up in a psych ward."

The word "home" hit her hard. She hadn't allowed herself to dwell on it, on the family she had left behind. Her memories were hazy now, like dreams she could barely recall, but the thought of seeing them again tugged at her heart. She felt her resolve waver, her mind twisting under the weight of his words.

Zincubus took a step closer, his hand settling on her shoulder in a disturbingly paternal gesture. "This world will grow old for you, Sekowah," he murmured, his voice almost gentle. "They've used you. The prophecies are rubbish, fairy tales, nothing more than hope and belief, a self-fulfilling prophecy they created out of desperation. They created you to be their icon of solidarity. You were never a person to them. You were a tool."

Sekowah narrowed her eyes, "They believe the prophecies. I don't doubt that."

"Of course they do," Zincubus countered. "Belief is powerful. But don't be fooled. They took away your childhood, your parents. Think of your mother and father—they're still there, and they miss you. Jade is not the child they love. You are."

Sekowah fought the tears that threatened to spill. His words wrapped around her, pulling at old wounds she had tried to bury. She was no stranger to grief, but the confusion, the ache of betrayal he spoke of—that was new, raw, and painful.

"You didn't answer my question," she said, her voice barely a whisper.

"Would it make a difference?" Zincubus' tone was almost kind, his face open and earnest. Then, as if the conversation bored him, he shrugged and turned his back on her, walking slowly toward the water's edge. He shed his cloak, dropping it carelessly on the sand.

Sekowah stared after him, her heart a whirlwind of conflicting emotions. She looked out over the ocean, where sea mammals leapt through the waves and a whale blew a plume of mist into the sky. Everything in her screamed that he was a monster, but there was something else, too—a possibility that lingered like a shadow at the edge of her mind. *Was he telling the truth?*

Had she been too quick to trust Máhí, Jájá, the Nezkwah? Had they really manipulated her entire life for their own purposes? *Did they create me only to rally their people against him?* Her chest tightened at the thought, a horrible realization that perhaps she'd been nothing but a pawn in a war that predated her existence.

With her heart pounding, Sekowah took a slow, hesitant step toward him. She didn't trust him, but the chance to know, to understand... it was like an itch she couldn't ignore. She stopped briefly where her belt lay in the sand, her fingers brushing over a small blue vial. Without thinking, she tucked it into her tunic, and with leaden steps, she followed him.

· · · · • ◯◯ • · · · ·

T he cold pressure of the water tightened around Sekowah's chest as she and Zincubus swam together through the dark tunnel, battling the violent current. Her lungs burned, and every stroke felt heavier than the last. The water here was thick with churning silt, and the depth of it—cold, suffocating—pressed against her ribs. Every inch forward was a struggle. And yet, when she faltered, feeling her strength give out, Zincubus was suddenly at her side, gripping her arm, hoisting her up toward a pocket of air.

They surfaced together, gasping. Her breath came in shallow, ragged gulps. For a brief moment, she caught his gaze, and in that instant, there was a flicker of... something. Was it compassion? Encouragement? It disappeared as quickly as it had come.

"You can do this. Come on," he urged, his voice oddly calm, almost gentle.

Sekowah felt her resolve harden. She could feel the weight of her mother's ruby pendant pressing against her collarbone, a reminder of why she was here—of everything she stood to save. Nodding, she pushed herself onward, ignoring the fatigue and the throb in her head.

They finally reached the rear wall, breathing hard, treading water, where Zincubus pointed to her pendant. "The pendant is the key," he announced.

Sekowah glanced down at the ruby, taking in its finely cut edges, the intricate mesh of gold threads wrapping around it. How had she not seen it before? The jewel was shaped almost like a key, the cut of it too precise to be anything but intentional. The realization was both exhilarating and terrifying.

He nodded toward the center of the gate, where a symbol of the sun blazed in the light. "You'll insert the pendant into the center of the circle inside the sun symbol," he yelled.

The gates creaked under the pressure of the water, each moan echoing in the cavern like the growl of some ancient beast. The weight of the floodwaters behind them was staggering, straining against the metal, threatening to break free at any moment. Sekowah hesitated, swallowing back her fear. "The water... it will push us back out to sea. We'll drown!"

Zincubus' face twisted into a sardonic smile. "We can wait for low tide if you'd prefer. But the valley won't."

"No." Her voice was firm. She couldn't bear the thought of how much damage the flood might be wreaking, how high the water might be rising even now, swallowing everything she held dear. "We do this now."

Zincubus' face softened, almost as if he were proud of her resolve. "When the gates open, step into the side chamber." He pointed to a small alcove carved into the rear wall of the cave. "We'll pull the gate in front of us as a shield. It's our only chance."

Sekowah nodded, adrenaline surging through her as she mentally rehearsed the steps. She took a deep breath, steeling herself, and then they both dove down.

Underwater, she searched the gate for the symbol he had described. Her fingers traced the etching of the sun, feeling the grooves and ridges under her fingertips. There, in the center, was a small hole, waiting. She pressed the pendant forward, her fingers trembling, and slid it into place.

The effect was instantaneous. The ruby blazed with a fierce scarlet light, illuminating the entire cavern with a wavering, otherworldly glow. The water around them seemed to shimmer and pulse with life, as if it had been set alight from within. Then, with a violent shudder, the gates burst open.

A tidal wave of water surged forward, roaring as it tore through the newly opened barrier, slamming the gates against the side walls of the alcove. Sekowah and Zincubus clung desperately to the bars, gripping the metal until their hands went white. The force of the flood was indescribable, a sheer wall of raw, furious energy, dragging debris from the valley with it—uprooted trees, shattered pottery, splintered wood, remnants of what had once been homes and orchards. All of it churned around them, a maelstrom of destruction.

"Hold!" Zincubus shouted over the roar, his voice barely audible above the torrent.

Sekowah's arms quivered as she tightened her grip, every muscle in her body straining against the relentless pull of the water. Her fingers dug into the bars, and she gritted her teeth, her knuckles going numb. She felt her strength slipping, her grip weakening as branches and rocks crashed against the gate, threatening to tear it from her grasp.

Hold on, she told herself, her thoughts a desperate chant. *Hold. Don't let go.*

The water poured out in a seemingly endless rush, the flood's fury unmatched. It seemed as if an eternity passed, the roar and pressure unyielding. But slowly—agonizingly slowly—the torrent began to lessen, the pressure dying down, the wall of water thinning until it was a quiet river, flowing steadily through the cavern.

At last, there was silence, broken only by the gentle lapping of ocean waves against the cave walls as the river became a stream, and then a trickle.

Sekowah let go of the bars, her arms shaking, her body spent. She barely registered the scratches on her hands, the bruises on her skin, or the mud that covered them both. All she could feel was the bone-deep exhaustion, the kind that seeped into every cell, leaving her hollow and raw.

Beside her, Zincubus let out a triumphant yell. "Whahhhoooo!" he bellowed, his face split into a delirious grin. But as he turned to her, the joy in his expression twisted, darkening into something predatory. His eyes narrowed, and in one swift motion, he pulled a dagger from his belt.

"Forgive me," he murmured.

Sekowah's stomach flipped. His sudden betrayal didn't surprise her; she had expected nothing less from him. Instinctively, she dropped into a defensive stance, her mind racing through the training she'd received. *Distract. Evade.*

Her body was trembling with fatigue, her muscles on the brink of collapse, but she forced herself to move. She raised one arm high, feigning a strike, while her other hand slipped into her tunic, fingers wrapping around the vial she had taken from her belt.

She swallowed its contents, as the word rose from her lips in a whisper, holding all the power she could muster: "Fish."

The transformation was immediate. Her body twisted, her bones and muscles re-shaping, her skin shimmering with blue light as she felt herself dissolve, reforming into something sleek, agile, untouchable. For a brief, blinding moment, she was nothing but light and water, her molecules scattering, reassembling. Then, with a final burst, she was whole again—and diving into the pool below, her new form gliding effortlessly through the murky water.

Zincubus plunged in after her, his dagger slashing wildly. But Sekowah, now a dolphin-like sea creature, was beyond his reach, her streamlined body cutting through the water with practiced ease. Around her, the water teemed with life—a pod of similar creatures, rays gliding gracefully, warriors of the water tribe encircling her in a protective formation. She clicked and squeaked, calling to the pod, the sound reverberating through the water in waves of sonar, guiding her, grounding her.

The water was thick with silt and valley debris, clouding her vision, but her new senses were sharp, each click bouncing back to her, mapping the space around her. She could feel Zincubus thrashing behind her, his dagger flashing in the murky light, slashing blindly. She heard the anguished squeals of the sea tribe as he landed blows, the water tinged with the scent of blood. Rage simmered in her, but she forced herself to stay focused, to keep mo ving.

The creature beside her nudged her, urging her to follow as the pod swam in tight circles, confusing Zincubus, leading him away from her. She stayed close, letting the pod shield her.

Zincubus, his air running low, finally abandoned the pursuit. He turned, his movements slowing as he swam toward the surface, desperate for air.

Just as he breached the surface, something dark and massive rose from the ocean depths. A giant squid, its eyes glistening with eerie intelligence, its tentacles extending like a dozen reaching hands, wrapped itself around him, pulling him down with relentless strength.

Sekowah watched, her eyes wide, as Zincubus struggled, his dagger flashing one last time before the squid's powerful arms wound tighter, dragging him deeper, past the swirling silt, out toward the open sea. His screams, garbled and bubbling, faded into the depths, lost to the vastness of the ocean.

The water grew still, the sediment settling like dust in an empty room.

Sekowah, trembling, swam back toward the cove entrance. The gates creaked in the silence, revealing a small, glimmering tunnel that sparkled like the inside of a geode. Beyond the gates lay a path—a portal shimmering with promise.

A pang of longing shot through her. *Beyond the gates... home.* The word filled her mind, warm and bittersweet. She could almost hear her father's laughter, the smell of her mother's kitchen on Sunday mornings. For a moment, the image was so clear, she could almost believe she was there, standing in their little kitchen, the hum of the television in the background, the warmth of her father's hand on her shoulder. But she was here, floating in the depths of another world, a queen with a valley to protect. The heart within her pulsed with a rhythm all its own, but the ache in her mortal heart was undeniable. She let herself hover there for a moment, swishing her fins and tail, feeling the pull of both worlds, feeling the weight of the choice that lay before her.

Chapter Forty-Three

RETURN

It felt like a lifetime had passed since she first arrived in this strange world. Sekowah thought back to who she had been then—just a girl who polished rocks, who studied biology, who dreamed of becoming a scientist or maybe a geologist. That girl seemed almost like a stranger to her now. Sekowah was Nezkwah. She was Queen. She had a people to care for, a land to rebuild. This was her home. It was where she truly belonged.

She scanned the cove floor for her pendant, and found it, glistening on the cavern bottom underwater. She turned in circles—gracefully, sadly—morphing back into her true form. *Return to true form*, she told herself as her form dissolved and rearranged itself at her command. She resurfaced for air and peered down the glistening tunnel that led back home. Water continued to peacefully flow through the aquifer and out to sea. The gates would need to remain open until all the water had receded.

She limped through the jagged interior of the cove, every step a reminder of what she had endured. The stones bit into her feet, slick with salt and blood, but she kept moving—drawn by the promise of open air and stillness beyond. At last, she emerged, breath ragged, the sky above eerily calm, indifferent.

Water streamed from her body as she collapsed to her knees on the sand. Around her, the remnants of chaos lay strewn like battlefield relics: her chainmail, her belt, shattered vials gleaming in the sun. Near the shoreline, Zincubus' black cape sprawled across the sand like a fallen shadow. His boots sat neatly beside it, absurdly pristine. A grim offering. Proof that he was no longer whole.

Naked again, vulnerable but no longer powerless, Sekowah glanced at the chainmail. Its cold weight, its bitter memory, made her stomach turn. She left it where it lay.

It was the cape that beckoned.

The fabric was heavy, soaked in blood and ruin, but she draped it over her shoulders, fastening it with deliberate care. It smelled of smoke and regret. She slid her feet into his oversized boots. They swallowed her, but she stood taller.

There was something darkly triumphant in the act. Not just survival—but reclamation. She had worn her pain. Now, she wore his defeat.

The cliff loomed above her, and the climb back up seemed endless. But she was driven by something fierce and unbreakable, a fire that had been forged through trial and suffering. She scaled the rock face, hands raw and trembling, until she reached the top and collapsed in the tall grass, gasping for breath. She took a moment to settle her thoughts, to regain her strength before rising to her knees, which shook from the effort, and stood.

Máhí was nowhere to be found.

Tahgeet lay nearby, her great body battered, feathers scorched and torn, her chest rising and falling in shallow breaths. She knelt by her, placing a gentle hand on her flank. Her eyes opened slowly, and she heard her thoughts, soft and strained: *Find Máhí. She needs you.*

Sekowah's heart lurched, and she scanned the field. A trail of crushed grass led away from Tahgeet, toward a patch of shadow beneath a thicket of trees. She scrambled to her feet, fear tightening her throat as she followed the trail, praying silently.

Then she saw her: Máhí, cocooned in a thick, white web, tiny spiders still weaving their silky strands around her. Her face was barely visible, her wings pinned beneath the sticky threads. But even from here, Sekowah could see the slight movement of her chest as she fought for air.

A knife. I need a knife. Without delay, she sprinted clumsily back to Tahgeet, and rummaged through Máhí's saddle bag, finding a small dagger tucked neatly beneath the flap of the bag.

Working quickly, Sekowah sliced through the sticky threads with care, freeing Máhí's face, then her arms, and finally the rest of her body. The webbing peeled away in thick layers, leaving Máhí blinking and stretching her wings in the sunlight.

Without warning, Máhí pulled Sekowah into a fierce hug, the first authentic embrace they had ever shared. "Thanks," she murmured, her voice softened with gratitude.

Sekowah closed her eyes, allowing herself to melt into the hug. She hadn't realized how badly she needed this, how starved she was for connection, for family. She felt the walls around her heart loosen, just a bit, as if this hug was the beginning of something deeper.

They pulled apart, and Sekowah's gaze drifted back to Tahgeet. She was still lying in the grass, her eyes half-closed. She checked her belt, realizing she had one green vial left. Kneeling by her side, she poured the healing potion onto her tongue. Her eyes fluttered shut, then slowly opened, brighter and clearer. Her wounds began to knit together, downy feathers regrowing over her burnt skin. Within moments, she was on her feet, nuzzling Máhí affectionately.

Máhí stroked her neck, murmuring softly to her, but her eyes stayed fixed on the cliff. "What of Zincubus' dragon?" she asked, her voice laced with pity and anger.

Sekowah looked down to the beach below, where the green dragon lay sprawled on the jagged rocks, lifeless. Its once-mighty body was twisted, broken, a creature of immense power reduced to ruin. She felt a pang of sadness for the dragon, an unwilling hostage in Zincubus' selfish games. Had it been thrown from the cliff in its final struggle, or had it chosen to leap rather than endure its master's cruelty? She couldn't know, but the thought haunted her.

They stood in silence for a moment, looking out over the sea. The turquoise water was marred with debris from the valley: shattered trees, fragments of rooftops, broken branches—all drifting in the tide, pulled toward the horizon. A dark plume of silt clouded the water near the Cove, a reminder of the flood's devastation. The valley had been saved, but at a terrible cost.

Sekowah sighed, the weight of everything pressing down on her. "What happens now?"

Máhí's voice was steady. "We rebuild. But first, we return the emerald."

They mounted Tahgeet, and Sekowah strapped herself in as the great beast lifted them into the sky, carrying them inland and away from the coast.

B elow, on the beach, a hooded figure watched them disappear into the distance. The figure moved silently across the sand, stopping by the boulder where Zincubus' staff lay propped against a rock. They picked it up, examining the worn wood.

Overhead, seabirds circled, calling out in eerie, echoing cries.

The figure held the staff aloft and stepped closer to the surf, where waves lapped against their bare toes. With one gloved hand upon the staff, the figure began to sing—not in words, but in tones old as bone, stretched thin with sorrow and rage. The sound was low and resonant, a melody woven with breath and breathlessness. The song shifted—rose and split—into a lament for something long buried, then surged with fury and memory.

The staff pulsed.

Where the hand touched it, cracks along the ancient grain glowed amber, like veins lit from within. The figure sang louder, voice riding the wind. Sparks ignited along the shaft's ridges, timid at first, then growing bolder. A final, piercing note split the silence—flames bursting forth from the staff's tip, coiling upward in twisting, violet-orange tongues. The fire consumed what power remained in the memory of the wood. It danced, alive, crackling with a strange intelligence, casting shifting shadows that stretched like tendrils across the sand.

The figure lowered their hand, and tossed what remained of the charred staff into the hungry waves, humming faintly in time with the fading echoes of the incantation.

Above, the seabirds had fallen silent.

With a final glance at Tahgeet as they ascended into the currents, the hooded stranger climbed a rock, then dove gracefully into the water, disappearing beneath the waves as they swam toward the black pyramids, their silhouette soon swallowed by the vastness of the sea.

Back in Obsidia, Máhí and Sekowah descended into Zincubus' dark chambers. The air was thick and stale, the lingering shadows somehow heavier now that he was gone. Máhí moved with purpose, rifling through Zincubus' belongings. She lifted a leather-bound tome, its cover worn from years of handling, and flipped through its pages.

"It's his notes... from Inanna," Máhí murmured, her face hardening. Her fingers traced the inked scribbles. "I can't imagine what she went through down here."

Sekowah's eyes lingered on a heavy iron chain still bolted to the throne. "I can."

A folded map slipped from the pages of the book, and Máhí caught it. She opened it carefully, revealing a meticulous blueprint of Obsidia's twisted labyrinth. "This will come in handy," she said, tucking the map into her pocket. She glanced over her shoulder and narrowed her eyes, taking in Sekowah's current attire—Zincubus' oversized cape and clunky boots. "You look ridiculous."

Sekowah grinned, twirling with a flourish that made the cape billow around her. "What? You don't like my new look?"

Máhí raised an eyebrow. "Leave it here. It gives me the creeps."

Sekowah tightened the cape around her shoulders defiantly. "Oh, no. I'm taking it back with me. Evidence of his demise."

Máhí rolled her eyes. "Fine, but you can't wear it back. You'll give everyone the wrong impression."

Sekowah's mouth slid into a smirk. "I'm naked underneath."

With a groan, Máhí cut a hole in a shaggy animal skin that lay across Zincubus' throne and handed it to her. "Here. Better than traumatizing the whole valley."

Sekowah wrinkled her nose but slipped it over her head, grumbling. As she folded the cape, a purple mushroom fell from one of its pockets. Curious, she picked it up and ate it, savoring the earthy, slightly sweet taste.

Máhí's eyes widened. "What was that?"

"Just a snack," Sekowah said innocently, gesturing to the shelves lined with jars of mushrooms. "Zincubus ate them all the time. They taste like chocolate."

Máhí snatched a jar and tucked it into her satchel. "We'll study them later. For now, *no more eating random mushrooms.*"

Sekowah stifled a giggle, feeling a warm, pleasant sensation spread through her limbs. "Sure thing, boss."

Guided by Zincubus' map, they made their way to the emerald vault. The emerald lay within, a glowing beacon of green light that washed over them in waves of warmth and peace. Sekowah knelt by the cage, awestruck, her heart swelling as she reached o ut.

Máhí's voice was soft. "Go on. Take it."

Sekowah lifted the emerald, cradling it with reverence as Máhí wrapped it in a fur blanket. The gemstone pulsed gently in her arms, filling her with a deep, resounding calm. She felt whole, as if a missing piece of her spirit had been returned.

Máhí gave her a smile, her voice laced with relief. "That is officially your responsibility now."

· · · · ◯◯ · · · ·

Map in hand, Sekowah led Máhí to an underground cave entrance. Smoke wafted out from under the door.

Sekowah nodded at her. "Go on."

Máhí hesitated outside the door. "You go. You're the Queen."

Sekowah held tightly to the emerald. "I killed Zincubus. You owe me."

Máhí huffed but shoved the door open. Inside, a purple dragon lay sprawled on a mound of glittering gems, lifting its head with a lazy hiss. It snorted a plume of fire, singeing Máhí's remaining top feathers.

Sekowah stepped forward, unwrapping the emerald and holding it up. The dragon's demeanor softened immediately, and it lowered its head, murmuring in smoky, rumbling tones.

Máhí crossed her arms, sighing. "She wants her rubies."

Sekowah rolled her eyes, speaking in soothing tones to the dragon. "We'll return what's yours, but we need your gems for now. They'll be restored once the aquifers are repaired."

The dragon grumbled but relented, sliding off her pile with a reluctant growl. Now that it was visible, they realized the enormity of the pile beneath her. "How are we going to get them back to the aquifers?"

Máhí shook her head. "How should I know?"

Behind them, a Moorigato cautiously stepped through the cavern door—the same warrior that Sekowah had saved on the battlefield. Next to him, was a female Moorigato, and their child. He bowed his head to Sekowah and knelt on one knee in allegiance.

"Hello again," Sekowah greeted him with kindness.

"There is no distance between our people. We see you. Sekowah. You are the bridge between the swampland and the valley. The aquifers connect us. What befalls the mountains, also befalls the valley, and makes its way to the lowlands," he said, his voice steady.

A smile broke out across Máhí's face and she raised her eyebrows. "The Moorigato people have been enslaved for too long. We will make it right again."

As he rose, a shuffle could be heard in the corridor outside, as more Moorigato filed into the cave, solemn, humble. He continued. "For our freedom, we work with you, together. When the task is complete, we return. We ask only that the land from here to the sea be ours. As far up the coast as the cliffs and as far down as the great swamp goes... until the coast becomes rock." He stepped closer to Sekowah, a seriousness in his eyes. "You walk between the worlds. You stand on the grounds of your ancestors. You see what cannot be seen and hear what the others cannot hear. Your ancestors did not forget you. Do not forget us."

Sekowah watched him with curiosity, his voice like gravel, and his skin covered in scales. He looked horrifying to her, but she could see through the veil of ugliness, into his heart, his energy field shimmering around him and his people, a peaceful lavender and mint. She thought him thoroughly earnest and took his clawed hand in hers.

"Freedom is not mine to give, as I am not your captor. He is gone and you are free of him. Nor do I own the land. What you choose to do and where you choose to go is yours to decide. All I know is that it is my intention to call you friend and as a friend, to bring no harm to you or your people."

The Moorigato shared glances among themselves, and the room lifted in spirit.

She dropped his hand and walked the room to greet the others. "If you should choose to help us, I promise I will not forget. And should you find yourselves in need, as your friend, I will stand by you."

CHAPTER FORTY-FOUR

THE CAVE OF SONG

As they soared through the sky, Sekowah took in the full extent of the devastation in the Jasper Valley, her heart growing heavier with each mile they covered. The floodwaters had receded, leaving behind a landscape utterly transformed. A long scar of churned earth cut through the valley, raw and exposed, where once lush meadows and blooming orchards had thrived. Trees had been ripped from their roots, leaving dark, gaping craters like empty eyes staring up at her. Boulders, displaced by the torrential force, lay strewn across fields, blocking pathways and crushing everything in their wake. Thick layers of mud caked the once-green land, tangled with branches and debris, and the orchards—those beautiful orchards that had sustained the valley and been a pride of the Nezkwah—were gone. Only splintered trunks and scattered fruit remained, like the remnants of a broken promise.

Below, small clusters of Nezkwah and Zahnene moved among the wreckage, working in silent determination. They moved rocks, cleared paths, gathered what little could be salvaged, but their energy was dim, drained. Sekowah could see it in their body lights—once bright and vivid, now dull and veined with deep red, like the embers of a dying fire. As she and Máhí flew over the ruins, the silence felt as heavy as the valley's grief, broken only by the steady rush of the wind and the soft beat of Tahgeet's wings.

Sekowah's heart ached, her spirit feeling fragile. This was her responsibility now, her problem. She was supposed to protect it, to heal it, and yet here it lay, shattered. She could still see the faces of those who had fallen in the battle, hear their voices in her memory, and she wondered how she could ever begin to make things right.

· · · • ⟨⟨⟩⟩ • · · ·

They flew in silence to the far northeastern mountains, where Sekowah had never ventured before. The mountain peaks rose sharply, crowned by a natural castle of towering crystals that glittered in the sun. Light caught on their smooth, angled faces, splitting into countless rainbow shards that scattered across the sky. At the base of the crystal formation, ancient trees clung to the rocky ground, their thick roots wrapping around boulders as if anchoring them in place. Flowering bushes spilled out over the ledges, and butterflies flitted among the blossoms, their wings catching flecks of sunlight.

They landed at the base of the pinnacle, and as Sekowah dismounted, she found herself transfixed by the view. From this high vantage, she could see the entire valley stretched out below, still beautiful, but scarred. Her eyes moved over the once-vibrant wildflower fields, now dull patches where the flood had swept through, stripping the land bare. The thought of Elo and his bees saddened her. She had promised him she would protect his wildflowers, his sanctuary, and now... there was nothing left for them. The bees would have no nectar, no pollen to sustain them through the winter. She felt her failure pressing in, a weight she could barely stand beneath.

Tears welled up, blurring her vision. She covered her face, and for the first time since the battle, she let herself cry openly. She was beyond exhaustion, beyond sorrow. She was utterly spent, stripped bare of hope.

Máhí placed a steadying hand on her shoulder and gave her a gentle pat on the back. "Come. It's time. This will lift your spirits," she said softly. From her saddlebag, she pulled out the emerald, handing it to Sekowah with a reverence that made her pause. Then, Máhí led her to the entrance of the crystal cavern.

Sekowah followed, clutching the emerald close to her chest. As they walked down the winding passage, the walls sparkled, like stars scattered through the darkness. The crystals lining the walls seemed to pulse gently with their own inner light, guiding them deeper, until the passage opened up into a massive chamber.

A skylight high above let in a column of sunlight that struck the cavern floor, casting a radiant pool of light in the center. Around the skylight, countless tiny crystals glimmered, casting flecks of rainbow light across the walls, making the entire chamber feel alive. The floor was a mosaic of gemstone tiles, polished so smooth that they reflected the light like a mirror.

And there, at the heart of the cavern, was a jade statue of a woman. Sekowah knew instantly who it was. Inanna. The figure was serene, with a face of calm wisdom and compassion, her hands resting on a round, empty belly—a womb shaped like an egg, waiting to be filled.

Sekowah kneeled in reverence at the base of the statue, bowing her head. "Thank you," she sobbed. A deep well of gratitude rose up in her chest and she was consumed by it. Joyful tears flowed freely, and she felt Inanna wrapping herself around her. Inanna's face was calm, forgiving, a peaceful energy about her. Her robes flowed from her and over the base of the pedestal.

With trembling hands, Sekowah unwrapped the emerald, taking one last moment to trace her fingers over its flawless, gleaming surface. She didn't want to let it go; it had become a part of her, a source of strength. But she knew where it belonged. She placed it gently into the hollow of Inanna's womb, fitting it into the small platform within.

As soon as it touched the jade, the emerald flared to life, its green light flooding the cavern with a brilliance so intense that she and Máhí had to shield their eyes. The statue absorbed the light, which shot through the crystals, bouncing from facet to facet, filling every corner with dazzling green radiance. The light surged upward, through the skylight, exploding into the sky above.

Sekowah felt something release inside her—a knot of tension, of grief, of doubt. The weight on her spirit lifted, and in its place was a profound calm. She felt connected to the valley, to the Nezkwah, to everything that lived and breathed in this place. She understood, finally, that the sacrifices made, including her own, were part of a larger story, one that stretched beyond her own desires, fears and even her own knowing.

Good of All.

The words resonated within her, no longer just a phrase, but a truth that she could feel pulsing through her. It was no longer about her own pain, her own wishes. She was part of something bigger, and this knowledge filled her with a quiet, unshakeable resolve. Whatever the valley needed, she would give. It was no longer about what she wanted or needed. *What will be, will be,* she reminded herself, and the valley's future would unfold as it was meant to.

She rose to her feet and extended a hand to Máhí, who took it, and together, they stood in silent reverence, letting the peace of the cavern settle over them.

A soft buzzing sound caught Sekowah's attention, distant at first but growing steadily louder. She turned, her eyes widening as a swarm of Zahnene filled the passageway, carrying strange instruments in their hands—steel drums shaped like flying saucers, ringed with gemstones, and long flutes made of gold. Máhí's face lit up with joy as the Zahnene filed in, forming a circle around the statue.

"What's happening?" Sekowah whispered, awestruck.

Máhí's eyes sparkled as she looked at Sekowah. "We're going to sing."

Máhí raised her golden spheres, letting them chime softly, and as if on cue, the Zahnene lifted their instruments. A gentle hum filled the cavern, a deep, resonant sound that vibrated through Sekowah's bones, soothing her spirit. Each Zahnene played a different note, creating a harmonious web of sound that wrapped around them like a warm blanket.

Máhí took Sekowah's hands and began to sing, her voice clear and lilting, weaving in and out of the hum like a bird darting through trees. The Zahnene joined in, their voices rolling through the cavern, building into a song that was both ancient and new. Sekowah felt her heart swell with the music, the notes pulling something deep from within her. She opened her mouth, hesitant, but let her own voice join the chorus.

The sound that escaped her surprised her—it was deep, resonant, a grounding harmony that filled the space beneath Máhí's lighter melody. The two voices intertwined, and Sekowah felt a surge of energy, a pulse of life that spread from her heart outward. She felt weightless, timeless, lifted by the sound until she was floating, her feet leaving the ground, as if she were held up by the song itself.

The music swelled, a crescendo that filled every crevice of the cavern, vibrating the walls so intensely that small bits of rock and sand began to trickle down. When it reached its peak, Sekowah felt herself completely overcome, suspended in pure, unbridled joy.

Gradually, the music softened, the voices fading one by one until silence settled over them like a gentle blanket. Sekowah drifted back down, her feet touching the stone floor, her heart full, her spirit renewed.

Hand in hand, Sekowah and Máhí walked out of the cavern, back into the sunlight. As they reached the cliff's edge, a tremor shivered through the ground, and Sekowah looked down to see a green light spreading beneath the soil, weaving through the valley in glowing tendrils.

They watched as the light touched the earth, coaxing new life from the ground. Wildflowers burst forth, fields of daisies and poppies spreading like waves across the valley floor. Cherry blossoms bloomed on trees, their petals drifting on the breeze like pink snow. Everywhere the light touched, life sprang up, a vibrant tapestry of green and color reclaiming the land.

Below, the Nezkwah and Zahnene looked on in awe, their faces lighting up as the valley transformed before their eyes. A great cheer rose from the people, echoing through the mountains, filling the air with joy. Máhí and Sekowah embraced, their laughter mingling with the valley's song.

And for the first time, Sekowah felt truly at home.

Chapter Forty-Five

A New Reign

Gavril stood alone on the balcony of Peregrine's Keep, his figure stoic against the dawn sky. The morning light painted the world in soft hues, but he felt none of its warmth. Every muscle in his body ached, not from wounds but from a grief that had settled so deeply it felt physical, pressing down on his bones and hollowing his chest. The battle had ended, but its toll was one that no healing potion could mend. His eyes, rimmed with exhaustion, stared out across the horizon, searching for a sign, any sign, of Sekowah and Máhí, who had been missing for two suns now. Anxiety knotted his gut; he feared the worst, but his spirit refused to accept it.

A charm of Zahnene flitted in with a tray of berrywine biscuits and honey water, placing it delicately on the table beside him, but he could only glance at it and nod a half-hearted thanks. His appetite was gone. He had been keeping vigil here since he'd returned from the battlefield, barely sleeping, watching the sky as though sheer will might bring the two missing figures back to him.

Jájá's absence weighed heavily on his spirit as well. He could still feel her presence echoing through the Keep, like a quiet warmth that was suddenly gone, leaving a chill in its place. He and Vesper had loaded her body on a wagon for the rites, laying her to rest with the dignity she had lived by, and still, the processions hadn't ended. Wagons continued to roll between the Daylight Meadow and the valley, carrying the fallen back to their resting places, a solemn tide of loss. Though Zincubus had been defeated and his forces scattered, victory had come at a cost too steep to celebrate.

The Keep was suspended in an odd balance of grief and relief. As Vesper's top commander, Gavril had been asked to take Jájá's seat temporarily, to stand in her place until they knew with certainty what fate had befallen Máhí and Sekowah. But the honor felt hollow, wrong. The previous night, he had stood alone in the grand hall, staring at her empty throne, his hands resting on its back as if he might feel some lingering warmth from her there. But it was cold, and he could not bring himself to sit in her place. He was merely a guardian, he told himself—a keeper of the memory, not a replacement.

A sound of laughter cut through his thoughts, startling him from his ruminations. The balcony doors burst open, and Mardig and Ylva strode in, looking far too lively for the early hour. Ylva was carrying a mug of lilac wine, her cheeks already flushed, while Mardig trailed behind, grinning as he bit into a lemon pastry.

Gavril raised an eyebrow. "I see you found the cooking quarters."

Ylva stuffed a blue pastry into her mouth and grinned, her teeth stained blue. "These are incredible. I don't know what they are, but I could eat a hundred of them," she said, barely pausing to swallow.

"Ah, those," Gavril said with a smirk, recognizing the pairing ceremony initiation treats. "You may want to leave those..."

But Ylva was already eyeing the grounds below. Her gaze caught on a tall figure with dark hair and a commanding posture—Tourik, one of the young Lirian warriors who had caught the attention of more than a few of the Dokar. Ylva's eyes gleamed with mischief. "And who is that?"

Gavril sighed. "Or not."

Mardig pointed to the mountain peaks where the twin waterfalls had previously stood. All that was left were two mountain peaks, divided by one quiet, clear waterfall, which trickled down through the valley peacefully.

Gavril looked down at the camps below, where Lirian and Dokar warriors mingled, sharing stories, mending armor, laughing together as comrades. *The time of all wars is over*, he thought. This alone was a great relief.

His gaze drifted out over the valley far in the distance, past the mingling troops, past the wreckage, to the northern edge where the devastation met the line of trees. He blinked, barely believing what he was seeing. A thin tendril of green light was spreading from the distant peaks, snaking its way across the ravished land, leaving behind patches of new growth—wildflowers, grass, even young trees—sprouting in its wake. He followed the path of light as it rolled through the valley, like the stroke of a painter's brush, restoring the land with every inch it covered.

Gavril sucked in a breath. "The emerald," he whispered, a smile breaking across his weary face. "It's been returned to the Cave of Song." If the valley was healing, then Sekowah and Máhí must have succeeded.

They were alive.

Ylva and Mardig looked out over the valley, following his gaze as the tendrils of green light continued to weave across the landscape, reviving the fields.

In that moment, as Gavril watched the valley come alive once more, he felt Jájá's presence near him, reminding him of her devotion. Gavril turned back to the balcony doors, leaving Ylva and Mardig to their lilac wine and pastries. He needed to prepare the Keep for Sekowah's return. There was work to be done, and this time, he would be ready to stand at her side, not as a commander, but as her steadfast friend.

· · · · ⟨⟨⟩⟩ · · · ·

Sekowah walked the winding paths of the garden maze outside Peregrine's Keep, her footsteps soft against the dewy grass. She wore a flowing green dress inspired by Inanna's statue, the fabric catching the sunlight and shimmering like leaves touched by morning rain. A rich, royal blue velvet cloak hung over her shoulders, embroidered with the same ancient symbol that adorned Inanna's chest—a tribute to the woman who had guided her from afar. On her head, a delicate crown of gold and silver, woven with small, fragrant roses, rested lightly, as if it had always belonged there. Around her neck lay Jájá's ruby pendant, warm against her skin, a reminder of the fierce wisdom that had passed down to her.

At her side trotted a small llama cria, orphaned by the recent flood. The cria darted back and forth, its wide, curious eyes exploring everything at once. He sniffed at the flowers, pawed at the earth, and even tried nibbling on a leaf.

"Don't be naughty, Duke," she chided with a soft laugh as the llama stomped down on a centipede that had dared to cross his path.

Bug. Bug. Bug, he thought, his golden eyes brimming with innocent outrage. *Stinky bug.*

"Yes, Duke. Stinky bug," she replied, her tone indulgent. "But leave it alone."

Hungry. Hungry, Duke insisted, padding close to her, his head tilted up in a look of absolute devotion.

"All right, you charmer. Let's go eat," Sekowah said, giving him a gentle pat. She lifted the hem of her dress and headed back toward the castle, Duke scampering along in her wake, his little hooves tapping eagerly against the stone path.

The path curved near the fountain of the weeping nymph, whose stone hands overflowed with water lilies. There, beneath the canopy of a flowering ginkgo, waited Perrin.

His golden wings were folded neatly against his flanks, bandages still wrapping one of his muscled forelimbs. His striped fur rippled slightly in the breeze, and his bright eyes gleamed with quiet alertness. When he saw her, he dipped his head—not in submission, but something older, more sacred.

You came back. His voice rang in her mind, warm and deep.

Sekowah stepped forward until her fingers brushed the velvet of his mane. *This is my home.*

He nuzzled her arm, careful not to unseat the roses in her crown. The cria squealed and darted behind her, uncertain whether to worship or flee.

She smiled and pressed her forehead gently to his. The contact lit a quiet current between them—wordless memories, shared pain, the terrifying weight of that moment when the bullet had struck him and he'd crumpled beneath her. The sound still lived behind her ribs. Her eyes stung. She traced the line of feathers along his wing's edge with reverent fingers. *I owe you more than breath.*

Perrin's thoughts curled around hers like a purring fire. *You owe me nothing.*

Sekowah dropped to her knees beside him, the cloak pooling around her like a fallen sky. She rested her palm on his chest, over the faint scar beneath his fur. "Then we rise together," she murmured aloud.

A breeze stirred the garden, scattering petals. Perrin extended his good wing and draped it around her, tucking her close. The cria bleated in protest at being left out and flopped dramatically at their side.

Your court grows unruly. Perrin quipped, eyeing the llama's antics.

Sekowah laughed, pressing her face to his neck. "Then let them see their queen begin with loyalty."

· · · · ⬭ · · · ·

Inside, the Banquet Hall had been transformed into a vibrant celebration of life and renewal. Cherry blossoms, roses, pine boughs, and lilies adorned every surface, filling the air with mingling scents that were both fresh and comforting. Lirian and Dokar alike danced to lively music, and the tables along both walls overflowed with fruits, vegetables, herbs, and desserts that had been painstakingly gathered and prepared. The hall buzzed with laughter and conversation, as warriors from every clan shared stories and toasted to their hard-won peace.

Gavril had organized the celebration for the summer equinox, as a gesture of respect for their new alliance. He had left the details to Ylva, Mardig, and Sekowah, each adding a touch of their own culture to the festivities. It was a rare blend of customs, a patchwork of traditions that had somehow come together beautifully.

Sekowah slipped through the towering doors, which were cracked open just enough for her to peek inside. She watched as Duke scampered through the opening, his soft ears twitching with excitement at the sounds and smells. Inside, Ylva and Tourik were dancing for each other, moving with both elegance and humor. Ylva's steps were bold, her eyes bright as she performed a traditional Dokarian dance, her hips swaying and hands gesturing in a language older than words. Tourik, with his massive arms folded across his chest, watched her with a captivated grin, his eyes gleaming.

Mardig, too, had been pulled onto the dance floor by Braylyn, a tall Lirian warrior with laughing eyes. They moved clumsily at first, stepping on each other's feet, but soon their laughter filled the hall, drawing cheers from the crowd. Sekowah's heart swelled with pride and relief at the sight. It was hard to believe that just several dozen suns ago, they had all trudged back from the Daylight Meadow in silence, burdened by the weight of the final death march. Now, the shadows of grief were beginning to lift, transforming sorrow into cherished memory.

Near the back wall, a new portrait hung alongside those of past kings and queens—a likeness of Jájá, painted with quiet dignity, her gaze unwavering, her presence as fierce in death as it had been in life. Gavril was supervising as a group of Zahnene hung it, his expression solemn as he ensured they found the perfect spot. Máhí approached him, her feathers neatly pruned and her indigo cape draped to cover the patches of feathers still growing back.

"A dignified sacrifice," Gavril murmured, his voice rough with emotion.

Catching sight of Sekowah watching from the doorway, Gavril offered her a small nod and a wink. The night before, he had shared his soul's musings with her, and together they had made a decision: he would remain as Commander of the fleet, while she would ascend as queen of the Nezkwah. She and Vesper would rule together, yet separately, as was the custom when Jájá had first taken her throne. Her union with Gavril, should it come to pass, would be one of choice, not obligation—a partnership forged by love, if and when they both chose it.

Sekowah's heart fluttered as Vesper, still looking weary from the recent trials, approached the throne at the front of the room. He raised his arms to quiet the crowd. "Friends! Hear this!"

The music faded, and all eyes turned toward him. Sekowah could feel the weight of the moment pressing on her, the significance of everything they had endured together. She smoothed her dress, took a steadying breath, and prepared herself.

Vesper's voice, though strained, held steady. "We have lost many dear to us," he began, his words carrying a gravity that silenced even the most jovial guests. Heads bowed in acknowledgment, faces turning somber.

"We have lost our homes, our livelihoods," he continued, a murmur of agreement rippling through the hall.

Then, he lifted his mug high, his voice rising with renewed strength. "However, we have not lost our dignity. We have not lost our spirit. Much has been gained." He gestured toward the crowd. "Many among us have broken the bonds of slavery. Others still have fought battles only their own hearts can know."

Several Zahnene lifted their own mugs and raised Jájá's portrait higher. Vesper's voice grew softer, reverent. "To those who gave their lives for this peace." He took a long drink, and the crowd erupted in a thunderous cheer, lifting their mugs in unison. "To those no longer with us. We will not let their sacrifice be in vain! We will rebuild. We will prosper!"

He motioned to Mardig and Ylva, who joined him at the front, standing shoulder to shoulder with him. "Today, we join our nations together in peace. From this day forward, there are no borders between us. We are one people."

A murmur of amazement swept through the hall, then hands reached out, clasping those around them in a chain that spanned the room. For a moment, the hall was united, a living testament to the promise of peace.

"And now," Vesper said, his voice resonating through the hall, "please welcome the valley's new Queen."

Elo stepped forward with his flute, lifting it to his lips. A delicate, regal melody filled the air, silencing the murmurs. The doors at the back of the hall swung open, revealing Sekowah framed in the doorway, her silhouette bathed in light.

A hush fell over the crowd as she made her entrance. She walked slowly down the aisle, her steps graceful, each one deliberate, acknowledging every group in attendance. Nezkwah, Lirian, Dokar, Zahnene—all bowed their heads as she passed, each gesture a silent promise of loyalty.

Sekowah felt a wellspring of gratitude rise within her, mingling with pride. *I have earned my place among them,* she thought, her heart swelling with purpose. Here, she would serve these people with all she had, as they had served each other.

She reached the front, where Gavril waited, a soft smile on his lips. He took her hand and kissed it, his eyes conveying a warmth that grounded her. Then he stepped aside, allowing her to take her place on the throne. Sekowah sat, letting the joy and pride radiate from her as she looked out over her people. Her subjects rose to their feet, their applause a resounding echo of acceptance, filling every corner of the hall.

The music surged once more, and the celebration began in earnest.

F ar from the jubilant halls of Peregrine's Keep, a hooded figure moved through the shadowed passages of Obsidia, her footsteps echoing in the silence of the abandoned fortress. She entered Zincubus' former observatory, a place thick with the residue of his dark magic. A line of crystal skulls glinted in the dim light, dormant but waiting.

With a wave of her hand, Inanna brought the crystals to life. One by one, the skulls flared with inner light, casting strange reflections around the room. She touched the center skull, and an image bloomed within it, like the surface of a still pond disturbed by a single drop.

The vision showed a shoreline, but not one from this world. It was the soft shores of Hilton Head Island, South Carolina. A mansion sat amongst palm trees and cypress, overlooking the endless blue of the Atlantic Ocean. In the driveway, a sleek black Jaguar convertible gleamed in the sun. Beyond the mansion, a figure emerged from the waves—a man, without clothes, battered and bruised, his skin marked with jellyfish stings and the lingering red rings of squid suction bruises.

Zincubus.

Inanna's lips curled into a small, knowing smile. She called out, her voice low and commanding. "Krag!"

A tall figure appeared in the doorway—a guardian draped in black leather, with violet eyes and hair as dark as midnight, flowing to his waist. In his arms was a small, green dragon, its scales glimmering like emeralds. His powerful wings, black as night, shifted slightly as he stepped forward.

Krag looked into the crystal, his gaze narrowing as he studied Zincubus stumbling onto the beach, slogging through the sand toward the mansion's stone steps. "Interesting," he murmured, "He's built another empire among them."

· · · • ◯◯ • · · · ·

A long a winding trail deep within the Great Smoky Mountains National Park, a campfire crackled under the open night sky. A group of hikers sat around it, swapping stories, their faces lit in shades of gold and shadow as they roasted marshmallows and sipped from battered thermoses. The smoky scent of burning wood drifted on the cool mountain air, and the only sounds were the murmuring voices, occasional laughter, and the soft chorus of night creatures singing from the trees.

One of the hikers, Eric Mendleson, pulled a perfectly toasted marshmallow from his stick and popped it into his mouth, waving his hand to cool the sticky sweetness. A lifelong environmental activist in his late forties, Eric had an air of weariness about him, softened by his wry humor and deep love for the wilderness.

"Alright," one of his fellow hikers leaned back, stretching his legs and tossing a challenge into the firelight. "Strangest thing that ever happened to you on the trail. Let's hear it."

Eric grinned, a tentative glint in his eyes. "Yeah, I got one for you. Happened a couple decades ago."

"What trail?" a young man asked, leaning forward.

"Right here in the Smokies," Eric replied. "Atagahi Lake."

A murmur of skepticism swept through the group. "Atagahi Lake? Come on, man. That's just a legend," a hiker chimed in, shaking his head.

Eric raised his eyebrows, his face deadly serious. "Atagahi is only a fantasy to those who aren't allowed to find it," he said, his tone so solemn it silenced the laughter.

One of the younger hikers rolled his eyes. "Whatever. Just ignore him. Go on."

Eric leaned in, his voice low and steady. "So, I came out to enjoy some nature. Some time alone. It was my first attempt at the Appalachian Trail, start to finish."

A woman across the fire caught his eye. She was older, with long, white braids falling to her waist, lavender-blue eyes that reflected the firelight, and a green baseball cap embroidered with a symbol he didn't recognize: a circle within a circle, with an eight-pointed star in the center. Next to her sat a young man with raven-black hair braided down his back and black felt boots on his feet. They both watched him intently, their faces serene but alert.

"Go on," the young man said quietly, lifting a harmonica to his lips. He played a single, haunting note that lingered in the cool air.

The group chuckled, but Eric felt a chill creep up his spine. He swallowed and continued. "Right, so there I was, on my own, setting up camp for the night. I'd just put some water on for tea when I heard something... something coming from a cave nearby. I went to check it out, and... I thought I saw antlers in the shadows."

"A buck?" a guy in a football jersey chimed in, sounding skeptical but intrigued.

Eric shook his head, trying to find the words. He lowered his voice. "No, not a buck. It was... something else. I'm telling you, it was like an alien or something. It had massive wings—feathered, like an owl. And antlers. Huge, like a buck, with stones hanging from them. Gemstones, maybe, glowing in the dark. It was... beautiful. Terrifying. It... *she*, I guess," he laughed awkwardly, "she kind of seduced me, I think."

The fire crackled in the stunned silence, and for a second, Eric's story held them all in thrall. Then someone snorted, and the spell broke. Laughter erupted around the circle, jeers and playful insults thrown his way.

"Shut up, Eric!"

"Lay off the mushrooms, dude!"

Eric chuckled with them, scratching the back of his neck. He'd been expecting that reaction, and it didn't bother him. Not really. He took a sip of his tea, letting the warmth settle him.

But not everyone was laughing. Across the fire, the woman with the lavender-blue eyes nodded thoughtfully, her gaze sharp and unyielding. She wore an expression that was half-smile, half-recognition. "Hey. Who's to say? It's a big universe, right?" Her voice was soft, with a strange, lilting accent that Eric couldn't quite place.

He nodded back at her, his heart strangely comforted by her understanding. "Exactly," he replied, grateful for her support. "Thank you."

The guy in the football jersey leaped to his feet, eager to take the spotlight. "Alright, alright, I got one! Wait till you hear this..."

As the new storyteller launched into his tale, Eric took the opportunity to study the woman and her companion more closely. They shared a quiet smile, exchanging whispered words only they could hear, as if they existed in a world slightly removed from the one around them. The firelight danced across their faces, casting shadows that made them look ancient, otherworldly.

For a moment, Eric felt the edges of reality blur, felt himself drawn toward something just out of reach, something deep and strange that he could sense in the night air. The woman's words echoed in his mind.

It's a big universe.

THE END

Chapter Forty-Six

Hunted

Book Two Teaser

Beyond the former borders of Mount Lira, a new village was springing to life amidst the rolling, late-autumn meadows. Dokar warriors and villagers, their numbers stretching back as far as the eye could see, were hauling the last of their supplies toward their new homeland. It was a weary but determined procession—dozens of creaking wagons, most laden with dried roots, herbs, and seeds to last through the cold moons, and a few others carrying the precious seed for spring plantings. The scent of crushed lavender and sage wafted from the baskets, weaving an invisible trail through the damp, earthy air. As the convoy pressed forward, warriors flanked both sides, keeping a sharp watch on the underbrush and the darkening skies, aware that with every step, they were drawing closer to the perilous border of Gold territory.

At the rear of the convoy, Gavril rode alongside Ylva and Tourik, his saddle squeaking with each step as the leather loosened in the moist air. He'd promised to escort the Dokar safely to their new lands, and though the journey had been long and arduous, he was relieved to know that wells were already being dug, and the first stone shelters had been raised. Simple, sturdy dwellings built by hand, each shelter would house a hundred or so families, grouped together for warmth and survival through the coming cold. It was no palace, but it would suffice, and come spring, the Dokar would be ready to plant and harvest, finally self-sustaining and no longer reliant on the valley's provisions.

The convoy traveled in near silence, save for the occasional murmur of conversation or the soft hum of a lullaby from a mother soothing her nestling. The youngsters, however, darted about like birds, flitting from wagon to wagon, their wings rustling as they jostled and teased one another, sometimes scrabbling over spilled nuts that tumbled from the baskets with each jolt of the wheels over rough terrain. Their laughter, innocent and unrestrained, was a rare spark of joy in an otherwise somber march.

But when the convoy stopped unexpectedly, and the horses at the front shifted uneasily without moving forward, Ylva handed her reins to Tourik and lifted herself into the air to get a better view. Her gaze sharpened as she rose above the line of wagons, and her expression tightened.

"Can you see what's happening?" Gavril called up to her.

She hovered a moment longer, her eyes narrowing. "No trouble I can see... Mardig—he speaks to someone. And... there's something on ground." Her voice held a note of apprehension.

Without another word, she descended back to her horse, and Gavril and Tourik immediately followed as she broke from the line, urging her mount to a gallop. The three of them thundered toward the front of the convoy, a sense of dread building in Gavril's chest as they neared the source of the commotion.

There, lying on the trampled grass, was a young Dokar warrior—his face pale, his leg severed at the knee, the stump bound hastily with blood-soaked cloth. Villagers knelt around him, their faces drawn with worry, murmuring words of comfort that fell on deaf ears. His eyes were glazed, staring unfocused into the distance, his breaths shallow and l abored.

Ylva dismounted first, her face stricken. "What is happen here?"

Mardig stepped forward to meet them, drawing them aside with a grim expression, his voice a low, urgent murmur. "No accident. He was part of group sent back to old encampment, to gather provisions and furs. But he returned alone... he brings terrible news." Mardig's eyes flashed with a barely-contained anger. "He says others are sacrificed."

Gavril's brows knit in confusion. Sacrifice? The word felt foreign and abhorrent—an ancient practice long outlawed among his people. He searched Mardig's face for clarification. "Sacrificed? This isn't something we—"

Mardig's eyes burned with fury. "Not by us," he spat. There was a shadow in his gaze, something dark and unspoken, something he could not—or would not—put into words.

The thought chilled Gavril. Though unlikely, he wondered if the Golds might have been behind such an atrocity. Their numbers were growing, it seemed, with every passing season, and their territory pressed ever closer to the borders. "The Golds?" he ventured, the suggestion slipping out as a whisper.

Mardig heaved a full sigh, his frustration palpable. "Your people," he said, his voice taut with bitterness, "have not marched into north territory in many harvests. You don't understand what hunts there. It is this that drove us to your mountains."

Ylva's face was taut with fear, her gaze drifting to the injured warrior whose blood was now a slow, steady trickle, staining the grass beneath him. "The giants," she said, her voice a whisper. She looked up, her eyes wide with dread. "They're coming."

ACKNOWLEDGEMENTS

The journey of writing this book was as winding as the story itself. It began as a screenplay idea meant for my eldest daughter, Morgan—who, I'm convinced, was a fae long before she incarnated in this world. But by page 87, it was clear this tale needed more than ninety pages to unfold. The characters demanded room to breathe, and their world refused to be confined. Having never written a proper novel before, the prospect of starting over was daunting. I hesitated. I second-guessed. I feared I wasn't ready. But the freedom to explore this universe in its fullness pulled me forward. Over six years, I taught myself to think and write differently. It was exhilarating and excruciating—often both at once. I worked with a coach, then an editor, and rewrote this book thirteen times. Somewhere along the way, I realized it wasn't just a book. It was a trilogy.

To my husband, Jeff—thank you for everything. You listened to every chapter with a mix of patience and playful critique. You brought me food when I forgot to eat. You argued passionately about character arcs and plot twists. You paid the bills so I could lose myself in this process. This book belongs to you as much as it does to me.

To Morgan—this story belongs to you, ethereally and eternally. You didn't just inspire the characters and the world—you helped birth it. You arrived in the eleventh hour with your artistic brilliance, crafting the cover, illustrations, and final revisions. Without your energy, this story would still be swirling somewhere in the void.

To those who guided this book into being: writing coach Sam Severn, editor Amy Karas, agent Nicole Resciniti of The Seymour Agency, beta readers Jenna Avery and Rita Roberts, writing colleague Cary Bayer, and writing inspiration Teresa Gabelman—thank you for elevating my craft with your insights and encouragement. A special thank you to artist Edward Kann for early collaboration, and to linguist Frederico Schroeder, who created the Nezkwah language, Selematla. Thank you for giving my characters their voice. *Si wi naynet may mitlak kaynen.*

Stories are not invented. They are remembered. I believe they live in the collective conscious, swirling about in the quantum madness of our subatomic existence, ever knocking on the doors of our hearts to be birthed into this small corner of the material world. So, to the keepers of the eternal and infinite wisdom, I thank you for allowing me to download this one to the mortal realm.

ABOUT THE AUTHOR

Jo Hannah Afton is a novelist, screenwriter, and multidisciplinary storyteller with a background in Communications and Theater. Her work spans genres and mediums, from feature films (including a Lifetime TV release) to optioned scripts and serialized television development. Her writing blends myth, memory, and female-centered narratives that explore the inner worlds of her characters across time and space.

Jo brings decades of experience to her craft, including poetry, photography, and graphic design. When she's not writing novels, she's designing for her online shops or capturing the world through a creative lens. She lives in the Southeastern United States with her husband Jeff, daughter Morgan, and her soul dog, Tupelo.

Visit www.johannahafton.com to explore her latest projects and publications.

www.ingramcontent.com/pod-product-compliance
Lightning Source LLC
Chambersburg PA
CBHW030646020726
47493CB00006B/1893